Raves for the Previous Valdemar Anthologies:

"Fans of Lackey's epic Valdemar series will devour this superb anthology. Of the thirteen stories included, there is no weak link—an attribute exceedingly rare in collections of this sort. Highly recommended."
—*The Barnes and Noble Review*

"This high-quality anthology mixes pieces by experienced author and enthusiastic fans of editor Lackey's Valdemar. Valdemar fandom, especially, will revel in this sterling example of what such a mixture of fans' and pros' work can be. Engrossing even for newcomers to Valdemar."
—*Booklist*

"Joseph Sherman, Tanya Huff, Mickey Zucker Reichert, and Michelle West have quite good stories, and there's another by Lackey herself. Familiarity with the series helps but is not a prerequisite to enjoying this book."
—*Science Fiction Chronicle*

"Each tale adheres to the Lackey laws of the realm yet provides each author's personal stamp on the story. Well written and fun, Valdemarites will especially appreciate the magic of this book." —*The Midwest Book Review*

WITHDRAWN FROM COLLECTION VPL

NOVELS BY **MERCEDES LACKEY**
available from DAW Books:

THE HERALDS OF VALDEMAR
ARROWS OF THE QUEEN
ARROW'S FLIGHT
ARROW'S FALL

THE LAST HERALD-MAGE
MAGIC'S PAWN
MAGIC'S PROMISE
MAGIC'S PRICE

THE MAGE WINDS
WINDS OF FATE
WINDS OF CHANGE
WINDS OF FURY

THE MAGE STORMS
STORM WARNING
STORM RISING
STORM BREAKING

VOWS AND HONOR
THE OATHBOUND
OATHBREAKERS
OATHBLOOD

BY THE SWORD
BRIGHTLY BURNING
TAKE A THIEF
EXILE'S HONOR
EXILE'S VALOR

VALDEMAR ANTHOLOGIES:
SWORD OF ICE
SUN IN GLORY
CROSSROADS

Written with **LARRY DIXON:**

THE MAGE WARS
THE BLACK GRYPHON
THE WHITE GRYPHON
THE SILVER GRYPHON

DARIAN'S TALE
OWLFLIGHT
OWLSIGHT
OWLKNIGHT

OTHER NOVELS

THE BLACK SWAN

THE DRAGON JOUSTERS
JOUST
ALTA
SANCTUARY

THE ELEMENTAL MASTERS
THE SERPENT'S SHADOW
THE GATES OF SLEEP
PHOENIX AND ASHES
THE WIZARD OF LONDON

And don't miss:
The VALDEMAR COMPANION
Edited by John Helfers and Denise Little

CROSSROADS

EDITED BY

Mercedes Lackey

DAW BOOKS, INC.

DONALD A. WOLLHEIM, FOUNDER

375 Hudson Street, New York, NY 10014

**ELIZABETH R. WOLLHEIM
SHEILA E. GILBERT
PUBLISHERS**

www.dawbooks.com

Copyright © 2005 by Mercedes Lackey and Tekno Books

All Rights Reserved

Cover art by Jody A. Lee

DAW Book Collectors No. 1346.

DAW Books are distributed by Penguin Group (USA).

All characters and events in this book are fictitious.
All resemblance to persons living or dead is coincidental.

If you purchase this book without a cover you should be aware
that this book may have been stolen property and reported as
"unsold and destroyed" to the publisher. In such case neither
the author nor the publisher has received any payment for this
"stripped book."

The scanning, uploading and distribution of this book via the
Internet or any other means without the permission of the publisher is illegal, and punishable by law. Please purchase only
authorized electronic editions, and do not participate in or en-
courage the electronic piracy of copyrighted materials. Your support of the author's rights is appreciated.

First Printing, December 2005
2   3   4   5   6   7   8   9

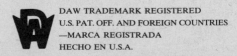

DAW TRADEMARK REGISTERED
U.S. PAT. OFF. AND FOREIGN COUNTRIES
—MARCA REGISTRADA
HECHO EN U.S.A.

PRINTED IN THE U.S.A.

Acknowledgments

Introduction copyright © 2005 by Mercedes Lackey

"Transmutation," copyright © 2005 by Larry Dixon

"The Feast of the Children," copyright © 2005 by Nancy Asire

"Death in Keenspur House," copyright © 2005 by Richard Lee Byers

"Dawn of Sorrows," copyright © 2005 by Brenda Cooper

"Horse of Air," copyright © 2005 by Rosemary Edghill

"A Change of Heart," copyright © 2005 by Sarah A. Hoyt and Kate Paulk

"All the Ages of Man," copyright © 2005 by Tanya Huff

"War Cry," copyright © 2005 by Michael Longcor

"Strength and Honor," copyright © 2005 by Ben Ohlander

"The Blue Coat," copyright © 2005 by Fiona Patton

"Safe and Sound," copyright © 2005 by Stephanie Shaver

"Song for Two Voices," copyright © 2005 by Janni Lee Simner

"Finding Elvida," copyright © 2005 by Mickey Zucker Reichert

"Darkwall's Lady," copyright © 2005 by Judith Tarr

"Naught but Duty," copyright © 2005 by Michael Z. Williamson

"Landscape of the Imagination," copyright © 2005 by Mercedes Lackey

CONTENTS

CROSSROADS:
AN INTRODUCTION

by Mercedes Lackey

Once there was a computer programmer with ambitions—
one might say delusions—of being a writer.

Actually she'd had ambitions for a very long time. As a
kid, she had written Andre Norton pastiches and illustrated
them too (and somewhere she still has some of those illus-
trations) and occasionally told them as bedtime stories to
the kids she babysat. As a teenager she continued to write,
submitting short story after short story to her high school
literary magazine (and she has some of those somewhere
as well). And in college she created an ongoing story arc
about a team of psychic spies that she wrote as letters to
amuse a friend.

She actually went so far as to take a creative writing
honors course with the one college professor who was interested in science fiction and fantasy. His advice: find out
what you like, break it down to see what you like about it,
then do that. It was good advice, and she's been following
it ever since.

Writing kind of went by the wayside for a while as she
(OK, *I*) struggled to make a living. But when things weren't
quite so hard, I went back to the writing, pounding stuff
out on an old typewriter for fanzines. Good heavens, someone even had a set of those things they asked me to auto-
graph recently. I was joking when I offered to buy them

1

back; but truth to tell, I have a lot of affection for those old zines and stories. I had a lot of fun writing them.

But then one day, at the point where I was actually that computer programmer, something switched over and I decided to get serious.

A novel of Valdemar was not the first book I tried to write. Actually, the germs of that first book became the books I co-wrote with James Mallory. But it was the second. And *Arrows of the Queen* was the first one I actually finished.

By that time I had written and actually sold several Tarma and Kethry stories—also in the same world—and some Darkover fiction. Most sold to Marion Zimmer Bradley, but some also sold to fantasy magazines. That was the point where C.J. Cherryh volunteered herself as my mentor, looked at the book, said "Commit trilogy," and it all proceeded from there.

I was incredibly lucky to hook up with Elizabeth Wollheim and the folks at DAW with this first effort. It has been a great relationship all the way.

Even better, the whole world seems to have inspired other people to want to come play in it. Each person has had his or her own take on it that has made it just that much more varied and interesting, and come up with things that made me smile, made me cry, and sometimes made me say, "Boy I wish I had thought of that!"

Two volumes of Valdemar short stories have been published already, and you hold in your hands the third. It's been a great trip so far, and even better for having all these wonderful folks along for the ride.

TRANSMUTATION

by Larry Dixon

Larry Dixon is the husband of Mercedes Lackey, and a successful artist as well as science fiction writer. He and Mercedes live in Oklahoma.

Prologue

VALDEMAR weathered the Mage-Storms, and all the nations and peoples of Velgarth worked to stabilize in the aftermath. In the north of Valdemar, Darien and his compatriots returned from their quest to find Darien's parents. Errold's Grove, Kelmskeep, and the newest Hawk-brother Vale, k'Valdemar, forged ahead alongside the western refugees while in the east, ancient Iftel opened its borders for the first time, and to the south Hardorn and Karse were no longer the threats they once were.

The trouble now, though, was from within. A trade baron named Farragur Elm and a coalition of major tradesmen, distributors, and warehousers seized all resources in the vicinity of Deedun and created a putative secessionist movement, using the entire—stolen—livelihoods of the region's workers as leverage. The strong arm of the plan was a mercenary force, once under Haven's pay, hired over to Elm's side. The Crown sent Heralds, Guard Regulars, and Cavalry to test the situation. In the first engagement with the mercenaries, Cavalry officer Hallock Stavern was mortally wounded, and dragged back to camp—whereupon he was put in medical isolation as an untreatable casualty. He heard a commotion outside, and discovered that a gryphon, sent from Kelmskeep in the north to scout the situation, dove in and smashed a mercenary attack against Valdemaran troops—but was himself gravely hurt. The gryphon, given only the crude medical treatment available and expected to expire soon, was housed with Stavern. They shared each others' company with stories of their homes and loves. Hallock told the gryphon, Kelvren, about his wife Genni. Charmed by the tales of Genni's love for the man, Kelvren is soothed, but then Hallock critically weakens—and would have died, if not for Kelvren's desperate Healing spellwork to save him.

It came at a great cost, though, because aside from his terrible wounds going septic, Kelvren was sliding into an agonizing death as a result of using literally *all* of his magic capacity to heal Hallock—and it was not coming back. . . .

***

Darkwind k'Treva handed over a strip of paper. "Here's trouble."

Elspeth turned away from the Lord Marshal and read the paper's battlefield shorthand aloud. "Gryphon, male. Defended First Company Sixteenth. Wounded. Recovered from field. Initial aid bad. Disposition: Gryphon near death, from attempt to heal Guard officer by spellwork. Healers unable to aid further." She frowned as she put that dispatch aside from the rest, and tapped her command baton thoughtfully on her chin. "We'd better tell Treyvan and Hydona."

"Mmm. You know how they are. Protective," Darkwind observed. He leaned forward against the most massive of the many strategic planning tables in the Haven palace. It held charts far more detailed than the great map inlaid on the wall in the main court room. "They'll be concerned. You remember those parental instincts of theirs from when we first met. With Jerven and Lytha getting older, they treat every other gryphon as clueless little fledglings to be herded about and taught not to fall into wells." He murmured to a page, who nodded and left immediately.

Less than half a candlemark passed before there were results.

"Unbarrr the way," a deep voice boomed from behind the double doors as palace guards hastily tried to open them. An imposing male gryphon shouldered into the room, causing the guards to stumble back as the heavy doors swung against them. Truth be told, he liked the feeling of people trying to get out of his way. And no wonder people did, considering both of the resident gryphons' reputations and relative power—and sheer presence. Treyvan had a wicked beak and formidable talons that were, at the moment, sheathed in wood-and-leather coverings to protect the Palace's floors. He was golden brown, with shadings of pure metallic gold and darker sable, with golden eyes the size of fists. Completely aside from being a predator the size of a horse, Hydona alone could wither a tree just by staring at it, or should the mood strike her, restore it to life. Treyvan was smaller, just as powerful magically, but faster, stronger, and more direct in action. Together, they put forth a presence in Haven felt in more ways than just the body heat they radiated. Treyvan's crested head flicked side to side, then homed in on the main table and its dozen or so planners and pages. "Who isss it?" he demanded, with no preamble.

Elspeth retrieved the dispatch slip and looked it over for any new clues she might have missed in the dozens of lines of code. She finally shrugged, holding the paper up. "It doesn't say. Dispatches can be annoyingly vague, I'm sorry. It's just how they are," she offerred.

"And concsserrrned about all grrryphonsss isss how I am. No morrre than that?" Any excuses about field vagueness clearly did not placate the beast that stalked toward the largest planning table. Respected friend of the Crown's or not, Treyvan had long ago established that he wasn't someone to obstruct, for any reason. Lesser commanders, analysts and staff alike, parted to make room. Elspeth handed over the dispatch, and Treyvan accepted it delicately with the tips of his talons.

"It might be from one of the Vales duc west of there, but that would be more than a hundred miles. It wouldn't have any good reason to be in this region, would it? Maybe it got lost," a lieutenant suggested, but that only gained him a loud click of Treyvan's beak, snapping a warning. "He," Treyvan said sternly. "The grrryphon isss a 'he,' not

an 'it,' sssoldierrr. Flesssh, bone, blood, beak," and he
clacked his own for emphasis, making a sound like branches
snapping, "talonsss," and he flicked up thumb and forefin-
gers of his right "hand," causing subtle magical sparks to
split off, "and mind asss sssharrrp asss any herrre." A
nearby sergeant visibly winced, and tapped the lieutenant's
shoulder. They made themselves scarce, each giving a weak
salute to Elspeth before fleeing.

Darkwind snorted a barely suppressed laugh. "Another
stellar triumph for interspecies diplomacy, Treyvan. Good
work."

The gryphon Adept ground his beak and clicked it softly.
"He sssstrrruck sssomething that annoyed me. I cannot
abide usss being thought of asss lesss than yourrr equalsss.
Hissstorrry ssshowsss that—" he growled.

Darkwind interrupted, "Maybe he thought of you all as
something *more* than equals. You don't call an Avatar or
sacred vision 'he' or 'she.' Unless you're very good friends.
I'm sure he was just overwhelmed by the dazzling thought
of—"

Elspeth rolled her eyes and sighed, giving a wave of reassurance to the staff as they backed off. The Lord Marshal
raised a brow, then drifted to another table, shaking his
head. A few adjuncts stayed. Elspeth snapped her fingers.
"You two. Featherheads. Come visit my world," she said,
and loudly tapped her baton on the map.

Treyvan loomed beside Darkwind and studied the map,
twitching his massive wings a few times. "K'Valdemar
Vale," Darkwind surmised, and tapped a fingertip on the
map symbol. "He might be from there. Firesong's new
roost. They're near Kelmskeep, they've got a wing of
gryphons, and they're threatened by the land grab. Assuming Kelmskeep and k'Valdemar are on good terms, they
may have gotten gryphons to fly scout. Bondbirds can only
do so much. Range and stamina would all be improved by
a healthy gryphon."

Elspeth folded her arms. "Yes. Well. It sounds like all
aid available's been given to *him*," and she eyeballed
Treyvan, "and it's failing. We only have so many Heralds
and Healers, and they're more concerned about the hundreds of troops digging in. I don't much like the news
from the north." She reached out and tapped her baton

against the largest of the table maps. "It's more delicate than you might first think. For reasons we still don't understand, these insurgent leaders feel justified in seizing power and using force. But if we go in and squash that dissent—militarily—we send a poor message to the rest of Valdemar."

"And allies and rival states," Darkwind pointed out. "The famed free country of Valdemar, open to refugees and the oppressed—its population pounded into submission." He leafed through other dispatches, laying them out to match their approximate places of origin on the map. "But we have heard the Bell ring twice since this began. This situation cannot stand, but handling it poorly could do great long-term damage socially." If anyone was aware of things in the long term, it would be one of the Hawkbrothers who'd think of it.

"Socially, yes, but our agents report the situation began economically. We've just sent the Skybolts and what regulars we can spare. Turning in on ourselves, after so many outside threats—it doesn't feel right. The timing of it. I don't think we know enough about action at the front . . ." she trailed off, seeing Treyvan—pacing. His raptorial eyes, crystal-sharp, appeared to be focused on nothing in particular, as if he was preoccupied. "What is it?" she asked of him, while a clerk handed her a new stack of notes to be signed.

The gryphon turned his attention back to the others by the table, explaining for the adjuncts' benefit. "Therrre arrre many waysss forrr a grrryphon to die," he began, rolling his Rs and hissing the sibillants in the accent all gryphons bore when speaking Valdemaran. "Assside frrrom the usssual overrrcasssting risssksss, frrrom headachesss to unwanted combussstion, overrrworrrk of magerrry can lead to deadly maladiesss, in grrryphonsss. It isss why we take sssuch carrre. The more unssskilled the casssterrr, the morrre enerrrgy isss usssed forrr a ssspell. The ssspell purrrpossse itsss dirrrective ssstrrructurrre— trrriesss many posssible sssolutionsss to compenssssate forrr the lack of prrrecsssisssion. Each attempt usssessess powerrr, and then demandsss morrre forrr the next attempt to begin. Without knowledge of the ssspecif—"

"The point?" Darkwind asked, cutting off what might

have become one of Treyvan's infamous lectures on magic theory.

Treyvan shot Darkwind an indignant glance. "You humansss have lesss rrrisssk in magerrry becausssse you can live without it. We live by magic powerrr morrre than food and drrrink. It isss one of hundrrredsss of rrreasssonsss why even cssenturrriesss afterrr ourrr crrreation, we rrrequirrre *trondi'irn* forrr consssstant help jussst to sssurrrvive. We arrre sssusstained by the converrrrsion of magical enerrrgy jussst to live, brrrreathe, and move. If a grrrryphon pushesss too farrr, vital sssystemsss will ceassse theirrr functionsss. Even losssing too many featherrrsss can kill a grrrryphon, becausssse we mussst collect the frrrree-field, orrr asss Masssterrr Levy callsss it, parrrticulate magical enerrrgy thrrrough them into the featherrr corrresss, ssssocketsss, and frrrom therrre into the interrrlacssed sssysssstemsss of . . ."

"That point you were getting to, Treyvan?" Darkwind prompted again.

"Hurrrhhh. Free-field enerrrgy isss denssserrr sssincsse the Ssstorrrmsss, and ssso, easierrr to sssift frrrom the airrr. A grrrryphon ssspellworrrkerrr, asss the dissspatch indicatesss thisss one isss, could heal himssself, if he could heal anotherrr. But the changesss sssincsse the Ssstorrrmsss have made mossst of Valdemarrr—hazy. Like a fog, magically. And any . . . dozen . . . thingsss could be wrrrong, jussst frrrom indissscrrriminate ssspellworrrk alone."

Darkwind nodded. "*Indi'ta kusk,* for example. *Tcha'ki'situsk.* In k'Leshyan, gryphon heavy injuries translate to 'ruins.' Most deep injuries cascade into worse bodily failures, and are ultimately lethal. If it is, say, a nullment ruin, *hirs'ka'usk,* then even what we consider 'normal' organs will falter as a result of the magic conversion organs waning."

"Small wonder our Healers are lost. Magical *organs*? Converters? More unpronounceable words?" Elspeth could only shrug. "We don't know who the gryphon is or what the injuries are, and we have a thousand other problems right now. What are we going to do about it?" Elspeth and Darkwind both glanced meaningfully at the Gryphon Adept while stacks of fresh dispatches were handed over.

The gryphon narrowed his eyes. "If you don't do sssomething, I will."

"You probably should, sheyna," Darkwind answered bluntly, sensing an opportunity and taking it. "Consider yourself assigned. We're in deep right here. All of our heavy magic work is going to be stopping a very uncivil war. And if there are no objections, if you can go north, I want you to take a writ of authority and your badges of rank with you, and help out up there. At least establish a teleson link if you get the chance. We are only getting so much back by Herald and courier. I'd like your eyes, and your power, up there. Your gryphon's your priority, but the rest—best discretion."

Treyvan nodded firmly, and let his hackles smooth down as he turned to exit. The two door guards he'd bullied through before flung open the doors as the gryphon closed in on them. Treyvan eyed each of them, and paused—then rumbled, "Sssorrry about earlierrr," and stalked briskly down the hall.

In a word, Kelvren was miserable. The rain persisted, and the too-small tent he'd been allocated had long since fallen down over him. The tent poles had slanted forward to begin with, and when the wind picked up they'd fallen all the way. It left his rump and tail out in the rain, and the canvas of the tent draped over his head like a very soggy, ill-designed cloak's hood.

He'd managed to inch his hindquarters up enough that they weren't mired in the mud, but that was it. The trouble was, he felt so heavy. Not lethargic, like he'd been drowsing in the sun. That was different. This was simply the feeling that his wings weighed too much, and that his muscles weren't up to the task of moving him. If he still had his teleson set, he could call for help. He could have called for help before he was even wounded—but it was long lost back where his skirmish took place and was probably since crushed under horse hooves. Kelvren was a weak Mindspeaker to begin with. The teleson amplified what he was able to muster, and without it, he probably couldn't Mindspeak past his tail.

The Healer that had tended to him after he'd saved Hallock Stavern's life had long since departed to the Front—and she hadn't known even the basics of gryphon anatomy. She'd confessed to Birce she'd used draft animal Healing techniques on him, in fact. The indignity of it! She'd better not tell *that* to anyone else or she'd have Silver Gryphon Kelvren to answer to. And she didn't want *that,* he told himself.

His secret bravado was fading away with every minute of this storm. He feared some sort of awful infection from his wounds was causing his inertia. The day seemed hopeless, and tomorrow he'd be weaker still. He could feel it. *This was no way for a hero to end.* He thought again about a famed tapestry picture he'd admired as a youth, back at the city of White Gryphon. It was many centuries old, of Skandranon, the Black Gryphon, wings spread, standing majestically atop Urtho's Tower with all the people of the Kaled'a'in looking up at him adoringly. The moon and stars shone behind the hero and made a halo around his body.

That, young Kelvren Skothkar had beamed, just days before joining the Silver Gryphons for training. *I want to be like that. I want to be a legend.*

It seemed like it might work, too. He trained hard, and emulated the ancient hero in every way that he could—superb flyer, vicious fighter, fine strategist, *stupendously* skilled lover—well, at least *he* thought so—and when the choice was to be bold or prudent, he went with bold. And reputation was vital—everyone knew who Skandranon Rashkae was in ancient times, even the dreaded enemies Ma'ar and the *makaar.* Kelvren didn't precisely boast, but he always made certain everyone knew who he was, and knew every deed. He knew he'd be a hero if he tried hard enough. A glorious legend!

Instead, he was like *this.* Mud was splattering up onto his chin and breastfeathers from the constant rain splashing the soil in front of the tent. Miserable. There was constant, throbbing agony from his wounds. The whipstitching felt like a line of fire. No one was coming to help him either. His friends at Kelmskeep and k'Valdemar had to be searching for him—but he was weak, and without a teleson he couldn't tell them where he was—and there were none with the soldiers, not a mage or Herald or even a hedge-wizard, who could Mindspeak or send word. He was angry, and anger was turning into one of the things that kept him going. They didn't bring him enough food, for one thing. There was no one to come clean him, no one to see to his

needs. No one to groom him. No one to *admire* him. All
the basics of gryphon well-being were absent.

And he was stuck on the ground.

Murky as the sky was, he couldn't help but gaze up at
it. A Tayledras proverb said, "When once you have tasted
flight, you forever after walk the earth with your eyes
turned skyward, for there you have been, and there you
will ever long to return." Never before was it so heart-
breakingly true. If he had bothered to count the number
of times he'd twitched his heavy wings, gathered up his
shaky haunches to leap, and almost surged forward to
flight—but stopped, knowing he couldn't—he would probably feel even worse.

He'd been on his feet earlier in the day, when the down-
pour ceased for a while. He'd shambled around through
the underbrush and high grasses of the hillock they'd put
him on. Well away from the troops, the townspeople, their
homes, their goods, and their horses.

*As if I'd eat the horses, anyway. Of course I wouldn't.
Unless they were offered.*

Someone down there had probably seen him eyeing the
corral, too. He felt like someone was always looking his
way. He saw no smiles when he caught the locals at it
either. It definitely did not fulfill the ever-so-vital require-
ment a gryphon had: to be admired. This was more like—
well, it was what it was—being kept purposely at a distance.
Twice today he'd felt an overwhelming emotional wave,
like a sour crop forcing its way up, that he simply wasn't
wanted here. He swayed on his feet then and sat down
abruptly, cracking the bushes underneath him when he
thought about it. It just didn't feel right to be like this.
They had to know what he'd done for Hallock, and what
he'd done for Valdemar—didn't they? Didn't that count
for anything?

It counted for something. He just hadn't realized, when
he was walked to the tent and given an uncooked pork
haunch, just how true what they'd said was.

It's the least we can do.

Apparently, it was.

He'd been put out here, with pleasantries about having
free space to roam around and no crowding. How diplomatic a way to tell him he'd been literally put out to pas-

ture. It took an effort to even heave a sigh when he thought about it. He had belly cramps. He attributed them to the food, the weather, and to his discontent. And, he *itched*. He felt like he was getting parasites under his feathers, and didn't have the spare strength to gnaw and scratch at them. And now, here he was—the brave skydancer—soaked, stuck, under a tarp, having a thoroughly unwanted mud-bath.

It just couldn't get much worse, he thought, *except there is a Tayledras saying that thinking those words is the first sign that it will definitely be worse.*

There was so much noise from the rain and thunder that he didn't hear someone approach until they were close enough to startle him. He felt suddenly furious at himself that instead of lurching to his feet ready for a threat, he only flinched. His eyes must have looked especially intense, as a result, because the boy who came toward him immediately backpedaled. The boy had on loose, heavily patched pants and over-large boots, and the rain sluiced off of his wide-brimmed—and also quite patched—sun hat. Right now the hat only seemed to serve as a way of directing rain down his back. He carried a sack in both hands that for all the world appeared to contain—and be completely covered in—mud. He looked about as gaunt as Kelvren felt, and his untanned skin had irregular patches of very dark brown, like the hide of a wild horse or domestic cattle. It wasn't like anything Kel had seen before on a human. Then again, like seemingly everything else in this part of the world, the dark splotches could have just been caked mud.

"Sir Gryphon, sir? 'S time for your feeding. Is that all right, sir? You hungry?" The boy's voice was strained with fear, and the words were obviously forced out between nearly clenched teeth. In fact, those teeth chattered a little from the rain as the wind picked up. "Come to feed you? Sir?"

"Hurrrh, yesss, come. Clossserrr. I won't eat you. What did you brrring?" The insult the boy delivered was galling. Come to *feed* him, like he was some animal in a pen? Did they have any idea who he was? What he was? He tried to stand, but instead just felt pinned by the soaked canvas. "Thessse polesss fell down. Come help with them firrrssst."

The boy looked around for a dry place to put his load, and since there was none, he settled on a thick clump of tallgrass to cradle the sack. It was still in the rain but out of the immediate muddy water. Hitching up his pants, he clumped through the sludge to the edge of the canvas, pulled it up, and met Kelvren's eyes full-on. Apparently up this close to a gryphon for the first time, the boy looked like a squirrel who just that moment realized that the pretty shadow closing in on him was an owl. Ten heartbeats passed before the boy moved another inch.

At that precise moment between ten and eleven heartbeats, the canvas weakly arched over Kelvren's head collapsed completely from the weight of the rain on it, leaving only the curve of a muddy beak sticking out.

Kelvren closed his eyes and sighed. *From the miserable to the absurd. I did wonder,* the gryphon thought, *and now I know. It does get worse.*

Treyvan walked to the recital chamber Hydona was using as a classroom. The sunlight from the dormers glinted on seven knifeblades, and illuminated the swirls of dust from feathers and age stirred up by the belt-fed brass overhead fans and the wings of the three gryphons already in the room. Sixteen people, a few in Herald's Whites, were in a loose semicircle strewn with books, folios, and large multi-colored drawings. They all seemed comfortable, propped up on dozens of mismatched pillows, and Hydona looked most comfortable of all lying on her belly on a short stage. Behind her, the two gryphlets, Jervan and Lytha, were doing their best to hover without flapping their wings. The lift that gave gryphons their ability to fly was in their bones, and it was a discipline to try and hover solely by mental control without moving any air by wings. Lytha looked to be a prodigy, almost a yard from the floor, with all four feet dangling down as if she was held in midair like a boneless cat. Jervan only managed to get his forelegs and wings to stay up without too much effort. He held himself in place and cried out, "Rrrampant!" then used his new position as an opportunity to bat at his sister's tail more easily.

Treyvan swept in and told Jervan, "Leave yourrr sssissst-errr alone orrr I'll feed you to the Companionsss," reached out, and bumped Jervan with a wingtip. The gryphlet's wings snapped out straight from his sides, changing his center of balance in his partial levitation. He fell over backward, whistling high-pitched laughter, while his sister joined in—but she sounded smug.

"Tyrrrant," Hydona trilled as her mate approached. "Come to conquerrr?" she teased as Treyvan tapped beaks with her and then turned his head upside-down to accept an ear nibble. "You sssee, ssstudentss, you mussst be prrreparrred to maintain yourrr worrrk durrring any dissstrrraction." The seven knives she held suspended point-down in midair between the stage and the students didn't waver. In fact, it appeared that she paid no attention to the knives at all. "Thisss isss why you essstablish sssolid anchorrr pointsss when beginning worrrk. Rrrelative posssitionsss mean rrrelative forrrcsse. When you know the posssitionsss well, you can then concssentrrrate on what might affect thossse posssitionsss. Contrrrol isss in how you sssensssse the changesss in thossse posssitionsss. and compensssate. Thisss isss why ssso many trrraditionsss ussse diagrrramsss and patterrrnsss in magic; they arrre waysss of trrrracking posssitionsss asss powerrr isss moved and changed. In thisss way you can ussse finessse, and lesss powerrr, by accurrrate percssseption. Morrre awarrrenesss meansss using lesss brrrute forcsse."

"Unlesss you like brrrute forcsse," Treyvan teased.

"Unlesss you have a mate that interrruptsss you consssstantly durrring yourrr prrracticsse. Then brrrute forcsse isss authorrrized, and you may ussse the knivesss on him," she replied in the same tone. Gryphlets cackled from behind her, and most of the students laughed outright.

"You wound me," Treyvan complained.

"I wisssh," Hydona replied, and chewed on his other ear. "But I need you arrround ssso I don't torrrment the ssstudentsss asss much. What isss wrrrong?" Her tone changed from mocking to concerned as she sat up on her haunches.

"An unknown grrryphon'sss been grrrounded, up norrrth," Treyvan admitted. "He isss at one of the sssupply line villagesss but therrre isssn't anyone who knowsss what'sss wrrrong with him. Rrreportsss sssay he isss without magic, and not doing well."

"You ssshould go," Hydona answered immediately. Gryphlet heads popped up from behind the stage. "I'll sssee to yourrr ssstudentsss and herrrd thossse two without you forrr a while."

"Hurrrh. Arrre you sssurrre you want me away?" Treyvan prompted.

"You can go away asss long asss you need to, loverrr," Hydona purred. "becaussse I know who you'rrre coming back to."

***

The rain had finally let up to just a haze and the boy had gotten the tent back up while Kelvren wobbled away through the field to relieve himself. He limped back, wings dragging in the tallgrass, and crawled into the tent. The gryphon bumped a wing and dislodged one of the four poles doing so, but the boy quickly sloshed around to prop it back up. Kelvren was almost turned completely over onto his stronger side, trying to get to some of his worst itches with his beak or talons when the boy said, "I'll get your food, sir. Just wait right there."

Kelvren openly growled.

"I'll be herrre. Why would I want to leave thisss palace?" the gryphon snorted. "All the sssilk tapessstrrriesss and dancssing girrrlsss arrre rrreason enough to ssstay."

"It's not so bad, sir, just depends what you compare it to. That's what I always tell myself." He returned with the sack and plopped it on the slightly less muddy tent floor.

"Not ssso bad? I am sssoaked to the bone. I can barrrely walk, I look terrrible, and I have beetlesss and twigsss underrr my wingsss. Do you underrrsssstand? *Beetlesss and twigsss.*"

"Ticks, too, probably," the boy shrugged. He undid the knots on the sack and left it open like a feedbag in front of the gryphon. "We get a lot of ticks around here. When it rains, they climb as high as they can up on the grass." The boy took his hat off and shook it toward the outside— an exercise in futility if there ever was one, since the hat had so many open patches in the weave, he may as well have been wearing an angler's net on his head.

Kelvren itched all over again, thinking about that.

"Thanksss," he growled, but the boy must have thought he was referring to the food.

"Y'welcome sir. I have to wait for the sack when you're done, so please don't tear it up much. I don't have too many."

Kelvren nosed into the bag and tasted at it with an extended tongue. He hadn't expected prime cuts, but it looked and tasted as if he was getting the least wanted body parts from whatever animals they had at the time. There were a couple of knuckle joints, and what looked like some backstrap from a—well, he wasn't sure. Could be pork. Could be horse. Could be deer. Could be tax collector. He hoped for horse. A short leg here, a few feet of entrails, six chicken feet and a hoof. Well, that part was identifiable at least.

It might be best just to eat it all, without looking too closely.

The boy was as far back against the side of the tent as he could manage, knees folded up to his chest and hands holding the hat in front of him. He stared at the gryphon.

Kelvren pulled his face out of the sack and regarded the boy. "Don't be afrrraid," he said, blood dripping continuously off his beak.

"Yes, sir. No, sir. Not afraid, sir."

"Hurrrh," Kelvren growled, and got another few pounds of the stuff down his gullet. "Ssso. Why sssend you up herrre? What did you do wrrrong?" the gryphon asked. He was only half joking.

"Lot of the town figures you're really dangerous, sir. And they need all able bodies down there, but I don't really count so much, and some of the folk, they want to stay with what stock they've got left to 'em in case you went down there, you know, on a rampage or somethin'. Monsters always rampage, they said."

Kelvren narrowed his eyes and peered out of the tent, letting his mood smolder for a long while. "Alwaysss," he growled.

"That's what I'm told, sir."

"Ssso. I am a rrrampage-to-be, and they sssend a boy to brrring me food? You mussst be verrry brrrave."

"Not so brave, sir. I get the work no one else wants, and I go with it. Gets my mum and me a little coin. Privy needs cleared out, fence strung through swamp, cleanup after calving, I'm who they get. Like I say, isn't so bad depending what you compare it to. There's folk out there losin' limbs and eyes and all. I figure I'm doin' all right. An' if somethin' happened to me, they said they'd just get someone else, so it's all proper."

"You'rrre herrre becaussse they can do without you if I ate you, and you'rrre—content with that?"

The boy shrugged and smiled. "Not like I want to get eaten, sir, but if I did get all killed, I'd still have had a life. Been told I shouldn't have, enough times, I figure I'm lucky havin' even a short one." He pinched the edges of his hat, staring at the water drips that fell from it while Kelvren finished the remains in the bag. "It might not be such a bad thing, anyway. They say you go to a really nice place when you die, where everything's warm and pretty. It's supposed to be a place where folk really like you no matter what. You probably know how it is, bein' a monster and all. No one can really be welcome everywhere."

Kelvren nudged the bag a few inches sideways toward the boy. "Ssso I am learrrning."

The boy picked up the bag and knotted the cords. "An' anyhow, I have my mum, an' she's good to me no matter what, even now that all's this happened. She said we were just about to get rich, too, which woulda been nice. Still, all the army trouble can't go on forever." He wiped his bloodied hands on his trousers. "Uh—thanks for not tearing up the bag or eating me," he said cheerfully, and put his soggy hat back on.

"Anytime," Kelvren replied, still mystified by the boy's logic.

The boy smiled, and waved back as he tromped out through the muddy field toward his town.

***

"This haze is . . . intolerable," Treyvan growled in Kaled-'a'in, lashing his tail in anger. "I can't do any better with my distance viewing, and that Herald with that FarSeeing Gift just left for the Deedun front. The Storms haven't so much made things unreliable as they've made them . . . hurrh . . . unfamiliar. This all would have worked five years

ago and now it is giving us nothing. All we know is where
the target is. And just a glimpse.''

"Did the glimpse show you anything useful?" a small
voice crooned from below Treyvan. The gryphon turned
his hawklike gaze down past his magic instruments to the
hertasi in the vast room with him. The little lizard creature
looked up at the gryphon with a wide-eyed but unafraid
expression.

"Rrrhhh. A Changecircle near by a Valdemaran Guard
camp. A gryphon body in a tent. Head down, wings flat."
Treyvan pondered. "Signs of heavy injuries but tended to.
Looked like Far Westerner, but he was no gryphon I know.
I couldn't read an identifying radiant—" Treyvan snapped
his head up suddenly. "No radiant aura, Pena. No distinc-
tive life glow to Mage-Sight. No wonder it was so hard to
find him. He wasn't shielded, there was just nothing there
to shield. I was looking for gryphon aura traits, but I must
have passed him by a dozen times since he seemed to only
come across as a common animal from such a search."

The *hertasi* looked alarmed. She obviously knew what
that meant. "*Hirs'ka'ursk* you think? He'll be dead soon,"
is all she could think of to say.

"We'll see about that," Treyvan growled, with an under-
tone of determination, and stalked to a massive cabinet.
He reared up onto his haunches, laid both claws flat on the
upper corners, and dug his thumbtalons into the sockets in
the trimwork. He twisted them and spoke "*hiskusk,*" and
the sound of long metals rods shifting and clanging into
place sounded from inside. The cabinet unfolded. Mage-
lights inside gleamed off of teleson sets, a massive leather
and brass harness, steel fighting claws, a narrow breastplate
and more. Treyvan pulled out and shouldered on one side
of the harness, while the *hertasi* rushed in to clip and buckle
the other side of it. More *hertasi* rushed in after three sharp
whistles from the gryphon, and preparations for a flight
gained momentum quickly. Three telesons were wrapped
and packed into a flat case, and at a nod from the gryphon,
the fighting claws were packed as well. Treyvan called out
instructions of what must be brought, and side pouches
were stuffed with arcane materials and clipped to the harness. Before long, a swarm of the little lizards were ready-
ing him for flight and unlacing his talonsheaths. When

Treyvan reached the outdoors, he shook his wings and tested the harness for fit. Another pair of *hertasi* affixed his ornamental breastplate and cinched it tight, while another one added several more pouches to his flight harness. "Pena. That downed gryphon is going to need a *trondi'irn*. Get Whitebird ready for travel right now. Tell Hydona I am going north."

Pena, the senior *hertasi*, turned to her charges still inside. "Get Whitebird ready for travel right now. Tell Hydona that Treyvan and I are going north."

Treyvan gave Pena a look of disbelief, even as she turned to clamber into heavy insulated clothing. He opened his beak but was stopped short by the senior *hertasi* poking a stubby finger up at him. "You know how this works, Treyvan. If you need supplies, you can't stop mid-spell to go fetch them. You get caught up in your magic and you know it. You don't get fed enough, you get cranky. And if *you* got hurt yourself, who would see to you?" Pena nodded firmly, slapped her tail once on the pavestones for emphasis, and pulled her hood and glass goggles on as they were handed to her by another *hertasi* scampering by. "Now just pay attention to where you fly and give me a smooth ride, understand?"

*****

Hallock Stavern, leaning on a greenwood stick that was either a too-short crutch or a too-long cane, glared at the clerk in the tent with him, and stabbed a finger on the papers and palimpsests heaped on a table that was obviously once a door. It still had the handle and hinges. "Now you listen to me, I want answers, son, and I want them now. Is help coming from anywhere for the gryphon? Anyone, anywhere? I've got the rank to push you into Karse in your shorts if you so much as—"

The clerk held up a hand, looked up at the officer, and snapped completely. "No, you listen to me, you overbearing bastard. The dispatches were sent and there is nothing new from Haven. Nothing. *Nothing*. You understand? Look at this." He slammed his ink-stained hands on the stacks of documents. "This is what I have to deal with. Every bleeding soul in this camp, and three other camps, want messages, and they're all demanding them of me. Send me to Karse *naked* if you want. Please! It will get me out of here, but until you get twenty more clerks to replace me, you will damned well wait like everyone else! Sir!"

Hallock rocked back slowly. He narrowed his eyes and crossed his arms, as the clerk sat down. After a long moment he replied, "I should damn well promote you for talking to me like that, son."

"There's no need to wish a curse on me, sir," the clerk replied. "I know what the gryphon did for you. We all do. But no news is no news. When I know something, there'll be a runner sent for you."

Hallock frowned but had to accept it. "I'll be making the rounds of wounded, then. But I'll come back. Good luck."

The clerk didn't even look up as he resumed scrawling notes on teetering piles of papers. "Same to you, sir."

Hallock caught himself rubbing at the wide scar on his forehead, then hobbled his way out into the mess of the encampment. Woods had been cleared on either side of the main trade road, which had become the main thoroughfare of a tent city—well, a city designed by a drunken mob, maybe. There were no straight lines to get anywhere, and tents clustered around every tree that was too heavy to clear cut. Ropework between those trees appeared to have been done by myopic giant spiders during fits of seizures, and anything from canvas to blankets had been strung up as shelter. The poor tinder gained from the smaller felled trees made the cook fires underneath the canopies smoke and struggle for life. The main local source for firewood was a nondescript sort of scrubby, scrawny bush with annoying short thorns. It grew all over for miles, except for a former Changecircle at the edge of the camp. No one wanted to even set foot on that Circle, even though it was set perfectly atop a circular mound that probably had the best drainage, and view, of any of this mud-ridden swamp.

The most orderly part of the whole encampment was on either side of the wide road to the river's edge, where the grain mill was. The miller moved in with a family in town, and volunteered his home as a command post. Most of the officer corps had settled into the mill tower, which was the tallest building for many miles around. The rooms above the grindstones served as operation planning rooms for security reasons. In truth, it was mainly because the rooms were warm, dry, and had fireplaces—some comfort despite the incessant grind of the millstones.

Hallock should technically be in there now, but the drone of the mill gave him a headache. So did the thick concentration of junior officers arguing tactics, where they tried to justify staying inside where they were "needed." Most of the staff at the mill mean well, but they didn't seem to understand: an army can not be administrated—it must be led. After the southern border wars, the turmoil of the Storms and the strife the Changecircles brought, one leader after another retired from service. Few command veterans had stayed in field service after all of that. Stavern's First, his commander of the Sixteenth Regiment, had been the most experienced field commander the Guard could send northward at the time. He knew the protocols as the woman's subordinate, but he hadn't known her well. She'd fallen when Hallock had. The morning that he'd been cut loose from the Healer's tent and the yellow ribbon removed from it, he heard the horns sounding the mourning notes. She had been buried already.

And here he was.

A new stripe tacked on the sleeve.

A new ribbon under the badge.

Brevet promotion. First of the Sixteenth, Captain Hallock Stavern.

A senior officer, maybe, but still one of the regulars in his heart.

Filthy and unpleasant as the cantonment was, at least here he was with the Guard. He hadn't gained his previous rank by nepotism or bribery, he'd gained it by genuinely believing in what the Guard could be, and his soldiers knew. Just the fact that he was in the muck, waving off occasional offers for help, and took his time checking in on the units didn't go unnoticed. If he had to plod along on a crutch to see to the soldiers' well-being, rather than pass by in a driven carriage, then that's how it would be done, and the mill be damned.

He stopped in at one of the larger tents, an open-front, thirty-pole affair where cots and poorly strung hammocks were every one filled with the wounded. The most open section of the ill-set compound tent held a score of uni-

formed women and men with boiling pots of water, sorting
rough buckets of more-or-less straight wood. Six of those
in the hammocks were unconscious, but two were snoring,
so that was a good sign. The ones awake were, healthily,
complaining of officers and strategies. These twenty-some
souls were the barely ambulatory Guard soldiers who were
left over from most of the northern clashes. As was the
Valdemaran tradition, if they weren't fit to ride or march,
they had been put to work. Those that still had full use of
their hands were engaged in basic fletching. All Guards that
were rated for field combat knew how to make arrows,
bolts, and spears of several types, of whatever native materials could be scrounged.

Supply trains were on the way from the south, and a
wagon or two arrived every few candlemarks during the
day. Proper, larger tents were being unloaded even now by
a mix of the Guard and the local, but now largely unem-
ployed, populace. Harvest crews would never come, so the
large households that depended on them for their crops
now faced hardship. The stalks and rushes from the grain
harvests wouldn't be collected, and peddlers who sold the
baskets and other wares made from them would have no
goods, and so on down the line.

The locals were being compensated for their goods and
work, but a government chit didn't change the fact that so
soon after the terrors of the Storms, when hope was building up again, their livelihoods had been smashed.

Still, where there is life there is hope, he thought as he
looked around the convalescents' tent. *And here I am alive
to see it. And I'll see Haven again and walk its streets again
with Genni.*

"First. Sir." The senior officer of the tent gave him a
salute with her one unbandaged hand. Even that was unexpected; most decorum went out with the slop in places like
this. "Good t'see y'back with us," she said, and it didn't
take a genius to read the subtext.

"Thanks, Corporal. You being seen to well here?"

The obvious answer came right on cue. "Well as can be
expected, sir." A couple of others chuckled—no matter
what region you were from or what Valdemaran dialect
you spoke, some answers are utterly predictable. Things
sobered up quickly as she spoke her mind. "Whole thing's

been a bit of a toss, honestly. It's not a proper deployment, we say, 'cause we're moving against, well, our own really. Ain't a one of us feels right bein' here 'cause of moving on fellow Valdemarans. We ought not be fightin' our own." The senior enlisted man nearby coughed, discreetly trying to wave the corporal down from making some kind of blunder. She gave him a rude gesture with a few fingers. " 'Ey, it's true. We talked 'bout it an' that's how we all lean. First's got the right t' know how we feel, even if we are stuck as gimps." She looked back to Hallock. "Might be a black mark on m'record to say all that, sir, but just the same, I'd as soon not get promoted in the Guard over fightin' my own countrymen."

Hallock leaned a little less on his stick and eyed everyone there who'd meet his gaze. "It's not exactly treasonous to say this kind of thing, but it bends some regs. Someone with less ribbon than me might bust down hard on you over what you just said. So why tell *me* this, of all people?"

Hallock felt himself unexpectedly moved from the words that followed. Right here were all of his country's virtues summed up in a few minutes of hesitant confession. The corporal spoke up first.

"Because you're here, sir. I mean, we coulda writ it up, an' sent it all official. Or could've gotten a clerk t'pass it 'round in rumor-mail. But fact is, sir," she hesitated, but then saw others nodding. "Fact is, sir, we get put off duty roster, there ain't much use for us. 'Cept as idle hands an' cot-warmers—but we ain't got idle minds, an' we're still Guard even if we get stuck off t' bleed-in-place." Another soldier grunted at that particularly derogatory term for convalescents.

"We told you, 'cause you came here to us. Not us to you. An' that means a bunch to us gimps."

Murmurs of agreement came from around the tent. A junior enlisted footman added, "You bein' so close to bein' one yerself, sir, we figured you'd understand better than the mill." The group nodded to that as well. "Isn't everyone gets magic-saved by a—" and he looked around for suggestions. "By one of those. Gods and spirits got t'have plans for you, sir, that kind of thing just doesn't happen to regular folk like us. We figure y'gotta be somethin' amazing for that t'happen."

Hallock steadied himself on his staff again, and licked his lips. "There is something amazing, at that, but I'll tell you what," he began. "We were under orders and got hit hard. A gryphon none of us had ever met struck out of the sky like a thunderbolt and near laid down his life to help Valdemaran soldiers just like me and you. Then he near killed himself just so I could get home to see my wife." He looked to each of them, completely holding their attention. "Every one of you here lost blood, bone, or tooth defending your fellow soldiers. You didn't even know their names, but you bled for 'em just the same, so they could get home to *their* families." He shook his head and leaned on his walking stick more heavily. "You're lookin' the wrong way here. You think *I'm* special because a fury shot out of the sky and fought to save Guard? To save *me*? Hell, no." He paused for a few breaths, looking at each of them again. "*You're* all amazing because you're like *him*."

***

Kelvren slept far longer than he'd intended, and it was a sleep with unsteady dreams. These dreams were more like sharp images, that struck and faded like the pluck of a bowstring, leaving afterimages and the memories that spun off from them. The worst were ones of his body coming apart, splitting open from each of the wounds he'd suffered until he floundered, drowning, in a deep pool of all his blood. The other dreams were less grisly—there was sky, in most of them, in the deep blue of chasing dawn, or the dazzling blaze of white only seen when emerging from one cloud towards another in bright day. There was the view of the Londell River, and Lake Evendim, and the descent into Errold's Grove. Some memories were sexual—which was no unusual thing for a gryphon, especially him. He'd been on quite a few backs over the years. Skydancing, solicitous crooning, laughter, and intimate nibbling were well recalled, then they'd fade away until another of those bowstring images shocked into his mind. His friends at k'Valdemar—Darian and Snowfire, and Steelmind and that insufferably enigmatic Firesong. And his *trondi'irns,* who made him feel so good, and got him prepared so finely for his assignations—and then it was back to the sex dreams again.

"Sir? Time for your feeding, sir." The boy with the mottled skin was back, looking under the flap of the tent.

Kelvren rolled onto his belly, startled. He immediately regretted it, crushing his sheath. He yelped and then kept his eyes closed a while, seeing only dazzle.

"Sir? You all right? You made a funny noise."

Kelvren coughed twice and answered, "Funny forrr you. Not ssso funny forrr me." He winced and slowly opened his eyes. "I may have brrroken sssomething I'll need laterrr. Urrrh. Food?" he asked, ears flicking forward. "Or isss it what you brrrought lassst time?"

"Uhm. It's not the, ah, exact same as last time. Some of it's new colors. And I brought some bread that didn't turn out right, but they didn't want me to tell you that. They figured, if you didn't know it was burned, you'd maybe think it was a treat."

Kelvren's eyes went to slits and he stood up on all fours, but kept his head down as he exited the tent. As he came out into full sun, despite the haze left from the heavy rain before, he swung his head to bear dead on the village.

"A trrreat. I am wearrrry of thisss disssrrressspect. You. Boy. What isss yourrr name?"

"Boy. I mean, that's what most people say to call me, is Boy. My full name's Jeft Roald Dunwythie. The Roald part's named after the king, o' course. No relation. But like I say, most everyone here knows me as Boy. So I'll answer to that if you want."

"Hurrrh. Do you like being called Boy?" Kel asked.

"It's not as if I have to like it, sir. Boy's what they call me." At the gryphon's unblinking gaze, he finally admitted, "No, I don't much like it. My mum gave me a proper name and, if it's good enough for her, it should be good enough for anyone else. If things was right. But things ain't so perfect in this life. They are as they are."

Kelvren turned away. Half a minute passed before he returned his gaze to the young man. "Jeft Rrroald Dunwythie, if you learrrn nothing elsssse frrrom me, I wisssh it to be thisss. Hold it clossse to yourrr hearrrt and never forrrget it. *It doesss not matterrr what otherrrsss call you, asss*

much asss it matterrrsss what you ansssswerrr to." The
gryphon limped away heavily, and stamped some tallgrass
down on the other side of the tent for several minutes. He
shook out his feathers, feeling renewed strength despite his
restless innards. His anger and pain were transitioning into
resolve, and a Plan. "And asss sssoon asss I am done making rrroom, we arrre going down therrre to get my next
meal. If they *expect* a rrrampaging monsssterrr, they'll find
out I am *not* that. They've ssseen me hurrrt and delirrri-
ousss, but I ssswearrr to you—they'll neverrr forrrget what
I am like when I am hungrrry, annoyed, and *deterrrmined."*

Kelvren Set into the first part of his Plan. *Principles of
magic,* he thought, *learned early on. Transmutation. Turn
what is useless into what is usable.* He hobbled toward, and
then past, his companion. *If I cannot preen for beauty, then
I will preen for effect.* He laboriously groomed—badly—
wincing several times from the persistent agony of his
wounds. He took a few deep breaths and stared up at the
sky when he was done. *If I am going out of this life,* he
thought, *I am not going as a disrespected animal shoved
away to rot. If I die, I am damned well going to do it with
a full belly, and the satisfaction of knowing I ruined some
idiot's day.*

The gryphon limped around to face the young man. Bandages askew, feathers at all angles, and his stitches exposed,
he looked to be in poor shape to anyone's eyes.

"Brrring your sssack, Jeft. Time forrr fun." Jeft did just
that, crashing along through the tallgrass and brush to catch
up. "Why arrre you ssso dissssresspected that they give you
the worrrsssst jobsss?"

"It's my face, I think. I'm not any different from the
other younglings here, 'cept my face."

"What isss wrrrong with yourrr facsse?" Kel asked, pausing ostensibly for Jeft to close in on him, but in reality, it
was because he was having trouble moving well. His right
side haunch folded up on him, and jarred his lanced shoulder badly, eliciting a short whine. "It looksss fine to me.
You have good marrrkingsss."

"That's just it there, sir, these, uh, markings," he confirmed as he stopped beside the gryphon, pointing at the
splotches that randomly covered his face. "People think my
face is really ugly. They say it's 'cause my mum married a

far-southerner, and he had bad blood in him, an' so I came out like this, all ugly from both sides, they say. And there's nothin' can be done about it, so I just do what I do." He hoisted the heavy bag up again.

"And yourrr fatherrr?"

"He died. He was one of the traveling harvesters, an' when he went away up northwest, he got crushed by one of those big carts, they said. Mum took it hard and still hasn't gotten better after that. Anyway. He's in a better place now."

Kelvren levered himself up gingerly, mulling that over, then snorted at the flies pestering his wounds and resumed his trek. "I am . . . sssorrry you—hurrh!—have—*kah! sketi!*—lossst yourrr fatherrr," he said breathily, tripping on brush. "I have not ssseen mine in fifteen yearrrsss. We sssend messsagesss but—ah. It isss not the sssame as sssharrring sssky with him."

"Sky's prob'ly where my father is," Jeft smiled. "We always did like talking about birds, me and him, so's maybe he's a bird now. He'd like that a lot 'cept, I guess he couldn't get stew an' scrapings as a bird."

Kelvren could see that soldiers and villagers were taking notice of them as they closed the distance to the encampment. Kel angled toward a recently cut tree stump and suddenly fell against it.

"Sir? Master Kelvren, sir? What's wrong?" Jeft dropped the bag and crashed toward the gryphon. "You're bleedin' again, sir, an' that, uh, sewin' they did on you's torn up some. Sir?" He waved at the flies, to little effect, and then Kel could feel the boy's hand on his eartufts. "Sir? You hear me? Can I help? Sir?" He was sounding desperate.

Slowly Kelvren opened an eye, toward Jeft. "Hurrrh. It isss—all forrr effect," he wheezed, and smiled as best he could. "Ssso brrrave. You rrrun towarrrdsss me when the rrressst of yourrr village would rrrun away."

"Well—I was scared, too!" he blurted, and then confessed, "I mean, if you—I—I'd be in a lot of trouble. Mayor said you were my problem now, an' I bet they'd whup me if you died." He pulled back his hand and wiped it on both of his eyes, under the brim of the sun hat. "It—I just don't want you t'die, all right? An', an', if y'need a healer, or somethin', I'll run get you a healer—" Jeft looked all around, and saw a dozen Guard soldiers were headed their way at a brisk walk. "I, uh—I think maybe help's coming, sir?"

Kelvren rumbled softly. "Yesss. Ssso they arrre. Heh." He closed his eyes, to rest. "Let the gamesss begin."

***

Hallock heard a commotion from the town while walking around the last of the convalescents' tents. In a Guard encampment it wasn't unusual to hear occasional incidents ranging from fist brawls to dirty-song competitions, or some poor soldier getting dressed down at top volume. This was the first one Hallock had heard, though, that began with shouting and running, and finally, laughter—and not all of it human. There was just that one loud, descending burbling voice that mixed in with the rest, but it put Hallock into motion. Quick-walking with the stick in his hand, he rounded the mill road and followed it toward the sounds—which came from the main mess tents.

He saw a mix of backs in Guard uniforms and locals' work clothing, and then a flick of a large feathery wing above them. Then there was another ripple of laughter. He pushed his way forward, finally collaring a lieutenant to help him reach the center of it all.

There he found someone who appeared to be a town official, judging by his necklace. He was getting up off his knees, where apparently he'd been vomiting into a large sack—though on second thought, yes, it appeared he had been vomiting because his head had been *in* the sack. Now the man was coughing furiously into a handkerchief and attempting to wipe his face down. Some of his attendants were trying to calm down a few Sixteenth and Guard regulars who were still shouting and provoking the man.

Kelvren sagged sideways against a trestle table, with one wing slack on the ground and his bandages askew and seeping. The platter on the table was filling up. Soldiers brought their own bowls over to pinch off a bit of meat or bread and set it down on the platter. When they spoke something to Kelvren, the gryphon nodded or smiled—but even from this far away, Hallock could tell that the creature was exhausted. Kelvren reached for a bowl and some of the food on the platter, but his taloned hands shook too much to keep hold of the bowl. A strange-looking boy stuck close to the gryphon, and was there in an instant to catch the bowl and load it up with food.

"First!" someone called out, and the air filled with a mix of expletives, intakes of breath, and "Sir!" aimed nowhere in particular. All Firsts were Captain in rank. Over a hundred Guard soldiers instantly *Weren't Involved And Were Doing Something Else When It Happened.* Whatever "it" might have been. Some soldiers saluted and then swiveled around in the mud to find who they were supposed to be directing it at. "It's Stavern!" someone else called out, and then a small cheer followed. "Welcome back, sir!" called a junior rider, who jostled around the retreating official to reach Hallock. He saluted again, apparently just to make sure he'd been seen saluting at all, but was also grinning. "Your gryphon friend there, well, we've just been taking care of him, sir. He wasn't getting treated none too well, so, we just helped him out some." The rider shooed people out of the way to get Hallock over to Kelvren's side.

The gryphon swayed a little, and his eyes pinned and dilated several times as he recognized Hallock. "Ah! My fine frrriend Hallock Ssstaverrrn," he purred. "How isss the belly?"

"Feels tight."

"Hurrrh. Mine, too. Thessse arrre good people, thcssse sssoldierrss of yourrrsss. Know the value of a good meal." A couple of dozen chuckles from all around told Hallock that he was missing something.

"Kel, you look—"

"I know how I look," the gryphon growled threateningly, then mellowed the next moment.

"Then I hope you don't feel like you look."

Kelvren swallowed, twitching his ears and keeping his eyes closed as a bowlful of food went down his gullet. He sighed loudly and opened his eyes again to lock onto Hallock's own. "Well-known fact. Feeding a grrryphon isss good luck." He sighed. "Thisss *sssketi*-chunk therrre, the . . . what isss it called. Officsse warrrmerrr. That," He indicated the retreating official and his staff, with his beak. "Ssseems he left orrrderrrs that I wasss to be given a sssackful a day of the ssscrrrapsss unfit forrr the ssstewpot.

I took inssssult." He swung his head around to indicate the soldiers in the mess tent with him, several of whom were still coming by to drop bits of their ration into what had become the gryphon's food tray. "Ssso in the ssspirrrit of equality between alliesss, I came herrre and sharrred the sssack with him. He looked well fed, and ssso in the ssame ssspirit, added sssomething to the sssack himssself beforrre leaving, I think."

A couple more soldiers laughed outright, then stifled themselves at Hallock's withering look. The rider turned Hallock aside and whispered confidentially, "He was in awful shape when he came limping down, sir. An' we knew what he'd done for you o'course. So when he asked so polite for help, well, we couldn't refuse. We brought 'im here to get him fed, an' sent word for the——well, anyway, things just went as they went. Some of the regulars, well, they crowded the mayor there, and——"

"Mayor? That was the mayor?" Hallock sighed. He put up a hand to halt the explanation. "So some of you pulled the sack of—scrap—over the mayor's head."

"And pulled the ssstrrring," Kelvren finished with a hint of triumph. "Policssy change wasss enacted immediately upon esscape from the feed bag."

Hallock frowned and asked, "Wait. Why would the mayor have anything to do with whether you got fed, anyway?"

The rider interrupted. "I know that one, sir. Guard feeds Guard, and buys meat and grain from whoever's nearest. The gryphon's a foreigner, so's when the accounting's done, the hospitality comes from the local senior diplomat. That's the mayor. I figure he thought the gryphon was gonna die soon anyhow, so why use the good meat he can sell to the Guard instead?"

Hallock nodded, and unhappily took in Kelvren's disheveled appearance. "I see. So. You. It was regulars that did it all, right?" The rider nodded. "You. There. Regular. It was horse that did it all, right?" The woman nodded. "All right, then. Clearly, there were no witnesses, and no laws or regulations provably broken." He waved a hand around loosely to dismiss the whole affair. "As you were." He angled in close by Kelvren, who reached up with a shaky taloned hand and pulled him close in against his head. Hallock was pressed against the gryphon's warm, feathered neck, cheek and jaw.

"It wasssn't too much, Hallock Ssstaverrrn. I jussst—wanted the sssame rrressspect of any Valdemarrran warrriorrr. Not . . . hurrh, what would Darrrien sssay . . . the firrrst sssalt frrrom the table. "His stoic demeanor faltered. "Therrre'sss nobody forrr me herrre."

Hallock squeezed a few of the neck feathers, each wider than his spread hand. "I'm here, Kelvren. And believe me, there are many here who admire you for what you've done for me." Hallock saw that where the gryphon's feathers had been cut away in clumps along his side and flanks, bandages had fallen away and seeping wounds glistened. "You have wounds coming open again, Kel, we need to get you out of here. You look like you are in terrible pain."

Kel held him there for a few more heartbeats, then patted the man's back before pulling back to meet eyes again. "A good meal helpsss, and the good will of otherrrsss. And ssseeing you, my good frrriend. What would Genni think of thisss day, mmm?" The gryphon shifted his weight, flinched, and let the wing he was trying to move lay where it was. "I do hurrrt, yesss. And I need a placsse to ssstay. And to get clean."

The gryphon lowered his head to the table, and let its weight rest on the curve of his beak while he kept his eyes closed. He sagged a little more with each breath. Hallock held out his hand and rubbed the gryphon's mud-crusted brow ridge. "I know somewhere you can stay, my friend. We'll take you there."

Kelvren lifted his head and looked sidelong at Hallock, with a slight grin. "You know what I sssaid beforrre. Pain sharrred isss . . . pain halved. I sharrred half of my pain with the mayorrr . . . and I feel much betterrr now."

***

Hallock gathered up a squad and they helped Kelvren trudge from the mess tent through the cantonment, a pair under each wing and one at each shoulder. Soldiers came out from almost every tent and watched the slow progression. Some came over to ask if they could help—everyone seemed to know who the creature was, or at least what

he'd done. Jeft followed along, looking worried each time
the gryphon slipped or groaned. When they passed one of
the corrals, several horses pressed in closer to see what this
curiosity was. "Why aren't they terrified?" one of the soldiers wondered. "He's a huge predator, shouldn't they be
bolting?"

"We do not . . . ssscarrre mossst crrreaturrresss . . . unlesss we intend to. It isss . . . a peculiarrrity of usss," Kelvren wheezed. His exhaustion was showing, and he stopped
to rest.

"You have a lot of those," Hallock teased. "Hoy, look.
That dapple gray, that's Dughan, my mount when my forehead got redecorated."

Kel made an effort to look over, but still his head hung
low.

Hallock tried to keep the gryphon's mood light. "I'm
ordering that you be fed well. Some of the men were suggesting we make up a fake squad, to allocate the food for
you. It's an idea with some merit—but I think I carry
enough weight now to have you cared for outright." He
spoke instructions to a runner and then sent her on her
way ahead of them. When they arrived near the convalescents' tent Hallock had visited earlier, the sorting barrels
had been pushed to the back and several cots had been
folded and pushed aside. Nearly everyone was awake, and
every eye was wide. Enlisted men spread out a canvas
tarpaulin on the cleared space, and the squad gingerly
guided the gryphon in. Kel all but collapsed on the spot,
and sprawled sideways onto his good—or rather, less
injured—side, panting. An unhappy private, nearly pinned
by the gryphon's fall, crawled out from under that side's
wing.

"Healer Birce will be here soon," Hallock reassured Kelvren, knelt down beside him. "Devon, too, on his usual
rounds. They'll fix up those plasters for you when they
check everyone else." He waved over a folding stool and
set it in front of Kel's beak, patting the canvas. "Here . . .
a place for your head." He grunted, and lifted Kel's head
to rest flatly upon it.

After a candlemark of reassuring talk and gawkers coming to see the beast that saved the captain, the Healers
arrived to tend to all the self-named "gimps." In the hours

that passed, a couple of dozen soldiers asked the captain if they could touch Kelvren, and after the first one scratched at his brow ridges for half an hour, Kel consented to all.

***

The cloud cover broke and Treyvan and Pena found themselves in searing sunlight. They'd made a short Gating to shorten their flight time, but then found themselves with a strong tailwind and Treyvan calculated it'd be quicker to fly directly for as long as that lasted. Despite the desperate circumstances, Treyvan found himself feeling good about it. He hadn't been on a truly long flight since the return to Haven from the Plains. Now feeling the sun on his back, the magic tingling through his feathers, watching the terrain roll on below, he exulted in the glory of flight.

:Pena,: he Mindspoke. *:You don't need a rest soon, do you? I have good thermals ahead.:*

:Oh, no, you go on ahead. I'm thinking about new tunnels around the Collegium and the embassies, and where to tap a new hotspring. And where to set in a new baking oven.: Treyvan felt the *hertasi* pat his back. *:An idle mind is my workshop. But, Treyvan, aren't we due to make another Gate attempt?:*

:Soon,: he replied. *:If I recall my maps right, we should be in range of a clean Gating within the candlemark. I'll try to anchor high up to correct for any targeting drift. We can fly the difference from there. I'll find us a good landmark by the main road, mark it with a lasting mage-light, and send word to Whitebird by teleson. We'll set an arrival time. When she gets there, I'll try another Gate to bring her in to where the gryphon is.:*

:Aren't you the clever one!: Pena chuckled in his mind.

:Just trying to keep up with you,: Treyvan answered, and laughed out loud as he soared higher.

***

Kelvren dozed off and on, as best his wounds would let him. The humans were given drugged drinks to reduce their pain, but Birce was not willing to risk mixing such stuff with a gryphon's unknown anatomy. It was very hard to

get good rest when parts of your body were simply screaming at you and throbbed with every breath. Still—the attention, the full belly, and the company gave him new strength.
When he was able to, he answered questions and shared
scores of stories about his exploits and his people with dozens of eager listeners. He related the story of Hallock's
Healing, but felt a pang of wistfulness when Hallock's wife
Genni was brought up, because Kelvren was acutely aware
he had no mate to go back to should he survive this. And
by this age, he *should*.

The night swallowed up the sky, and he lost all track of
time between naps. Most of the rest of the convalescents
were asleep, their night dosages in full effect. He raised his
head, looking up to the starry sky, seeded by sparks from
the camp's fires. He whimpered softly.

*This wasn't what Skandranon was like—he would never
have been laid up with such injuries, wasting away. And
they have to be looking for me—Darien and Firesong and
the others; they must be able to send me help or bring me
back. I know that great legends usually involve great
funerals—but I don't want to die.*

"Sir? Y'there, sir? You awake?" He heard Jeft's voice
at his side and turned an eye that way without lifting his
head. "Oh, good, you're awake. Sir, I, uh, my mum wanted
to see you. I fetched her here." The young man waved
someone in. A woman in trews and blouse carrying a large
basket knelt beside him, and licked her lips.

"My lord gryphon," she said in a voice gentled down as
if talking to a scared child, "Jeft's talked so much about
you, I wanted to see you myself. You—" and she glanced at
where Jeft stood back by Kel's flank, "—you've treated
him well, better than most people ever have. I—wanted
you to know it is appreciated. He's never really had many
friends, and even then they didn't consider him an equal.
But then here you are, this—wonder dropped into our
lives—and you talk to him as a *person*. Not as a servant.
You've done us a great honor."

Kel listened to every word and raised his chin up then
laid his head sideways. "The honorrr isss mine, Lady. . . ."

"Ammari. Not a Lady, though, my lord gryphon. I am
just a seamstress and artisan." She looked down at her

hands when she said this. There was something in her tone
that was deeply sad for a moment.

"Hurrrh. Jeft isss a brrrave—" and he paused, "I won't
sssay 'boy.' But he isss brrrave. Sssmarrrt." He brought his
head up and shifted his weight from his sideways slouch,
which sent lightning shots through his body from each stitch
and scab deep into him. "Urrrh. Ssso. Welcome to my
palacsse."

Ammari pulled back the cloth cover from the basket, and
hesitantly pulled out a scrub brush. "Jeft said that—that
you didn't look—uhm, that you needed some cleaning up.
And he knew you were in pain. When he gets hurt, he
comes to me, so he thought if you were in pain—I should
come to find *you*." She asked, apprehensively, "You won't
bite me if I do this badly, will you?"

Kel smiled but took his time to answer. "Haven't the
ssstrrrength to bite, Ammarri. You have no fearrrsss
frrrom me. But. You arrre herrre forrr morrre than tending
to my filth." He glanced back to where Jeft was pinching
and toying with the tattered feathertip of one of his pri-
maries. "And it isss not jussst about him, isss it?"

Ammari swallowed and nodded to Kel. "It's—about
both of us. I've never been like this beforc—I feel so lost.
My husband—" She caught Kel's eye. He nodded. "You
know, then? Jeft must have told you. I've been alone with
Jeft all this time, and we work so hard, but—when all of
this happened, it just—it's just been too much for us. I've
been trying to find work here at the camp—honorable
work, I mean. But it's so hard." She reached out to Kelvren's face, but let her touch fall instead along his neck.
His hackles looked black in the dim light. Flakes of dirt
crumbled away off of feathers. "I'm sorry—words don't
come easily about this. I feel selfish being here, when
you're so badly hurt. But, with what happened—you're
magic. And—magic does bad and good in this life, and
you—you're good magic. Everyone talks about what you
could do. What you did do. I don't know where else to
turn, and Jeft thinks so much of you." Ammari pulled her
hand back and wiped her eyes, where tears had welled up.
"I just—is there any work I could do for you—is there
anything you can do to help us?"

Kelvren let out a long, descending sigh and rested his head again. "Sssoldierrrsss have been coming herrre all day. My flessh issss brrroken, but my earrrsss arrre sssharrrp. They come to sssee the oddity—the thing that sssaved sssome of them. Sssome come in, want to touch featherrrsss orrr talonsss. They want to have sssome luck rrrub off on them. Hurrrh. Foolisssh—they want luck frrrom sssomeone who had all of *thisss* happen to him?" He snorted.

"Lord gryphon, *any* of those injuries would have killed a man. You survived how many? A dozen? Two? Cut, shot, stabbed, lanced through, even? And still you can speak? Even walk?"

"Hurrrh. I am ssstill dying," Kelvren replied distastefully.

"Lord gryphon, we are *all* dying. But if you'll forgive me for being so bold, sir, until you are dead, you are still living."

Kelvren stayed silent for a while, and Ammari started brushing out feathers while Jeft picked away at the larger clumps of dirt around Kel's hindlegs. "You know, my husband would have loved to have been here with you. He loved birds and kept feathers when he found them out on his travels. Yours would be a prize, if you dropped one."

Kel looked sidelong at the woman.

"Jeft sssaid that you werrre about to be rrrich. What of that? Isssn't money what sssoothesss illsss in Valdemarrr?"

Ammari smiled a little—a flicker of pride, then the sadness again. "When the Changecircle came—we—had just lost my husband. I was unconsolable. I ran into the circle in my grief. I just—clawed at the ground, crying out for someone to bring him back. Somehow. I knew there was magic there—else how could it have appeared?—but by morning, there was still no help. I clawed at the ground while I cried—I cried so much." She paused in her work. "When daylight came, I saw that my hands were—different. There was something in that soil that made my hands glimmer in the light." She resumed brushing. "My man was not back. But maybe he provided for us in his own way. I found a way to sift this from the soil and bind it, so that it would adhere to cloth and leather. No one but Jeft and I would go into the circle—so it remained ours alone. Almost all the money I had I spent to buy the land the circle was in.

I made jars and jars of my solution. And there it sits." She sighed. "Before all of this strife, traders were going to carry some to Haven, and Deedun, and—well, you understand. I staked all I had on a luxury item, and now no one wants it and no traders will come for it."

Kelvren rumbled a little and then asked, "Thisss—sssubssstancsse of yourrrss. Do you have any to ssshow me?" The glint of speculation was in his eyes.

Ammari set the brush down and brought out a kerchief from her blouse. Even in the meager light, it shone with an irridescence like oil on water in bright sunlight. Jeft beamed when he saw it. "My mum's special. She's smart. An' I helped, with the makin' of the stuff."

Kel admired the cloth as Ammari twisted and turned it around, showing its shimmer. "And thisss—ssubssstancssse. Isss it expensssive? Doesss it poisson, or ssstink, or come off easssily? Doesss anyone elssse know of it?" He added, with a hint of shrewdness, "And doesss it bind to featherrrsss?"

***

By noon of the second day, Kelvren's plan was in motion. Through Hallock, he arranged the purchase of several jars of Ammari's mixture. It positively blazed in the full light of day. Small wonder she knew it would make her wealthy! With his guidance, several of the convalescents trimmed away particular stray and partial feathers from around his wounds, painted them with the bright substance, and set them aside to dry.

Transmutation, he thought. *Though I fade, I still have resources.* When he had time to rest, the pain actually sharpened his thoughts—it was only when he moved that it overwhelmed him completely. *I can turn what little we have into something important, whether I can fly—or even walk—again.* He *had* to be of use—he couldn't bear to slide off into oblivion meekly. So, then, what was there to do? Assuming he couldn't move, he had to somehow use what he was rather than what he could do. He was unique in the camp—an oddity. He had reputation here, even a growing mystique.

The elements were there: the soldiers' superstitions about

how he was good luck. A tent full of invalids making
arrows. And to bring it all together, Ammari's secret, beautiful mixture, that shone like—
  Magic.

                              ***

  The history was told lovingly, in the way only someone
who loved tales, and had actually experienced a part of
them, could tell a story.
  *Far off to the west, there was a city made of hope and
light. It was made to honor its peoples' savior, and named
for him. White Gryphon was built of terraces and sweeping
walkways carved from a white cliffside overlooking a perfect
bay. In the centuries since its founding, its wings had gradually spread out around the bay, enfolding it as a loving protective bird would cover its nestlings from cold or rain. Its
wings, in fact, truly did appear to be wings—canopies and
promenades swept in complex curves on a massive scale, to
outline individual feathers when seen from the sea and barrier islands. The city center was a huge complex of overlapping towers making the hackles, breastfeathers and lower
mandible. The highest and widest complex, crested the whole
of the city in a stylized beak, with its eyes and ears facing
north. In summer, the sunrise cast the shadow of a raptor
across the bay waters, and at noon the eyes of the beast
were completely concealed by shadow. At sunset the water
reflections shimmered upon the creation and the sun's colors
blazed upon it while the thousands of small lights and fires
came up one by one to greet the stars for the oncoming night.
  To the immediate east was the more conventional side of
the city that had sprawled out as more housing, workshops,
and trade centers were needed—but past that, the terrain became terrible indeed. Forest that became impassable. Trees
as broad as eighty men thrust up to a canopy three hundred
feet tall, above treefalls and hidden rivers as deep as oceans.
Deadly ravines lurked under simple ground cover, and
nightmarish beasts hunted anything that ventured in.
  Past that came hundreds of miles of marshlands and desert, two entirely different kinds of forest, and then mountain
ranges and a jungle. Then grassland, and finally after all of
that, the other great forest. The Pelagirs.*

Gryphons need the help of trondi'irn, *though, like me, sometimes gryphons learn some healing along with other powers. Yet, one pair endured the venture for over six years, alone, blazing a trail eastward from White Gryphon, until they found their city's long-lost brethren.*

"... That pairrr was Trrreyvan and Hydona. When I call them the Grrreat Onesss, it isss becaussse they arrre the brrravessst explorerrrsss of ourrr time. And they arrre her- rre, in Valdemarrr. They helped everrryone sssurvive the Ssstormsss. And Hallock Ssstaverrrn *knows them.* Essscorrrted them around Haven—perrrrsssonally!"

Jeft looked up at Kelvren in amazement, having utterly forgotten the bow-wrapping he'd been tasked with, tangled between his fingers. The few other locals and Guard in attendance, and all of the convalescing soldiers had similar expressions. It wasn't just that they had a six-hundred- pound, taloned, killing fury telling them fireside stories, it was that these stories were uplifting. His tales fired the imagination in ways no one had expected. Most of the sol- diers would probably never see active duty again, but in- stead of being stuck with the wasting-away grousing of lousy encampment and the same old blather, this creature they'd first thought would be an intrusion instead had be- come needed because *all* of his tales were new.

"And you got here because of that trail they found?" one of the horsemen asked. Kelvren nodded. "An' so did all these strange allies that came with th' Hawkbrothers?" Kel nodded again. "An' these trondi-urn people could fix you up?"

There was a collective holding of breath as that question halted the mood.

"Yesss. But that isssn't to be. Ssso. Let usss sssee just how tough I rrreally am, mmm?" The gryphon tried to play it off. "We ssspend time togetherrr herrre. It isss a good exchange. You learrrn about farrr-away landsss and amaz- ing culturesss. I learrrn about mud and sssmoke." People laughed. "And fletching. I finally get to sssee some arr- rowsss that arrren't going *into* me." There were a few chuckles at that, and someone in the back cracked, "Oy, I never really *aimed* at you, y'know!" The jovial mood was returning.

"Hah! You asssume you *could!*" he retorted. "I *have*

dodged arrrows, you know. Jussst not enough of them. The one the city was named for, Ssskandrranon, talesss sssay he could fly thrrrough whole brrrigadesss of archerrrsss and emerrrge unssscathed."

"You ever notice that the older a story gets, the more invulnerable the heroes are?" one of the enlisted women snickered.

Kelvren answered in complete seriousness, "Oh, no. No, thisss isss trrrue. Thessse thingsss . . . they arrre important for usss. Grrryphonsss—we *need* to be known. Trrreyvan and Hydona, Kuarrrtess and Ussstecca, and Tusssak Kael the Elderrr. Zhaneel the Ssswift and Aubrrri the Ssstalwart, and Kecharrra—herrr name came to mean "beloved" in ourrr language. They have meant asss much to usss by legend asss they did in life, and accomplisssh asss much by legend asss by deed. Ssskandrrranon Rrrassshkae isss known to all of usss becaussse he *wasss* that amazing. And now—he isss known to you."

Kel's facial feathers fluffed and he held his head high for a few moments. With his stories, he had done his part to make his heroes immortal.

***

Above the mill, at midday, there was suddenly a bright flash. What appeared to be a hole in the sky, rimmed by an everchanging glimmery edge, showed through to a landscape of low grass beside a wide roadway. The light came from a column of mage-light the height of two men on the other side of the hole, bright enough to be noticed by people below. A hulking shadow eclipsed the light, and observers below shouted and pointed up. The shadow burst through the hole and huge wings snapped outward to stop its arcing fall. It flapped ponderously to level its flight before circling over the encampment. Whatever it was, it wanted its outline to be clearly seen before landing.

Treyvan spied the Command flag at the mill, circled the Guard camp four times, and glided to land in the road between the rows of carriages. The door guards readied pikes and called for reinforcements, and a junior officer went pale when he popped his head out. Treyvan stood with his wings up, then sat on his haunches to be received.

Pena stayed on his back, as yet unseen, and appeared to be simply another bundle of cargo.

Then a familiar figure stepped into the road from the mill's entry. Hallock closed on the gryphon and hailed. "Ambassador Treyvan! This is unexpected! It has been too long since I saw you last." He gestured for the door guard to go back to vigil, and waved off questions from junior officers, still walking forward with the aid of his walking stick. "Welcome. Are you here about Kelvren? He's in a bad way. Because of me, I fear, I was the one he Healed."

"Kelvrrren, you sssay? The wingleaderrr frrrom k'Valdemarrr?" Treyvan's knowledge of gryphons was encyclopedic. He could recite the names and positions of hundreds. "Hurrrh. Wherrre isss he? Frrriend of Firrrresssong'sss. A badly wounded grrryphon isss harrrd to find by ssspell. If Firrrresssong hasss not aided Kelvrrren, the sssituation mussst be grrrave indeed." Treyvan turned to accompany Hallock, and paused for Pena to dismount. She peeled off her helmet and goggles, and tucked them under an arm while she walked alongside the others. Hallock filled in the senior gryphon on what he knew of Kelvren's condition, talking continuously until they neared the convalescents' tent.

They heard *singing*. Not just from inside, but from the eighteen soldiers standing outside, lacquering sheaves of arrows. In the middle of the song, a gryphon voice—thin and strained—nonetheless boomed a line, and made the others grin. The soldiers outside halted singing one by one, and moved backward as one as Treyvan, Pena, and the captain approached. Only a few remembered to salute. They had come to know Kelvren, a terribly wounded gryphon—but *this* was a fully healthy gryphon stalking toward them, bedecked in regalia of rank, all but dwarfing the captain beside him, with a little lizard creature padding along beside them.

:I can hear you,: Treyvan Mindspoke toward the gryphon he heard. *:I have come to help you. And a trondi'irn is on the way.:*

* * *

Inside the convalescents' tent, the singing went quiet voice by voice. Kelvren turned his head from side to side, and upward, as if searching for something. Something was about to happen, and everyone in the tent could sense it. Kelvren cut short a whimper of pain as he rolled himself over to his belly. "I hearrrd—" Kelvren croaked, and then his eyes fixed outside, locked onto an approaching shadow. A *large* shadow.

Captain Stavern stepped around the edge of the tent, nodded behind him, and then came someone Kelvren thought he would never see in his lifetime.

The breastplate adorned by the badges and bars of rank, the impeccaby tooled harness, and the teleson headpiece around the feather-perfect gryphon's brow ridges and fore-crest, crafted to be as much a crown as anything—it could be no one else.

Completely against his will, Kelvren shuddered all over. Breath seized in his throat. He blinked his eyes out of their stare and lowered his head. The fletchers and attendants dropped their work completely or set their tools aside, all eyes on what—*who*—had just walked across the threshold of the tent's oiled-canvas floor. Then everyone who stood or sat went down to one knee and bowed their heads in recognition when Kelvren spoke the words—

"My Lorrrd Trrrreyvan."

The power of the senior gryphon's arrival could be felt radiating into the tent, like sunlight sinks into the skin on a summer day.

"Rrrissse, all," Treyvan said. Kelvren's head felt light, as if he was about to pass out. Treyvan stepped to within arm's reach of the stricken gryphon, and then bowed his own head in turn. "Wingleaderrr Kelvrrren Ssskothkarrr of k'Valdemarrr. The Crrrown hasss sssent me to sssee to yourrr well-being."

What Treyvan said next made Kelvren certain he was hallucinating.

"You arrre firrrrssst grrrryphon on sssite in thisss engage-ment. I name you Wingleaderrr of thisss forcssse asss sssoon asss you arrre fit forrr duty."

Motes of light swam in Kelvren's vision. This must be a fever dream. It was Silver Gryphon standing practice that whoever was on scene first was automatically the senior of that engagement—"Incident Command"—the reasoning being that they knew the situation, by being there first, better than any who followed. It held, regardless of rank, until there was a formal exchange of power. It meant that *he* was now empowered *to command Treyvan.* One of the *Great Ones!* It was mindboggling.

Enough so that Kelvren passed out on the spot.

***

Much happened while Kel was adrift. The supply tent across the mud path from the convalescents' tent was emptied out so Treyvan could always be near Kelvren.

Treyvan used several spells—though relatively minor, they were impressive to watch, because to enhance his precision he used simple light effects to burn off any excess energy. He used Magesight and sweeps of power to discover which of Kelvren's magic-conversion organs were still alive and responsive, and several probes to test the state of the still-unconscious Kelvren's injuries. Jeft stood by his gryphon friend's side and asked—very possessively—exactly what Treyvan was doing. Treyvan explained that he was taking away Kel's pain and deepening his sleep, to help him regain strength—and to keep him from trying to move and make his wounds worse.

Jeft wasn't the only one who acted proprietary about Kelvren. To the inhabitants of the convalescents' tent, this was *their* gryphon.

Hallock Stavern called a muster on the main road, and each company stood in formation while he introduced Treyvan and Pena. He made it very clear that unless it directly contravened "high end" regulations, the gryphon was to be treated as captain—"or better." He held up the proof that the Crown wished it so, and added that the little lizard with him was Treyvan's personal assistant. Treyvan made a formal pass by each company. He nodded to each company's senior officer and gave them polite greetings—but it was also calculated so they got a very clear view of his rank markings by being close up to him.

Birce and Devon stood humbly while Treyvan thanked

them personally for their good work, and astonished them
when he suggested to Hallock that they be listed for
commendation.

Treyvan explained to the mill officers how a teleson
worked, and contacted Haven with one to report on Kelvren. The overworked clerk that Hallock had needled before was set in front of the device, and thanks to the link he
might actually have some sleep possible in his near future.

Pena was well on her way to becoming the most popular
creature in the camp. Once word had been spread that any
fast-moving lizards in camp weren't to be shot at, she'd
become a blur. Not only were Kelvren's needs being tended
to and materials brought to Treyvan, her abilities as a chef
transformed the dull fare the convalescents ate into events
to be savored. She bolted into the woods and returned with
foraged materials half a candlemark later that by the end
of the day made a basic stew bear delightfully complex
tastes. The condition for off-duty soldiers getting any of her
dishes, though, was that time must be spent assisting the
convalescents and Treyvan. They never wanted for help.

Ammari spent more of her waking hours in the tent with
the "gimps," as they'd now laughingly begun referring to
themselves. One of the southerners pointed out—wisely—
that a word is only truly an insult if you take it as such.
Making it a joke, instead of derogatory, takes the power
out of it, and makes it your power instead.

It reached its zenith when one of the fletchers asked Jeft
to bring another basket of arrowshafts, and Ammari heard
her son answer back, "That's *Boy* Jeft to you, gimp!" The
whole group fell about laughing.

That laughter was what awoke Kelvren. He blinked a
dozen times, cleared his mind, and found the pain that had
been his constant, unwanted companion had dulled its
screaming to barely a whisper. He still felt unbearably
heavy, but lifted his head, and found Treyvan was there,
and real.

Treyvan spoke to him with respect. "Wingleaderrr Kelvrrren. You have sssurrrvived woundsss that would kill
thrrree grrryphonsss. I am imprrresssed by yourrr
willpowerrr—and yourrr durrrability. And yourrr compasssi-
onate sssacrrrificsse."

Kel smiled a little at that. Praise from Treyvan! "Wasss

it not what ssshould be done? Hallock Ssstaverrrn had hisss Genni to rrreturrrn to. Hisss mate. I have no mate, but I have wissshed it ssso. I would not let him lossse hisss, if it cossst my own life forrr it. He lived the drrream I have. It ssshould not perrrisssh. You—you have Hydona. Can you underrrsssstand?"

Treyvan nodded gravely. "I would claw out the hearrrt of the sssun if it meant keeping herrr sssafe. And my young—the sssame forrr them."

Kelvren looked into the middle distance, as if caught in daydream. "It would be good to have sssuch perrrfect daysss as Hallock Ssstaverrrn and you have had. And young, yesss."

"In time, Kelvrrren. In time. Yourrr legend grrrowsss."

"Legend?" Kel looked bemused. "Legend."

"Yesss. I know that I will tell of you. And you ssshall rrrecoverrr. Whitebirrrd—ourrr *trondi'irn* frrrom Haven— isss on herrr way. In the meantime, if yourrr mind isss clearrr enough, I would like to know yourrr wissshesss."

Kelvren choked out a chuckle. "I want nothing lesss than to give incssident command overrr to you!"

Treyvan smiled reassuringly. "Verrry well, but I name you my rrresssident advisssorrr. I am currriousss—what arrre thessse people doing with yourrr cassst-off feath-errrsss? They trrreat them with—rrreverencsse."

Kelvren rumblechuckled. "Ssstorrriesss, my Lorrrd Trrreyvan. Belief, and ssstorrriesss." He sobered and continued. "I told everrryone in thisss camp that would lisssten about ourrr people, ourrr herrroesss, and the deedsss we have accomplisssshed. I wasss all but csserrrtain I would die sssoon. I *had* to tell ourrr ssstorrriesss. Yourrr tale wasss one I told. My Lorrrd Trrreyvan, you arrre one of the Grrreat Onesss. When you arrrived, I thought I wasss feverrred. When you deferrred to me, I thought I wasss mad. Beforrre you arrrived, I knew my end russshed towarrrdsss me. I knew that I had to end making a differrrencsse." He paused to rest for a few moments, then resumed after several deep breaths. "The sssoldierrrsss trrruly believe that to sssome degrrree, I am invincssible. They sssaw I sssurrr-vived thessse woundsss, and knew I prrrotected theirrr own. They believe that what I am—what I do—isss magic of a mosssst potent kind. Ammarrri and Jeft—they paint thessse featherrrsss of mine in Ammarrri'sss liquid light. The fletcherrrsss—they sssnip thessse parrrtsss of my ssshed featherrrsss and bind them in with the norrrmal feath-errrsss. And they shine—to thessse peoplesss' eyesss, they *look* magical. And the sssoldierrrsss who recsseive thessse arrrowsss believe they arrre now gifted with sssome of my powerrr."

Understanding dawned on Treyvan, and he sat up straight.

"If thessse sssoldierrrsss go into battle with thessse arr-rowsss they will feel morrre confident. It will rrreinforcsse theirrr brrraverrry. It could be enough to help them win, if it comesss to that." He glanced around the parts of the camp he could see, and spoke more softly. "My lorrrd Trrreyvan. I will confide my beliefsss. We arrre not like otherrr crrreaturrresss, who wonderrr if a deity even carrr-esss if they exissst," Kelvren continued. "We grrryphonsss werrre not crrreated by godsss, we werrre crrreated by a man. We werrre made forrr a *purrrpossse*. We werrre not crrreated to fight warrrsss, though we have. We werrre not made to rrressscue, to thwarrrt, to chassse, or kill. I believe we werrre made to *inssspirrre*. With all my bonesss and hearrrt I feel that to *inssspirrre* isss the ultimate of what Urrrtho wanted of usss."

Treyvan cocked his head, his attention completely absorbed by what Kelvren told him.

"*This* isss what I wasss made forrr. When I sssaw ssso much missserrry herre—felt it frrrom them, felt my own life fading—I had to combine the worrrsss cssircumsssstanc-ssess in sssome ssspecial way—I needed to trrransssmute ssso many bad thingsss into good thingsss. It became clearrr to me when I came down frrrom that hill jussst to eat. Sssoldierrrsss wanted to ssssharrre theirrr food with me. They wanted to sssupporrrt me, touch me forrr luck. I rrrealized. What bound it all togetherrr wasss *wonderrr*. They believed in sssomething grrreaterrr than they had the day beforrre, jussst becaussse I wasss herrre. And ssso." He gestures with a few taloned fingers toward the industrious fletchers. "I put sssimple plansss into motion, and theirrr belief imbued the motion with powerrr, and it moved on itsss own."

"Without a single spell left to you," Treyvan murmured, incredulous.

Kelvren closed his eyes and with some effort, pushed himself up to a sitting position, wings still flat on the floor. "Thessse people arrre watching usss. What they sssee rrright now will matterrr to them the rrressst of theirrr livesss, and they will tell theirrr children and the hissstorrry will sssprrread. It may be—a minorrr legacssy—but I hope that even if I fall, it will be in the tale that I *trrried. Even if I die, I will not have not failed, becaussse to the lassst I did not give up.* I am sssomething extrrraorrrdinarrry to them. Therrre arrre no enchantmentsss on the arrrowsss, but the arrrowsss arrre not falssse. They *arrre* magic becaussse the sssoldierrrsss believe in them."

***

The arranged time for Whitebird to arrive was nearing. Treyvan sent word to the mill that, to bring in his *trondi'irn,* he would open a Gate to connect partway to Haven, and that anything they needed to send through in half a minute could pass through after his specialist from the other side arrived. He caught Hallock biting his lower lip as he sat by the slumbering Kelvren.

"What trrroublesss you, Firrrssst?"

"It's the Gate. A doorway to just step through to be closer to Haven."

"Clossserrr to yourrr Genni," Treyvan shrewdly noted.

Hallock nodded. "Closer to my Genni. I miss her so much, it's impossible not to think of being with her every moment. And returning to her is precisely what Kelvren diced his life on. I could just resign my command, and step through a door to be a few days' ride from her. But I can't do it." He looked Treyvan in the eyes. "I do have a command here, and I owe it to my troops. But as much as that—I have to be at Kelvren's side."

Treyvan was silent for several minutes, finally saying delicately, "You musssst rrrealize he isss unlikely to sssurrrvive thisss."

Hallock held a fist in his hand. "I'm not knotting a yellow ribbon for him yet." He gestured out toward the rest of the camp. "And I have my soldiers to take care of. They just lost their First, and I've replaced her. It would be too much for me to leave now. I can't risk them getting someone with no field experience in my place."

"You arrre a good leaderrr, Hallock Ssstaverrrn. The grrreatessst of leaderrrsss arrre at the forrrefrrront of battle, wherrre the powerrr of theirrr prrresencssse can be felt by thossse they command. He isss a parrrt of hisss forcsse, not ssseperrrate frrrom them. The Haighleigh sssay that a wissse chief isss a man who sssaysss "I was beaten," not "My men werrre beaten." You sssee the rrreality of battle widely, immerrrssse yourrrsssself in it, and ssset yourrrsssself apart frrrom thossse who debate it asss theorrry· frrrom afarrr."

"This may be so," he agreed, "and thank you for the compliment. But just the same, I have to admit there's a lot of me that wants to go through that Gate of yours." He turned toward Kelvren. "But I'm not leaving him."

***

Three light wagons laden with injured troops, and a courier on back of a pony were lined up, two horselengths behind Treyvan. The gryphon mage sat in front of a rope laid out on the road, which marked where the Gate aperture would be. He stared toward it, but not at it—as if he looked past it deep into the earth. He spread his wings and flapped them slowly, drawing his arms up and tracing talons through several motions, culminating with a wide gesture of two halves of a wide circle.

A short crack of thunder came from in front of the gryphon, and made everyone flinch. The horses looked none too happy, but didn't run. Then the air simply opened up. Forest, grass, and another road were brightly lit by a column of light on the other side of the Gate, and rippled while the edges of the Gate stabilized. Foreclaws still up, Treyvan sidestepped to its right and called out, "Now!"

The light was eclipsed by three horses running toward the hole, and then they were there in the camp, swerving off to the side at a gallop. "Go!" Treyvan called, and the horses pulling the line of wagons churned hooves toward the Gate and went through. The courier on the pony surged through the hole last, and then the Gate was allowed to collapse. Treyvan dropped back to all fours, swaying and panting.

Two of the horses bore *trondi'irn* Whitebird, her assistant, and a heavy load of supplies. Whitebird's appearance was striking—she dressed in a half dozen shades of blue, and her hair was past shoulder length and as snowy as the third "horse" that had come through. A swarthy man in a Herald's uniform was astride a mare Companion, and dismounted to speak earnestly with Captain Stavern. Treyvan walked briskly toward the convalescents' tent, and the *trondi'irn* fell in behind him.

Whitebird let her assistant take the horses as she walked the rest of the way to the tent. When she saw Kelvren dozing, she stared, mouth open. "Oh, you poor thing," she gasped.

She rushed to Kelvren's side, resting her hands on his shoulder, his wing, and down his flank. She leaned in to smell him, taking in his scent from beak to rump. A minute later, her assistant came in laden with cases and pouches. They extracted instruments and vials from them and took samples from the wounds, judged the colors they turned, and set them aside on a complex anatomical chart. Kelvren roused from slumber—barely—and rolled a glassy eye sideways to view the two new people.

"Oh, good," he murmured, and then drifted back to sleep.

Whitebird glanced at Treyvan with an unreadable expression, then stood to stand near him. She spoke in Kaled'a'in. "Trey—this looks very bad. He has such strong infections I can smell them. I don't know how he's lasted this long unless it's divine providence or pure willpower. We'll get to work on him immediately, but I'll be honest with you, it's definitely a ruin." She wiped down her hands with a wet cloth that smelled of vinegar. "Right now, it looks like *hirs'ka'usk,* and if you don't find a way to rejuvenate his magic, he'll be lost to us in days. I can give him medicine and prime his body for a rejuvenation, but if you can't infuse him with power, the best I can hope to do is stabilize him as he is. No strength, no flight—for a life of a few months." The elder gryphon rumbled and nodded, and Whitebird bent to her work on Kelvren. "I'll be here for four or five candlemarks."

"She's beautiful," one of the men behind her said. "I think I'm in love."

"Grow some wings and I'm yours," Whitebird answered without looking up. "Until then, get me some hot water."

***

Ammari, Birce, Hallock, and Whitebird's assistant Rivenstone sat on folding chairs, huddled with Treyvan in the tent across from where Whitebird still tended to Kelvren's wounds. Jeft stayed by her, fetching whatever Pena did not.

"Whitebirrrd and I have conferrred with Firrresssong and Hydona by telesssson. What we attempt—we do not know what the rrresssult will be. If we take a longerrr-terrrm path, therrre isss a sssslight chancsse he will rrrecoverrr, but find hisss flight limited orrr gone. If we attempt thisss—rrrejuvenation—he will jusssst asss likely die frrrom it."

Ammari asked, "Why?"

Rivenstone answered her. "When his inner channels are opened up, it will be a surge through the feather roots—where gryphons collect ther energy and begin its conversion. The sudden rush of power into—by now—sensitized vessels might well boil out as heat. Or rather, boil in, and—ah—cook him. If we can keep the inrush to a steady flow, we may be able to draw it out of him before it becomes too much." He steepled his fingers, resting his elbows on his knees. "I must be honest with you all. No gryphon has *ever* been drained so completely as Kelvren has."

Treyvan laid out a spread of pages from one of the *trondi'irn*'s books. "We only have thisss frrrom the hissstorrries—an infusssion method unusssed sssince Ssskandrrranon'sss time. What effect it will have now, we can barrrely prrredict." He looked off to the northwest. "Firrresssong isss bessside himsssself—he wantsss ssso much to be herrre. He carrresss morrre about Kelvrrren than Kelvrrren prrrobably knowsss. He sssaysss everrryone frrrom Lorrrd Brrreon to the Ghosssst Cat Clan wantsss Kelvrrren back. He sssaysss the Clansss arrre holding rrritualsss and lighting firrresss to guide Kelvrrren home to them."

Everyone was silent for a moment.

"So," Hallock began. "The questions are, do we try this

method, can it be done, what is required for it to be done, and what will we do if it fails or succeeds?"

"If it fails," Rivenstone answered, "he will be his own funaral pyre."

"But the firrrssst quessstion isss what the rrressst hinge upon. Kelvrrren hasss rrresssolved that even if he diesss he hasss done well. I doubt he would want to lingerrr in a living death. Ssso I sssuggessst that we procsseed."

The others agreed. "We will need a sssite to prrreparrre," Treyvan stated. "And I confesss, it isss no sssmall rrrisssk to me. We need a placsse clossse by, but sssafe from casssual interrrferrencsse—becaussse in a matterrr of a day, I mussst consstrrruct a node."

There was an uncomfortable silence.

Finally Hallock asked, "What's a node?"

"A confluence of magical power," Rivenstone replied. "Like streams run to a lake, a node is where lines of force converge. But since the Storms, those lines have been largely dispersed. If Treyvan tried to use his personal power, he could wind up like Kelvren is, and Kelvren still wouldn't be healed. So he has to use an outside source of power—a node. There aren't any nodes around here, so we need a place to make one. Safely. Quickly."

Ammari raised her hand shyly. "Uhm. Will a Changecircle do?"

***

Being gryphon through and through, Treyvan was very physical about his magic—but to human eyes he looked utterly mad while he worked. He had gotten volunteers to go into the Changecircle and dig holes in specific places, with the deepest in the very center, a man's height in depth. He dropped particular stones in the holes and covered them up, and paced around the Changecircle, muttered to himself, then did things his gathered audience found inexplicable. Many times he leaped ten feet in the air and suddenly dove down, thumbs locked, as if trying to push a stake into the ground with his forefeet; other times he would slink along the ground and turn his head side to side before jumping up to circle in the air over the site.

Shafts of light erupted from the ground periodically, equidistant around the circle. Treyvan walked around each one, then drew glowing lines in midair toward the center of the circle, and subdivided them. More shafts of light shone, higher this time, where those lines crossed, and then wavered. Treyvan growled and leaped on one that was brighter than the rest, and the others became evenly brighter.

He warned loudly that no one was to enter the Changecircle for any reason, and took to the air, flew a circuit across the Changecircle, and then arced back to the convalescents' tent, where Kelvren was awake after his *trondi'-irn*'s drug-enforced sleep. Treyvan murmured to Pena, who dashed off after something. Hallock intercepted Treyvan.

"Kel was just giving me his opinions about this political and military situation, in case the worst should happen," the captain said. "And I have to say, I'm impressed. You should hear this." He looked down at the notes he'd written. " 'In this conflict the Guard is already beaten, because they do not want to fight their fellow Valdemarans. And this insurgent militia, brought to bear arms against the Guard and Heralds, are also beaten for the same reason. In their hearts—regardless of blades, arrows, and horse— they cancel each other out. Therefore, the battle is between the mercenaries and the callous bastards who incited this, who owe no allegience to this country and have no affection for it—and those mercenaries hired by the Crown, who do feel affection for this country, but hold no pressing regard to spare that militia or their hired counterparts. So to make this conflict collapse, the motives must be attacked, without swords and arrows piercing flesh, and thus make the mercenaries cancel each other out. Create a collapse within this insurgents' power structure, and the mercenaries fold up. Then may Valdemarans be brothers again, and meet in taverns to give thanks and apologize to each other, rather than soak their beloved soil in the blood of their brothers."

"Hurrrh. The Shin'a'in sssay, 'therrre are only two pow-errrsss in a warrr—the sssworrrd and the ssspirrrit, and the sspirrrit will alwaysss win out.' If Kelvrrren wasss a warrrl-orrrd, we would all sssurrrely be in trrrouble," Treyvan said in all seriousness. "Hisss ability to find powerrr in the mossst minorrr of thingsss isss unnerrrving."

Hallock looked back toward Kelvren. "I think he really *needed* to tell me all of that. It seemed very important to him, even though it exhausted him to say it."

"He wantsss morrre than anything to feel effective," Treyvan observed. "But, I sssupposse, ssso do we all." Pena arrived by his side and offered an unlatched case which Treyvan delicately reached into. He pulled out a fist-sized sphere of glass, perfect in every dimension. With a calculating look he asked Hallock, "Do you know what a Heartstone isss?"

***

It was dusk.

Whitebird set the last of the empty bottles and cups aside, then arose from her knees beside Kelvren. "Those should strengthen you," she said encouragingly, "and keep you going through what's to come. Everyone is ready."

Kelvren stood up on all fours for the first time in days. He shook all over from the muscle strain, but he did not buckle. Whitebird folded her arms, squeezing herself in worry. Ammari shuffled close from the rear of the now-emptied tent. Kelvren pulled his shoulders back and raised his head to look her in the face. "Thisss isss a tale that tellsss itsssself," he rumbled wearily, forcing a raised-crest smile. "Pena hasss sssomething forrr yourrr ssson. If my ssstorrry endsss this night—hisss ssshall go on. I have a favorrr to assk of you, Ammarrri. Yourrr—liquid light—sssparrre a few jarrrsss for Genni Ssstaverrrn. Frrrrom me." He lifted his head up to his shoulders' height, and Ammari cupped his lower jaw in her hands and rested his beak against her bosom. She tucked her chin down and kissed him on the curve of his beak. "You'll be all right, Kel—you will be."

His breath was hot against her body, and he trembled as he turned aside and took his first step toward the circle. "If I am not, I ssshall fly with yourrr husssband firrrsssst of all."

Whitebird, Rivenstone, and Pena stepped in instantly to

help him from the tent, but he warned them off. With wing-tips dragging, Kelvren trudged to his fate on the hill.

Spectators had gathered, but guards kept them a hundred feet from the Changecircle. They parted to let him through as he approached, and several murmured encouragements to him.

All of the "gimps" were there among them.

Treyvan awaited him several horselengths from the edge of the faintly-glowing Changecircle. "It isss not too late to refussse thisss," he said to Kelvren in Kaled'a'in. "You may ssstill live if we use the other method."

"Live. But not fly, or rrrun even? Neverrr climb a back again? I'd rrrather die," he chuckled weakly. "No—I must try this."

Treyvan shrewdly asked, "You already have planssss for what you will do if thisss rejuvenation ssssucceedsss, don't you?"

Kelvren smiled slyly. "Oh, yesss. A few. If you'rrre in a fairrr fight, you didn't plan it properrrly. If this worksss, it will mean more than if I lingered on. It will be a gloriousss life—or a gloriousss death." He dipped his head solemnly. "Thank you for giving me the chancsse at eitherrr, my lord Treyvan."

Treyvan bowed his head, mirroring Kelvren's own motion. "The sssite has been prepared. You must go in alone, and lie down in the exact centerrr. When I rrreleassse the sssequencsse, you mussst rrraise your wingsss if you can, and breathe deeply. In that insssstant, cassst your ssself-healing ssspell. If you can ssstand, then ssstand. If you can—" He paused, obviously trying to hide something. "If you can fly then, fly. Ssstraight up, as far as you can."

Kelvren said the obvious. "If I can't fly then, I burn."

Treyvan looked down. "Yesss," he said softly.

Kelvren stared at the center of the circle. His heart beat harder as he stepped across the circle's edge, and more than a hundred people held their breath.

Pena stood at Treyvan's side, with a look of dismay and sorrow on her face. "He doesn't know it's a Heartstone—does he," he asked Treyvan.

The gryphon mage looked down at her with a look of resignation. "No. He doesssn't know."

Pena's eyes glittered from the reflected lights that were

starting up from the ground as Kel approached the circle's center. "It is probably best that he doesn't."

Whitebird and Rivenstone walked up beside them. "Treyvan's made a minor node," Pena explained to Whitebird and Rivenstone, "But it's channeled into a Heartstone—a purposely fragile one. It's why Treyvan used glass. When the spell reaches its height, it will consume itself. Even a tiny Heartstone will release its power in a saturated burst."

Treyvan nodded. "I didn't tell him. I completed the node hourssss before I buried the glasss sssphere. And the control pointsss I burrried, arrround the rrressst of the cssircle, are not to draw the power in from outssside. They are to contain the power and dirrrect the burst upward from the center. If his sssysssstem ressstartsss—he will absssorb it. If it doesss not—hurrrh. He will only feel pain forrr a few sssseconds."

Ammari and Jeft approached the four that were speaking Kaled'a'in. "What're you all talkin' about?" Jeft asked.

"We arrre—wishing Kelvrrren luck." He stepped toward the circle and spread his wings widely as Kelvren neared the center. "It isss time."

Pena ushered the humans back to where the Herald and his Companion stood even with the soldiers, locals, and patients who came to see the fate of their gryphon. Dusk descended further, making the light from the Circle even more apparent. Kelvren neared the center and walked around the packed earth there, until he faced the crowd.

He lay down on his belly, and carefully and deliberately folded his wings.

Treyvan stepped to the edge of the Circle, sat on his haunches, and pulled his wings straight back behind him. Faint beams of light broke through the ground around the perimeter. The light of the nearer control points visibly pulled toward him as his wings swept slowly back. Treyvan spread his arms wide, curled his claws toward the sides of the Circle, and swept his wings forward again. The light pushed back and caused the next nearer points to flare brighter.

Kelvren watched Treyvan—and then looked at every one of the gathered crowd. A sharp eye could see that tears ran from his eyes and dripped from the hook of his beak.

He laid his head down flat on the ground and his wings slumped.

The sixty control points around the perimeter blazed fully now, all of them matched columns of light tapering to a foot high. Treyvan went back to all fours and walked a horselength farther from the crowd, and stopped again at the edge of the Changecircle. He sat up, raised his forearms higher than before, and swept his wings back then forward again, harder. All the perimeter lights swayed inward and another ring of them blazed up from the ground in unison. Another massive flap of his wings, and a third ring shot up and steadied, encompassing Kelvren. Arcs of energy extended from one light to another, seemingly randomly, and then all at once they made a stable, steady pattern which looked like a stained glass rosette.

Treyvan held his own breath for a moment, and said in Kaled'a'in, "Wind to thy wings, sheyna."

Treyvan snapped his wings open.

A boom of thunder struck the crowd.

Inside the circle, a rising ring of light closed in on Kelvren in the center.

And consumed him.

Daylight surged upward from the circle's center, and the briefest shadow of wings flickered in it before everyone watching was blinded by it. Treyvan's irises pinned to width of a finger. He peered resolutely into the light.

There was movement.

There was the shape of a gryphon—getting to its feet. Standing. Its wings were unfolding, and raising up.

Except it was not a shadow against light.

It *was* light, and everything else was shadow compared to it.

Treyvan stepped back, one step. Two. The figure in the center rose up onto its hindfeet. It was Kelvren, but he was radiating light like nothing Treyvan had ever seen before. His body color wisped away, replaced by a glow from inside the feather shafts themselves. The edges of every feather gleamed and rippled in a yellow-white radiance, like the edge of burning paper. His eyes more than glowed—they shone outward in tapered rays of light, wherever he looked.

Kelvren raised a hindfoot, then the other, and stepped

up into the air. Calmly, he shone there, suspended off the ground, watching everyone.

And with a single wingbeat, the gryphon of light shot up into the air as a streak, and was gone. He went up higher, until he was a bright speck in the sky amidst the stars.

No one could say a word.

The mote of light descended a minute later.

It shone even brighter than before, and swept over the encampment, making shadows shift as if a new sun was lighting the night up. Kelvren's flight was effortless.

He backwinged once, and with the lightest of touches, settled atop the mill with his wings spread wide, and regarded everyone below.

Hallock, Pena, Ammari, Whitebird, Rivenstone and Jeft staggered, stunned, to Treyvan's side. "What—just happened?" Ammari asked.

"I have no idea," Treyvan admitted.

"Just look at him," Whitebird gasped. "He's beautiful."

"That's the damndest thing I've ever seen," Hallock said.

"He looks just like that tapestry back at White Gryphon," Rivenstone gasped.

"That's my gryphon," Jeft said.

The gryphon of light stayed atop the mill for ten minutes, then he sprang up from the mill's roof and dove to alight in front of the crowd, banking in to brake and hang in midair without a single wingbeat. His eyes swept them, one by one, and murmurs of astonishment came from nearly everyone.

Kelvren spoke.

"I have become—sssomething morrre than I wasss beforrre—but my hearrrt and allegiancssesss arrre unchanged. Ssso hearrr me," his voice boomed. "I know what I mussst do. The forcssesss at Deedun know little of magic. Theirrr sssoldierrrsss arrre mosssst likely bewilderrred by magic; and by now, they know what a sssingle grrryphon can do. I believe they will rrresssspond to what they can sssee, and by that, even the sssimplcssst of magic is made magnitudesss ssstrrrongerrr. He who isss afrrraid isss half beaten." He lifted his from the ground and fanned his wings as he rose, suspended in midair. "I will ssstrrrike, and I will ssshed no blood. And I do it in the name of the

Guarrrd, the Herrraldsss, and the Crrrown. Forrr all of you. Forrr all of usss. Forrr Valdemarrr!"

The crowd erupted into cheers and shouts.

The light from Kelvren's eyes flared brighter, and swept over to Treyvan. "You underrrsssstand," he said, his voice seeming distant. Kelvren gazed upon the rest, where they'd gathered with the convalescents. The illumination surrounded them all, sharpening the shadows. "My frrriends— I will neverrr forrrget you."

And with those last words, Kelvren rose, did a wing-over, dove down from four winglengths up and slammed his claws down to the ground. The earth trembled, and loose earth momentarily heaved up to knee height. The resulting crater ignited into a white, scintillating brightness. When Kelvren leaped into the sky, the sunlike glow stayed. Then with several massive wingbeats, the gryphon powered away from the crowd, driving up debris and dust, and with each downstroke his brilliant wings surged brighter. Below him, a jagged incandescent line two wings'-width wide crackled up from the shimmering focal point, and split away from its origin. The shimmering swath on the ground directly followed his flightpath. He swept through his skies, leading the line of sunfire from the Changecircle, through the camp, to the great Trade Road. He followed the Trade Road precisely, and the brilliance followed him on the ground. With each wingbeat Kelvren absorbed more magical power from the air, and the swath trailed him as light, following every twist. He coursed faster with each wingbeat than any gryphon he had ever known of. He flew for hours, tracing the Trade Road below, leaving a trail of light all the way to Deedun.

And it did not fade.

Mercenaries and militia alike looked up in astonishment, uncertainty, or stark terror at the figure that shot past them by the time an arrow could be nocked.

Candlemarks passed, and the path of coruscating light etched into the road still did not fade.

Only when he reached Deedun did Kelvren backwing and hover in midair in front of the tallest of the High Keep's towers. He stared at it, and concentrated.

The citizens of Deedun saw, line by line, the crest of

Valdemar, three stories high, burn itself into the wall of the keep's tower, and blaze like daylight across the city.

And like the wide line of light the length of the Trade Road, it too, did not fade.

Kelvren turned his gaze across the city. Citizens, guards, militia, and mercenary alike were coming out of buildings, all lit by the bright path that came from the far distance through the center of the city. Kelvren knew that with the sheer power he'd put into his mage-light spell, the crest of Valdemar would not fade away for a month or more.

He smiled.

Then the gryphon of light soared into the sky, becoming a bright star, and went home.

***

Captain Hallock Stavern and the Sixteenth Cavalry, three companies of Guard Regulars, and Kerowyn's Firebolts advanced steadily along the Trade Road. The militia they met offered no noteworthy resistance, and laid down arms almost apologetically. The Herald with the Crown's forces adjudicated the conditions of surrender, town by town, and left the locals with their pride. The mercenary company hired by Farragur Elm and his cohorts all but disbanded, demoralized by the showy display of magic they could not possibly match.

Kerowyn held her Firebolts back from taking the city. She was of the opinion that it would be damned unseemly for a merc company to take over the city rather than the Crown's Guard regiments—especially since so much of the troubles had been caused by *other* mercs.

When the Guards rode in and liberated Deedun, "Chancellor of Prosperity" Farragur Elm and his several of his insurrectionists barricaded themselves in the High Keep. Others guilty of the thefts that financed the power grab were, over time, discovered, arrested, and jailed. In time, Elm himself was dragged, screaming obscenities, from the very tower that Kelvren had marked.

Treyvan conferred with Whitebird and all the mages he knew, still amazed by what had happened. They finally deduced what Kelvren had done. When the power of the

Heartstone dissolution surged upward into him, Kelvren Healed himself, but there was too much chaotic raw power, flooding in too quickly. Kelvren used the simplest, but most stable, spell that any mage knew—mage-light—and quelled the chaos of raw power into a tuned current. Instead of ending the spell, as mages normally did when they had enough light, he let it flow through him. The ordeal of having no magic in his body had left his channels and conversion organs needy, and they filled to capacity, then into his bones, then into the feathers themselves. Then with so much free-floating energy in the air, his every movement brought in more.

The road of light was far more than a psychological ploy. The rate he cast it matched the rate the power was absorbed as he flew, and it burned off enough energy for his system to stabilize.

Firesong reported by teleson that Kelvren returned to k'Valdemar the night after his rejuvenation, still as bright as a sunrise. He flew over the Clan fires, Kelmskeep, Errold's Grove, and the Vale purely for effect.

And so the mill was gradually emptied of officers, and the village was freed from the Guard camp, and trade was reestablished along the great glowing Road. The light faded slowly over the fortnight since Kelvren's flight, but it wouldn't leave anyone's memory anytime soon.

Before long, it was time for Treyvan, Whitebird, Rivenstone and Pena to go back to Haven. They said their good-byes, and with a small bow, Pena gave an oilskin-wrapped package to Jeft.

Jeft opened it up, and inside were three gryphon feathers, bound with strips of leather, a folded scrap of paper, and a small leather pouch attached to them. Inside the pouch were six gold coins. His mother read the message.

"Jeft Roald Dunwythie. My friend. If you grow tired of being 'Boy,' with this, you will be welcomed into Hawkbrother lands and accepted as our own. Your mother will be welcome also. So speaks Wingleader Kelvren Skothkar of k'Valdemar Vale, Ally of the Crown of Valdemar."

Ammari felt tears in her eyes, and she hugged her son as strongly as she ever had. They gazed up at the encompassing sky, and listened to the birds together.

And by the end of that month, Captain Hallock Stavern

returned triumphantly to Haven, and to the arms of his beloved Genni.

***

Darkwind handed over a paper slip to Elspeth. "Mmm. Oh this is good. Repercussions from the Kelvren affair. Says here, some mayor demands reparations for the gryphon's presence in his village. Cites him as a hazard, detrimental to the town's morale, and an insult to the dignity of his office."

Elspeth browsed the slip, shrugged, and handed it off to a passing clerk to be handled. "Sounds like a healthy gryphon to me. What's next?"

THE FEAST OF THE CHILDREN

by Nancy Asire

Nancy Asire is the author of four novels, *Twilight's King-doms, Tears of Time, To Fall Like Stars,* and *Wizard Spawn*. She also has written short stories for the series anthologies *Heroes in Hell* and *Merovingen Nights,* and short stories for Mercedes Lackey's anthologies *Flights of Fantasy* and *Sun in Glory*. She has lived in Africa and traveled the world, but now resides in Missouri with her cats and two vintage Corvairs.

THE evening service had ended and the night candle burned brightly on the altar. From the steps leading to the Temple, Pytor watched his fellow villagers as they went off to what would normally have been a well-earned meal after a long day in the fields. As priest of this small Temple for fifteen years now, he knew each of them as well as he knew his own kin. Unlike so many other priests, he had come home after being elevated from an acolyte to a fully practicing member of the Sunlord's representatives on earth. Born in the village of Two Trees, he had returned, drawn by the quiet of the place and a family history that spanned generations. He had offered to come after the old priest who had served Two Trees since before he had been born had died. Not for him was the life some priests craved—cities and towns were too crowded, too noisy, too full of people who sought status and power. He was more than satisfied to minister to his villagers, people he had known since birth.

But as he watched the last of his neighbors leave the Temple, Pytor suddenly shivered, though the summer evening was far from cold. This evening, one of the most terrifying situations he had ever faced as a priest had loomed before him, one that could presage even more horrible times to come. But he had made his choice and now he must weather its outcome.

"Pytor."

He glanced over his shoulder at his sister who waited for him to close the Temple for the night and join her for dinner. Sunset light revealed the concern on her face, the searching look in her eyes. He was going to have to tell her; he had no choice. She would find out soon enough.

Then what would she think of him? Would she see him as a failure? Less of a priest? And could he live with that?

"Selenna." He smiled, turned and led the way back inside. Shutting the doors, he doffed his ceremonial robes, and led the way to the room that served as his residence. Attached to the back of the Temple, it was the only home he had known for fifteen years, a simple place that contained everything he owned in this world.

:*Tell her,*: that suddenly ever-present voice in his mind whispered. :*You'll have to tell her eventually and the best time to do it is now.*:

"I'll have dinner ready in a moment." she said, bustling around with preparations for their meal. She glanced over her shoulder. "Take care of your cats first. You know they're waiting for you."

He smiled somewhat sheepishly. Not only his sister, but the villagers teased him unmercifully about his fondness for the feline kind. He had always loved cats, a love fostered, no doubt, by growing up surrounded by at least two or three cats living in and around the house, not to mention those that had taken up residence in the barn.

"Here," Selenna said, extending a plate full of cold and finely chopped sausage left over from the midday meal. "Should keep 'em quiet 'til they go out mousing."

Pytor took the extended plate, smiled his thanks, and opened the door to the yard behind the Temple. Sure enough, he was greeted by a group of his cats, their tails lifted in expectation. Here was Tom, the big brown-and-white tabby; Puss, the all-white cat with green eyes shouldered forward, followed by the dainty little girl, Patches. And there, sitting back as if to say he was above all this pushing and shoving, was the newcomer. Pytor had named the recent arrival Sunshine, because he sported a coat of the oddest shade of gold, a color rare enough in these parts to have attracted attention. Sunshine looked up at him, the fading light turning his eyes into fiery points of topaz.

:Tell her now,: that voice whispered again. *To set things right between you, she has to know.:*

Pytor put down the plate and stepped back, letting the cats gather around their meal. Sunshine finally took his place at the plate, eating with a daintiness his companions lacked. There was something strange about that cat. Ever since he had wandered into the village several months ago, odd thoughts had filled Pytor's head. Thoughts that could, in this day and age, lead to inquisition or, even worse, the cleansing Fires.

Thoughts that had finally blossomed into the actions he had taken this evening.

He shook his head and went inside. Selenna was patiently waiting for him to join her. How could he tell her? How could he explain what troubled him so? Would she understand?

"Pytor." Selenna reached across the table and patted his hand. "You be too worried 'bout this. From what you told us tonight, we got no choice. You know that."

"I do," he responded. "I just don't like it. I don't like it at all. Can't you see? It's not simply that we're disobeying the new laws. We could be putting our very souls in peril."

She snorted, a very unladylike noise but one that spoke of her practicality. "You've said over and over we could put our souls in peril if we *don't* do this. That we must stand up for what we know Vkandis Sunlord wishes for his children in this world. How could he look down on us and be pleased if we let the children be put to the Fires?"

And there it was . . . the lurking fear that had plagued him. Only five days left now before the Feast of the Children, when a priest came to the village all the way from Sunhame to test the children.

Test the children. What a bland way to put it. In the old days, that was exactly what it had been. Priests went from city to city, town to town, and village to village to test children for their talents. Talents that were now becoming spoken of in whispers as "witch powers" and were said to be evil in the sight of the Sunlord. But Pytor knew better . . . by the Light of Vkandis, he *knew* it was not so.

Even when he had studied for the priesthood, things had started to change in Sunhame. The Son of the Sun was no priest *he* would have chosen, had he had been Vkandis Sunlord, to be the God's representative on earth. And through the years, the Son of the Sun's actions had proved him right. Far more interested in temporal power, Hanovar had gathered priests around him who told him exactly what he wanted to hear, all eager to increase whatever powers and positions they thought were rightfully theirs.

"What we're doing—" He started and abandoned his words, and tried again. "It goes against what I've been taught. Our allegiance to the Son of the Sun is paramount. But I know what's going on in the priestly circles is *not* what I was led to believe Vkandis wants for his children. How could he wish to destroy those of us he granted these powers to at birth?"

"More the reason," she said in her quiet voice, "to give 'em a chance to grow into those powers in a place they won't have to live in fear. Najan be our cousin. He's told of the place we're going. It be not that far off, and he's lived there over a year. Two Trees be close enough to the border so we can make it there in three days. A few priests be there already. You know that. Other families followed 'em. They be afraid of what could happen to their children who have talents when the Feast of the Children comes. What be so different 'bout this time?"

He cleared his throat. "It's you . . . I don't know how I could live without you. We're all we have left of our family, what with Father gone, Mother dying last year, and your husband the year before. Both you and I are childless. If anything happens—"

"You be avoiding my question," she said and smiled slightly. "What be so different 'bout this time? And who be the one to say I won't come back? Once the children be safely 'cross the border, Najan will take care of 'em and I can come home."

Here it is, Pytor thought. *Here's where I tell her or trust Vkandis to keep my secret.*

"You know I have confidence in you and Najan. And it's not that the children will be too close to the border of Valdemar. Neither Karse nor Valdemar seems too concerned with what goes on in that territory." He sighed. "What I've *not* told you, is this: the priest who's coming to Two Trees is Chardan."

For a moment his sister's face went totally blank. Suddenly, sadness replaced the emptiness of her features, a sadness that spoke more than anything she could have said.

"Yes," he said softly. "Chardan. My friend from my earliest days of study in Sunhame. The one I swore an oath to, promising there would never be anything between us. I'll have to lie to him, Selenna, about those children. *Lie!* And in doing that, I'll have to break my oath to him."

To say nothing of what might *happen if Chardan detected the lie.*

"But what happened to Durban?"

Durban, the Red-robe priest who had become a Blackrobe, who had come year after year to Two Trees and who, despite his talents as a demon summoner, had seemingly possessed a soft spot in his heart for the inhabitants of this small village. Durban had never pressed too hard and, Pytor suspected, had consciously overlooked those children who might be growing into their talents.

"Durban died a few months past," Pytor said. "I didn't want to tell you because I knew—"

"I'd worry 'bout the upcoming Feast," she finished his dying sentence. She stirred the greens on her plate, her face gone still and thoughtful. "But it wouldn't have changed things, Pytor. I *always* worry 'bout the Feast."

He glanced up at the ceiling. "What am I to do? How can I lie to Chardan?"

:There's nothing wrong in doing such a thing if it's done for Vkandis and for the love of his children,: that voice whispered in his head. *:Don't take more upon yourself than you ought.:*

If he had not known better, he would have sworn his sister had heard the same voice. "Which be worse?" she asked. "Lying to an old friend and betraying a childhood oath, or doing what you know be best for the children of this village?"

"Oh, you're clever," he said, "throwing my own words

back at me. Yes, Selenna, there's a higher power to answer
to here than a childhood oath. But if he doesn't believe
me . . . what if he tries to go into my mind—"

"Now why would he do that? He be your friend," she
stated. "You been tested, time and again. Not once, *ever,*
did you show a hint of any so-called witch powers."

"But times are different now, and that difference can
turn friend against friend. Remember what happened with
Zarvash and Tomasio?"

"Never *did* think Zarvash worthy of much more than pig
slop," Selenna responded bluntly. "He be an evil, grasping
man. He'd betray his own mother if it meant a few more
gold pieces in his pouch."

"That's true, but he did report Tomasio to the priesthood, and Tomasio went to the Fires."

:There are worse things than going to the Fires,: the voice
in Pytor's head murmured. *:The Sunlord sees all and re-
wards accordingly.:*

Pytor rubbed his forehead, attempting to dispel that
inner voice. "Well," he said, sitting up straighter in his
chair. "I guess there's nothing to be done for it now. We've
cast our fates to the Sunlord's mercy. You and the children
will be leaving at first light tomorrow. Vkandis willing,
you'll be over the border before Chardan is close to Two
Trees."

"And I'll be back, Pytor," she said, squeezing his hand
in hers. "Don't worry 'bout that. I can take care of myself.
And Najan . . . Oh, don't look so horrified. He's always
been a free spirit, a trader and tinker by nature. He comes,
he goes. No one knows where he's been, or that he lives
'cross the border. But I can find him."

Pytor knew that for truth. Though a woman wasn't supposed to travel unless accompanied by a male relative,
those rules weren't strictly enforced out here in the back
of beyond. A woman *could* make a trip by herself, if she
thought the need was great.

After Selenna had returned to the house she and her
husband had shared, Pytor was left alone with his own misgivings. Now that his plan had been set into motion, he
could foresee a hundred ways it might go wrong. Not for
one moment did he believe the new thinking emanating

from the Son of the Sun. Once an eagerly anticipated ceremony, the Feast of the Children was turning into a day
every family dreaded. In years past, it had stood as a
marker of the passage from childhood to adulthood; the
child making that passage tossed some valued possession
of theirs into a fire to signify entry into a new phase of life.
Now they, themselves, could be thrown to the Fires.

Unless, of course, they could be suborned by the priests
into becoming one of the newly powerful Black-robes,
those summoners of demons and possessors of a magic
Pytor suspected did *not* flow from the hands of the Sunlord.
He wore his own robes of red proudly; the last thing he
wanted was to be seen as a figure that inspired fear, not
love.

He stepped outside to retrieve the cats' plate. Tom was
gone, and Puss and Patches were stalking something in the
grass over by the bushes. Only Sunshine remained, cleaning
his whiskers. When Pytor picked up the plate, the cat
looked up, a satisfied expression on his face. Pytor reached
down and stroked the cat behind his ears, the simple act
settling his emotions.

"Where did you come from?" he asked conversationally.
"Who's missing you? You were far too well cared for to
be homeless."

Sunshine's response was a throaty purr.

"I hope I'm doing the right thing," Pytor continued,
finding nothing odd in holding a conversation with a cat.
"I can't see Jovani, Chelsah, Bhobar, Lispah or the twins
go to the Fires. And I *know* they would." His heart gave
a sad little jump in his chest. Chardan wouldn't hesitate a
moment to make the decision to rid the world of those
children. As much as he cared for his old friend, Chardan
was no Durban.

The admission pained him. Oh, Sunlord, how it pained
him. But he had seen the change come over Chardan years
ago, as Chardan had become intent on ascending through
the ranks of the priesthood and assuring himself a position
of power in the future. Pytor simply could not understand
what had happened to his childhood friend. The world was
far too much with Chardan, and the dark side of that world
seemed to be winning.

And that fact made Pytor's decision to shield the children even more important.

:The Sunlord requires much of us,: his inner voice said, warmth present in its tone, *:but not more than we can give. There's no limit to his love for us. He only wishes us to love him in return and share that love with all his children.:*

And, as a priest, he should know that better than most. Pytor smiled. His sister was right. He must place his trust in Vkandis, certain he had made the correct decision.

If things went wrong . . . well, there *were* more terrible things than death.

The following day passed in a blur. Selenna and the children had left for the north, but not as early as planned. A sudden summer storm had boiled up during the night and drenched the countryside, delaying a morning departure. Normally, the villagers would have hailed this storm as beneficial, but with travel held to narrow country roads, most merely lanes, rain seemed a bad omen. Choosing not to see it so, at the morning service Pytor had blessed the rain as a gift to the surrounding fields. He further assured the children's parents that Vkandis had given everyone a bit more time to say farewells.

It had been extraordinarily difficult to stand at the edge of the village and watch Selenna and the six children set off to the north, though his sister, ever the practical and enterprising one, led the small caravan.

The families of the departing children had seemed lost now that their children had gone. He had said comforting words, made comforting gestures, but had no comforting thoughts for himself. And now, of course, he must rehearse his explanations—if such were ever needed—as to the absence of the six children. Two Trees was hardly a large village, and the yearly census would show there were fewer children to be found if anyone came looking.

And that was exactly what Chardan would be doing.

Chardan.

Pytor bowed his head. What could he say to Chardan? The ready responses he and Selenna had concocted had seemed more than sufficient at the time, but would they hold up under Chardan's questioning? The fact all six children were cousins could explain why they had set off to visit a dying grandmother before the God took her. Such an event could preclude mandatory presence at the Feast of Children. The children's parents had agreed to journey to the grandmother's home to flesh out the deception, leaving not more than three hours after their children had departed. And now, in a village far emptier than it had been in the morning, Pytor wondered if it was enough.

Chardan was no fool, and Pytor was uncertain as never before how he would react when he looked his childhood friend in the eyes and had to lie.

Morning dawned as one of those glorious summer days when all seemed right with the world. Some of the gloom had lifted from Pytor's heart overnight, and he felt considerably more confident in the outcome of his plans. Even Pytor's cats sensed his increased optimism: when he went outside to feed them, everyone, even Sunshine, had gathered close and rubbed his ankles thoroughly before settling down to their breakfast.

And now, he fell back into his priestly routine. He cleaned the Temple, thoroughly swept the yard around it, and made sure he had a sufficient supply of night candles. As he inventoried what few medicines he kept in a small chest in his room, he thanked the God he had a more than competent midwife living but one village away.

With fields in constant need of weeding and watering, the remaining children of Two Trees would be off helping their parents. The village, therefore, lay strangely quiet, save for the occasional barking of an exuberant dog. In the past, this had been a time when Pytor had devoted his waking hours to contemplation and study of the Writ. It should have been again, but, far back in the depths of his mind, he still worried about what could happen when Chardan arrived.

Sunset, and another evening service passed without incident. The night candle lit, Pytor sat down to supper, missing his sister's company. By now, she and the children should be nearly halfway to their destination if the roads and lanes held firm. This knowledge, of course, only emphasized it would be all too soon that Chardan came knocking at his door. Suddenly, the sausage he was chewing tasted like

dust. His heart beat faster, and he closed his eyes. Calm . . .
he needed calm. If he could achieve a state of serene composure, *if* he could maintain that state through Chardan's
visit, then his deception would be complete.

The door to his room stood open, admitting the evening
breeze. He drew another deep breath and cast a wary eye
on what remained of his supper. His appetite had gone and
the thought of finishing what lay on his plate upset his
stomach. Ah, well. The cats would thank him for the
extra portions.

As if called, he felt the soft sensation of fur against his
ankles. He leaned down to pet the head of his visitor, and
started. It was Sunshine. Sunshine, the stand-off cat, the
one so far as he knew had never entered a building. Yet
there he was, sitting now at Pytor's feet, staring at him with
the total inscrutability of his kind. Pytor rubbed Sunshine's
head again, glad of the diversion from his gloomy thoughts.

:You worry too much,: the voice said in his head, the
voice he had not heard in several days. *:Vkandis protects
those he loves. Have faith in your God. Has he let you
down yet?:*

Pytor smiled. No, the God had never let him down, but
then he had never been party to a deed that, at least in
these days, seemed to fly in the face of what the God demanded. Three days remained until Chardan arrived. Three
days to perfect his attitude of calmness in the face of possible exposure as a renegade priest. Only three days.

:And all our days are held in the God's hands,: the voice
said. *:What are you, man, in the scheme of unfathomable
eternity?:*

He bowed his head and silently acknowledged his doubt
as proof of his own mortality. He could no more understand what Vkandis had in store for the world than an ant
could of what a man planned as he walked across the fields.

He had no choice. He had cast dice in this game and
must wait on the outcome of their tumbling.

The following day held nothing but rain. Unusual for this
time of year, the rain fell slow and steady, keeping the
entire village indoors. What was good for the fields unnerved Pytor. This should have been the last day of his
sister's journey with the six children, but now he was not

sure. What fell from the dark sky today had more than
likely fallen to the north the evening before. This could
delay crossing the border into the no-man's land that lay
between Karse and Valdemar.

A sodden gathering had waited for him in the Temple
to begin the evening service. As he threw himself into the
ritual in an effort to diminish his own fears, Pytor sensed
the unease that gripped the villagers at his back. And now,
held to his room by the gently falling rain, he prayed again.
One more day and he would have to face Chardan. One
more day and his sister and the children would surely be
safely across the border and out of reach of the Black-
robes who would consign the children to the Fires for no
other reason than they were different.

A seething emotion welled up in Pytor's chest that he
recognized instantly. It was anger, pure and simple anger.
How dared those charlatans decide who lived and who
died, especially the very young whose lives were new and
full of promise? How dared they? Nowhere in the Writ
that Pytor was familiar with was there any mention of such
depravity . . . nowhere! Once again, he was confronted by
the fact the priesthood was changing, that earthly matters
were swiftly supplanting heavenly ones, all in the name of
temporal power!

Despite the weather, he left his room and stood outside,
his face lifted to the darkening evening sky. The rain felt
good on his flushed face and its coolness served to calm
his mood. No good would come by railing against what he
could not change. Again, he knew he had no choice. He
must trust in his God, and rest sure in the knowledge he
was doing the God's will.

Hoofbeats broke the stillness of the village the following
late afternoon. Pytor looked up from weeding his small
garden, amazed to see Iban riding his way, his old plow
horse dark with sweat.

"Sun's Ray," Iban got out. His breath coming fast, he
slid off his mount's broad back and sketched a brief bow.
"Horsemen to the south."

Pytor glanced over his shoulder as if he could see beyond
the edge of the village.

"Who?" he asked, struggling to remain calm.

"Don't know," the farmer said, wiping his brow with the back of his hand. "Don't look like nobody 'round here. Be four of 'em, and they got a wagon with 'em."

Pytor felt the blood leave his face. Chardan! A day early! That was the only answer. Or could it be—

"Traders?" He was proud his voice remained steady.

"Don't think so, Sun's Ray. Not enough of 'em. And from what I seen, they be dressed in black, all of 'em."

Chardan.

Pytor closed his eyes briefly. Now, not only would he have to face Chardan, but a day before he was ready.

"Make sure everyone knows the priest from Sunhame has come sooner than expected," he said slowly. "And, for the God's sake, remember what you're all to profess to. Do you understand?"

Iban's sun-browned face paled at Pytor's words. "Aye, Sun's Ray. I'll tell 'em. You can trust us!"

And the farmer scrambled up on his horse's back before Pytor could add another word, off to warn the villagers that auspicious company was arriving,

"Well met, Pytor, well met."

The voice was as he remembered it . . . cool, deep and utterly confident. Pytor bowed slightly as Chardan dismounted in front of the Temple. Not much else had changed about his childhood friend either. Unless one noticed the even finer cut to his black robes, the glint of more gold than was seemly for a priest to wear, and the subtle hint that the food in Sunhame was tempting beyond belief.

Pytor took Chardan's hand in greeting. "I'm sorry to be so ill prepared. You came earlier than expected."

Chardan waved a dismissive hand. "All the more time to talk to you, old friend." He glanced around, his eyes cataloging the cottages that stood around the Temple. "Besides, I'm not used to all this riding about. Simply put, I want to get this over and return to Sunhame. You really should change your mind and join us there. Nothing can be accomplished here in this backwater. You're made for better things that this."

Pytor said nothing.

"So," Chardan said, again taking a slow look at the village. "Everyone's out in the fields, I take it?"

"They are," Pytor replied. "We have no inn here, as you well know. I'm not sure where—"

"I'm sure your villagers can make room for my three companions. As for me, I can suffer a night in your bed, old friend. Durban said you always took to the barn when he was here. Sorry to put you at such inconvenience, but I'll be gone by tomorrow afternoon."

Pytor smiled what he hoped was his most disarming smile. *Tomorrow. Oh, by the mercy of Vkandis, let me be strong until tomorrow night.*

The noontide sun beat down like a burning hammer. That alone could account for Pytor being slightly light-headed, but what he faced now was enough to cause cold sweat to gather on his brow. He hoped Chardan would mistake it for honest sweat produced by the heat, and not an indication of guilt.

Pytor had managed to make it though yesterday afternoon with no sign of his growing unease. Chardan had presided over the evening service, the villagers reacting to the senior Black-robe's presence with suitable awe. But the night Pytor had spent in the barn had been one of the most unnerving in his life. He had spent most of the night in prayer and rose fuzzy-headed before dawn to participate in the morning service. Now, standing before the Temple in the blazing noon sun, he prayed again for the strength he felt he sorely lacked.

"Where are the rest of the children?" Chardan asked in a deceptively quiet voice.

The children who had remained, who had never given any evidence of talents or powers, shifted slightly. Their parents, who had grouped themselves on the other side of the Temple's doorway, kept their expressions as neutral as they were able.

Pytor drew a deep breath, forced himself to meet Chardan's eyes, all too aware the three junior Black-robes were watching him carefully.

"According to my records, old friend, there should be six more children living in this village."

"There are," Pytor said, struggling to keep his voice as devoid of emotion as Chardan's. "They're all cousins. Unfortunately, their grandmother is dying, and they left with their parents to be with her before Vkandis calls her home."

There. He had done it. Lied. Actually lied to someone he had pledged faith to.

"Hmmm." Chardan glanced down at the list he held in his hands, a list Pytor suspected contained the names of everyone who lived in Two Trees, their ages and their sex. "Interesting. And your sister, Pytor? I missed her company last night. Where is she?"

This line of questioning caused Pytor's heat to jump in his chest. "Visiting our cousin Najan," he replied, his mouth gone dry.

"The itinerant trader? And why would she go visit him now?"

Pytor shrugged his shoulders. "Who knows what goes on in a woman's head?" It was a safe response for a man to give, though Selenna would have excoriated him had she heard.

"Hmmm."

Pytor held his face to an expression of polite attention, certain Chardan watched his every move from the corners of his eyes.

"Well," Chardan said at last. "Since impending death of a family member grants adults and their children exemption from the Feast of the Children, I suppose we're done here. Once again, old friend, I congratulate you on the condition of your village and the souls you minister to. We could have been treated no better in the larger towns we sometimes visit." He folded the paper he held and lifted his right hand in blessing. "Go with the love of the God who watches over all," he said, his voice deepening into stentorian depths. "Turn to his Light and away from all things dark, and flee in peril of your very souls from anything that verges on the edge of witchery! May the blessings of Vkandis Sunlord be upon you all!"

The villagers and their children responded, as was custom and ritual, "May it be so."

For a moment, Pytor's knees threatened to give out. Relief flooded his heart. Could it be over? Could he have actually—

"Pytor," Chardan said, his voice pitched so only Pytor could hear. "A word with you, if you please."

It was *not* over. Not by a long shot. With legs feeling heavy as lead, Pytor followed Chardan to the rear of the Temple. His four cats lay in what shade they could find, sleeping deeply in preparation for their nightly hunts. Chardan glanced at them with an expression of extreme distaste.

"Don't know why you keep such creatures around," he said. "Too independent, though I suppose they're good for killing mice. Now," he continued, "you and I need to have a talk. What are you hiding, Pytor?"

Pytor stared at Chardan, his heart in his throat. How did his old friend know— The answer came with that thought. *Old friend.* How could he keep a secret from someone he had regarded as a brother, with whom he had shared his most intimate thoughts? There was no hope for it. Another lie, piled up on top of the ones he had told already.

"I can't hide anything from you, Chardan, you know that."

"Then why am I sensing something you're not telling me? It has to do with the children, doesn't it, Pytor?"

"Most assuredly not," Pytor answered, allowing the barest hint of hurt indignation to enter his voice. "Why would I lie to you?"

"I'm not sure. But I sense it. Those six children—when Durban was here, just last year if my notes are right, he said there might be the possibility of those six showing witch powers. Is that what you're hiding from me, Pytor? Do they possess forbidden talents?"

Pytor simply stared. What could he say? What could he do?

"I'm sorry, my friend. I want to trust you . . . I've *always* trusted you in the past, but this is something I can't led go based simply on our old friendship. I must go into your mind."

O Vkandis! Shield me now! He'll find out for sure and it will be the Fires for me!

"You have every right," Pytor said, amazed his voice sounded steady. Behind Chardan, Sunshine lifted his head, blinked, and stretched. Wandering over to where Pytor and Chardan stood, the gold cat sat down next to Pytor, leaning up against him in a feline display of affection.

"This won't hurt, and I'll be brief as I can," Chardan said, staring into Pytor's eyes. "I'm sorry it's come to this, but witch powers cannot be allowed. Even in those we love and care for. The Sunlord's people must be pure and turn their faces from darkness."

A dizzy sensation overwhelmed Pytor. He thought he was going to fall, but another portion of his mind assured him he still stood steady on his feet. But even more powerful than the thrust of Chardan's mind in his, came the sudden warmth and comfort emanating from the gold cat leaning against his leg. Into his mind, blotting out the rummaging of Chardan's, flowed a feeling of peacefulness, of affection, forgiveness, and, above all, of a love he could no more understand than fly. A barrier rose in his mind, a flaming bulwark erected between his innermost thoughts and Chardan's probing. Nothing could hurt him now; nothing could hurt him ever. Wrapped in the hands of a power greater and more indescribable than anything he had ever experienced before, he was only dimly aware of the tears seeping from his eyes and spilling down his cheeks.

And, suddenly, he was released and stood fully back in the present day world.

"I'm sorry, old friend." It was Chardan's voice. The Black-robe reached out and steadied Pytor. "I'm sorry I ever doubted you. Your mind is clear as sunshine. You've hidden nothing from me. Durban must have been mistaken, for you have no suspicions about the six children he mentioned. And I doubt you'd ever try to lie to me. The God knows you've never been good at it, even back in our childhood days."

Pytor drew a deep breath. "You did what you had to, Chardan. You're forgiven, if I have it in my power to forgive."

The gold cat meowed softly, stretched again and wandered off to lie down in the shade.

Later, after evening service and lighting the night candle, Pytor sat in his room, only now feeling full strength returning after his ordeal. Chardan and his fellow Black-robes had left Two Trees immediately after Chardan had searched Pytor's mind. Pytor hadn't even lit the candles after dinner, preferring to remain in the warm darkness, his mind gone a total blank.

Suddenly, clearly as if seen in bright sunlight, he beheld

his sister and the six children safely across the border; they had found Najan and the other people who had fled Karse in the face of growing persecution. They were safe! He had wagered mightily and, through what grace he dared not question, they had all won.

:You trusted in your Lord,: the voice inside his head said softly. *:And, as such, you were rewarded. Remember—the God loves all his children, for he made them, each and every one.:*

He heard a soft meow and turned to see Sunshine standing in a corner of his room. For a moment, time seemed to stand still. Though no candle burned, the gold cat stood surrounded by a glory of light, a wondrous golden halo that cast shadows on the walls. And he grew in size, his coat changing to rich cream, and his face, legs and tail darkening to brick red. For a long moment, man and cat stared at each other, and Pytor could have sworn the cat smiled.

And then, so swiftly Pytor could not comprehend it, Sunshine turned away and was gone.

:Vkandis watches over those whose hearts are pure,: the voice said, fading off to a mere whisper. *:Never doubt that the Sunlord loves those who love and care for others! For that is why he made us all.:*

DEATH IN KEENSPUR HOUSE

by *Richard Lee Byers*

Richard Lee Byers is the author of twenty-five fantasy and
horror novels, including *Dissolution, The Rage, The Rite,
The Black Bouquet,* and *The Shattered Mask.* His short
fiction has appeared in numerous magazines and anthologies. A resident of the Tampa Bay area, the setting for much
of his contemporary fiction, he spends much of his leisure
time fencing foil, epee, and saber.

THE living eyed me with emotions ranging from hope
to dislike. Mouth agape, eyes wide, smallsword still
sheathed at his hip, chest hacked to bloody ruin, the corpse
stared up at the high ceiling with its painted scene of
nymphs and deer. I stooped to see if his eyes still held the
image of the man who'd cut him down. They didn't. That
trick has never worked for me, nor, so far as I know, for
anyone.

Stout and balding, a man in his middle years like myself,
Lord Baltes asked, "Are you learning anything, Master
Selden?"

I straightened up. "It's too early to say."

Lanky and sharp-featured like so many members of the
Keenspurs, Tregan snorted. "Surely it's clear enough what
happened. Venwell had the bad luck to blunder into the
thief, who then had to kill him to make his escape."

"Is that what your magic reveals?" I asked. A talent for
wizardry ran in the Keenspur blood, and in addition to

serving as his brother Baltes' lieutenant, Tregan was house mage.

His mouth twisted. "No, actually. The signs are muddled. But it's common sense, surely."

"Maybe," I said, inspecting a floral tapestry spoiled by eight long rust-brown streaks. The murderer had evidently used it to give his weapon a thorough wiping. "I'd like to see the room where the wedding gifts are on display."

"What will that accomplish?" asked the sorcerer. "The killer took the ruby tiara. It isn't there for you to examine anymore. We sent for you because Marissa claims you know your way around the stews and thieves' dens down by Stranger's Gate. You should be hurrying there—"

"You sent for him because he's the one who caught the salamander and so kept the city from burning down, and the Greens and Blues from slaughtering one another," Marissa said. Lithe and long-legged, she'd been the principal sword-teacher to the Green faction as I was for the Blues. "He has a knack for puzzling things out."

"I hope so." Baltes waved his hand. "The room is this way." Tregan, Marissa, and I followed him, and an assortment of his kinsmen and servants traipsed along after us.

The remaining gifts—begemmed goblets, gold plates and trays, rings, bracelets, armor, glazed jars of spice and unguents, furs, and bolts of velvet and silk—glowed in the candlelight. Relatives, political allies, and trading partners had sent presents from as far away as Errold's Grove.

I'd walked a warrior's path my whole life long, first as a mercenary, then, primarily, as a master-of-arms, though I still occasionally rented out my blade if the job didn't require actually riding off to war. So perhaps it was no surprise a splendidly crafted broadsword, with emeralds gleaming in the hilt and scabbard, caught my eye. I hankered to pick it up and try a cut or two, but that would have been gauche and inappropriate.

So I kept my mind on the task at hand, wandered about, inspected the heaps of gleaming treasure, and tried to think of something useful. "Are we certain," I asked, "that only the tiara is missing?"

"Yes," Baltes said.

"I need to confer with my colleague," I said. "We'll only

be a moment." Conscious once more of the animus with which so many of Baltes' people regarded me, I led Marissa into the next room.

"What have you figured out?" she whispered, brushing back a strand of her short black hair.

"Nothing for certain."

"Curse it, Selden, I'm the one who urged them to send for you. Don't make me look a fool."

"Believe me," I said, "I want to unmask the killer and recover the bauble as much as you do, and not just because Baltes will reward me. To lay the feuds to rest for good."

For years, the fifty noble houses of Mornedealth had divided themselves into factions of ten. Each of the five disliked the others, but the Greens and Blues, the most powerful, detested one another with extraordinary virulence. When the fire elemental's depredations fanned their mutual hatred and suspicion, their enmity nearly plunged the city into outright civil war.

Strangely enough, that turned out to be a good thing, because it threw a scare into every noble with a particle of sense. In the aftermath, Pivar, a leader of the Blues, led a campaign to quell the factions. The forthcoming wedding represented the culmination of his efforts. When Baltes, a widower, married Pivar's youngest daughter Lukinda, it ought to lay the rivalries to rest for good and all.

But only if the wedding came off as planned. On the surface, there was no reason why the murder and burglary, no matter how unfortunate, need prevent it. But my gut warned me that, if left unresolved, such an alarming, inexplicable calamity could bring the old malice and mistrust creeping back.

"So," said Marissa, "what did you want to talk about?"

"First, tell me about Venwell. Did you train him?"

"Yes."

"Was he an able, seasoned swordsman?"

"Very much so."

I sighed. "I was afraid of that. Now I need to know how hard I can push these folk. I have things to say they won't like. I won't mean to denigrate their honor, but some may take it that way."

She snorted. "Wonderful. Because they don't like you."

Understandably so, I supposed, since for years, I made my living teaching Blues how to kill them. "I don't know that you dare push them very hard at all."

"Damn it, I have to do the job they brought me here to do. Will you back me up?"

She made a sour face. "Well, I did get you into this, even if I'm starting to regret it."

"Let's rejoin the others."

"What do you have to tell us?" Baltes asked.

"Milord," I said, "I'm no sage—far from it—but as Marissa told you, sometimes I have an eye for what's odd about a particular situation. We have several oddities here. For starters, neither the sentries nor the watchdogs outside detected an intruder, nor have we found any sign of forced entry."

"What of it?" Tregan asked. "As I understand it, there are thieves skillful enough to sneak into any house."

"Perhaps," I said. "But consider this also. Venwell died of cuts to the chest. He saw his killer. Yet he perished without even trying to draw his blade."

"Perhaps," Tregan said, "he froze."

Marissa shook her head. "No. I schooled him too well."

"It's possible," I said, feeling as if I were about to dive from a cliff, "he knew his slayer. If it was someone he trusted, that would explain why he took no alarm until it was too late, even though the killer had a naked sword in his hand. Similarly, if the culprit was someone who lives here in the mansion—or is currently a guest—he wouldn't need to sneak past the guards and hounds, or break open a window or door."

For a moment, everyone just gawked at me. Then a footman said, "But everybody liked Venwell."

"That may be," I replied, "but a thief still couldn't afford to let him report that he'd seen him stealing the tiara."

"Ridiculous," Tregan spat. "Ours is a wealthy and honorable house. No one here would steal the gift."

"Not even a servant?" I asked. "Or the least of your kin, perhaps burdened with gambling debts?"

"No," Tregan said, "I don't believe it."

"Have you wondered," I said, "why the thief took only a single article? A housebreaker could surely have carried away more. But if the murderer never left, if he needed to hide his plunder here in the mansion for the time being, he might have reckoned that the more he stole, the harder it would be to conceal. Or, if he's a member of the household, it might have shamed him to take more than he reckoned he truly needed."

Skinny and sharp-nosed like Tregan but younger, a Keenspur named Dremloc stepped forth from the mass of observers and planted himself in front of me. *Here it comes,* I thought. At least it looked as if he meant to deliver a formal challenge. I had a fair chance of surviving that, as I wouldn't if he and all his outraged relations simply assailed me in a pack.

"You Blue bastard," he said. "I say you're a lia—"

But just before he could articulate that unforgivable word, Marissa sprang between us. She glared into his eyes, and he flinched. Since she'd trained him, he knew how deadly a combatant she was, and accordingly feared her more than he did me.

"Master Selden," she said, "is under my protection. Is that clear?"

Dremloc scowled, but also inclined his head.

Baltes turned to me. "Do you have more to say?" he asked.

I had a nagging sense that I should. That I'd missed things a sharper eye and brain might have discerned. But it would have only have undermined his confidence in me to say so. "You've heard my conjectures, Milord. They point to an obvious course of action. Search the mansion, find the tiara, and hope its hiding place reveals who took it."

The assembly growled at the prospect of having their quarters and belongings ransacked. Tregan said, "Ridiculous." Evidently it was a favorite word of his.

"No," Baltes said, "it isn't. Master Selden's guesses are only that, but they seem plausible. We will search the house, if only to lay the suspicions he's roused to rest, and you, brother, will try once again to locate the tiara with your sorcery."

We organized ourselves into search parties and formulated a plan. I cast a final admiring glance at the broadsword with the emeralds in its hilt, then set forth with my companions.

The Keenspur mansion was enormous. It took well into the morning to complete our search, and even so, we didn't look everywhere. Some hiding places simply seemed too unlikely to bother with, and I wasn't bold enough to suggest that we rummage through Baltes' or Tregan's apartments, even if I'd believed it would serve a purpose.

Our mundane search failed to produce the tiara, nor did Tregan's divinations fare any better. At the end of it all, standing before Baltes, the magician, and their tired, irritated relations and retainers, I did indeed feel "ridiculous."

"I'm sorry, milord," I said. "I thought I'd reasoned my way to the truth, or a part of it anyway, but it appears I was mistaken."

Tregan sneered. "Will you now make inquiries among the robbers and knaves, as we told you to in the first place?"

"Yes, milord." I certainly had no better plan.

As I walked to the door with as much dignity as I could muster, I heard Dremloc and another young blade muttering in my wake. "This is like sending a weasel to escort the chickens safely into the coop," my would-be challenger said.

"What do you mean?" his companion asked.

"I don't claim to understand any of this, why the tiara was taken or Venwell had to die. But you can bet your last copper a Blue is responsible."

The seed of suspicion was already sprouting.

For the next week, I went about mostly in disguise, in the costumes of other lands or with false whiskers gummed to my chin, prowling all night and sleeping by day. Reasoning it would be difficult for a woman to wear the tiara in Mornedealth, I began my investigations among receivers of stolen goods who specialized in moving them safely out of town. When that availed me nothing, I moved on to the commoner sort of thieves' market, and bribed whores and tavern keepers to tell if any of the city's more accomplished housebreakers had lately boasted of a coup, started spending lavishly, or was lying low to avoid hunters like myself. That was of no use either. If any of the city's rascals had knowledge of the tiara, it would take a shrewder, subtler agent than me to tease out the information.

Meanwhile, Mornedealth commenced a slide back into

the hateful, bloody days of yore. Hotheaded young Keenspurs started wearing green tokens, their friends from other
houses followed suit, and the fools among the supposedly
defunct Blues would have felt cowardly had they not responded by displaying their own colors. Soon the Reds,
Yellows, and Blacks took up the old practice, too. From
there, it was a short step to insults, mockery, and scuffles
in the street.

Baltes, Tregan, Pivar, and other leaders of the noble
houses did their best to quash the unrest, and at their behest, the City Guards assisted. Thanks to their efforts, the
quarrels among the resurgent Blues and Greens, and members of the lesser factions, ended short of grievous harm to
any of the principals. But it was only a matter of time
before our luck ran out, and I feared that as soon as it did,
the blood-feuds would resume in earnest.

All because of a crime that, on the surface, had nothing
to do with the grudges and rivalries of old. It was perverse,
mad, yet it was happening.

In due course, I trudged back to Keenspur House to
report my lack of progress.

Somewhat to my surprise, when a lackey admitted me to
confer with Tregan and Baltes, I found the latter wearing
the broadsword from the wedding gifts. It was contrary to
custom to put such a present to use prior to the nuptials,
but I could understand why he'd succumbed to the
temptation.

I explained what I'd accomplished, or rather, what I
hadn't. It didn't take long, as accounts of failure rarely do,
so long as a man resists the urge to make excuses.

"I'm beginning to think," said Tregan, sneering, "that
your success in catching the salamander was a fluke."

I was starting to wonder myself, but still had enough
pride left to resent his contempt. "Should I infer, milord,
that your efforts to solve our problem with wizardry have
proved as futile as my own?"

The question made him glare.

"Tell me the truth," Baltes said. "Is there any point in
your poking around the slums any further?"

I sighed. "I can't be certain, but probably not."

"Then don't. Tell me what I owe you for your time, and
the steward will pay you on your way out."

Now that—his assumption that I wasn't merely stymied but defeated—truly stung me, and perhaps it was the injury to my pride that finally goaded my brain into squeezing forth some semblance of a fresh idea.

"Please, milord," I said. "I don't want your coin, not until I earn it. I have a further course of action to suggest."

He cocked his head. "What?"

"I'd like to take up residence here from now until the wedding."

"Why?"

I didn't know myself, really, but had to improvise some sort of answer. "Maybe if I become more familiar with the murder scene, some new insight will occur to me. Or, failing that, maybe I can at least stop the robber from returning and doing any more harm."

"Nonsense," Tregan snapped. "You're reverting to your first idiot notion, that one of our own family, or loyal retainers, is responsible for the atrocity. You want to spy on us in hope of identifying the culprit."

"No," I said, and wasn't sure if I was lying or not. I was halfway satisfied that none of the household was guilty, yet likewise suspected that some secret awaited discovery within these walls.

"You're aware," Baltes said, "that the old folly of Green and Blue has flared up again. I'm struggling to put the fire out, and I fear your presence here will feed it. You surely won't feel particularly welcome."

"I can tolerate that," I said. "Please, milord. I want what you and Lord Pivar want, to put the feuds and factions behind us forever. If there's even the slightest chance that my presence here will help accomplish that, or simply lead to the apprehension of Venwell's killer, isn't it worth a try?"

"Perhaps," Baltes said. "Stay for the time being, and we'll see how it goes."

So began my sojourn in Keenspur House. As the head of the family had warned, few of his kin exerted themselves to show me hospitality. It might have been even more unpleasant if I hadn't kept to my nocturnal habits, sleeping the mornings away and roaming the mansion late at night.

looking for clues that had eluded me before, trying to imagine what had happened on the night of the murder.

Any huge old pile, no matter how opulent, can turn into a shadowy, echoing, spooky place after the servants turn out the lamps and everyone goes to bed. So it was with the mansion, and perhaps it was that eerie atmosphere that prompted me to recall Venwell's wide eyes and gaping mouth, and to infer what they actually signified.

Marissa was wrong. The lad had frozen. Because he'd faced a supernatural assailant, and any man, no matter how well trained a swordsman, can succumb to terror in such circumstances.

Yet Tregan swore the killing had nothing of the mystical or otherworldly about it, and much as he disliked me, he seemed sincere in his desire to identify the culprit, so what was I to make of that?

I returned again to the suspicion that the thief dwelled within the mansion. I thought of our search, and one area we'd neglected. Because the family kept it locked, Baltes had the only key, and thus it scarcely seemed a likely or convenient hiding place. It was, moreover, the sort of place folk rarely visit by choice.

But, though I still possessed no certainties, merely a collection of vague suspicions and intuitions, I decided I wanted to visit it, or at least inspect the entrance. I found an oil lamp that was still burning, lifted it from its sconce, and set off through the hushed, gloomy chambers and corridors. Portraits, busts, and statues seemed to glower as I passed, and suits of plate armor standing on display looked misshapen as ogres.

Then a pair of figures skulked from the shadows to bar my path.

It was Dremloc and his crony. Each was only half dressed, with feet bare and shirt unlaced. But despite the inadequacy of their attire, they'd taken the trouble to arm themselves. The flickering yellow light of my lamp gleamed on the smallswords in their hands.

"Don't be stupid," I said. "I'm here to help your family, I'm Lord Baltes' guest, and if that's not enough for you, Marissa would take it ill if you harmed me."

They didn't answer, just stalked forward, further into the

circle of lamplight, and then I saw what I'd missed before: their eyes were closed.

Happily, I didn't freeze, though I admit a chill oozed up my spine. Retreating, I set the lamp down on a table, drew my broadsword, and yelled for help. The Keenspurs spread out to flank me, then rushed in.

Somnambulism didn't hinder their swordplay. The slender thrusting blades streaked at me, and I dodged and parried frantically, meanwhile striving to keep either of my opponents from working his way around completely behind me.

Even if I'd wanted to kill them, I didn't dare, for fear of their kindred's retaliation. But neither could I simply defend and defend until one of them got lucky and slipped an attack past my guard. I feinted at the crony's face, and he jumped back. His retreat bought me a moment to concentrate solely on Dremloc. I parried his next thrust, feinted high, then made a drawing cut to his knee.

To my relief, the blade sliced his flesh precisely as I'd intended. His leg gave way beneath him, and he fell. But, barring ill fortune, he'd survive and even walk again.

I heard rushing footsteps as the other youth charged at my back. I spun, parried his thrust, stepped in close, and bashed his jaw with my weapon's pommel. Bone cracked. He reeled, dropped, and lay motionless, his trance knocked into true insensibility.

It was then that help finally came rushing into the room, in the persons of Baltes, Tregan, and six of their household guards.

"By the Goddess," Baltes said. He wore a robe, nightshirt, and slippers, but, like my assailants, carried a sword— in his case, the sword with the emeralds. "What's happened?"

"Milord," I panted, "I regret this. But I had no choice. Your kinsmen attacked me."

"No," said Dremloc, ashen, voice shaky, clutching at this bloody knee. No longer sleepwalking in any obvious way. "Don't believe him. We found him looking at that jade statuette yonder as if mustering the nerve to pocket it. We told him to leave it alone, and he drew on us."

The fabrication startled me, and it took me a moment to reply. "That isn't so. You and your kinsman were sleepwalking. Possessed, or under some sort of spell. You attacked me."

Despite the pain of his wound, Dremloc managed a laugh. "That's stupid. Wyler and I were drinking and playing at knucklebones in my room. We got hungry, came downstairs to raid the larder, and found this Blue whoreson looking shifty."

"If that was the reason you left your quarters," I said, "would you have brought your swords? The same influence that controlled you before is tampering with your memory."

Baltes looked to Tregan. "Tell me," the Keenspur leader said, "if there can possibly be any truth to this."

"As you wish," the warlock said. He closed his eyes, murmured under his breath, swept his hands through mystic passes, and swayed from side to side. The darkness flowed and thickened around us, and a bitter taste stung my tongue.

Tregan opened his eyes once more. "There was no magic involved."

"No!" I said. "Somehow, you're mistaken." I pivoted toward Baltes. "Milord, do you truly believe I'd steal from you, when you already offered me gold, and I refused it? Is it likely I'd pick a fight where the odds were against me, in a house full of my adversaries' kin? Or that I'd be the one to cry for help if I did?"

Baltes scowled. "Perhaps it was simply ill will and folly that made the three of you brawl, and no one has the courage to admit it."

"No, Uncle," Dremloc said. "I swear, it happened as I told you."

Meanwhile, I made the corresponding assertion in different words.

"Master Selden," Baltes said, "I suspected no good would come of having you here, and you've proved me right. In other circumstances, I might be inclined to punish you for it. But Pivar and the other Blues—former Blues, I should say—hold you in esteem, the wedding is only two days hence, and I'm loath to do anything that might stir the old animosities. So just get out."

"Milord," I said, "I was about to follow up on an idea when all this happened. Apparently, our unknown enemy somehow discerned my intent, and used Dremloc and Wyler to stop me. That must mean the notion has something to it. I beg you—"

Baltes' hand clenched on the hilt of his sword. "I've had enough of your foolishness! Go now, or I won't answer for your safety."

I looked at all the Keenspurs and Keenspur servants glaring back at me, and I went.

Afterward, I resolved to put the affair behind me. Since Baltes had discharged me, it was no longer any of my concern, and I'd been lucky to come out of it with my skin intact. But I'd never had much of a knack for minding my own business, and after a morning of moping and grumbling around my school, I went to see Pivar.

He'd already heard I'd disgraced myself among the Keenspurs, but received me anyway, for the sake of the services I'd rendered him in the past. I told him my side of the story, and couldn't judge if he credited it or not.

"I'm glad you escaped unharmed," he said, sitting on a marble bench in the conservatory where he often received callers, if their rank and business was such that formality was unnecessary. Sunlight streamed through the high windows, and the scent of verdure tinged the air. "But you can't let go of it, can you?"

I grinned. "You understand my foibles, milord."

"Well enough to realize you're here because you want something of me. What?"

"Can you tell me about the early years of the feuding? It was already well underway when I first came to Mornedealth, and I never bothered to learn the details."

"I don't see the point of your learning them now, but all right. I have time to chat for half a candlemark or so."

Some of what he told me, I did, in fact, already know. How the factions began as supporters of one or another racing team, silly as that seemed. But eventually the talk turned to a wizard named Yshan Keenspur.

"He was their House mage before Tregan," Pivar said, "from which you can guess that he was an older man. That, in turn, might lead you to imagine him as a prudent, cool-headed fellow who would try to prevent the rise of the factions, but you'd be wrong. He was one of the instigators, as rabid and bloody-minded a Green as ever was. Perhaps he simply had a choleric temperament, or saw it as a way to increase his family's power. Or maybe he dabbled in Dark Magic, and it twisted his mind. There were rumors, but then there always are, whenever a sorcerer is disliked."

"What became of him?" I asked.

"For all his powers, he came to grief in a street brawl, when three Blues set on him at once. He died trying to lay a curse on us. But so what? It happened long ago."

"Maybe not long enough." I explained my suspicions, to the extent I understood them myself.

Pivar shook his head. "You realize, the Greens—the Keenspurs, I mean—would find this allegation even more offensive than anything you've suggested hitherto."

"I suppose."

"On top of that, it doesn't actually explain the theft of the tiara. According to your postulations, the culprit took it to rekindle the hatred between Green and Blue. But why would anyone anticipate that it would have that result?" He smiled a humorless smile. "Even if, somehow, that's how it's working out."

"I don't know," I said, "but I have figured out what we ought to do next." I told him.

"No," he said at once. "If I insulted Baltes and his kin with such a proposal, it could shatter the peace for good and all."

"Something dangerous is lurking in Keenspur House," I said, "and you're about to send your daughter to live there."

"But not immediately. She'll marry there, but she and Baltes will spend their wedding night, and the following week, at his hunting lodge. Even if your wild hunch is right, that buys us some time. Let's get the bride and groom wed, our two houses united. Then, perhaps, you and I can broach this matter, if you still deem it necessary."

It was the best he had to offer, so I tried to rest content with it. I failed.

Every great house employs dozens of servants, but when it hosts a wedding, even they aren't enough. The steward, cook, and groundskeeper all have to hire extra help, and accordingly, nobody expects to recognize everyone he sees.

Thus, clad as a common laborer, my grizzled brown hair stained black as Marissa's, with my sword, a pry bar, and a lantern hidden in a sack, I found it easy enough to slip back into Keenspur House. I then skulked to the one quiet precinct of the mansion, a chapel where a few votive candles glowed before icons, and stone stairs descended into the earth.

I lit the lantern, strapped on my sword, and headed down. Before long, I came to a door of vertical iron bars. It was locked, but the fact did little to allay my suspicions. Magic that could turn sleeping men into puppets could likely manipulate a lock as well. I broke it with my lever and continued on.

The steps debouched into dank crypts, festooned with webs the spiders spun to snare the beetles, and smelling faintly of incense, embalmer's spice, and rot. The lesser Keenspurs lay behind graven plaques in the walls. The principal lords and ladies had their own private vaults, where stone sarcophagi, the lids often sculpted into likenesses of the occupants, reposed on pedestals in the center.

I assumed Yshan had rated one of the latter, and found him quickly. If his marble likeness could be trusted, he'd possessed the sharp features characteristic of his line, honed beyond the point of gauntness. It gave him a look of fanaticism and spite, which the sculptor had accentuated by rendering him with glaring eyes and a scowl instead of the usual expression of serenity.

I inspected the lid of the sarcophagus, trying to discern whether anyone—or anything—had opened it recently. I couldn't tell. Not unless I opened it myself.

Assuming I could. It looked damnably heavy for a lone man to shift. But I meant to try. I set the lantern down, then, with a dry mouth and sweat starting beneath my arms, tried to work the pry bar into the crack between cover and box. The iron tool scraped the stone.

The lid flew up and to the side, like the cover of a book, straight at me.

It could have shattered my bones, but my reflexes jerked me backward, and perhaps that robbed the impact of some of its force. Even so, the sculpted marble slab slapped me like a giant's hand, knocking me into the wall. I fell, and the lid fell with me, crashing down on top of my legs.

Meanwhile, Yshan, who had, by dint of either magic or prodigious strength, flung his graven image at me, reared up from the sarcophagus. He was relatively intact. The embalmers had evidently done their work well, and his box had protected him from rats and worms. But his face was shriveled, flaking, and streaked with black leakage. His right eye had gone milky, while the left had crumbled inward. A few slimy strings stretched across the vacant socket.

He held a sword, and the glow of the lantern just sufficed to reveal a thick layer of grease coating the blade. When I saw it, I finally comprehended all that had eluded me before.

But I didn't have time to dwell on it. Not with the dead thing stepping out of the coffin, and my legs pinned. I struggled to free myself, and managed to drag my feet out from under the lid.

Just in time. Yshan's sword flashed at my head, and I flung myself out of range. It was the only move that could have saved me, but it put the dead man between me and the doorway. Now, I had no choice but to fight.

I scrambled up and snatched for the sword at my side. Yshan cut at me, and I parried.

The impact jolted my arm, and his weapon nearly smashed through my guard. He was as unnaturally strong as I'd feared.

In other circumstances, wary of his might, I might have fought defensively. But if I hung back, it would give him the chance to cast spells, and I feared that even more than the force of his blows. So I attacked hard whenever I was able.

I drove my point into his chest, but it didn't balk him even for an instant. Why should it, when he was already dead, his vital organs still and rotting? The only effect was to trap my blade. He whirled a backhand cut at my face. I ducked beneath it and yanked my sword free.

He cut down at my head. Still in a crouch, I just managed to parry, and once again, his stroke nearly hammered through my guard, almost broke my grip on the hilt of my blade.

But not quite, and I discerned that he'd struck with such ferocity as to shift himself off balance. I straightened up, feinted, deceived his awkward attempt at a parry, and slashed his one remaining eye from its socket.

He snarled like a beast, exposing yellow teeth and dark, oozing gums. But he didn't falter as most any mortal creature would have done. Instead, he struck back immediately, and his aim was as accurate as before.

As I dodged, I thought, a hit to the vitals hadn't stopped him, nor had blindness. What if nothing could? I struggled to quash the panic welling up in my mind.

I opened my guard a hair, praying that he'd think it an error, not the invitation, the trap, it truly was. That he'd make a particular indirect attack I'd noticed he favored. It seemed likely. It was a combination well suited to exploiting the seeming defect in my defense.

His arm extended, and I immediately stepped forward and to the side, without waiting to see where his blade was actually going. If I'd guessed wrong, it had an excellent chance of winding up in my guts.

But I hadn't. He made the move I expected, I avoided it, and placed myself on his flank in the process, surprising him. Before he could pivot to threaten me anew, I gripped my hilt with both hands and cut with all my might.

I didn't quite lop off his sword hand. But I shattered the wrist bones and left it hanging useless.

Yshan reached to shift his weapon to his off hand, but I was faster. I beat the greasy blade and knocked the hilt from his now-feeble grip. The sword clanked on the floor.

Even then, with his terrible strength and resistance to pain and injury, he might have gotten the better of me if he'd simply assailed me like a wrestler. But he hesitated, and I cut at his leg. My sword bit deep, he fell, and I attacked the same spot twice more, until I was certain I'd done enough damage to keep him from getting up.

Then I concentrated on his head, driving stroke after stroke into his skull while avoiding his flailing hand. Finally he collapsed and lay motionless.

I studied the mangled, seemingly inert carcass for a few heartbeats, then turned and strode toward the exit.

At my back, a harsh voice hissed rhyming words.

The patch of floor beneath me turned to soft muck, treacherous as quicksand. I sank to my knees in an instant, and as I floundered, Yshan began a second incantation, no doubt to finish me off while the ooze held me helpless.

I cast about, spied the open sarcophagus, and tossed my broadsword into it. Then I stretched out my arms, and, straining, succeeded in hooking my fingertips over the lip of the stone receptacle. I heaved with all my strength, and dragged myself up and out of the sucking slime. In the process, I noticed the tiara lying inside the coffin, not that I cared anymore.

I grabbed my sword and leaped at Yshan.

Some shapeless phosphorescent thing was rippling into full existence above him, but it vanished when I cut into his chin and silenced his conjuration. I finished removing his jaw, severed his head, cut the tongue out, and hacked off his fingers. Afterward, I still wasn't certain he was altogether dead, but reasonably confident I'd deprived him of the ability to cast any more spells.

That should have been the end of it. But I hurried back the way I'd come because I feared it wasn't.

Practitioners of Dark Magic don't always pass from the world as easily as normal folk, especially if they leave a dying curse behind. While the feud between the Greens and Blues raged, Yshan had apparently rested easy. But the prospect of peace roused him, and he resolved to avert it.

He had the power to observe things at a distance, and so discerned a sword among the wedding gifts, its blade smeared with grease as such fine weapons generally come from the maker. He decided to switch the sword for the costly one his family had interred with him. Baltes and Lukinda had received such an abundance of presents that it seemed unlikely anyone would notice the substitution.

Yshan emerged from the crypts late one night, had the bad luck to encounter Venwell, and killed him to silence them. He then gave his sword a more thorough cleaning than any common housebreaker, eager to flee, would have done. It couldn't have even a drop of blood on it if it was to pass for a new weapon.

He made the substitution, stole the tiara simply to bolster the impression that an ordinary thief had invaded the mansion, and returned to his vault. In the days that followed, the enchantments he'd laid on the emerald sword began their work. First, a glamour made Baltes yearn to wear the blade without delay. I'd felt the power myself, if only I'd had the wit to realize it. Next, its influence nudged the Keenspurs back toward the rancor of yore.

And through it all, Tregan never sensed supernatural forces at work because Yshan had trained him and held some tricks in reserve. Tricks that allowed him to operate without his successor detecting it.

I doubted he was detecting anything now, either, and that meant I had to get upstairs fast. Because I suspected the warlock's sword had a final trick to play.

The Keenspurs were holding the wedding in their great hall, before hundreds of guests. Lukinda was plump, freckled, and pretty in her gown of shining white, the priestess, matronly in vestments of green. Baltes wore the emerald sword. From the looks of it, the ceremony was nearing its conclusion.

"Stop!" I bellowed, starting up the aisle. "Lord Baltes, throw away your sword! It's cursed!"

Everyone turned to gawk at me, and I realized what a peculiar spectacle I must be, clad like a laborer, my legs filthy, a blade in my hand.

Then Dremloc cried, "It's Selden!" The dye in my hair wasn't enough to fool him.

Several of the Keenspurs rose to bar my way. "Get out of here, lunatic," said one, hand on the hilt of his dagger.

"You don't understand," I said.

Nor were they disposed to listen. As they advanced on me, and all the other guests gawked at us, Baltes whipped Yshan's sword from its scabbard and lifted it to threaten his dumbfounded bride.

The priestess grabbed his arm, but he shook her off and shoved her reeling. Nobody else saw, because they were all looking at me, and I could do nothing. The entire length of the hall, and the folk intent on ejecting me or worse, separated me from the altar.

Which meant that despite all my efforts, Baltes would commit the atrocity Yshan had intended. Then the Blues would rise up in fury, the Greens would have no option but to defend themselves, and any nobles who survived this day would prosecute the blood-feud for years to come.

Or so it seemed. But it turned out that someone had

heeded my warning after all. Marissa hurled herself at Baltes and grappled with him. She softened him up with a knee to the groin, then twisted his arm. The emerald sword dropped from his fingers.

As soon as it did, he stopped struggling. "Blessed Goddess!" he whimpered, his voice full of horror. "Blessed Goddess!"

By then, people were finally taking note of what was happening before the altar. I cast about and found Tregan. "The evil's in the blade," I reiterated. "Surely you can sense it now."

He peered at the fallen weapon, then growled, "Yes." He muttered words of power, swept his right hand through a pass, and a ragged darkness swirled up from the sword. People cried out and cringed, but Tregan had the demon, if that was what it was, under control, and it couldn't hurt us. It wailed as it withered away.

Afterward came explanations, and reassurances to the frightened Lukinda and her understandably agitated kin. During the course of it all, Baltes, still white-faced and shaky, told me, "Master Selden, I owe you a hundred apologies. What can I do to make amends?"

I grinned. "Finish the wedding, invite me to the feast, and give me a purse heavy with gold."

Marissa said, "I think I'm due a split."

DAWN OF SORROWS

by Brenda Cooper

Brenda Cooper has published fiction and poetry in *Analog, Oceans of the Mind, Strange Horizons,* and *The Salal Review,* and been included in the anthologies *Sun In Glory* and *Maiden, Matron, Crone.* Brenda's collaborative fiction with Larry Niven has appeared in *Analog* and *Asimov's,* and their novel, *Building Harlequin's Moon,* appeared in 2005. Brenda lives in Bellevue, Washington, with her partner Toni, Toni's daughter Katie, a border collie, two gerbils, and a hamster. By day, she works as the City of Kirkland's CIO, applying her interests in science, technology, and the future to day-to-day computer operations and strategic planning. She writes for *Futurist.com* and can sometimes be found speaking about the future, and suggesting that science fiction books make great reading. The rest of the time, she's writing, reading, exercising, or exploring life with her family.

B ARD Jocelyn paused at the crest of the hill and looked down at the peaceful town of Sunny Valley spilling between two sets of lower hills below. The midday sun washed the houses and fields in bright, cheerful warmth, as if the town smiled up at her and Bard Silver. She turned to look back, where Bard Silver trailed behind, one slender white hand against her side, the other wiping sweat from her forehead. Jocelyn wanted to push down to Sunny Valley, buy supplies, and keep right on going. But Silver needed a break, even if she wasn't complaining.

Standing sideways, Jocelyn watched Silver struggle up the last few steps to stand beside her on the crest of the hill. Soft midsummer wind blew tendrils of ash-blonde hair across the younger woman's white face, obscuring the light freckles on her nose. Silver was pretty enough to draw a crowd anywhere; between the silver eyes she drew her nickname from, her alabaster skin, and her slender height, she looked more like a fairy-tale princess than a young Bard fresh to her Scarlets.

Might as well be nice to the girl—it wasn't her fault her beauty was so like Dawn's, not any more that it was her fault the powers-that-be in Bardic had decided Jocelyn needed a partner. She didn't, of course. She'd been just fine on her own the last five years. She sighed. "We'll take a break here." She gestured toward a convenient tumble of white-and-gray rocks, then dug into her pack and pulled out two red apples, handing one to Silver.

Silver settled on the sheep-cropped grass, took the apple daintily, and bit into it. "Thank you."

Ashamed of her curtness, Jocelyn stepped into her pleasant performance voice. "No problem." She picked out a flat rock, sat down, and took a bite of her own apple. "Do you have any questions? Is there anything you'd like to know?" Maybe Silver wanted to know about their trip—they were going to walk a circuit all the way to the border and back, and would be expected to perform, and listen for news, starting in just a few days. This was, after all, Silver's first long journey away from Haven.

Silver nodded and finished her apple in thoughtful silence. Then she turned toward Jocelyn, a small mischievous gleam in her eye. "I want to hear the story behind *Dawn of Sorrows*."

Jocelyn sat back against the sun-warmed granite rock and crossed one long leg over the other. This was why she hadn't wanted to travel with anyone. "I don't tell that story."

Silver laughed nervously. "You're famous for 'Dawn of Sorrows.' But no one knows the real story, just the song. I thought—" she looked away, as if suddenly shy, "—I thought maybe you'd be willing to tell me. I know the song tells the story, but there must be more details. I want to write a song that matters some day."

Jocelyn bit back a suggestion that no one should want to write a song like "Dawn of Sorrows." She finished her apple. She didn't have to answer Silver, not right away. She was the elder by seven years, after all. She threw her apple core into the woods for the ants, then captured the most unruly bits of her own red hair with her left hand and looked down. From this distance and height, the people working the ripening fields looked like brightly colored moving dots. But she remembered looking down on another town. . . .

Despite the day's warmth, she shivered.

She'd managed not to talk about Dawn for at least five years, and not to sing the song herself for almost as long. It was impossible, of course, not to hear it. "Dawn of Sorrows" was one of those songs that took on its own life and became part of the repertoire of nearly every minstrel and bard. Some days, she wished she'd never written it. She hadn't written anything else since.

Maybe she *should* talk about it, maybe that would teach Silver that adventure wasn't always easy, that sometimes it tore you right up. Jocelyn sighed. Bard Dennis had assigned her to travel with Silver for a full season. She'd have to talk to the girl eventually.

Jocelyn had pushed Silver by setting a hard pace, and the girl had kept up. She'd asked for silence and Silver had let her have a polite and respectful quiet. She didn't deserve to have her first question rebuffed.

Jocelyn took a sip of water and settled back. "Sorry. I guess I'm a little touchy. I'll start by telling you Dawn's story . . . her story from before I met her."

Silver sighed, a smile edging her pale pink lips, anticipation brightening her eyes. She pillowed her head on her scarlet cloak and closed her eyes, relaxed and still, as if she listened with her whole body.

Jocelyn nodded in silent approval—the Bardic Gift was akin to empathy, and when Silver focused her energy on listening as hard as Jocelyn focused hers on storytelling, they'd both feel Jocelyn's emotions. She whispered, almost to herself, "I hope you're ready to hear the story."

Silver opened her eyes and regarded Jocelyn gravely. "Try me."

"Dawn lived in Johnson's Ford, a border town near

Hardorn. I call it a town just because it had a name, but it was really just a handful of houses. Maybe thirty people or forty. Not a bad place, not really, but like other border towns: raiders and bandits swooped down from time to time, bellies grumbled and old people died when the winters were hard, and the granaries never overflowed. Other small towns nearby traded with them, but they didn't get much news or many minstrels or Bards. So the people of Johnson's Ford didn't understand the big things shaping up in Valdemar, like Elspeth becoming the first Herald-Mage since Vanyel."

Jocelyn paused, watching a lone hawk circle lazily just above her eye level. If only she could fly alone like that today. "No, Johnson's Ford mostly worried about surviving the storms that plagued Valdemar that year. Oh, the impending war with Hardorn had grazed the town, rattling nerves and stealing young men. But Johnson's Ford was far from anything strategic except the ford itself. . . ." Jocelyn let her voice trail off. She was taking too long, making the story hard to get into. She closed her eyes and focused her breath deep in her belly, letting her loss and pain creep up so it would fill her, her story, with true emotion. Her breath quickened.

Silver opened her eyes, as if curious about the long pause, but she closed them again, content to wait.

Jocelyn swallowed. "The year before Elspeth's return, a pack of black wolves that had been twisted by Ancar's mages came through town, and Dawn's husband, Drake, and two other men died defending their homes. A nasty death, as quick and as unexpected in Dawn's life as a lightning strike. She kept living in the little two-room house that Drake died for, alone except for their daughter, eight-year-old Lisle. Oh, Dawn was pretty enough that she did get a few offers from other men, but she turned them all down, for she had been truly in love with Drake.

"Dawn had no other family in Johnson's Ford. Lisle became her anchor, her ground. They were inseparable. They worked side by side, minding the sheep in the morning and weeding the fields in the afternoon. Neither had the Bardic Gift, but either could have been minstrels, and they sang together when they worked and sometimes they sang for town gatherings."

Silver's eyes were bright with curiosity. "So what did Dawn look like?"

Jocelyn cocked her head, studying the other woman. "A little like you." She arched an eyebrow, shook her head. "But not so light, or so thin. Her eyes weren't silver, they were dark and warm, like walnut. . . ." She shook her head again.

Silver frowned, puzzled. "So she'd already lost her husband, before you even met her?"

"Yes." Jocelyn paused. "So the first stanza of her song happened before I met her. That's the only part of the song I didn't see." She took a deep breath and threaded her fingers through her hair.

"I took my journeyman trip alone, and for a purpose. Selenay had given word that Valdemar was her people and not her places. She sent Heralds out to tell the people along Hardorn's border to leave, but there weren't enough Heralds available, so some Bards were selected as well. Our goal was to take Selenay's message to every single person near Hardorn." She glanced at Silver, caught her pale eyes with her own. "We were to use our Gift to convince them, if we had to. You know, that business about it being okay to use your Gift on the business of the crown."

Silver nodded, smiling wryly. "I know the rules." She sat up, picking at the grass beside her in small, nervous motions.

"I'm sorry." She'd been Silver's age the year she met Dawn. So why did Silver seem so much younger than she remembered being herself? Jocelyn uncrossed her legs and bunched her red cloak under her knees to serve as cushioning. "That was the year the Companions searched Valdemar high and low for Mage Gift.

"I was walking the last half mile or so to Johnson's Ford when a lone Companion trotted past, her head up, her nostrils flared as though she smelled something good. I remember how it felt for her to pass me. Just for a moment, I wished she would Choose me. But of course, I already had my scarlets, and though I wouldn't refuse a Companion, I didn't really hope for one anymore.

"But I was going down the same road, and I'd never seen a Choosing take place. I quickened my steps, turning a corner just in time to see the Companion stop in front of a little girl and her mother. The girl had dark hair, the mother light. They both had pert noses and wide eyes and slender builds. It was, of course, Dawn and Lisle. Both were beautiful, and the Companion in front of them was beautiful, and all together it called up all every Choosing song and story I'd ever heard." She could see it in her mind all over again, as if the Companion and her Chosen stood in front of her right then. Even now, years later, it awed her. "There are no words for the grace with which the Companion bowed down to that little girl and lowered her gorgeous head so her bright blue eyes met Lisle's dark ones. I stopped no more than twelve feet away from them, and I swear I felt something flow between the Companion and the girl, some magic like the magic in a room when a Master Bard weaves his or her Gift into a powerful song.

"The girl held her arm up and she spoke the Companion's name, 'Tamay.' I could hear the love in that one word, even from twelve feet away. Surely Dawn heard it, too." Jocelyn paused again, for effect.

"Tears began to flow down Dawn's face.

"Lisle didn't notice.

"Tamay knelt even farther down, and nuzzled the girl. Lisle climbed up on Tamay's foam-white back, and clutched Tamay's bright white mane, her eyes shining with pleasure.

"Tamay stood completely still, unnaturally still, looking at Dawn. Dawn stood her ground, gazing back, brown eyes into blue. They stood that way so long my legs began to shiver from standing. There was a conversation going on between them that I couldn't hear. And all that time, Lisle sat on Tamay's back and twisted her hands in her new Companion's white mane and watched her mom's face.

"Finally, Dawn nodded. She wiped her eyes and took three steps toward Lisle. She reached up, took Lisle's small hands, and kissed them, smiling up at her daughter through damp eyes. She whispered, 'I love you, honey. Take good care,' just barely loud enough for me to hear, and her little girl whispered back, 'I love you, Mommy, and I'm sorry.'

"Dawn said, 'Don't ever be sorry,' and let Lisle's fingers slip from hers.

"The Companion turned and passed me by. She gave me

a look that didn't need Mindspeech to read. She might as well have spoken out loud and said, 'Take care of this woman for me.' "

Jocelyn paused. This was the heart of the song, and she wanted to be sure Silver felt it. Silver had turned her head, but when she turned it back to see why Jocelyn had stopped talking, tears glistened in the corners of her eyes.

Jocelyn noted the tears, smiled, and kept the story moving. "I reached for Dawn, but she had already fallen to her knees in the dirt, head buried in her hands. Sobs shook her whole body. I knelt by her side, my hand on her slender, heaving back. I sang softly, soothing her as best I could."

Silver's voice was soft and warm, concerned. "And that's when the last stanza starts."

Jocelyn nodded. "Her tears were pure sorrow. I'd never heard such a forlorn sound before, and haven't since, not from animal or human. I wanted to help her more than I'd ever wanted anything, for her sake, and for Tamay's and Lisle's, too. For all of our sakes. Seeing Lisle's Choosing felt like a symbol of all that Valdemar holds dear, all the love, all the sacrifice, all the magic. It showed me what Ancar wanted to take from us." She glanced back down at the peaceful summer scene below them, and spread her arm out over the town, encouraging Silver to see the peace.

"When I'd thought about Choosing before, I'd only seen the joy and shock and bewilderment of it, never the price. Companions choose who they choose, of course, and usually it's not first or only children; usually it's a blessing to the family left behind. Surely, Lisle must have a special part to play, but that's not part of this story."

"Did anyone ever write a song about Lisle?"

Jocelyn shrugged. "I don't know. Remember, she'll just barely be getting her Whites by now. I never stayed in Haven long enough to watch for her." Jocelyn shrugged. "Most Heralds live unsung lives. It's easy to forget that. There are so many songs about Heralds, but there are many more Heralds than songs about them. Many parents and families of people who come to Haven, whether Herald or Bard or Mage or Healer, well, their pain is unsung as well." She stared down at her knotted fingers. "That's why I wrote 'Dawn of Sorrows,' for Choosing, and all the love and pain and sacrifice and promise of that moment. Dawn's pain would have gone unnoticed, a single sacrifice in a flood of things surrendered to save Valdemar from Ancar. Except I gave people her story for remembrance. That's what Bards do."

Silver twisted her hands in her lap. "I haven't yet written anything that many people sing." The wistful yearning in her voice echoed in her eyes.

Jocelyn stood up. "Your life will surely yield opportunities. Come on, there's only a few hours until dark. We should get moving." She bent down to gather up her battered leather pack and fiddle case, and when she stood back up, she saw the disappointment on Silver's face. She sighed. "Yes, there's more. I'll tell you more of the story tonight."

"Thank you." Silver's voice sounded small. She shouldered her own nearly-new black leather pack. A flute case hung below her pack, tied in with purple ribbons, and she carried a gittern case that looked as new as her pack. "Will we stay at an inn tonight?"

Jocelyn shook her head. "Not if you want the rest of Dawn's story. It doesn't make me want to sing. They'll have plenty of minstrels and even Bards in a town this close to Haven—they won't expect us to sing."

Silver fell silent, and Jocelyn started down the hill, setting a good, hard pace. Silver's footsteps behind her reminded her of Dawn following her, and she walked faster, leading them downhill through tall dry grass and yellow mustard flowers. If only she hadn't tried so hard to help Dawn. She struggled to distract herself by counting the small suncup butterflies flashing white and orange over yellow mustard flowers and tiny blue wild onions. She picked up speed, nearly jogging down the water-rutted path.

After an hour, the footsteps behind her began to fade and Jocelyn stopped, looking back. Silver's cheeks shone red with exertion and her shoulders drooped. Jocelyn heard her own rattling breath and stopped. She waited for Silver to catch up, then said, "I'm sorry. I didn't mean to walk so fast."

Beads of sweat stood out on Silver's forehead. She breathed in little hard gulps. "I didn't know how much you'd mind talking about Dawn." She licked her lips and brushed damp hair from her face, looking at Jocelyn earnestly. "I thought I was asking about a song, but I guess I was asking about more. You don't have to tell me."

Hot tears suddenly licked at the edges of Jocelyn's eyes. She turned her face away a little, hoping Silver wouldn't see them. "I know." She took a long drink of water, felt it fall like a welcome river in her mouth. She'd been pushing Silver too hard, but maybe she'd also been pushing herself too hard. "I'll slow down some. Tell me about the first song you wrote." She started off again, not looking at Silver, but measuring her pace.

Silver was quiet for a few steps. When she spoke, her soft voice barely carried to Jocelyn. "I always made up songs, as long as I can remember. I'm sure my first songs were about my family. What about you? Did you sing about your family?"

Jocelyn flinched. How come everything Silver said poked at her? Had she really become such a pincushion? No wonder Dennis had looked so concerned when she wandered back to Bardic a month ago for rest. "I sang about the boarding school I was raised in, and about some of my teachers. Maybe we should just walk for a while."

Behind her, Silver's answer was to start humming, and then singing, a summer harvest song. If Silver had asked her to join in, Jocelyn would have refused, but the younger woman's quiet singing acted like a balm, letting Jocelyn enjoy the late afternoon sun warming her face and steady, quiet hum of bees in the flowers. By the third song, Jocelyn began to sing along, and before they even made it all the way off the hill and onto the main road, she realized she was smiling and her pace was naturally slower.

The road to Sunny Valley was wide enough for two carts to pass each other easily. Although the hard-packed road was empty for long stretches, they were greeted by kids on horses going between farms, and carts most likely headed between towns or even to Haven.

Jocelyn remembered to stop a few times under shade trees. Silver would get used to traveling, and they'd make better time in the future. After all, this was only day two of a three-month journey.

They stopped at an inn in Sunny Valley to refill their waterskins and purchase a loaf of fresh bread, a skin of red wine, and a round of deep-yellow cheese. As the skinny, dark-haired innkeeper handed them their packages of food, he said, "There's room. We have a local minstrel who plays here, but he never minds being joined by Bards, long as they share the takings. Says it helps him learn new songs."

Jocelyn glanced at Silver, letting her choose.

Silver shook her head. "We'd rather push on tonight."

The innkeeper grumbled good-naturedly. "You folk from Haven. Always hurrying." He turned to his next customer, and Jocelyn and Silver headed back for the road.

Two candlemarks later, after setting up a quiet camp by a thin stream, they perched on an old log, a small fire at their feet throwing tiny sparks up into a darkening sky. Jocelyn broke the bread in half while Silver parceled out the cheese and one more apple each.

Jocelyn set her plate on her lap, and took a long sip of the wine. Her stomach fluttered, but at least the hot tears didn't return. No point in waiting, the words wanted to come out. "So we left the story with me and Dawn in the middle of the road, and Dawn in pain, and me feeling her pain, and on my way to Johnson's Ford to convince people I'd never met to leave a town they'd struggled to build their whole lives.

"Well, I might as well have promised Tamay I'd take care of Dawn, and besides, who could have left her? So I sat there with her and fed her water and sang to her, and she let me stroke her back even though she'd never seen me before. Finally, she pushed herself away from me and looked deep into my eyes. Her voice trembled as she said, 'Thank you.'

She glanced at Silver, finding Silver's pale eyes staring at her, waiting. Silver still looked like Dawn, and still, like Dawn, looked like she needed Jocelyn. Except Silver had her own scarlet cloak, and her need was simple and healthy, unlike Dawn's naked, scraped-raw tenderness. Jocelyn cleared her throat. "I stood and helped her up. We walked back to town just as the sun was setting. She moved slowly, as if she were an old woman, as if every movement hurt. Perhaps it did. Perhaps her grief was so heavy it weighed on her bones.

"Johnson's Ford didn't have an inn, so Dawn led me home with her for the night. I really should have called a town meeting right then, maybe stayed one night, and gone on, but I didn't. I stayed a week.

"Dawn's house had two beds, hers and another that must have been Lisle's, but Dawn didn't offer it and I couldn't make myself ask. Besides, I'd been traveling a few months anyway, and the floor wasn't as hard for me as Dawn's sadness."

Jocelyn stopped and took another pull of wine, leaving her plate untouched.

Silver spoke softly, compellingly, a voice full of promise. "You loved her, didn't you? The first time I heard 'Dawn of Sorrows,' I thought it must have been written by a man."

Had she? They'd never been lovers. But she knew every line of Dawn's face, every curve of her slender arms. She knew the shape of her fingers (long, slender, with one pinky shorter than the other). Even after all this time, she remembered how warm Dawn's hand had felt in hers. Even though she'd only had weeks with Dawn, she still stopped by streams and pretty trees in bloom, and wished Dawn were there to point them out to.

She swallowed hard. "I loved her beauty and her loss, and her story was so romantic and so tragic, and I'd seen the most recent part of it. So maybe I *was* star-eyed about her. But there's nothing romantic about helping someone with such deep grief. So . . . even if maybe you've found a grain of truth, it didn't feel that way the days we spent in Johnson's Ford.

"I talked to the mayor that next morning. I told him about the Choosing, and he helped me get news out that Selenay had sent me to talk to the town.

"I met with about twenty townspeople that night. Farmers and hunters; strong and tough, sure of themselves. The women held their little ones like they were gold, especially the older boys, watching me carefully. Their faces were stoic and still as I told them Selenay wanted them to abandon Johnson's Ford.

"When you've worked your whole life to keep a town together, when you've built the buildings with your own hands, you don't much want to just pick up and leave. After the first amazement at having the Queen's words sent to them, the meaning of the words sank in. Some of the parents understood right away, but most people's faces stayed stones to me, and I knew I hadn't convinced them. So I told them I'd sing to them, every night, and that they could find me at Dawn's house most of the day if they had questions. I only sang a few songs that first night. Even though I put as much of my Gift into those songs as I could, the town didn't just jump up and start packing.

"Another mage-born storm slammed into town that night, and by morning the streets ran with water and the river had risen noticeably, but still no one agreed to leave. Between me and the storm, it took four days before anyone started to pack. Those four days are their own story that I'll share some other time.

"Each night, I sat with Dawn after I came back in, wet from walking home from the Mayor's house in the storms. We kept a fire going, talking a little and singing a little and staying quiet a lot." Jocelyn started to reach for the wine again, but changed her mind and picked up the bread. She chewed slowly, watching the little fire. "So it took four days for the town to start packing. It began with three women who had little kids, and their husbands, and then a grandfather and then a young couple that had just gotten married. By the sixth day I was there, everyone finally decided they didn't want to be the last one in Johnson's Ford, and they all started making plans to leave. Some had family in other towns, but most were just going to walk away from the border, walk farther into Valdemar and hope.

"Except Dawn.

"Dawn came up to me, her eyes big and dark and suddenly full of fire instead of sadness. She said, 'I don't want to go with them. I want to help you keep other people safe. I want to go with you.'

"She took me aback, completely. She looked so brave, and so damned lonely. I reminded her I was traveling toward danger, and wouldn't be going back to Haven until winter. I thought maybe that was it, maybe she wanted to get to Haven and saw me as the easiest way to get near Lisle. But she stood in front of me, looking like she'd looked when she stared into Tamay's eyes, rooted, curious, and full of dread.

"She said, 'I want to do something that matters. All my life I've just lived, and loved the people I loved, and I've been lucky. I had the best husband and the best little girl

in the world. They're all gone now. Even Lisle, even if I
get to live near her, well, she'll have her own life. Tamay
told me all about the Collegium and about how Lisle would
have important jobs for Valdemar, how she was special.
Tamay convinced me my little baby was special for more
than me, that it was time for her to grow up. Now it's time
for me to do something that matters, and the only thing I
can think of is to go help you.' She took my hand, the first
time she voluntarily touched me. 'You can use someone
familiar with living near the woods and hills of the border,
I know you could. I can't just run away with everyone else,
and I can't start over, not yet, not until the war is over.
Lisle's gone off to help in her way, and I want to help in
mine. I need to.'

Jocelyn shifted uncomfortably, and stirred the fire.
Dawn's eyes had drilled into her so hard, needed her to
say yes so badly. "I didn't have an argument for her; I
understood her. We were allowed to accept local help. I
could probably even bring her back to Haven and find her
work somewhere, maybe even at the Collegium. But first
there was a war on. I wish I'd told her no, every day I wish
I'd told her no."

"I took her.

"The next town was about the same size as Johnson's
Ford, and we stayed outside of it in my tent, storm-
drenched and shivering, for the first night. The second
night, an older couple made room for us in their barn. That
town took five days to convince to leave. Then we went to
Killdeer, which was big enough for an inn. A Herald came
through there the day after we got there, reinforcing my
message, so we were off again." Jocelyn paused, reaching
for water.

Silver shivered. "I was only thirteen that year and mostly
I heard about everything—I wasn't involved, except I did
get to see the gryphons come into Haven. I remember *that*.
So you must have only been twenty."

Jocelyn closed her eyes. "I felt older."

"And Dawn, how old was Dawn?"

"I don't know. I suppose she was in her late twenties.
Lisle couldn't have been more than ten when she was Chosen, and women marry young out in the hill country like
that. I bet she wasn't ten years older than I was."

Silver took a bite of cheese and reached for the wine. The last light had faded; Silver's white face and light hair looked almost ghostly in the firelight. "But she listened to you, followed you, right?" She sipped the wine. "Because you were a full Bard?"

Jocelyn shook her head. "Not everyone follows you because you're a Bard. Not in Haven, and not out here. You'll learn that eventually." She steepled her hands under her chin, musing on Silver's question. "I think she needed someone, and maybe it mattered that I was a Bard, but maybe it mattered more that I had seen Dawn's loss, and been there for her. I was young, and any other year, I probably wouldn't have been a full Bard yet. I think a few of us were tested into full Scarlets because Valdemar needed us. That was a scary year with new-found Mages and Ancar's army and the storms. Very little was done the way you'd do it in peacetime." Jocelyn took her own sip of wine. Silver was right—she really had been young. Younger even than Silver, if just by a year or two.

Silver said, "You've traveled alone ever since. Didn't you like having someone to travel with?"

The fire snapped and popped, holding Jocelyn's gaze. The presence of the other woman did feel good. And Jocelyn wasn't responsible for her. Even though Silver was younger, she was a full Bard. While Dennis was correct and Silver could learn from Jocelyn, they were more equal than Jocelyn and Dawn had ever been. Silver had education as well as enthusiasm, even if she had lived in the city her whole life. Maybe . . . maybe Silver could be a friend. Or more. Dawn could have been more, but there hadn't been time. . . .

Jocelyn threw two new logs on the fire and watched it lick up their edges in bright tendrils, then bloom. The new light played on her feet. She didn't have to decide whether or not to trust Silver, not yet. But she did have a story to tell. She finished eating and then slid down so her back rested against the log. Next to her, Silver took out her metal flute and started polishing it with a clean cloth until firelight glittered back from its bright surface. Jocelyn cleared her throat. "We had fires like this at night, small and cozy, and we talked. After a while, Dawn began to talk about Lisle and Drake. She told me doing something, even just helping me find my way from place to place, helped her to feel less lonely. Oh, I still heard her crying sometimes at night, especially when it was cold and wet and we shared a tent and lay close, each of us swaddled in blankets, but still near enough to share body heat. The coldest, scariest nights, we even held hands.''

She'd never told anyone that. But then, she hadn't told the story at all for years. Oh, she'd told plenty of stories and sung plenty of songs to countless people she didn't know. But this was different. It was like . . . like talking to Dawn had been.

"After we'd been traveling two weeks, we had two more towns to go, and then I was due to head back. I still planned to take Dawn with me. We came to the first of the last two towns, up over a hill, kind of like where you and I sat today when I started this story. The sky hung low and oppressive over us, a gray at midday that was almost black. Lightning flashed in the far hills. It wasn't raining, but it had, and would, and the air itself felt full of water, as if drops might materialize all on their own. In the damp darkness, smoke filled the bottom on the valley, persistent and thick and ugly. Bright embers showed where the largest houses had once been. We walked down into it. We had to. Whoever, whatever, had burned the town did not seem to be there, and maybe there was someone we could help.

"Dawn clutched my hand when we saw the first two bodies. Children. Two children. They had been running, and fire had somehow caught them. Dawn's eyes were huge, her face pale, and at first she stopped and her fingernails dug into my palm and her body shook. I had seen the dead before, but something seemed unnatural. The nearest burned building was quite a distance away. It looked like the children had just burst into flame running, not like they ran, flaming, from a fire. It sounds like a small difference when I say it, but it was a big difference to see. It struck us both silent. Part of me didn't want to go any farther into the town, no matter what, didn't want to take another step.'' The memory hurt, the moment she should have, could have, changed her mind. Jocelyn stood and stretched and paced once around the fire and sat back down, keenly aware of her own restlessness. "But you know, when you're out there, and there might be someone you can help, you remember you're a Bard, that you're more than just a court singer. You just are."

Jocelyn looked up into Silver's eyes. Did Silver understand this, in her bones? Did she know what life she'd chosen? Silver nodded, as if answering Jocelyn's unspoken question.

"So we walked forward. We didn't talk about it. We dropped each other's hands, but we kept going, looking around. The stench—all the things that had burned but were never meant to burn—stuck to us, covering us, and I wanted the sky to rain and clean us off. It didn't. The sky just glowered above us instead. We saw more burned bodies, crisped, dark. Some houses still smoldered, others stood untouched.

"A fat brown dog ran between two houses. It looked lost, but healthy. It stopped and stared at us, then it barked plaintively. And then . . . then it burned. Fire flashed alive on it and in it, a blanket of blue fire. It went from standing to burning."

She swallowed. "Dawn screamed." She paused, swallowed again. The words clawed their way out of her throat, dry and hot as flame. "And burned." Tears ran down her cheeks. "And burned." She gestured toward the fire. "Not like if that campfire caught my clothes, but completely. In seconds, I could see her bones. She didn't . . ." Jocelyn choked. "She didn't even scream for long. I ran. I didn't scream. I . . . I just ran."

Dawn's arms—no, *Silver's* arms—Bard Silver's long slender strong arms, circled Jocelyn's shoulders and Jocelyn turned her face into the other woman's chest and burrowed, holding on. She should never have let Dawn go in there. She should never have let Dawn travel with her in the first place. She should have gone alone. She should have died instead, or at least died, too. Magic. She lifted her head, looked away, talking in broken words. "It was . . . she was killed by . . . a spell triggered by sound. That killed them all—the whole town—" Jocelyn wiped at her eyes and nose and reached for a waterskin. Her hands shook so hard Silver had to help her pull the stopper out. She drank deeply. "I learned that when I got back to Haven—learned sound started the spell, and learned that it faded quickly. If we'd come into town the next day, all the gruesome sights would still be there. But we could have talked or laughed or screamed. The Palace sent one of the White Winds mages to read the spell as soon as I got back to Haven and told my story. He said . . . he said it he thought it was Ancar's mages testing a potential trap. They killed that whole town just to test a spell."

"You know it wasn't your fault she died," Silver whispered awkwardly, earnestly.

Jocelyn pushed a little away from Silver, reached down to touch the dirt, to ground herself. She drew in the smell of the fire, of the night. "I know. My head knows. But I could have been more careful."

Silver sounded confused as she said, "But wasn't magic new to Valdemar? Weren't you still inside the borders, where magic hadn't even worked just months before? How were you supposed to know?"

Jocelyn didn't answer. Her head said the same thing, all the time. But . . . but Silver was so young. And *she* was saying the same thing. Silver was a year older than Jocelyn. So . . . so Jocelyn really had been young that year. She hadn't felt young. She'd forgive Silver if she made a mistake—she was on her first trip and couldn't even walk a good day's pace yet, even though by the end of their trip, today's walk might seem short. If she could forgive Silver almost any mistake, why couldn't she forgive her own younger self?

"Look," Silver said, "I'm sure it doesn't help to tell you Dawn died doing something she wanted to do. You must have heard that before. But you did the very best you could. And then you wrote her a song, and your song made a difference."

"How? Dawn's dead."

"Right." Silver's voice was soft, musical. A Bard's voice. Surer than Dawn's had ever been. "But now, when kids are Chosen, now a lot of towns do something extra for the parents, or for the other family left behind."

Jocelyn looked up. Was it true? Why hadn't she noticed? "Really?"

Silver returned the smile. "Really." Silver picked up her gittern, unwrapped it, and started the refrain for "Dawn of Sorrows:"

"Dawn of sorrows, sacrifice
Yield up all you love in life"

Jocelyn's took a breath and opened her throat. She took up the first stanza, focusing on the notes, on her voice, on singing as strong as she could. By the end of the song, her voice sounded clear and steady.

This, she suddenly understood, was why Dennis wanted her to travel with someone. Maybe she'd write another song. It was too early to tell what that song might be, of course, but . . . maybe even a song about something that wasn't quite so painful. There were, after all, happy moments in Valdemar.

She looked over at Silver. Tears glittered like gems on the younger woman's smooth, pale cheeks but she sang through a wide smile, and her eyes were warm behind the wetness.

Warmth bloomed inside Jocelyn. It took her a moment to recognize it as happiness, to notice that she, too, smiled as she sang, even though tear tracks still stained her own cheeks.

HORSE OF AIR

by *Rosemary Edghill*

Rosemary Edghill's first professional sales were to the black & white comics of the late 1970s, so she can truthfully state on her resume that she once killed vampires for a living. She is also the author of over thirty novels and several dozen short stories in genres ranging from Regency Romance to Space Opera, making all local stops in between. In addition to her work with Mercedes Lackey, she has collaborated with authors such as the late Marion Zimmer Bradley and the late SF Grand Master Andre Norton, worked as an SF editor for a major New York publisher, as a freelance book designer, and as a professional book reviewer. Her hobbies include sleep, research for forthcoming projects, and her Cavalier King Charles Spaniels. Her website can be found at http://www.sff.net/people/eluki

THERE are places in Valdemar where the Heralds can't go.

Well, actually, this isn't true. Heralds and their Companions are welcome everywhere from Keyold to the Crookback Pass. Heralds are the voice and hands of King Sendar—it's Queen Selenay now, but it was Sendar who reigned when I put on my white leathers for the first time, and old habits are hard to break. Heralds bring news and gossip, defend the weak, embody the Crown's justice.

Do good in the world.

It is a sacred trust to be a Herald, and it is a public thing. You are *always* on display whenever you are in public. People tend to think of Heralds as being more than human—as far removed from them and ordinary concerns as our Companions. Above pettiness, injustice, fear, and weakness.

The first lesson you learn from your Companion—and at the Collegium—is that you must never disappoint them.

Sometimes it is—was very hard. To be always watched, and always judged by a standard no human could possibly meet.

And because they believe such things of Heralds, the people behave differently when Heralds are among them. Some try to act as they believe a Herald would, and that can be a good thing. Some hide—both their bodies and their words—out of fear, out of awe, out of guilt.

Some lie. Some tell too much truth.

Even in Haven, where they see Heralds and their Companions daily, it is the same. The people turn a different face to the Heralds than they do to one another. They talk of different things.

And so, when I say that there are places in Valdemar that a Herald cannot go, this is why. If the Crown would know what the people speak of when the Crown's greatest mystery is not before them in a glory of blue leather and silver bells, it must send other eyes.

I must go.

It has been twenty years since Shavanne and I rode over these roads on circuit. The bells that ring out my journey now are copper and brass, twined about my walking staff.

I walk everywhere now. I could not bear to ride.

When I returned to the Collegium after Shavanne was killed, everyone said I would be Chosen again—it was only to be expected. It was the last thing I wanted; for months after I was well in body I wandered the halls of the Collegium, soul-sick and, perhaps, half-mad at the death of my Lady Heart. Everyone said that, too, would pass; in time my soul would heal.

Even my fellow Heralds, those few who knew what it was to survive the death of that which should survive both death and age, said I would love and be loved again.

I had no desire for that. Shavanne had been life and joy to me. I could see no purpose in accepting anything less, and I could imagine nothing more.

Perhaps it would have been different if I had possessed one of the Great Gifts, or even a powerful one, but I had no more than minor Mindspeech and perhaps—no one was every quite sure—a trace of Empathy, enough to hear Shavanne's voice, and with her death, even that was gone. I did not miss it.

I knew that she, of all beings, would not wish me to squander my life in vain regrets and hopeless yearnings, and I tried to honor what I knew were her wishes. The anger at my loss—Valdemar's loss—faded, and even the bitterness, in time.

But no one Chose me, and it was a relief.

When a year had passed, I knew it was time to take up my service to the Crown once more in whatever fashion I could. The King's Own had shown me the way.

There are places in Valdemar that a Herald cannot go. I had all a Herald's training, and loyalties, but I was not, precisely, a Herald. I put off my white leathers for a coat of motley, and took up my belled staff.

Paynim the tinker was welcome everywhere in Valdemar. My father had been a tinsmith; we both thought, when I was Chosen, that my apprenticeship in his shop had been for nothing. How wrong we both had been. A tinker can find work anywhere, and stay as long or as short a time as he pleases. He need, carry with him no more than the tools of his trade, and no one is surprised when he wanders on. I wandered where I was sent—even into Hardorn and Karse—and in twenty years I had crossed and recrossed Valdemar a dozen times.

Where there was need of a Herald, all white leather and silver bells, I sent for one. Where merely sending a report back to Haven was wanted, I did that, too. I quickly learned the circuit of every Herald; it was easy to pass messages and receive orders.

My friends kept my secrets, as I wished, and as the years accumulated, fewer and fewer that I met knew that I once wore the White. It is more comfortable that way. If they wonder who I am, and why they bring me messages and take my reports away, they do not ask.

Herald Niniyel and Companion Teroshan had brought me a message; there are many fairs and market days throughout the warm dry months, and Heralds and tinkers both attend many of them. The message was an odd and improbable one, but it is my task to turn the unlikeliest of rumors into hard truth, and until I have seen—or not seen—what I have been sent to see, I do not waste my time wondering about it in advance. A wise man never needs to borrow trouble since fools give it away free, as my father always told me.

Yet this time I did wonder out of season, for the message Herald Niniyel had brought me said there was a witch in the Armor Hills.

That alone was reason enough for me to go.

Since Vanyel's time, there has been no magic in Valdemar. The Mind-Gifts of Herald and Healer are not sorcery, as they use the term beyond our borders. But lately that has changed. There is even a Mage College in Haven now, though it is new and I have never seen a Brown Robe on my wanderings. But the world is filled with wonders that I have not seen with my own eyes—a Karsite Captain with a Companion, for example.

But it is a byword of the Bards that the memory of the common folk is longer than any History, and so the country folk have never ceased to speak of witches when they encounter anything uncanny.

A fortnight and more of steady walking lay between me and my destination, but it was summer, a good time to walk the roads. The Armor Hills are north of the East Trade Road. They are not so distant from Haven as many other places, but Sumpost and Boarsden are the nearest villages, and they are not large. To the north, Iftel is their border; on the east, Hardorn.

I had been told that the witch of the Armor Hills was said to be a woman grown—that in itself was odd, for notable Gifts generally appear first in childhood. Further, it was said that all the Armor Hills paid her tribute, for she had the power to call a man's soul out of his body, which is a power that could not be explained by a misunderstanding of any of the Mind-Gifts I knew—so perhaps the tales I chased were true, and what I sought was indeed a witch.

*   *   *

At first, there was nothing for me to see. It was difficult enough to find the people themselves, for the Armor Hills is a wild and unforgiving place, and the houses of its folk are scattered and hidden. The people there subsist by hunting and trapping, and gathering the bounty of the wild, for though I saw many small gardens—once I had found the people—I had also quickly discovered that everything that is not up is down; it is impossible to find a level tract of land to plow or plant. It is an article of faith with those who dwell there that the land is too poor to take a crop, but I saw no sign of that. The small gardens flourished, and the woods and sharp-cut narrow valleys that I trudged through were lush with growth.

I mended pots, gossiped idly, and listened more than I talked.

A moonturn passed as I wandered from house to house. I had visited such remote places before, and knew better than to ask questions, lest I give offense, but soon I was accepted so far that one night's host would give me good directions to the next place that might have need of my services, and I no longer had to search out each house by myself.

People began to talk freely in my hearing, giving little thought to me as I sat over my fire in the dooryard, wrestling a cracked pot into working order or repairing an old skillet that must have lost its handle in King Roald's reign. That was when I first heard folk speak of the Moonwoman. Who else but she could be the creature I sought?

They said she was the offspring of a Companion and a Herald. I took no offense at hearing that; the common folk say odder things of us. They said her hair was as white as a Companion's tail—that, at least, was a thing nearly possible.

They said she could see the inmost thoughts of man, woman, or child, and could send their spirit from their body into light or darkness, calling it back at her whim. To placate her, they gave her anything she asked for when she walked among them.

These things did not sound at all encouraging, but what mattered most to me was that they said she would be at Midsummer Meeting. There I could see her—if she was, in fact, a flesh-and-blood woman and not simply a tale of the hills—and judge for myself for myself whether she had all—or any—of the powers claimed for her.

It took more work than I had imagined to gain an invitation to Midsummer Meeting. I had imagined, hearing the hill folk speak of it, that it was simply their version of one of the Season Fairs so common elsewhere, in Valdemar, and so a tinker would surely be welcome.

In fact, it bore more in common with a religious gathering, or a mustering of clans. Midsummer Meeting was where marriages were celebrated, babies acknowledged, and those who had died in the previous twelvemonth named. Trading went on as well, and music, dancing, and fine eating, but the true purpose of Midsummer Meeting was the exchange of information among the hill households, and a chance for a young hill son or hill daughter to meet someone from several valleys away.

But outsiders were not forbidden to attend.

Meramay was a young widow, plump and blonde, who had taken a shine (as the saying there went) to me. I had stayed with her ten days together, walking out each day in search of work, and returning at nightfall, adding my day's payment, in eggs or honeycomb or fresh-killed rabbit, to Meramay's larder. In truth, she could use all that I brought, for she lived entirely alone, and to take a living from the hills was a constant round of hard work, best shared by many strong backs.

I dealt with her honestly, telling her that I was lowland bred and born and would be moving on before the seasons turned. Still, there was comfort to be given and taken. She told me flatly the first night I stayed with her that she hoped to get a child with me, as she was seeking a new husband at Midsummer Meeting, and, as in many places, a woman's fertility was a far more attractive quality than her chastity.

It was she who invited me to accompany her to Midsummer Meeting; she wished to show off her current bedmate to her prospective suitors, much as a farmer would show the bull when selling the calf. I had long since outlived false pride, and so I was happy to say I would go with her.

"I only hope Moonwoman doesn't take against me," Meramay told me matter-of-factly. "She doesn't like a light-haired girl, and no man's going to cross her."

"You might darken your hair," I said casually, though my heart was beating fast; this was the first time anyone had spoken of Moonwoman directly to me. "The herbs are easy to find, after all."

Meramay shook her head decisively. "That'd be the same as lying, and they say she hates a liar worse than death and poison. She can see right into a body's heart, too."

There was no changing Meramay's mind, though I did wonder why, if she feared Moonwoman so much, why she was taking the risk of bringing an outsider to Midsummer Meeting. She did take the precaution of tying up her hair in a brightly colored scarf before we set out; apparently simply hiding her hair didn't count as lying.

And so we began.

Meramay carried a pack heavier than my own, and traveled, besides, with a cart drawn by one of the enormous brown-and-black dogs which are the usual beasts of burden in these hills, pulling carts and sometimes carrying packs themselves.

It took us three days to reach the place where Midsummer Meeting was to be held, but I had long since decided for myself that everything in the Armor Hills was three days' walk from everything else, most of it spent climbing one side of a hill and falling down the other. As we walked, I did my best to gain more information from Meramay about the mysterious Moonwoman.

Meramay said she had been here "for always," but Moonwoman had not been at last year's Midsummer Meeting, nor had word reached Haven of her before the spring, so I did not think that could be so. I was growing increasingly uneasy with what I heard of her; Meramay had never seen her, but she certainly feared her.

On the third day, just as we reached the meeting grounds, I found out why.

"Was her took my man," Meramay said, as simply as if she were remarking on the fine summer weather, or the flowers growing by the side of the trace. "Saw him out walking of an evening and followed him home. Then she Sang him out of my bed, will-he, nill-he, and that was that."

This was the first time anyone had mentioned music in connection wit the witch I was seeking. Did Moonwoman have Bardic Gifts? No proper Bard would use his or her powers so; I was not even certain that Bardic Empathy could so thoroughly compel someone against their will, certainly not the Gift of an untrained Bard.

I would have questioned Meramay further, though it was a chancy thing to do, save for the fact that we had arrived at Meeting Home.

It was the closest thing to a proper town that I had yet seen in the Armor Hills, though it must lie deserted most of the year. There were dance floors, open to the air; platforms of raised wood planks, where even now groups of dancers whirled, stamped, and spun to the sounds of drums and dulcimers, and even a few roofs without walls, where groups of hill women clustered together, talking and sewing and keeping a weather eye on the youngest children. Meeting Home filled an entire valley, and its floor was surely the largest flat space I'd seen since I'd arrived here. At one end of the valley there were a row of hearths, a great open-air kitchen flanked by tables enough to fill the dining hall at the Herald's Collegium.

I wondered, then, why I should think of that, for memories of the Collegium belonged to a life I had long since left behind me. They had nothing to do with the life Paynim the Tinker led.

Though the Meeting did not properly begin until the following night, the whole of the valley was already filled with bright clothes and bright colors, the sounds of music, and the smells of good cooking. There were more people here than I had seen so far in my entire visit to the Hills, and Meramay assured me that more would arrive before the Meeting Days began tomorrow night with the acknowledgment of the new children born in the past year. As I followed Meramay across the meadow to help her unload her cart, I saw unharnessed cart dogs lying everywhere, basking in the sunlight.

With Meramay to make my introductions, I was welcomed without trouble, and set myself up near those who had brought things to trade. I soon had as much work as I could fairly handle. Not much of my payment was in coin; there was little way I would be able to carry the bulkiest of the goods away with me, but I might well be able to trade them for smaller and more portable items—or for more costly things that I could fairly use, such as a new shirt, a hat, or a pair of breeches.

More people arrived as the day waned, and that night there was a feast the like of which I had rarely experienced, followed by dancing that would go on, I was assured, until dawn.

The dances of the Armor Hills are complicated ones, and after stumbling through a few sets, I excused myself and sat with those who were—to hear them tell it—older and wiser. When the ale jugs began to pass, I began to hear more of the Moonwoman.

Half of what I heard I discounted immediately, for not even the sorcerers of Karse and Iftel could do such things as were claimed for Moonwoman—or if they could do one, they surely could not do the whole.

Thus, I did not think she could truly turn men into wolves and women into deer, nor ride the wind invisibly, nor strike people dead with a touch. If she could do even a tenth of what was claimed of her, she would have been a greater Mage than Vanyel the Good, and I thought that unlikely.

What was plain to hear, however, was that the people of the Armor Hills feared her greatly, and would not cross her, though she took not only goods from their houses, but young men as well, none of whom had ever been seen again. I heard, further, that she was never seen beneath the light of the sun, which only increased the awe in which she was held.

The awe . . . and the fear.

It was fear, perhaps, that had kept them from petitioning for a Herald's services before now. In truth, I did not know. I heard as much admiration of Moonwoman as I did anything else, though only a fool would think he would hear honest and open criticism of one whom they felt wielded such power. Such reticence was, in fact, one of the very reasons I walked the roads, for awe and fear are close cousins, and neither is the sister of truth. It was plain that I had much to report to Alberich, but I could not leave just yet. I would have no good reason to give for my sudden departure.

Besides, I had not yet seen the woman, and there is a

saying in the taverns along the Exile's Road that truth is to tale as the worm to the fish: one may easily be swallowed up by the other.

On the first day of the Meeting, disaster struck, though at first Meramay and I both thought it to be a blessing. Several of the families that arrived brought strangers with them. In each case, the story was the same: they had been found wandering nearby, with no memory of who they were or how they had come to be where they were. The families that had found them led them around to those who cooked and those who traded, for these were usually the elder men and women of their households, and might have the best chance of naming them.

Of course I could be no help in identifying them; perhaps if Shavanne had still been with me, but not now. That they all came from the Armor Hills was plain; the folk there, whether blond or dark, have a strong look of one another. And all were within a few summers of the same age.

I returned to my work, turning over in my mind what could have caused this. A few moments later I heard Meramay scream, loud enough to be heard over the sound of my own hammering. I dropped my tools at once, and ran for her side.

"Garan! Paynim, it's Garan! Ceile, Joard, Magan—it's Garan!" She was laughing and crying, and hugging the neck of one of the men. He looked bewildered but polite. Elsewhere, I heard similar glad outcries as lovers and kin claimed those without memory.

"Moonwoman Sang him away, and now he's back!" she added.

When I had been a Herald, I could sense the tenor of emotion in the towns and villages I passed through. It required no Mind Gift to do so, Shavanne had assured me, only experience and plain common sense. As a tinker, I had not noticed such things any longer, and came to the conclusion that I had felt it before because everyone had been focused upon one thing: me. And I did not feel it later, since no one pays any attention to a wandering craftsman, or if they do, it is in ones and twos, and not everyone in the town at once.

But now once more I felt it, and as if I still wore Whites,

I could read the ripples of emotion as easily as a fisherman can read the ripples in a stream.

For Meramay to speak Moonwoman's name aloud was bad enough. To say what she had done—in fact, to accuse Moonwoman of doing something—was far worse. Even though no one moved from where they stood, I felt their displeasure, and I was not surprised when they began to drift away and move their goods away, until soon Meramay was standing alone.

Even Garan felt it. He made graceful apologies to Meramay, saying he had to get his family settled in, but still he left; he had been Sung away nearly five moonturns ago, after all, and the people who had taken him in were all the family he knew.

She gazed at me, eyes wide and hurt and frightened, just beginning to be afraid.

I knew then that we must leave at once, for the sort of sullen anger she had roused was the sort I had seen flare to violence more times than I could count. But she swore she would not leave without Garan; that he would not be taken from her twice.

I mustered every good argument I could think of in vain—that she knew now where he was and that he was safe; that she did not wish to kindle one of the stubborn grudges that might smolder for generations in a small enclave, beginning for a cause as trivial as a misheard greeting; that Garan would return to her when he had gotten a chance to think—but she would not go. Whether because it was impossible for her to leave Midsummer Meeting or because it was impossible for her to leave Garan, I did not know. I dared not press her too hard lest she turn against me and order me from the Meeting; I would not go in any event, and I thought she would need my help soon.

I was more right than I suspected.

The shunning of Meramay that had begun when she had spoken those fatal words grew like the lake ripples from a thrown stone, until her face was as grim as my own. No one wished her assistance at their cookstove, nor to add the dishes she had prepared to their communal table. But she was proud and stubborn, and still she would not leave. We sat alone together, I making my whole meal of the eggs and vegetable pies that were to have been her contribution to the feast, and Meramay too miserable to eat at all.

I had expected the dancing to resume after supper, though the trading and bargaining over knives and axheads, cloth and livestock, was over for the day. But instead of pipes and drums and fiddles, as the sun set over the valley and twilight filled it, the only sound I heard was that of a lone and distant gittern.

In my home village we play the twelve-string gittern only, though the six-string is the more common instrument in most of the kingdom, for it is easier to learn, and to play well. I recognized the faint silvery ringing of the double-stringed gittern long before I saw the singer.

She came walking down the valley, glowing like the full moon itself in the twilight, and if you had never seen a Companion, you would surely think that the hair that fell loose and rippling to her waist was as white as its coat.

And I thought I must know what she was, or half of it.

When I was a student at Haven, a child was brought to the Healer's College for treatment. Young Jaxon's skin and hair were as white as Moonwoman's, and the bright light hurt his eyes terribly. I had seen the boy arrive, and asked the Healers what might be wrong with him. Master Tiedor told me that like some animals, the boy had been born without color in his skin or hair, and none of the healing arts could cure that, or lend strength to his eyes. In animals, Healer Tiedor told me, the uncolored state does not cause weak eyes, but humans who are so afflicted cannot see in bright sunlight at all.

The Healers were able to help, with tinted lenses for Jaxon's eyes, lotion for his skin to heal the effects of the sun, and calm matter-of-fact advice to his parents. Though his parents had been hoping for a cure when they came to Haven, this was no disease, just a different way of being born, and to change it was beyond a Healer's skill.

So must it be with Moonwoman.

The people all turned toward her like flowers to the sun, and I felt a strong prickle of warning, though as yet she had done nothing but pick out a tune upon the gittern, a lullay I had heard many of the women sing here. It is written in a minor key, filled with sadness and longing, like so many of the old songs.

But now the sweet tune seemed to contain anger as well; I felt it prickle across my skin and I wished, longingly, for some weapon. But I had nothing more than an eating knife, and my belled staff.

Many of the men with whom I had shared ale last night had fallen into step behind her, and from all around, men and women drifted toward her in little groups, following as she paced slowly down the length of the valley. Some carried torches plucked up from around the dancing floors to light their way.

And then Moonwoman opened her mouth and sang.

To this day the experience seems unreal to me. Her words were of a father who has gone away hunting to feed his family and will never return; but the meaning had nothing to do with the words.

In Haven I had once been privileged to listen to a Master Bard enchant a whole hall of folk in just this way, standing upon a stage with a harp in his arms—but it was his audience that was his instrument. But the emotions Bard Ronton had conjured in audience were mild and peaceful, compared to the killing rage I sensed building in the people around me.

In a minute—or two, at most—it would crescendo into violence, and I could already guess its target. If we dared to run, we would only conjure the inevitable up faster. Meramay stood beside me, too terrified by what she, too, knew was about to happen to fall beneath the music's spell.

The music—and the musician.

By now the mob was close enough that I could see the singer's face clearly. Tears glittered in her pale eyes, and her face was set in a white mask.

She was as terrified as Meramay.

I could not let this happen, though I died trying to prevent it.

As Shavanne had died, swept downstream by floodwaters, her body battered against the rocks along the way, until she was impaled on a submerged tree branch that ended her glorious life as surely as a Tedrel spear.

We had nearly been safely across the river, risking the crossing because villagers downstream had to be warned about the flood. But the bridge ropes had been rotted through with age, and it had collapsed under our weight.

Shavanne had nearly gotten us both to safety even so, but the far bank was water-sodden earth and it had collapsed beneath her hooves when she tried to climb it. She had spent the last of her strength throwing me to safety, but doing so had pitched her back into the water.

I had felt each moment of her struggle to live.

I had heard her dying scream.

I would not again fail to save a life.

Not here, and not tonight.

I willed Moonwoman to hear me, as I stepped into her path and shouted with all my might, both in Mindspeech and with my voice. To stop what she was doing was our only chance; the people she had englamoured could not be reasoned with, nor would they feel they were acting in anything but self-defense.

Someone threw a rock.

It struck me in the shoulder, too small and flung from too far off to do more than sting, but in that moment I knew despair and felt Death step near.

Yet I would not surrender nor flee, for I was a Herald still, in my heart, even though no one could see.

I had never ceased to be a Herald.

"Stop!" I shouted again, and this time I felt Shavanne add her strength to mine.

Power roared through my veins like the waters of that long-ago flooded river. This was the Mindspeech such as I had never wielded it, strong enough to match Moonwoman's own gift, enough for all about me to hear.

She flung back her head as if I had struck her with a hand of flesh. The gittern fell from her hands, and she swayed, falling at last to her knees and burying her face in her hands, weeping.

All around me the hill folk roused, coming out of the trance into which she had Sung them. They gazed from Moonwoman to me with looks of awe, though I knew how quickly that would change to both fear and anger. The "sorceress's" power over them was broken at last—and they would quickly hate what they had lately feared—but they had no idea how.

I did.

The night wind brought me the sound of phantom silver bells.

:Now at last I leave you, Beloved. Be well.:

I knew now how I had lived through my terrible bereavement, and why I had never been Chosen again. Why should a Herald with one Companion have another? In all the years I had walked the roads of Valdemar, Shavanne had never left my side, and in the one moment when I truly needed her, she was there.

Perhaps it is not possible. Perhaps her presence in my mind was no more than an illusion, nurtured by long-delayed grief. Perhaps my Mindspeech was so powerful for lying dormant all those years.

But I know what I believe.

I did not wait for the folk of the Armor Hills to know their own minds, but took Moonwoman away with me while they still wondered and argued among themselves. I stayed only to gather up my pack and to borrow Meramay's hooded cloak from her. The goods I had gotten in trade here would be a fair bargain for it, and I knew that Moonwoman would not be able to stand the light of the sun upon her skin. And we would be traveling many days beneath the light of the sun.

I would be returning to Haven for the first time in many years, for I needed to give my charge personally into the hands of Healers and Bards—and there was certainly no safety for her in the Armor Hills now, even if she had wished to stay.

Along the way, she learned to trust me, and told me her story.

Her true name was Liah. She had been born in these hills nineteen summers ago, in a remote cabin similar to many I had stopped at during my visit here. Her parents, Andren and Colmye, were simple folk who knew little of the world beyond their hills and believed less. They had thought their daughter's milk-white skin and hair must be some sort of judgment upon them, and when the sickly child was painfully burned by the sun, they became certain she was a curse, for what else would take injury from the sun, source of all good?

Andren blamed his wife, of course, denying that the child was his.

I well knew the madness of grief. Even though his fear

and anger had led to suffering for so many others, I could understand why Andren had acted as he had done, even though I could not excuse it.

Andren put it about at the next Midsummer Meeting that Colmye's child had died; no one doubted his tale. Colmye never attended another Meeting—whether she would have endorsed his story to her own mother, even Liah does not know. Andren never ceased to reproach his wife for giving birth to a Moon-child, though he never raised a hand to her or to Liah.

Liah grew toward maturity seeing no one but her parents. Her father hated and feared her, her mother, shattered in spirit, retreated into a world of music. It was her mother's gittern Liah had been playing that night.

Her Gift manifested violently, as the Great Gifts often do. One night the smoldering anger she felt against Andren boiled over. She Sang him all her hatred and despair with the life she led until he fled the cabin into the night; in the morning her mother's screams awoke her.

She helped her mother cut her father down from the branch on which he'd hanged himself.

After that, I think Liah lost all hope. She knew she had caused her father's death; therefore all that he said of her must be true. She knew that she had the power to impose her will upon those around her with a song, and she had used her power to kill.

Her mother followed her father into death a scant few years later, wasted away with madness and grief. Though I do not think Liah caused that death, save indirectly, she blamed herself for it as well—and she blamed the hill people who had not come to her mother's aid, though by the time Liah had eighteen summers behind her, I do not know if many of them remembered Andren and Colmye at all, and none knew that there was a child.

In loss, in fear, in rage, Liah tried to become all that her father had thought she was. She found that people would believe anything that she Sang to them, and had used that single power to create a fantastic monster of herself. The men that she lured from their wives she compelled to forget their families, and even their own names, and sent them wandering through the hills; even she was not sure why.

Perhaps Garin and the others could be Healed, and their

memories restored. Healers would have to go to the hills to try to undo the damage Liah had done. Healers, and Heralds, and teachers as well. Life in the Armor Hills would change, perhaps for the better.

Liah would need Healing as well, and Training.

She must accept what she had done, and move beyond it.

Sometimes Healing takes a very long time. I am not too proud to say that I am proof of that, for anger and grief take strange forms, and can be stubborn enough to defeat the strongest Healer.

Yet if the heart is strong, Time heals all, in the end.

In Trevale, I will buy a horse for us to ride, now that Shavanne is gone.

A Change Of Heart

by Sarah A. Hoyt and Kate Paulk

Kate Paulk was born in Australia where, unable to decide what she'd be when she grew up, she took no less than three degrees. When bored with that, she married an American. She's now residing in Texas with her husband and two bossy felines. One of her stories will come out soon in an Illuminated Manuscripts anthology and she's working on a novel.

Sarah A. Hoyt was born in Portugal, a mishap she hastened to correct as soon as she came of age. She lives in Colorado with her husband, her two sons and a varying horde of cats. She has published a Shakespearean fantasy trilogy, as well as any number of short stories in magazines ranging from *Asimov's Science Fiction Magazine* to *Dreams of Decadence*. She's currently working on an adventure/time travel novel with Eric Flint. Her Three Musketeer Mysteries are upcoming under the name Sarah D'Almeida.

JACONA stank in the heat of a summer night. The stenches melded, mingled, and rolled onto Ree's senses like a physical assault—a cloying staleness of dinners, the acrid bite of wood smoke, the offensive punch of middens and animals and offal, of human sweat and too many bodies living too close together.

Ree remembered when the smell didn't bother him. He remembered—and shook his head and tried to forget. The new talents had their uses. Right now he could smell a collection of unfamiliar scents: leather, sweat, and steel. A patrol. Approaching.

Silently, he slipped back into the shadows of his refuge, the abandoned warehouse behind him. It had been deserted since last winter, when the magic failed. All that remained now was a maze of rotting timber and fallen stone, unfit for human life. Which did not bother Ree. He had not been human since the magic storms.

One of the disturbances had caught him, a few days after the magic went bad. He had been stalking a sleek rat that would have given him meat for a day. The rat had found an old cat waiting to die. Ree had pounced on the rat as it gave the cat an experimental nip.

Lurking in the shadows, he shivered, despite the heat of the night, as he remembered the blurriness and the queasy feeling—as he remembered opening his eyes to a different world. A different self. To a self equipped with cat claws and rat's tail, with cat eyes, too sensitive to movement and keen in the darkness—to a short coat of fur over his whole body. The fur had helped him survive the winter. His keener senses helped him avoid the patrols and the soldiers who killed hobgoblins like him.

At least he'd been lucky so far. But it was getting harder. Ever since the snow began to melt, there had been more and more patrols. Ree was the last of the street rats who sheltered in the ruined warehouse. The humans had been caught and taken off to orphanages or work gangs, and the hobgoblins had been killed. For all he knew, he was the only hobgoblin left in Jacona.

How long could he go on surviving?

Voices drifted to his ears. They had a strange accent, not like the regular patrol. And yet, they still smelled military. Ree tensed and breathed shallowly. The area around his refuge had been empty at night ever since Emperor Melles had declared a curfew so the hobgoblin patrols would not accidentally kill anyone's registered Changechildren.

Ree scrambled up through the debris until he could peer out from one of the many holes in the roof.

Outside, in the dark night, his changed eyes could see strangers. Soldiers. Real soldiers. At least no city patrol Ree had ever seen would dress in gray. City patrols believed in bright colors as a way of showing how important they were. The army believed in efficiency. Gray clothes and actually doing their jobs.

Ree held his breath. Soldiers were bad news. He ducked back into the dark before he reminded himself that only his changed sight allowed him to see them. And to hear them, as they drew nearer.

". . . can't believe no one's torn this dump down, even for firewood."

One of the soldiers laughed. Ree could not see which one. There were five, all burly and looking well-fed.

"Ever'thing round here's Army property now, anyhow. Ain't no one was gonna go through all that crap last winter just to steal a bit of firewood off of Army land."

An icy fist clenched around Ree's gut. He bit his lip, to avoid calling out. The army was efficient. Efficient . . . at killing hobgoblins and undesirables. At rounding up street rats for the work gangs. "More like they didn't want to meet the rats," said another man. "Every brat that's been picked up in this sector knows the rat hole."

They moved in close enough to be hidden by the walls of the building. Only the sound of their breathing, the sound of their movements told Ree they were still there and coming closer. And closer.

Ree stayed where he was, frozen. His hands reached back, to find support against a wall that was mostly crumbling rubble. He felt the dryness of plaster against his palms. Surely they would not enter his refuge. This place wasn't safe. For humans.

For him, and for the rest of the city's discards, it was home.

"Gah! Filthy vermin!" Squeaks and skittering joined the soldier's curse as rats fled the noise. A boot scraped in the rubble.

They had come in. Ree's chest hurt. His mind became a blank space filled with fear. Part of him—the part of him at the back of the mind, the part of him that was not fully human, not fully himself, wanted to run, to hide. But his working mind, his memories, knew better. To run meant to call attention to himself. It meant death.

The soldiers came closer. A spot of light danced erratically on the skewed beams near Ree's head. One of the soldiers had unshielded a night lantern. Though Ree knew he could not be seen from the ground, he had to fight the urge to run, to escape. To hide in a hole and be safe.

Heart pounding, he waited until the lantern was lowered and its light aimed away from his hiding place. Slowly, he crept out of his hiding place. Balancing his feet on crossed beams, he shifted quickly, feeling the slight shift of the wood beneath him, and leaping before the minimal movement turned to a rolling fall. He skipped and tiptoed and leaped till he reached a hole, barely big enough to let a slim rat-boy through.

Stretching his arms up to the hole, he balanced on one foot. As he lifted himself by the strength of his arms, the log rolled beneath him, and a shower of rubble trickled beneath.

"Up there!" The light of the lantern hit Ree.

Ree pulled himself up, pushing his head through the hole. He had to escape, to get away from the light, away from discovery.

"Outside, quick! It can't get far!"

Ree squirmed through the gap, pulling himself on his aching arms, feeling the jagged edges of the hole scrape his fur-covered body.

"Quick," a soldier shouted beneath.

Ree skidded down the sloping roof, twisting around to get his feet under him. A second from a precipitous fall, he managed to jump onto the next building. For a heart-stopping moment, he hung in the air, then his fingers latched onto the wooden eaves of the building across the lane.

His claws extended, instinctively, and dug into the wood. His feet scrabbled for a hold.

He heard shouts behind him. Strength he didn't know he possessed infused him. He pulled himself onto the steep-sloped roof. Scrabbling up it, he panted. His heart hammered in his chest. His throat ached with dryness.

At the top, he held on, his claws fully extended, biting into the age-softened wood. He eased himself down the shingled roof. His chest hurt. He swallowed. Once. Twice, trying to summon moisture onto his panic-parched tongue.

He'd survived. He was alive. But he was alone and unprotected. Where would he go now? The abandoned warehouse had been the closest thing he had ever had to a home. Well, the closest thing since his mother's home. . . .

Ree banished memories of a beautiful woman dressed in silks—of perfumed rooms—of her laughing. Her laughter had never been for him. Nor had there been any true joy in it. It had been a sham deployed in the service of the men who paid her. And more often than not Ree was locked out of her rooms while she entertained clients. Until . . .

Ree blinked to clear his burning eyes. His mother's home had never been home. His mother had never been a true mother. And besides, that was all done and over with. That was the other Ree, the human—the boy. The clawless, furless creature who was as nothing to this Ree. . . .

He swallowed hard, wishing moisture away from his cheeks. He was no weak human. Not anymore. He would not cry. He would think. The warehouse could not be the only available shelter in this town. He had to lose the soldiers, and then he could think about what to do next. At least climbing down to the ground was easy.

Streets here were swept at least once each day by one of the work gangs. With his night vision, Ree could scamper through them as if it were full daylight. He hardly thought about where he was going. And perhaps that was for the best. If he had nothing in mind and just turned on whim, the soldiers would find it harder to follow him. It would be harder to anticipate random movements.

Their voices grew fainter till even his enhanced hearing could hardly pick them at all. Ree breathed deeply. It was working.

As he came to a narrow lane between overarching buildings, he slowed down and looked around. His mad turnings had brought him to one of the tenement districts, where the shabby buildings leaned so close to each other they almost touched above the lane. Black alleys barely wide enough for a hand cart separated the buildings. The sun never reached the mud beneath.

He lifted his feet off the dismal muck and sighed. He needed to pick his way more carefully now. He had already trodden in more than enough to leave a scent trail even a human could follow.

Lifting his foot, he shook off the worst of the filth. These lanes had never been paved. They went from ice in winter to mud in summer, and since the magic died they had more than just mud and ice in them. He had been born somewhere like this. He'd played in these streets—or walked forlornly along them—when his mother locked him out of her rooms.

Ree crept slowly through the darkness, listening, listening. His enhanced hearing picked up the sounds of people in their houses—whispers, conversations, a sleeper turning in bed, a child crying forlornly.

Smells seeped over the ever-present stink of waste. A hint of stew that made his stomach growl, reminding him that he had not eaten since last night. Old beer, rancid as it mingled with older straw in the closed alehouses. Unwashed humans, ripe with sweat from days of work in the summer heat. Acrid smoke from cooking fires. The smells were signs of life in the darkness.

But the streets themselves were almost deserted. This area had once bustled day and night. But since the curfew, no one wanted to risk a crossbow. A shadowed figure in darkness could be mistaken for a hobgoblin, and who was going to say the soldier who fired the crossbow hadn't thought he was killing a monster? Certainly not the dead person.

The quiet felt wrong to Ree. Ominous. Even though he could never go out among humans again, Ree wanted to know people were still out there on the streets—feasting, fighting, flirting. People on the streets meant things were normal again, and normal meant that people would fear hobgoblins less. And not hunt a young street rat, constantly making his life a living hell.

He walked down the street, listening, listening for the sounds that told him at least people were still living in their houses, still safe. He felt a nostalgia for that life he'd never had, for that life that would never be his—for a family and a quiet snug home, where he could turn in his bed, pull the covers over his head, and be safe.

His ears, reaching for the sounds of normalcy picked up marching. Marching feet. His fur rose in hackles on his neck. Marching footsteps came from farther up the lane. He stopped. Then darted into the nearest alley.

"What the—" someone said, near him.

Panicked, Ree spun to the unexpected voice. A hulking shape loomed out of the blackness as the marching feet grew closer.

A hand closed around his neck. Ree's claws came out. He squirmed, scratching out with hands and feet to make the human in the army uniform let go. He had to. He had to defend himself, to force the human to leave him be. He somehow wrapped his body around an arm that seemed thicker than his chest, his feet kicking at the man's neck.

The hand let go. Ree tumbled to the ground, gasping. The dead weight of his attacker fell on him. Almost flattened him. Was the man dead? Had Ree killed him? There was a trickle of something warm-soft onto his neck, some liquid.

Oh, he could smell well enough the sharp, metallic tang of blood. But he didn't want it to be blood. He didn't want to have killed someone.

Oh, not the first time. Never the first time. But Ree didn't want to kill. He didn't want . . . Every time he killed someone, every time his instincts—no, the rat's instincts, or the cat's, took over and killed a human, Ree felt that he'd become a little less human. Eventually, his humanity would be all gone. Drained away.

He had lost too much humanity already.

Blood trickled onto his neck, draining away the man's life, and Ree wanted to stand, to squirm, to flee. But the marching steps approached and he held his breath and hoped, hoped they would pass without pausing.

Closer, he could hear their breaths, and smell the individual men. Not moving, Ree felt blood fall on him, felt the man shudder, stop breathing.

Along the main alley, the marching steps passed away. Slowly, slowly. Ree remained still. Holding his breath.

When the silence had lasted long enough, Ree dug his claws into the mud of the alley and pulled himself from beneath his attacker. His muscles seemed to have gone to water. His movement was too slow. Too slow.

I'm just tired. That's all. Tired. Give it a little while.

Pulling away from beneath the dead weight, he took deep

breaths. His nostrils filled with the smell of blood and filth. He stared at the man he had killed, shaking as he realized what it meant.

Dangerous hobgoblin. They'll hunt me down and kill me. There could be no doubt the dead man had been killed by a hobgoblin. Human murderers did not leave claw marks clear across their victims' throats.

He heard a sound. A breath. It came from behind him. He paused, shocked. He was not alone.

Ree froze, terror rising to choke him. Someone had seen him kill the man. He felt as if his lungs filled with freezing air.

Someone. There was someone. The person would call for help, and he would be killed like an animal. Like the animal he was. He'd killed someone with his claws, with his . . . He'd killed out of sheer panic.

The soft, muffled sound came from deeper in the alley.

For a moment, Ree trembled on the edge of fleeing, then he recognized the smell that lurked beneath the blood and worse. *Aw, crap. Not that.* He turned slowly, half dreading what he would see, half expecting it.

He stumbled in the direction of the breathing, in the direction of the smell.

The boy lay in the muck. It was hard to say how old he would be: younger than Ree, but not by much. He was all human, but he had the hollow, young-old look all the street rats got sooner or later.

Seen too much, Ree thought. *Felt too much.*

It was the gag and the way he had been tied up with his ragged pants that made Ree's gut churn. *Aw, crap. You poor thing.*

He fell to his knees besides the boy. He saw the momentary panic in the youth's eyes, and then an odd sort of relaxation, resignation, as if he'd given up the fight and consigned himself to anything fate wished to throw at him. As if the worst possible thing the boy could imagine had happened—and now something worse loomed.

Ree could well imagine what he looked like to this stranger, this shocked stranger. How would he have felt, in the old days, if a monstrosity with rat fur and broad, green cat's eyes knelt by him . . . touched him.

Gently, Ree reached for the knots. Just the knots, every

movement deliberate and slow. Still, the boy closed his eyes and tensed.

The knots were so tight it hurt Ree's hands to work them free. He would not use his claws to tear through the thin fabric: likely these were the only pants the boy owned. The gag was a little easier, although when Ree's eyes adjusted and he saw the bloody marks from a beating—probably administered with a rough-edged belt—etched on the boy's shoulders and face his claws nearly came out anyway. He stifled a hiss.

The boy opened his eyes. They were very large and sky blue, and looked at Ree with startled surprise. Slowly, the boy reached down and gingerly touched his wrist with his other hand.

He blinked at Ree. "What—" he started and swallowed and his expression changed to one of gratitude.

Ree felt queasy. He hadn't killed the man to rescue the boy. He had killed in an animal panic.

Gently, Ree held out the boy's clothes. But the boy was swaying on his feet and looked dazed, and Ree sighed. He dressed the boy as if he were a small child. And the boy let him.

By the time the boy was dressed, Ree realized he couldn't leave him here. Not like this. Not alone and dazed and hurt. But Ree had nowhere to go. And if anyone saw him . . . Especially with the dead man in the alley. The dead man killed by a hobgoblin.

If the boy refused to turn Ree in, they would hurt him. They would hurt him more.

Ree swallowed. "You know this part of town?" he asked.

The boy nodded. "I squat three blocks down—" He hesitated, as though he wanted to give Ree some kind of title.

"Call me Ree. And let's go. You gotta rest up, and we don't want no one finding us."

As they approached a rickety tenement building, the boy looked over his shoulder at Ree. "I live there," he said. "In the attic."

Ree nodded, not knowing what else to say.

The boy looked longer, as if waiting for an answer. "My name is Jem," he said.

"Jem," Ree repeated.

And Jem smiled, a brief, startling smile that made him look, of a sudden, much younger and much too old.

He turned away and walked fast, ahead of Ree, a new spring in his step. He took Ree up a steep, crooked staircase that climbed partway outside the building. Then he climbed up to the attic, a space made usable by some enterprising street rat. Jem's meager belongings sat in a neat pile by the hole in the roof Jem had used as an entry.

Despite his injuries, despite being human, he climbed nearly as well as Ree. Ree bit his lip. No point feeling jealous.

Jem was all human. He could do odd jobs for a copper coin, or get himself ration chits. Ree had no such advantages. But it was Ree who was unhurt and Jem who was ready to pass out.

"Get yourself down, so's I can clean you up," he said.

Jem nodded. His eyes, too big for his thin face, never once left Ree's face as he lay down. But there was no mistrust in that look. No fear.

How can you look at something like me, and not fear?

"I ain't going to hurt you any more'n I can help," Ree said roughly. "That big bastard cut you up good, and it's gotta get cleaned up or you'll get sick." He had seen what happened to wounds that were not cleaned. He knew the putrid wounds, the fever. No one deserved to die like that.

Jem swallowed, but he still watched as Ree dipped a rag into the water bucket. When Ree touched the rag to one of Jem's bloody welts, the boy gasped, and clenched his fists into his hair.

Ree supposed that hurt less. He tried to be gentle, but he had never tried to mend anyone's hurts before. He was better at killing.

He flinched from the thought, but looking at Jem's wounds, he could not summon up as much regret as he wished. He just hoped the big bastard had not torn Jem up too bad inside.

But Jem still got sick. His fever rose till he burned to the touch, and he twisted and talked in his sleep.

Ree stayed with him. The rat part—the animal part—wanted to go away. There was a horror of disease. Of death. Death and disease both attracted predators.

The human part of Ree was scared, too. How could it not be? He held onto Jem's hand through the day, and tried to quiet his screams, his mumbles. Tried to still his panics. And hoped no one heard. No one came.

What would people think if they found a hobgoblin and a human youth?

Ree talked to him through the day. Told him silly things. Sang to him, ballads he barely remembered hearing—in his mother's house, long ago. And Jem looked at him with wondering, blue eyes.

And never showed fear. Never fear. A twinge of fear from Jem, a twinge of horror at Ree's strangeness, and Ree would have been free to leave, free to go in search of a new hideout. Free to become a wild creature again. To forget he'd ever been human.

But Jem looked at him with confidence and trust and, in his brief moments of lucidity, grinned at Ree's jokes, smiled at them. Or reached for Ree's hand for reassurance.

So Ree stayed. And when he went out at night to refill the water bucket and steal food for them both, he always came back. Perhaps he was fooling himself. Perhaps he was using Jem to make himself feel human.

But he could not possibly live knowing how Jem would feel if he didn't come back. The idea of Jem's betrayal and disappointment was more than Ree could bear. It would have stripped Ree's soul bare of what humanity remained.

So he went and he came back. Sometimes, he caught rats. One good, fat rat made a meal when he skinned it and cooked it over a tiny fire.

In the past, Ree had eaten it raw. But Jem would have been shocked, scared. For the sake of Jem, Ree had to be human and eat with human manners, as he hadn't since the night the magic had changed him.

And each time, each time out, Ree feared he would be caught. Not just for his death, but because Jem might think he'd been abandoned.

There were more patrols now, and searches. Patrols that came too close for his liking talked about the killer hobgoblin, the one who'd killed the soldier, and how Emperor Melles himself was offering a whole gold piece for the hobgoblin's hide.

The thought made his stomach go all queasy. Not all

those soldiers would make sure he was dead before they started skinning him. And there were worse things . . .

Jacona had become a rat trap. Holding Jem's hand, as Jem slowly became stronger and more confident, Ree realized he could not stay in the city. Like his warehouse, it had become a trap.

The problem was, he did not know how he was to escape. The work gangs had not just hauled water to cisterns and replaced all the work that used to be done with magic. They had built a new wall around the city, to keep the hobgoblins out. The wall went all the way to Crag Castle, Ree had heard, and soldiers guarded it all the time. Jacona was a fortified rat trap.

No matter how busy the roads were, everyone who went through one of the gates was inspected. Ree had seen the frozen dangling corpse of a merchant who had tried to smuggle his son-turned-hobgoblin out of the city. He did not know if the man had died of the hanging or if he had frozen to death. Ree shuddered at the thought of what the patrols would do to Jem if they found them together.

He did not want to think about it. But he had to escape. It would be safer for Jem if he was just another human, with no rat boy to make him a criminal. Safer for Jem to be alone again. And safer for Ree, even though he had no idea what lay beyond the walls of Jacona.

Oh, he knew there were farms, and farmers, and roads that went to other cities. And he had heard there were wild places where a rat boy might be able to live without humans always hunting him. But he had never seen anything outside Jacona, never been beyond the tenements and warehouses of the poorest districts.

How could he escape?

The aqueducts had been broken by the winter storms after the magic began to die. The sections near the city walls had been knocked down by the work gangs who built the wall.

Ree had heard that no one knew when—or even *if*— magic was going to come back, so there had been no reason to keep something that would not be useful without magic. He had wondered sometimes if he would eventually change back without magic, but that did not seem likely.

As for the drains . . . Ree shuddered. The patrols would

not go there. That was where the Changerats and the even weirder hobgoblins had gone. The ones that were all teeth, claws, and poison. Like the patrols, Ree did not want to know what had become of them. And yet, it might be his only chance. A slim chance at life, as opposed to the sure death that would come to him if they found him in Jacona. And to Jem if they found him sheltering Ree.

But first he had to wait for Jem to be well, for Jem to be well enough to survive on his own.

"You're leaving?" Jem asked. He managed to look about two years old and very confused.

Ree nodded. Jem had stood up two days ago and he looked strong enough to survive, strong enough to do whatever he had done before meeting Ree. Why was it that Ree could not meet his eyes, and found himself looking at the floor as he said, "Stay away from the soldiers, Jem. You are—" He stopped short of saying that Jem was too pretty to be safe. He had not thought it, not thought it at all the whole time they had been together. Not consciously. Not with his rational mind. He had not. Jem was just . . . Jem. Ree looked up and caught a disturbing glimpse of broad blue eyes, like a summer sky. Threatening rain. "They are not . . . They do not have the restraints of the local patrols. They answer to no one.

"Jacona will be safer for you without me. You could stay here, get work, that sort of thing."

Jem made a sound. It wasn't quite a sigh or quite a sob, but it had a bit of both and more of frantic urgency. Ree looked up.

Don't let Jem cry, he thought. *Don't let Jem cry. He is just young and hurt and recovering from a lingering illness. His crying meant nothing. And yet, I don't know if I can bear to watch him cry.*

Jem looked like he was trying very bravely not to cry. He was biting his lower lip, hard.

Don't let him ask me to stay, Ree thought. *I can't stay. I can't.*

But instead of asking, Jem whispered, "My mother left me, on the street, when I was four. She gave me a sweet and said she would come back. She never—" He shook his head.

Ree started to say "Better than—" meaning to say *better than have your mother sell you to a customer when you're barely thirteen.* He remembered the fear, the frantic humiliation. He remembered being told about it, being sent to the room. He remembered running away.

For months, before, he'd noticed his mother's customers casting looks at him. There were men who didn't seem to care if you were male or female, provided you were a young thing, whose services could be bought. Who could not complain. There were men who didn't care what they did. Like that soldier, with Jem.

But as he was about to tell Jem this, Ree stopped. Because all through it, he'd been afraid Jem would follow him, Jem would come with him—that Jem would get caught by the patrols and hung outside the city walls to freeze to death. Or worse, now summer had come. And suddenly he wondered if his mother had been afraid of what would happen to Ree, if one of her customers found him. If one of her customers treated him as the soldier had treated Jem.

For the first time, he remembered his mother's face that day, without flinching. And it seemed to him there was concern in her eyes, overlaid with a harshness she had put there, a false harshness. He remembered she hadn't told him who the customer was. Or anything about him. Or how much he paid.

She'd told him just enough to make Ree run away and be safe.

Ree bit back tears, and forced harshness upon his features. He stepped close to Jem and did his best to growl, in his most threatening hobgoblin voice, "I'm tired of you. You're human and slight and weak. I don't want you with me. I can travel quicker alone, with my fangs and my hobgoblin senses, and my claws." He saw Jem look startled, scared, and he felt as though his heart were bleeding, but he pressed on. "If you come with me, I'll kill you. Like I killed the soldier."

Without waiting to see Jem's expression, to see the further devastation his words had brought to it, he turned around, he jumped out the window—he skittered and ran his way to the ground.

Running through the shadows to the abandoned washhouse, whose drains fed to the sewers and drains beneath the city, he wished he could remember how to cry. And he half-hoped a patrol would find him and kill him.

The washhouse was quiet, in shadows. No patrols in it, more was the pity.

Ree remembered it pretty well, from when his mother had come there with him, when he was very small. He didn't want to think of his mother. It hurt even more now.

He bent to the manhole and prized it open, his claws making short work of it. He had told Jem the truth. He would travel faster alone. And besides, if he got caught, he would die alone. He was a hobgoblin. A . . . thing. Part animal. He had no right to the company of a true human.

Jem would be safer without him.

Ree wondered if there was anywhere he could be safe. If a thing like him deserved safety.

The drains beyond the manhole smelled acridly of old waste. Ree stared dubiously into the shadows. Nothing came racing out to eat him.

Ree climbed gingerly down into it. Rusting steel rungs had been set into the shaft, so people had once come down into the sewers. That helped. He wasn't the first. And there would be some way to get around down there. It couldn't be all vertical tunnels and precipitously small shafts.

He hoped there were no guards on the outlets.

Ree listened for anything that might mean an attack. All he heard was water, dripping, trickling, and gurgling. He smelled more than water, even though last night's rain would have washed a lot of the worst away.

Once there had been spells on these drains, cleaning them so that only water flowed out at the end of them, spells to turn everything else into heavy dark mulch the farmers bought for their fields. Ree remembered watching them trade for the mulch at last summer's fair. Now everything went out to the river, although work gangs had built weirs to catch the worst of the solid stuff.

The rungs ended, leaving Ree's feet dangling. He used his hands to lower himself to the bottom rung, and stretched. His feet touched solid ground.

He sighed and let go. "Bit of a drop at the bottom," he said. And realized Jem wasn't there. He had got in the habit of talking to Jem. Of relating his actions to him. Even when he went out alone to hunt, he would come home and tell Jem everything.

Home . . . when had Jem's crash pad become home?

But it wasn't the place. It was because Jem was there. But Jem wasn't here. Jem would never be here again. And that was as it should be. Ree had no right to risk Jem, no right to—

He cut the thought off, and listened and peered into the darkness.

This part of the drain was quiet. Ree saw and smelled nothing animal. If there were Changefish in the water, he had no way to tell.

With no real idea which way to go, Ree decided to follow the flow of the water. There was a walkway along the side of the drain that must have been built so workmen could get in without having to walk in the water.

He walked in silence, senses straining for a hint of danger. There was none. Once, he heard animal squabbling far off. Whatever made it, it was too far distant to be a danger to him.

When drains joined the one he was in, narrow bridges crossed the channels.

He crossed them, following his drain and the water, hoping that it would lead to an outlet that would take him out of the city, away from Jacona. If he had not been always listening, sniffing for danger, it would have been an easy walk.

He did not know how long he walked, or how far. Darkness and the constant sounds of water played tricks on his senses, making it seem that he had been walking forever, and sometimes like no time at all had passed. Apart from the bridges where new drains joined his, everything was all the same.

Finally, the darkness began to lift. Ree hurried toward gray, eager to be out of the never-ending blackness. Soon, light glinted off the water, the chilly white light of moonlight. Ree hurried toward the light. Then stopped.

There was something there, at the grate waiting for him. Something big. As he drew closer, his heart started pounding. A hobgoblin had been tethered to the iron grate that sealed the drains. It looked looked partly like a snake and mostly like too many teeth. Its head swung back and forth at the end of its tether as it tried to reach him.

Ree gulped. He jumped back. His claws all came out. But he thought of himself—of how the soldiers would kill him on sight. And he did not want to do that to another hobgoblin. Whose fault was it, if he had chanced to be near a snake, when the changes came? It had not asked to become a hobgoblin, any more than Ree had.

"You don't have to hurt me," he said, and his voice came out small and frightened. "You're like me. I'm like you. I mean you no harm."

Slowly, he stepped toward the thing, toward the grate. The eyes, amid the teeth, glinted, he thought, with a hint of understanding.

He thought he was safe and then the creature launched. Ree just managed to jump out of reach, flatten himself against the wall, while the thing's too-sharp, too-many teeth closed near his bare arm.

"Why—" Ree yelled.

"You are nothing like me, kitten-rat boy. Snakes eat the likes of you," the creature spoke, hissingly, through its many teeth. "And my life is spared because I'm important and I can kill the likes of you . . . vermin."

Ree was pinned against the dank wall. Moving either way would bring him within reach of the thing's teeth. He could not go out. He could not go back. He could rush toward death or stay here till he starved.

He would never see Jem again. Ree flinched from the thought, because it was stupid. He would never see Jem again anyway.

Just then he heard a scream. He turned, at the same time the snake creature did.

Jem stood in the tunnel, away from the snake's reach. He had a crossbow. And he was screaming, a scream of rage through clenched teeth, as he pulled the string back on the bow.

The snake thing tried to jump, but it was tethered. And it moved a little too late. The bolt entered the mouth between the rows of teeth.

There was a roar and the thing jumped in the air. Then fell, and was still. And the smell came.

Ree didn't remember falling on his knees. And he didn't remember Jem approaching him. He had put the bow on his back, and he had a quiver with bolts. His hands were free. He held onto Ree's upper arms and pulled Ree up onto his feet.

"I know you told me to keep away from soldiers, but I saw the crossbow right at the entrance to a bar as I was following you," he said. "It was on the floor, near a table full of soldiers. I only had to go in a couple of steps. They never saw me."

He spoke very quickly, as if Ree would reproach him for disobeying his orders. But Ree's mind could only hold onto the central fact, the central surprise of the last few minutes. He looked up into Jem's big blue eyes. The eyes that were looking anxiously at Ree.

"You followed me?" he said.

Jem nodded.

"Through the streets and the tunnels you followed me? All alone, you followed me?"

"Wherever you go, I go," Jem said.

Ree blinked, wondering what he had done to deserve that kind of attention, that kind of devotion from someone like Jem. From someone brave enough to follow a hobgoblin through tunnels infested with worse creatures.

From someone brave enough to steal from soldiers after what had happened.

"I'm a hobgoblin," he said. "Not . . . human." A coward, who ran from everything. Who killed when he was scared. When the animal took over.

"Nonsense," Jem said. He managed to look sterner, more adult. "You're human, Ree. You're good. You saved me. Without you, I would have died."

"I killed the soldier by accident," Ree said. "Because the rat in me got scared. I didn't even know—" He shook his head. He did not want to remember lying under the soldier as he died. Did not want to remember the blood dripping onto him.

Jem shrugged. "Maybe. But no one forced you to free me. No one forced you to stay with me, to take care of me."

Ree swallowed hard. "What else could I have done?" Too many memories, too many things he wanted to forget.

The bloody welts on Jem's body, the way he had just . . . given up. . . .

"You could have killed me," Jem said. "You could have done what the soldier did."

Despite the years of being hard, of showing nothing, Ree flinched. He could never . . . not with anyone who did not want him as much as he wanted them. Even though weakness was dangerous, he could not be angry at himself for flinching, for showing emotion. Jem was safe. He could show his true self to Jem.

If Jem saw Ree's weakness, he did not show it. He pointed at the snake. "You could have done what he would have done. You're human, Ree. And I will follow wherever you go."

Ree shook himself. It seemed to him he'd been living in a long nightmare and just awakened.

He edged past the body of the snake thing, trying not to look at it. He took a deep breath, and extended his claws. "Let's get out of here." The bars in the grate were set wide, to let debris through. They should be far enough apart.

Jem nodded.

To Ree's relief, the grate was wide enough for him to slip through, even if he did lose some fur on his shoulders and hips on the way.

He and Jem stumbled out of the river, into the moonlight, looking at a strange new world that held nothing they knew. Low, rolling hills stretched to the darkness of mountains, and the silver moonlight gave it all the look of a ghost land.

Ree sought Jem's hand at the same time as the boy sought his. Their hands met, warm and moist. They stood there a moment, rat boy and street rat, facing a world of dangers they could not begin to anticipate.

"Well," Ree said finally. "Guess we'd better get going. Got a ways to go and a lot to learn."

"Yah." Jem squeezed his hand. "Got a whole world to find, out here."

They walked into the moonlight.

ALL THE AGES OF MAN

by Tanya Huff

Tanya Huff lives and writes in rural Ontario with her partner, four cats, and an unintentional Chihuahua. After sixteen fantasies, she's written two space operas, *Valor's Choice* and *The Better Part of Valor,* and is currently working on a series of novels spun off from her Henry Fitzroy vampire series. In her spare time she gardens and complains about the weather.

"I'M too young for this."

Although Jors had spoken the words aloud, thrown them, as it were, out onto the wind without expecting an answer, he received one anyway.

:So you keep saying.:

"Doesn't make it any less true."

:You are experienced in riding circuit,: his Companion reminded him. *:All you must do is teach what you know.:*

Jors snorted and shifted in the saddle. "So *you* keep saying."

Gervais snorted in turn. *:Then perhaps you should listen.:*

"I'm not a teacher."

:You are a Herald. More importantly, you are needed.:

And that was why they were heading northeast, out to the edge of their sector to meet with Herald Jennet and her greenie. To accept said greenie from the older Herald and finish out the last eleven months of her year and a half of Internship. The courier who'd brought the news of Jennet's mother's sickness had also brought the news that

152

the Herald able to replace her was already in the Sector but way over on the other side of a whole lot of nothing. It was decided he'd start his circuit from there and Jennet would backtrack the much shorter distance to meet up with Jors.

The girl's name was Alyise, her companion's name was Donnel, and that was pretty much all Jors knew. He couldn't remember ever seeing anyone of that name amidst the Grays during the rare times he'd been at the Collegium over the last few years and he only remembered her Companion as a long-legged colt.

The thing was, he liked being on the road and he much preferred the open spaces of the Borders to any city, so he went back on Circuit as fast as he could be reassigned. That didn't give him much time to learn about the latest Chosen and when he did meet up with other Heralds, he was much more interested in finding out what his year-mates had been doing.

"Jennet has got to be ten years older than I am. At least. And she's a woman."

Strands of the Companion's mane slid across Jors' fingers like white silk as Gervais tossed his head. *:What does her being a woman have to do with this?:*

"Women are better at teaching girls. They understand girls. Me . . ." He rubbed a dribble of sweat off the back of his neck. ". . . I don't get girls at all."

:You seemed to understand Herald Erica. I remember her continuously agreeing with you.:

"Continuously agreeing? What are you talking about?"

:Raya and I could hear her quite clearly outside the Waystation. She kept yelling yes. Yes! Yes! Yes!:

"Oh, ha ha. Very funny. " Jors could feel Gervais' amusement—the young stallion did indeed think it was very funny. "As I recall, Erica and I weren't the only two keeping company that night."

:We were quiet.:

"Well, I'm sorry we kept you from your beauty sleep and you needn't worry about it happening again for, oh, about eleven months."

:You do not know that the new Herald will find you distasteful. Raya told me that her Herald found you pleasant.:

Jors sighed. Pleasant. Well, he supposed it was preferable

to the alternative. "Thank you. But that's not the point. I'll be Alyise's teacher, her mentor; I can't take advantage of my position of power."

:You will be Heralds together.:

"Yes, but . . ." He felt a subtle shift of smooth muscles below him echoed by a definite shift of attention and fell silent.

:Inar says we will meet in time for us to return to the Waystation outside of Applebay before full dark.:

If that was true, and Jors had no reason to doubt Jennet's Companion, they were a lot closer to the crossroad than he'd thought. He glanced over his shoulder to check on Bucky and found the pack mule tucked up close where Gervais' tail could keep the late summer insects off his face. And that was another possible problem. Mules were mules regardless of who they worked for and mules that worked for Heralds could be just as obstinate and hard to get along with as any other. They'd be adding a new mule to the mix.

It was a good thing Companions always got along.

And speaking of . . .

"Why didn't Donnel contact you? Can't he reach this far?"

:Inar is senior to Donnel as you will be senior to his Chosen.:

"You'll be senior to Donnel as well, then."

:Yes.: Sleek white sides rose and fell as Gervais sighed.

Jors grinned. "Wishing Alyise's Companion was a mare?"

His grin broadened as it became quite clear that Gervais had no intention of answering.

"She's a good kid," Jennet said, glancing over at where the youngest of the three Heralds was carefully packing away the remains of the meal they'd shared. "Eager, enthusiastic . . ."

"Exhausting?" Jors suggested as her voice trailed off.

"A little," the older Herald admitted with a smile. "But you're a lot younger than I am, you should be able to keep up."

"That's just it. I'm too young to be doing this. I'm no teacher."

"You have doubts."

He only just managed not to roll his eyes. "Well, yes."

"Does your Companion doubt you?"

"Gervais?" Jors turned in time to see Gervais rising to his feet after what had clearly been a vigorous roll, his gleaming white coat flecked with bits of grass. "Gervais has never doubted me."

"Then, if you can't believe in yourself, believe in your Companion. And now that I've gifted you with my aged wisdom . . ." Grinning, she bent and lifted her saddle. ". . . we'd best get back on the road."

Lifting his own saddle, Jors fell into step beside her. "I'm sorry to hear about your mother."

"Yes, well, she wasn't young when I was born, and she's never been what you could call strong, so I can't say that I'm surprised. I'm just glad that the Borders are so quiet right now and that there was someone close enough . . ." She smiled so gratefully at him that Jors felt himself flush. "*Two* someones close enough."

Inar, given his head, had disappeared southward almost too fast for the eye to follow. One moment he, and his Herald, were a white blur against the gold of summer-dried gasses and the next, they were gone.

Gone. Leaving Jors alone with Alyise.

Alone with an attractive eighteen-year-old girl.

No. Alone with another Herald.

One he just happened to be responsible for.

Oh, Havens.

:She is a Herald. That makes her responsible for herself.:

:I was broadcasting?:

Gervais snorted. *:Donnel probably heard you.:*

Jors doubted that since Donnel—with a fair bit of that long-legged colt in him still—was dancing sideways away from a bobbing yellow wildflower. Alyise was laughing, probably at something Donnel had said. Their mule, right out at the end of its lead rope, turned his head just far enough for Jors to see that he looked resigned about the whole thing.

Which reminded Jors of something he'd meant to ask Jennet and forgotten. No matter, Alyise would know what had happened to their second mule.

"Spike?" She giggled. "Oh Jennet left him back at the Waystation supply post saying you'd have enough on your plate without having to deal with Spike, too. He's not a pleasant fellow although honestly, I think most of it's an act and he's really much nicer than he pretends. You know?"

Jors had no time to answer. He suspected she hadn't intended him to as she rattled on without pausing.

"She left a lot of her gear there except for the bits she gave to me. I seem to go through soap really, really quickly, I can't think why, I mean, we're all in Whites but if there's something to smudge on, I'll smudge. I may be the only Herald ever who really appreciated her grays. So Jennet gave me her extra soap and a tunic that was getting too tight for her—across the shoulders, of course, not in front because I'm well, a little better endowed there—but no worry about her being caught short because she didn't leave behind or give me anything she'll need because she's heading home. But you knew that, didn't you, because you were there when she left?"

The punctuating smile was dazzling.

The Waystation outside Appleby was much like every other Waystation; there was a corral for the mules, a snug lean-to for the Companions, a good sized, well-stocked storeroom, and a single room for the Heralds. The biggest difference was that the fireplace had been filled in with a small box stove, flat-topped for cooking and considerably more efficient at heating the space.

"Not to mention there'll be a lot less warm air sucked up the chimney," Jors observed, examining the stovepipes. This was new since this the last time he'd been by.

"I think it's less romantic, though."

"What?"

Alyise smiled as he turned. "I think a stove is less romantic than an open fire. Don't you think there's just something so sensual about the dancing flames and the flicking golden light?"

"Light." Jors cleared his throat and tried again. "We'd better light the lanterns."

She pushed russet curls back off her face with one hand, gray eyes gleaming in the dusk. "Or instead of lighting the lanterns, we could just leave the doors of the stove open and sit together close to the fire."

"Fire."

"Pardon?"

"You light the fire." His palms were sweaty. "In the stove," he expanded as she stared at him, head cocked. "So we can cook. I have to go check on Gervais."

:I'm fine.:

:Good.: He got outside to find his Companion standing by the door and gazing at him with some concern. *:She's . . . I mean, I'm supposed to be teaching her.:*

:Donnel says his Chosen is glad you are a young man. She has been with Jennet for seven months.:

:Hey, I've been on my own for eight and that's . . . : He paused as Gervais snorted. *:Yeah. Sorry. Way too much information. The point is, it wouldn't be right.:*

:If that's how you feel.:

:It is.:

:Good luck.:

:Oh, that's very helpful.:

:Thank you.:

Never let anyone tell you that Companions can't be as sarcastic as cats, Jors muttered to himself as he turned and went back inside. The curve of Alyise's back stopped him cold. Her pants hung low on the flare of her hips, low enough to expose the dimples on the small of her back just under her waist.

She smiled at him over her shoulder as she pulled a sleeveless tunic out of her pack. "I just had to get into something that wasn't all sweaty. I don't know what it is about spending the day in the saddle that makes me so damp, since Donnel's doing most of the work, but from my breast bands right on out everything is just soaked through. I guess the good news is that, at this time of the year, I can rinse them out tonight and they'll be dry by morning unless it rains, of course, but I don't think it's going to. There's really no point in having the village laundry deal with them." Her brow wrinkled as she pushed her head through the tunic's wide neck. "Does this village even have a laundry?"

"Laundry?" He tried not to stare at the pale swell of her

breasts as she pulled the tunic down and turned to light one of the lamps with shaking hands. He was not ready for this kind of responsibility.

"Men."

Was she allowed to laugh at him? There was too much about this mentoring that he didn't know.

"I don't suppose you even noticed," she continued, slipping out of her pants. "Ah, that's better. Shall you cook or shall I?"

"Me!" Cooking would be a welcome distraction. "You can tell me about your time with Jennet. So I know what you've covered . . . done."

"Okay; how much of . . ."

"Everything!"

Everything took them through dinner and into bed. Separate beds. Alyise seemed fine with that, Jors noticed thankfully, since he wasn't certain his resolve would stand up against a determined assault. Long after her breathing had evened out into the long rhythms of sleep, he lay staring up at the rough wood of the ceiling and wondered just how authoritarian he was supposed to be. All Heralds were equals, that was a given. Except when they weren't, and that was tacitly understood. *I'm just not ready for this yet.*

:Sleep now, Heartbrother.: Gervais's mental touch was gentle. *:Many tasks seem less daunting in the morning.:*

Jors woke just after sunrise to discover that Alyise had already gone out to feed and water the mules.

"I can never stay in bed after I wake up," she explained with a sunny smile. "My mother used to say it's because I was afraid I'd miss something, but I think it's because I didn't want to get bounced on by my younger sisters and I'll tell you, that habit stood me in good stead when I was a Gray because you know how hard it is to get going some mornings and the first up has the first shot at the hot water and there were mostly girls in my year; six of us and one boy. What about yours?"

"My?" When did she breathe?

"Your year; how many boys and girls in your year?"

"Oh. Three boys, two girls."

"How . . . nice."

He heard Donnel snort, realized she was staring at him,

and a moment later realized why. He'd gotten a little panicked when he'd seen her bed was empty and raced outside
wearing only the light cotton drawstring pants he'd slept
in. With the early morning sun behind him, he might as
well be naked. *Oh, yeah. This is going to help me maintain
some kind of authority.*

   :Authority does not come from your clothing.:

And that would have been more reassuring had his Companion not sounded like he found the entire situation entirely too funny. *:Maybe not, but it sure doesn't come
from . . . :* It occurred to him that while he was standing
talking to Gervais, Alyise was still staring. Appreciatively.
"I'll just go and get dressed. We'll be heading into Appleby
right after we eat."

And thank any Gods who may be listening for that, he
thought as he made as dignified a retreat as possible into
the Waystation.

Appleby wasn't so much a village as it was a market and
clearing center for the surrounding orchards that gave it its
name. Jors told the younger Herald all he knew about both
the area and the inhabitants as they rode in from the Waystation, but since his available information ran out some
distance before they arrived, Alyise took over the
conversation.

Her mother made a terrific apple dumpling but wouldn't
give out the recipe no matter how much Alyise or her sisters begged.

Donnel was very fond of apples, especially the small,
sweet pink ones that grew farther north.

She loved apples sliced and dried and hoped she'd be
able to buy some of last year's if they had a moment before
they left town.

Her grandfather used to carve apples and dry them
whole and they turned into the most cunning old men and
women dolls' heads.

Just when Jors was about to suggest she stop talking, she
finished her story about how an apple peel taken off in one
unbroken spiral would give the initial of true love when
tossed over a shoulder and fell silent, straightening in the
saddle and transforming from girl to Herald.

   :Neat trick.:

:Why does she need to be anything but what she is when she is with you?: Gervais asked reasonably.

:She doesn't.:

:And why do you . . . :

:Because I'm her teacher!:

:Herald Jennet was also her teacher. Do you think Herald Jennet behaved differently than herself?:

:Herald Jennet has had more time to be herself!: Jors pointed out.

Gervais tossed his head, setting his bridle bells ringing as they passed the first of the buildings. *:You are not Herald Jennet,:* he said as the first wave of laughing children broke around them.

:That's what I keep saying!:

The Companion carefully sidestepped an overly adventurous and remarkably grubby little boy. *:Maybe you should try listening.:*

And that was all he was willing to say.

Go not to your Companion for advice, Jors sighed. *For they will tell you to figure it out for yourself.*

Judgments in Appleby were, not surprisingly, mostly about apples. More surprisingly, Jors found Alyise to be an attentive listener—both to the petitioners and to him. Although she deferred to Jors as the senior Herald, she expressed her opinions clearly and concisely when asked for them and in turn asked intelligent questions when she needed more information. Having been more than a little afraid of what the day would bring, Jors was impressed and grateful that he could set aside personal doubts and concentrate on the job at hand.

Late that afternoon, when they'd finished with official business and had moved on to the more social aspects of being a Herald—trading the gossip that kept the far-flung corners of the kingdom telling the same stories—Jors glanced over at Alyise within a circle of teenage girls and wondered if it counted as a conversation when everyone seemed to be talking at once.

"Herald Jors."

He turned to see the eldest of the village councillors holding out a cup of cider.

"Don't worry, it's one of this year's first pressings. Windfall from the early apples. It has absolute no trade value, so you needn't fear you're being bribed."

A tentative sip curled his tongue. "Tart," he gasped.

"A little young," the councillor admitted, grinning. "And if you don't mind my saying, you seem a little young yourself to be teaching the ray of sunshine there."

"I've been doing this for a while, Councillor." On the outside, Jors remained calm and confident. Inside, a little voice was saying, *Oh that's just great. It's obvious to everyone.* "And Alyise is a trained Herald. I'm only here to help guide her through her first Circuit."

"Oh, I'm not criticizing, lad. And given that one's energy, it's probably best you're no graybeard. I imagine she'd be the death of an older man."

The councillor obviously believed he was sleeping with Alyise. That was a belief he'd have to nip in the bud. "Heralds aren't in the habit of taking advantage of their Interns."

"Advantage?" The elderly councillor glanced over at Alyise and began to laugh so hard he passed a mouthful of cider out his nose. "Oh, lad," he gasped when he had breath enough to speak again. "You *are* young."

There wasn't a lot Jors could say to that.

:You seem fine in the villages,: Gervais pointed out as they headed toward the Border.

:It's different in the villages.: Jors told him. *:We have well-defined roles and I know what I'm supposed to do.:*

:You've always known what to do in a Waystation before. You've always know what to do with another Herald before.:

He glanced over at Alyise who'd turned to check on the mules. *:I've never been responsible for another Herald before.:*

His Companion sighed and raised his head so Jors could get at an elusive itch under the edge of his mane. *:You're beginning to worry me.:*

There wasn't a lot Jors could say to that either.

Six days later Alyise handed him a mug of tea and said, "Is it because you like boys? It's just that I've been as obvious as I know how without coming right out and saying we should bed down together," she explained a few moments later, after they cleaned up the mess. "I mean, I was with Jennet for seven whole months and you're cute and well, it's been a while, you know."

He knew.

"Your ears are very red," she added.

Jors attempted to explain about being responsible and not taking advantage of her while he was in at least a nominal position of power. Alyise didn't seem to quite understand his point.

"You're a little young to take such a grandfatherly attitude, don't you think?"

"That's it, exactly."

She wrinkled her nose, confused. "What's it?"

She was adorable when she wrinkled her nose and some of the tea had splashed on her tunic drawing his eye right to . . .

"Maybe you should talk to Donnel about it," he choked out. "I need to check the um . . . mules."

"I just checked them."

"I meant the . . . um, stores!"

"Gervais explained to Donnel who explained to me and I think I understand the problem." Alyise smiled at Jors reassuringly when he came back inside. "I was kind of dumped on you unexpectedly, wasn't I? I mean, there you were, out riding your circuit, just the two of you hearing petitions and riding to the rescue and being guys together and all of a sudden Jennet finds out her mother is sick and you've got me. I know Heralds are supposed to be adaptable and all, but this is a situation that could take some getting used to for you, so I expect it's all a matter of timing."

"Good. So we're um . . . ." He tried, not entirely successfully, to pull her actual meaning from the cheerful flow of words.

Her smile broadened. "We're good."

"Okay." Still, something felt not quite right. *:Gervais?:*

He could almost see his Companion roll sapphire eyes. *:I dealt with it, Chosen."*

:But . . . :

:Let it go.:

Not so much advice as an unarguable instruction.

"So . . ." Jors brought his attention back to the younger Herald. ". . . there were some tax problems in the area we're heading for next. We should go over them in case they come up again."

"Jennet and I ran into a few problems just like this back last month. Well, not just like this, because that's one thing I've learned since I've been out is that no two problems are exactly the same no matter how much they seem to be and . . ."

He let her words wash over him as he pulled the papers from his pack. So they were good. That was . . .

. . . good.

Why did he feel like he was waiting for the other shoe to drop?

Last year's tax problems didn't reoccur, but new problems arose, and Jors did his best to guide Alyise through them. She was better with people than he was and as summer passed into fall, he allowed her to hear those petitions that dealt with social problems and tried to learn from her natural charm as she learned from his experience.

Given her unflagging energy and exuberance, he felt as though he was running full out to stay ahead of her and he never felt younger or more unsuited for his position as her teacher as when he saw her in the midst of a crowd of admiring young men.

Not that she ever forgot she was a Herald on duty, it was just . . .

:*Just what, Chosen?*:

:You're laughing at me again, aren't you?:

No answer in words, just a strong feeling of amusement. Which was, of course, all the answer Jors needed.

Frost had touched the grass by the time they reached the tiny village of Halfrest, grown up not quite a generation before around a campsite that marked the halfway point on a shortcut between two larger towns. A shortcut only because the actual trade road followed the kind of ground sensible people built roads on rather than taking the direct route more suitable to goats.

Jors had a feeling that without the mule tied to her saddle, Alyise and Donnel would have been bounding like those goats from rock to rock, Alyise chattering cheerfully the entire time as they skirted the edges of crumbling cliffs.

The Waystation was brand-new, the wood still pale and raw looking. No corral had been built for the mules but a rope strung between two trees would take the lead lines, giving them plenty of room to graze. While there was no well, the pond looked crystal clear and cold.

"If you have a Waystation," Jors said as they carried their packs inside, "you're more than just a group of people trying to carve out an uncertain life. You're a real village."

"And that's important to them, to be seen as a real village?"

"This was wilderness when the elders of this village came here with their parents. They're proud of what they've accomplished."

He reminded her of that again as they rode into Halfrest which was, in point of fact, nothing much more than a group of people trying to carve out an uncertain life. Livestock still shared many of the same buildings as their owners and function ruled over form. Only the Meeting Hall bore any decoration—graceful, joyful carvings tucked up under the gabled eaves gave some promise of what could be when they finally got a bit ahead.

"Because a real village has a Meeting Hall?" Alyise asked quietly as they dismounted.

He nodded and turned to greet the approaching men and women.

They had not had an easy year of it. There had been sickness and raiders and heavy rains, then sickness again.

"We had no Harvest Festival this year," a weary woman told them, pushing graying hair off her face with a thin hand. "With so many sick, there were few to bring the harvest in so when the fields were finally clear the time was past. We had little heart for it besides. But there are two pigs fattening, pledged for the festival last spring. One came from my good black sow, and I feel I should be able to slaughter him for my own use."

"He was pledged to the village," an equally weary looking man interrupted.

"He was pledged to the festival!"

As there had been no festival it would seem sensible to give the pig back to the woman who had pledged it, perhaps requiring her to give some of the meat to those in need. But this was Alyise's judgment and Jors sat quietly behind her, allowing her to make up her own mind with no interference from him. He glanced around the Hall, from the work-roughened and exhausted villagers to the sullen knot of teenagers clumped together by the door. No one looked hungry or ill used, just tired. They'd been working nonstop for weeks. It was no wonder they'd skipped their festival, all they probably wanted was a chance to rest.

"I have heard all sides of the argument," Alyise said at last. "And this is my judgment." She paused, just for a moment, and Jors had the strangest feeling the other shoe was finally dropping. "The pig was pledged to the Harvest Festival. Have the festival."

"But the harvest has been in long since and . . ."

"The harvest is in," Alyise interrupted, her smile lighting all the dark corners of the room. "I think that's worth celebrating." Before anyone could protest, she locked eyes with the woman who owned the pig. "Don't you?"

"Well, yes, but . . ."

"The sickness is past. The raiders have been defeated. And that's worth celebrating, too." The man who had protested the reclaiming of the pig seemed stunned by her smile. "Don't you think so?"

"I guess . . ."

"And the rains have stopped." She spread her arms and turned to the teenagers by the door. "The sun is shining. Why not celebrate that?"

Shoulders straightened. Tentative smiles answered her question.

No one stood against Alyise's enthusiasm for long. Soon, to Jors' surprise, no one wanted to. The pigs were slaughtered and dressed and put in pits to roast. Tables were set up in the hall. Food and drink began to appear. Musicians brought out their instruments.

"I'd have thought they were too tired to party," Jors murmured as half a dozen girls ran giggling by with armloads of the last bright leaves of fall.

"My mother has a saying; if you don't celebrate your victories, all you remember are your defeats. The food they're eating now won't be enough to make a real difference if the winter is especially hard, but the memories they

make, good memories of laughter and fellowship, that could
be enough to see them through." Alyise gestured toward
the carvings. "They know joy. I just helped them remember
they knew. You know?"

He did actually.

:Careful, Chosen.: Gervais adjusted his gait as Jors listed
slightly to the left.

"You lied to me." Alyise's Whites were a beacon in
the darkness. Which was good because he didn't think he
could find her otherwise. Except that she was on Donnel
and that made it pretty obvious where she was now he
considered it.

"What did I lie about?"

"You said that was apple . . . apple jush. Juice."

She giggled. "It was once."

"Jack. That wash apples jack." He wasn't drunk. Heralds
did not get drunk on duty even at impromptu Harvest Fes-
tivals where the apple juice wasn't. Which he wouldn't have
had any of had Alyise not handed him a huge mug just
before they left to toast the celebration and the celebrants.

Now the night was spinning gently around him and he
suspected that getting the Companions settled for the night
was going to be interesting.

Fortunately, it seemed that Alyise was less affected.

"Hey." He set his saddle down with exaggerated care.
"You had some of that, too!"

"Some," she agreed, the dimples appearing. "Come on
inside."

Her hand was warm on his arm. Then it was warm under
his tunic. And her mouth tasted warm and sweet. And . . .
Wait a minute. He pulled back although his hands, seemingly with a mind of their own, continued working on her
laces.

"I don't think . . ."

Her eyes gleamed. "What?"

He couldn't remember. *:Gervais?:*

*:She got you drunk and now she's taking advantage of
you.:*

:What?:

:It was Donnel's suggestion, but it seemed sound.:

The bunk hit the back of his legs and he was suddenly lying down holding a soft, willing body.

:*Help.*:

His Companion's mental voice held layers of laughter. :*Say that like you mean it, Heart-brother.*:

Actually, for a while, he wasn't able to say anything much at all.

Jors stood staring down at the pond watching the early morning sun tease tendrils of fog off the icy-looking water, trying to work the kinks out of muscles he hadn't used for far too long. Alyise was as enthusiastic in bed as she was about everything else and he'd been hard-pressed to keep up.

He guessed he had been a bit of an ass about that whole position of power thing. Still . . .

:*What is it, Chosen?*: Gervais' velvet nose prodded him in the back.

:*I'm still her mentor for another seven months. What if this changes things between us?*:

:*You think she will no longer trust your judgment because you have shared her bed?*:

Put that way it sounded a bit insulting. :*Well, no.*:

:*Then what is the problem?*:

There didn't seem to be one. Jors leaned against his Companion's comforting bulk and thought about it.

He wasn't Jennet.

Alyise was a Herald. That made her responsible for herself.

Donnel said his Chosen was glad he was a young man.

They had well-defined roles in the villages.

There was no reason for them not to continue sharing a bed as long as they both remained willing. No reason at all for it to detract from his ability to teach what he knew or learn what she offered.

Jors grinned. He had other nights like last night to look forward to and days of cheerful conversations combined with an enthusiastic welcome to whatever the road ahead might bring, and a high-energy approach to life that definitely got results since a village-wide party turned out to solve a petition about a disputed pig.

His grin faded as a muscle twinged in his back.

"Havens," he sighed, as he realized what the next few months would bring, "I'm too old for this."

Gervais' weight was suddenly no longer a comforting presence at his back but rather a short, sharp shove.

The water in the pond was as cold as it looked.

WAR CRY

by Michael Longcor

Michael Longcor is a writer and singer-songwriter from Indiana who wrote a dozen songs for the Mercedes Lackey album, *Owlflight,* released by Firebird Arts & Music. He's also had stories appear in the Mercedes Lackey anthologies *Sun In Glory* and *Bedlam's Edge.* Here, he tells the tale of a young Valdemaran soldier with a dangerous problem facing his first big battle and the bloody, final clash of the Tedrel Wars.

RURY Tellar pulled the blanket closer around his shoulders and stared into the yellow heart of the campfire. The blanket and the Valdemaran Guard surcoat were enough to keep off the night's cool, but still he shivered. His throbbing head didn't dim the whispering feelings crowding in; feelings of doubt, fear, hope, despair, cheer, loneliness and sadness—the massed feelings of an army camped close on the eve of battle.

It had started three weeks ago, soon after his seventeenth birthday and the call for the Oakdell village militia to march off and join the main army. The intruding feelings were very faint at first, like the not-quite-words heard late at night in the settling of an old house. They'd grown steadily stronger and now they constantly jostled his thoughts. His head ached with the pressure of other people cramming in. Sometimes he felt like his brain was the anvil from the blacksmith shop where he'd apprenticed, with strangers' feelings hammering and ringing on it like the smith's sledge.

169

Around him were the night sounds of an army encamped. Thousands of soldiers shifted in sleep, muttered in dreams, coughed, or whispered curses. The air smelled strongly of campfire smoke and more faintly of horse dung. Ten paces away, Aed snored in the tent alongside Milo and Snipe. Rury would likely have to nudge space to lie down between them when he finally turned in.

They'd been in the big camp for two days, waiting for the Tedrel army to come over the border. Somehow the brass hats knew the Tedrels would cross near here, and there would be plenty of them. Camp gossip said this would be the last battle of the Tedrel Wars, one way or another.

Rury was tired, but trying to sleep made it easier for the feelings of others to crowd in. It was better, a little, to sit and stare at the dying fire until his eyelids drooped and his head nodded.

At first he'd mentioned the headaches to the others, but stopped because his comrades might think he was shirking, or crazy, or worse, scared. He *was* scared. He'd do his best, though, no matter how afraid he felt. But he could *feel* when people around him were afraid, and their feelings ran through him, adding to his own fears.

It didn't help to know the rest of the unit was scared, too, except for maybe Sergeant Krandal. They were all young and scared and afraid to let it show, afraid of looking like cowards. Last night Princess Selenay herself had briefly visited the company campfire, shadowed by her bodyguard. She was young and lovely, and seemed brave and genuinely interested in them. Rury knew, even if the others didn't, that she was afraid of what was coming, too, no matter how brave her words.

"Trouble sleeping again, Tellar?" Rury jumped as Sergeant Krandal stepped into the firelight. It glinted on the silver-gray in his close-trimmed beard and the white horse of the Valdemaran arms on his blue surcoat. He was no taller than Rury, but built square and solid, where Rury was lean young muscle.

"Uh, just thought I'd get a little quiet time, Sarge." Rury shrugged. "Aed's snoring shakes the tent, and Snipe talks in his sleep."

Krandal smiled and shook his head. "Still having trouble with the headaches?"

"Ah, they come and go," said Rury. "Uh, maybe I better turn in anyway." He got up and walked to the tent. "G'night, Sarge."

"Good night, soldier." Sergeant Krandal said softly. He was concerned, and not for the boy's health. Mit Krandal had seen twenty-eight years of Guard service and thousands of young soldiers before his retirement to Oakdell two years ago. Rury Tellar was a good kid; well-liked, big and strong, with good fighting moves and the makings of a fine soldier. Krandal knew all the symptoms of a youngster facing his first fight, but Tellar's problem seemed more complicated and serious than that. He banked the fire and started walking. Instead of heading for his own tent, he steered toward the fires of the command tents a hilltop away. It was time to call in some help.

Even this late, the tents of the Communications and Intelligence sections bustled with candle-lit activity. Couriers came and went with the less pressing reports and orders. Urgent dispatches were sent off by the few Heralds who could make objects disappear, then reappear elsewhere. Others pored over big maps, keeping track of units, supplies, and numbers. They waded through seas of unrelated information, assembling tiny bits into bigger bits, and fitting it all into a hazy, incomplete picture of how things were.

Herald Erek Ranwellen pushed aside the reports scattered about his folding camp table, brushed away a stray lock of light-brown hair, and rubbed his eyes. It had been a long day. He felt ages older than his twenty-six years. His white leathers were mostly clean, but he longed for a bath and change of clothes. He should have turned in an hour ago like his Companion, Déanara.

He looked up at the sound of nervous throat-clearing to see a door sentry at attention before him.

"Yes, what is it?"

"Beggin' your pardon, Herald," said the soldier. "But there's a sergeant from the Pikes outside wantin' to see you."

"Did he say why?"

"No, sir. He just said to say you still owe him for turning a whiny little rich boy into a passable good soldier." The sentry's mouth barely twitched. "His words, sir, not mine."

Erek's eyes widened. He smiled broadly, to the sentry's wonder.

"Sergeant *Krandal*?" said Erek. " 'Iron Mit' Krandal's outside? Send him in, man, send him in!"

Sergeant Krandal's snap to attention and salute were parade-ground perfect, as was Erek's response. The grins and strong handshake that followed were less than regulation.

"Sergeant Krandal! I'll never get used to *you* saluting *me*."

"Aye, Erek . . . er, Herald." Sergeant Krandal's eyes twinkled. "Who'd have thought the company's biggest slacker would be chosen as a Herald. You even turned out a good soldier."

"Thanks to you, Sergeant."

"Maybe," said Krandal with a crooked grin. "A few hundred laps around the parade ground in full kit didn't hurt either."

"How is your lady wife?" asked Erek.

A shadow of pain crossed Sergeant Krandal's face.

"There was a fever, two winters past. She . . ." He looked away and waved weakly.

"I'm sorry. I didn't know."

"No way you would have. Anyway, I'm not here socially."

"What is it?"

"I need a favor."

"Thrust! Recover! Advance! Thrust!" Sergeant Krandal's voice cracked out the commands, and the Oakdell militia sweated through pike drill. Rury's tunic was damp under his armor, his hands sweaty on the spear shaft. They drilled two hours a day with the larger company, then Sergeant Krandal had them on the field for an extra hour after that. They needed it. The spears were half again as long as Rury, and the pikes even longer. They had to work together as a unit or people got hurt, even in drill.

They'd learned the basics of spear and pike back home, but there the militia's main job was fighting bandits and peacekeeping. The weapons were more likely to be sword, bow, or staff. The Guard, however, had decreed they were pike soldiers, so Pikes they had to become. For Rury, one good thing about drill was getting some small respite from the massed feelings pressing in. Those around him mostly suspended thought and feeling as they concentrated on the barked commands and responses.

"Rest in ranks," ordered Sergeant Krandal. The four rows of militia grounded the butts of their weapons gratefully and leaned on the shafts. The sergeant walked around the formation to face them. He upended the spear he carried and thrust it upright into the trampled sod.

"It took some doing to get these toys." He patted the short sword hanging off his right side, and the buckler, a small round shield two hand-spans in diameter, clipped at his left. All the militia members carried the same. "So you will oblige me by being proficient with them."

He had them lay down spears and walked them through various drills, drawing the sword with either hand and getting the buckler off the belt and up. They'd had months of training back home using larger shields and longer swords, and they were improving rapidly.

Aed Karlan, the group's self-appointed jester, muttered sidewise to Rury, "It's not enough we have to slog around with armor and pigstickers. We get to haul extra gear, too."

"You have questions, Karlan, or just gas?" said Sergeant Krandal. Aed flushed and stammered.

"Uh, just wondering, Sergeant. Why the extra weapons if the army thinks we're pike soldiers? Not that I mind 'em, but it'd be nice having a full-size sword and shield."

"That's simple enough," Sergeant Krandal replied. "Two lines of spears backed with two of pikes are a bit thin against a massed rush. Put a big force of heavies against you, or even an equal force whose front line cares more about running over you than staying alive, and you people will be playing kissy-face with the Tedrel. If that happens," he pointed at Aed's weapons, "those will give you a fighting chance. And there's no way to carry full-size weapons and still fight a spear in close order without getting hung up on your comrades." The sergeant smiled thinly. "I approve of soldiers asking questions." Aed looked relieved as Krandal continued, "but not soldiers talking in ranks. Karlan, you get wood and water duty tonight." Aed's look of relief melted.

"Dortha, front and center!" A dark-haired young woman

broke ranks and came on the double. "Run them through reverse-draw drills." Dortha was no-nonsense and as good a fighter as the men. After joining up she'd silenced snickers from the boys with a ready kick to the knee if they were lucky, somewhat higher if they weren't. She quickly got them into the rhythm of the drill, drawing the sword with blade reversed and pointing down, slashing up and across an enemy's face, then immediately sweeping back to stab face or throat.

Sergeant Krandal noticed the unit sneaking looks off behind him. He glanced back to see a small group of horsemen, most on brilliantly white mounts, turn off the camp road at the end of the drill field and trot toward them. The sunlight glinted off the armor and crown worn by the group's leader, and off the coat of the Companion he rode. Behind him a horseman bore the blue-and-silver standard of the King of Valdemar.

"Hold! Dress your ranks!" Sergeant Krandal snapped back to the militia. "I don't know why, but that's King Sendar coming to call. You lot follow my lead and show some respect, or you'll all spend the next week wishing you had!"

Sergeant Krandal turned back just as the group pulled up. He saluted and dropped to one knee. Clinking and rustling indicated the militia was following his example.

Now if they can just keep quiet.

Rury dropped to a knee with the rest. With the mindless rote of drill paused, he immediately felt the feelings of those around pressing on his mind. The militia were awed and a little apprehensive. Sergeant Krandal was mostly curious. From the king, Rury sensed an almost overwhelming weight of worry and sadness, but in front of it, like an army's standard in the charge, rode a spark of hope and pleasure.

King Sendar sat his Companion, leaned forward on the saddle, and smiled warmly.

"It's good to see you back in the field, Sergeant Krandal," the King said. The militia's eyes widened.

"It's good to be back, Your Majesty," replied Sergeant Krandal. "I may be getting old for this game, but I'm your man and Valdemar's to the end of it."

"I know that," said the king, "and I'm grateful." He

raised his eyes to take in the rest of the militia. "I'm grateful also, to every man and woman standing for our kingdom against the Tedrel. You may guess that I know your sergeant of old. I know, then, you are well trained. I see you are well-armed. This battle's outcome will depend on each of you. *I* depend on you. I know you will not fail me or Valdemar."

Rury felt his heart swell with pride, and sensed the same from his comrades. This was a king to follow, a king to fight for!

King Sendar sketched a salute to Sergeant Krandal, wheeled his Companion, and he and his entourage cantered back to the road.

All save one. One Herald, with the insignia of the Communications branch on his surcoat, remained behind. His Companion shifted with a delicate grace as he dismounted.

Sergeant Krandal walked over and saluted the Herald, then bowed deeply to his Companion, and it seemed to the gawking militia that the shining Companion returned the bow.

"My greetings to you, Lady Deanara." said Krandal. "You look even lovelier than usual." The Herald's companion dipped her head gravely and snorted.

"Dee says it's always a pleasure to meet the legendary Sergeant Krandal," said Erek, "and when's lunch?"

"We break in fifteen minutes or so," said Krandal with a grin. He turned back to the ranked militia.

"Back to work, people! You heard His Majesty. He's depending on you to save the kingdom. But don't get big heads about it!"

They sat on the grass in the common area between the company cook fires and the drill field. Lunch was cracked grain boiled with bits of sausage and what vegetables might be available, a staple of the Guard in the field. The troops had a dozen nicknames for it. The commonest and least profane was "Thunder Mud."

"The cooks are trying to kill us with this stuff," said Aed. "They sure cooked this until it's dead."

Sergeant Krandal snorted. He pulled a tiny bottle from his belt pouch, undid the stopper, and sprinkled a bit of reddish-orange powder on his food.

"Never let the cooks hear you gripe about the food," he said. "If you do, don't eat camp soup after that. Besides, any dish loses a lot when it's made for five hundred at a time. Perking it up's your problem."

"What's that stuff, Sarge?"

"Ground Karsite peppers. Guaranteed to put a little zip into anything the Guard dishes out." He restoppered the bottle, tasted his food, and nodded.

"Sarge," said Aed, looking to where Rury and Erek sat apart, with the Herald's white Companion standing behind, "is Rury in trouble?"

"We're all in trouble," muttered Sergeant Krandal. "It's just that we might be able to help Tellar with some of his."

Herald Erek seemed likable enough, but Rury had never met a Herald before, let alone had the personal attention of one. He was nervous.

"Guardsman Tellar," said Herald Erek after they got settled, "can I call you Rury?"

"Uh, sure," said Rury. "Am I in trouble or something?"

Erek smiled slightly. "Not with me, you're not. I'm just here to help with a problem you may have."

Rury felt the Herald's sincere concern, but he still didn't like where this was going. "I'm, uh, not sure what you mean."

"Let me make a guess," said Erek. "You think everyone around you is trying to climb into your head, or that maybe you're just going crazy." Erek's voice stayed calm, but it took control not to laugh aloud at Rury's open-mouthed, goggle-eyed response.

"What . . . how . . . ?"

"It's all right," said Erek. "May I touch your arm for a moment? It should help me help you." Rury held out his left arm in reply. Erek grasped Rury's wrist. His Companion, whom he'd introduced as Deanara, left off nibbling grain from a canvas bucket and swung her head to where Erek could place his free hand on her nose. Rury felt a gentle coolness brush his mind. A few moments passed and Erek released Rury's wrist.

"I was almost certain, but Dee confirms it." Said Erek. "you have a strong Gift of Empathy. I have a touch of it myself, though my major Gift is Mindspeech."

"It doesn't feel like a Gift," said Rury, "More like a curse."

"That's because you haven't learned how to keep other peoples' feelings out. It can go both ways, too. If you have strong emotions of your own, you can influence others around you."

"You mean like the rest of the militia?"

"Yes, especially with feelings like fear. They could feel afraid for no reason other than you're afraid."

Rury didn't want to think about what that might mean in a fight; the entire militia panicking because of him.

"Is there a cure?"

Erek chuckled, but cut it off. "Sorry. It's not a disease, so there's really no 'cure'. You can make it easier for yourself, though, and safer for your comrades. You need to learn ways to shield your feelings from others, and keep the emotions of others out."

"I could do that?" Rury looked like he'd been reprieved from a death sentence, which was just what Erek was trying to do.

They spent the rest of lunch break running over simple techniques. Rury seemed more relaxed at the end of it. Erek hoped it would be enough. Keeping out the random jitters of his comrades was one thing. Shielding against the raging emotions of two armies locked in mortal combat would be an entirely different beast.

The night was clear and cool, with stars twinkling in a black sky. No one looked at the stars. Soldiers glanced away from their fires toward the Karsite border, where an orange glow marked the encamped Tedrel horde. Tension and suppressed fear, thick and heavy, pushed through Rury's best attempts to shield his mind. His own fear kept intruding on his efforts to block out emotions of those around him.

Sergeant Krandal stood and stretched, wincing.

"Better hit the bag, people," he said. "We don't want to oversleep the party tomorrow."

"Sarge," said Snipe, "I heard the next company over is sleeping in their armor. Should we?"

The sergeant shook his head. "No, not unless you're sure you can actually sleep that way. If you have any clean, dry clothes with you, especially underclothes, change into those. Wouldn't hurt to keep your boots on either." He looked around. "Tellar and I will take first watch. The rest of you turn in."

They shuffled and muttered back to their tents. Sergeant Krandal had Rury take a position on the company's tent line, facing away from the banked fire. After noise from the tents settled down, he appeared at Rury's side.

"You might not feel like talking, Tellar," he said, "but tell me true, how's that empathy thing going?"

"It's better, Sarge. Really, it is." He paused, wondering if he should go on.

"But you still feel afraid," Sergeant Krandal said.

"Well . . . yeah, kind of."

"You'll be fine, lad." The sergeant smiled. "Every sane soldier is afraid at some time or another. It's what separates the good soldiers from the dead ones. A little fear is Nature's way of making you pay attention. If you feel afraid, use it. Stay calm and let it turn to something else, something you can use."

"What if I freeze up?"

"I doubt that'll happen. Let your training and reflexes take care of things while you deal with it. Herald Erek taught you ways to handle the Empathy, right?"

"Yeah, Sarge, but I'm not sure if I can make them work."

"Then turn in and practice until you sleep. I can handle the rest of the watch, and I want you fresh tomorrow."

"Sarge, I don't . . ."

"That's an order, Tellar," Sergeant Krandal said gruffly. "Go." His tone softened. "It'll be all right."

Krandal watched Rury trudge off, then muttered under his breath, "I hope."

Half a candlemark later, Erek and Deanara appeared at the edge of the firelight. Sergeant Krandal waved them in silently.

"Well?" he said, barely above a whisper.

Erek swung off Deanara, sighed heavily, and sat down. He replied in equally soft tones.

"I didn't get much farther than you did, Sergeant. The brass isn't about to pull one young pike soldier off the line this late in the game. I'm sorry." Behind him, Deanara gave a snort of disgust.

"I'm not surprised," Sergeant Krandal replied. "Guard policy is like Guard cooking. What's best for the army is usually hard on the individual soldier."

Erek nodded. "I did point out that an untrained Empath probably wouldn't survive the coming battle, and that the intensity and volume of emotion he'd face would leave him dead or insane." He sighed heavily. "They said there are hundreds, maybe thousands of young soldiers in this army who won't survive the battle, Empaths or not."

"They're right. So, what's to be done?"

"I spent what time I could teaching him shielding techniques. It wasn't much, but we have to hope it will do. We've simply run out of time. Can you shift him in the unit?"

"I could, but he's one of my best. And if he's capable of what you say, and he panics, he could take the whole unit with him. If he breaks, I'd just as soon it be where I can see him. I'll shift things so I'm behind him in the second line."

"So you can help if there's trouble?"

Sergeant Krandal stared into the fire a moment.

"So I can help him. And if it's the only way, so I can stop him."

Rury kept running the shielding exercises through his head as they donned armor in the dim light of predawn. Armor in the Guard was never completely uniform, even within units, except for what it had to protect. Leather and metal leggings covered Rury from crotch to foot. He pulled on a padded vest with separate, quilted sleeves, and over that a leather jerkin with small, overlapping iron plates stitched inside. More leather and metal covered arms and elbows, and an armored cowl covered throat, shoulders, upper back and chest. He looped the baldric suppporting his short sword over his left shoulder and secured it with a wide belt that also supported his water bottle, rations pouch, buckler and dagger. Reinforced leather gauntlets and a plain, well-made helmet finished the outfit. Rury bent and picked up his spear. He consciously felt the armor's weight only for a moment. Sergeant Krandal had been dril-

ling them in full kit since before they'd marched out from
Oakdell.

The sergeant appeared, wearing his armor as naturally
as if it were his skin. Stepping close to Rury he spoke
barely above a whisper.

"Remember, relax and let the training do the job. If you
feel fear, let it go to something else."

The sergeant stepped back and looked around at the militia, then smiled grimly.

"Boys and girls," he said, "it's time to go be soldiers.
Marching order, column of fours!"

They marched to the company's muster point, then
trudged to the valley in the dim red light of pre-dawn. The
upright rows of their shouldered weapons rippled as they
moved, like a field of grain waving deadly in the breeze. A
crow cawed harshly at their passing.

They reached the shallow stream marking Valdemar's
border with Karse and arrayed themselves there. Rury
stood on the front line with Aed and Snipe to either side.
Behind him were Sergeant Krandal and the others, their
presence reassuring. Perhaps five-score paces to his left
Rury could make out the King's standard fluttering bravely
in the breeze. To either side stretched the armored ranks
of Valdemar.

Muttering rippled through the Valdemaran ranks, as the
Tedrel Army crested the opposing hilltop. They came, and
came, and kept coming, armor glittering in the morning
sun. The measured tread of their march was like muffled
drums.

"That may be the scariest thing I've ever seen," muttered Aed.

"That's because you aren't them, looking at us." replied
the sergeant. "Look close. The front ranks aren't squared
off and hard lined like the ones behind. See how the officers are riding close on them. The Tedrel are running their
mongrel hounds out ahead. Those boys in front are nervous." He raised his voice. "I've seen more than my share
of fighters, and you people are better than that lot." He
grinned wryly. "Though it looks like it will be a while before we run out of Tedrels."

Rury knew the sergeant was trying to buck them up. Still,
he was glad of the confidence in Krandal's voice. As the

Tedrels filled the far slopes, the mutterings in his head grew to a low roar, even through the shields he tried to raise. The voices were back, and this time every voice was shouting hate and rage and desire for his death. For the first time in his young life, Rury seriously thought about the possibility of death, and that today he might die.

"Nice to see somebody remembered to invite the Tedrels," joked Aed. "So what do we do now?"

"We stop jabbering like a bunch of first-fight rookies, for starters," growled Sergeant Krandal, "then we settle in and wait. Stand easy."

The morning crawled on. The sun was well up now, glinting off the dew on the grass. Soldiers in the line held their positions, occasionally shifting their feet or drinking sparingly from water bottles.

Suddenly there was a cry as the Tedrel lines started moving. Their front ranks left the main body and advanced toward the little stream just ahead of Rury. They moved at a trot that sped up as they came down the slope.

"Dress your ranks!" shouted Sergeant Krandal. "Hold in place."

The Tedrels were up to a run, now, a wordless roar coming from their throats. Thousands on thousands charged down the hill, shaking the ground. Rury felt the vibration through his boot soles.

"Level weapons!" The front line of Tedrels reached the stream, lurching and splashing across.

"Hold steady!" Sergeant Krandal could barely be heard over the noise. *"Hold the . . ."* The rest was lost in crash, screams and drumming thunder as the lines slammed together and two armies each leaped for the other's throat. On either side of Rury, Tedrel fighters, unheeding of danger or unable to check their rush, impaled themselves on spear and pike points. For every Tedrel who did, two more fought to get past the spears and close with the fighters of Valdemar. The roar of clashing arms and screaming soldiers was deafening.

Rury nearly blacked out from the waves of emotion. He tasted bile in his throat. His head felt as if it would explode. A big Tedrel in bronze and leather armor knocked Rury's spear point aside with a shield rim and charged in. He hacked down and his sword bit into Rury's spear shaft with a crack. The shaft buckled. Rury saw death in the warrior's eyes, felt hate pouring from him as the Tedrel's sword came up again. The noise seemed to mute and time slowed to a crawl as Rury brought up the splintered remnant of his spear shaft and blocked the sword coming at his head.

Something happened, clicking into place in Rury's mind. The physical act of defending himself combined with the hurried training from Herald Erek and Sergeant Krandal's words.

"Stay calm. Let the fear and hate turn to something else."

He didn't need to stop the feelings, he just had to let them divert as they flowed into and through him. The hammering in his head and the sickness in his gut vanished. He felt the rage and fear of two armies coming to him, and felt it refracting, turning into . . . something else.

He held up the broken spear shaft like a talisman with his left hand and fumbled for his sword. The Tedrel swung again, but stopped short as Sergeant Krandal's spearhead hit the man's shoulder. The thrust didn't bite deep through the Tedrel's armor, but it hung him up.

The hours of training kicked in. Rury gripped his own sword, fist up and blade-down, and swept it out of the scabbard, slashing across the Tedrel's face. The cheek and nose-piece of the Tedrel's helmet turned most of the cut, but Rury's backhanded return stab took him just below the chin. The Tedrel dropped like a puppet with cut strings. His blood bathed Rury's sword and spattered his surcoat, filling Rury's nose with its coppery smell. A tidal flow of primal emotion roared into Rury, the greatest feeling of his young life. The dying Tedrel's anger, fear and lust surged and churned inside him, turning to something that felt strangely like love. Love of his enemies. Love of battle. Love of killing. At that instant Rury Tellar became an angel of death.

Spears and pikes stabbed from behind and around him as Rury's comrades fought to fill the gap left by his broken spear. Another Tedrel forced an opening with his shield and rushed at Rury, his war hammer swinging high. Rury calmly stopped the charge cold by thrusting the splintered end of his spear shaft into the warrior's face, followed with a sword stab over the shield's rim. Whether the sword struck the Tedrel's face or throat, Rury couldn't see. He heard the man cry out and felt him sag, but the Tedrel didn't go down. Rury tried to draw the sword back, but it was stuck, jammed in bone or armor. He released the sword and wrenched the hammer from the man's faltering grip, then brought it around to crash on the Tedrel's helmet. The blow threw the man's body back into the Tedrel line.

In the moment's respite, Rury dropped the splintered spear shaft and had his buckler off his belt and up, still gripping the war hammer. The weapon was no nobleman's decorative piece, just a steel head with a long, narrow hammer face and wicked points on back, sides and front, mounted on an oak haft nearly as long as his arm. Whatever its form, it was a hammer, and Rury had spent four years at the forge using one. Driven by his hard-trained muscle, the hammer rose and fell on the pressing Tedrel host. Armor and bone crushed. With nearly every blow a man went down. The Tedrel fought to get a return blow on Rury, but Sergeant Krandal bellowed orders, and the militia's spears stabbed and clicked like giant, deadly knitting needles, taking down any Tedrel who gave Rury too much attention. Bodies piled before them, making a barrier that let their spears and pikes reach across to dart and tear.

Every Tedrel who died in pain and fear and rage fed energy into Rury. Every blow was like a lover's touch, every scream a sweetheart's whisper. He wanted it to never end. He would kill until no one lived on this bloody field, just to keep the song of love and death singing through him.

The Tedrels fell back a dozen steps, and arrows rained down on the Valdemaran line. Armor and luck proved good enough for the Oakdell militia, and they took little hurt. But the Tedrels had pulled back out of reach of his hammer, and Rury stood with impatient resentment.

The roar of battle eased for a moment, and he heard cries of commanders, getting louder as they relayed orders. Glancing to his left, Rury glimpsed the King's banner plunging across the stream and deep into the Tedrel host. And then Sergeant Krandal was shouting at his back.

"Advance the line! The king is leading! Advance the line! Move up to support the king! Move it! Move it *now*! *CHARGE!*"

Like a hunting dog released from its leash, Rury scrambled up and over the slick line of Tedrel bodies, trailed closely by the rest. There was a shock of wet and cold on feet and shins as they splashed into the shallow stream, now running a muddy crimson. Past the opposite bank stood a locked line of Tedrel shields. This time it was the soldiers of Valdemar who crashed into a line of steel. Rury gave it no thought. He only wanted to regain that wonderful feeling that came with killing.

His hammer crashed down on a Tedrel's wooden shield, splintering the arm that supported it. Another blow smashed a helm. The rest of the militia were with him now, exploiting gaps made by Rury's relentless blows. The Tedrel line gave ground before the young demon with the hammer and those terrible, thirsting spears.

"No!" thought Rury. *"Stay! Stay and let me love you!"* He smashed the shield of a lone Tedrel left in an opening cleared of live enemies. The shield sagged down, but before Rury could strike the killing blow a spear head thrust past him and took the Tedrel cleanly. As the man fell, Rury felt the rage of a child whose toy was taken.

Take my *kill, will you? Thwart* my *love?* Rury turned to see Aed pulling back his spear.

Then let you *be my love!* Rury smiled as he raised his hammer.

Far up the line the King's banner trembled and fell. Rury drew back his hammer, ready to send it smashing down on Aed's helmet.

Instead, lightning struck Rury.

A bolt of searing emotion ran through his mind and body, rushing through his veins, so intense he felt his fingers and toes must be sparking and flaring. It was a wave of feeling that screamed of pain, despair, death and the loss of loved ones.

OUR BELOVED! OUR CHOSEN! THEY HAVE KILLED THE COMPANIONS! THEY HAVE SLAIN THE KING!

It was too much! Too much power. Too much pain and raw emotion. Rury's mind reflexively redirected the bolt, casting it back out across the battlefield. His legs buckled and he sank to his knees, felt the hammer pulled from his grasp. He heard savage screaming as he fell, something about the King's death. He glimpsed Aed swinging the war hammer wildly, and Sergeant Krandal roaring wordlessly, running into the enemy ranks with his spear gripped high.

And then the dark closed in.

Erek limped as he picked his way across the wreckage of the battlefield, closely followed by Deanara. His uniform and the Companion's trappings were torn and dirty, here and there stained with blood. Communications and Intelligence people weren't supposed to be front line troops, but after the Valdemaran reserves had been ordered out to intercept the Tedrel cavalry ravaging the countryside, every Valdemaran who could hold a weapon became a combat soldier. Even with his mental shields up, he'd felt the call of grief and rage that marked the King's death. He and Dee had thrown themselves into the battle as ferociously as any. Erek wasn't certain who had channeled that wave of emotion, but he had an idea, and he had to find out.

Around them was what the worst of the nine hells must look like on a sunny day. Nothing in the universe is so horribly, totally messy as the aftermath of a battle. The metallic smell of blood and pungent aroma of feces from the dying and dead hung in the still air. The injured moaned and screamed. Figures on the ground writhed or lay much too still. Others like Erek and Deanara picked their way across ground littered by broken weapons, discarded armor, and awkwardly sprawled bodies. It was difficult getting through some sections without walking on limbs, torsos or faces. The former front lines were marked by raggedly piled rows of dead, like windrows of cut hay ready for harvesting.

He found them twenty paces or so beyond one of the largest piles, to the right of what had been the Valdemaran center. Sergeant Krandal sat sprawled in a small cleared area, bareheaded and with part of his armor stripped off. Rury lay with his head cradled in the sergeant's arms, sobbing like a child. Both were bloodstained and filthy. Sergeant Krandal looked up at the Herald's approach.

"How did you fare, Sergeant?" said Erek.

Sergeant Krandal gave a pained, crooked smile. "Better than we might have hoped. We gave far better than we took, but we did take losses. Six dead that I know of. Aed

took an ax to the shoulder. Lots of walking wounded. Dortha's got the rest out with the company, mopping up." He
winced and shifted his seat, and Erek saw the sergeant's
outstretched leg seeping blood through a crude bandage
ripped from a surcoat. "I took a scratch on the thigh,
enough to make me stay put." Krandal looked down at
Rury, who was quiet now, like a child who had cried itself
almost to sleep.

"The boy seemed to master that empathy thing about
the time they closed with us. He fought like a Karsite
demon after that. That was mostly why we weren't overrun.
Then right after the King died, when we all somehow *knew*
he'd been killed, I was filled with grief and rage like I'd
never known. That's when I saw the boy go down. He
wasn't struck down, just dropped like he was dead. There
wasn't time to check on him then. We were all too busy
trying to rip out the Tedrels' throats with our teeth. At
least that's what it felt like. It was as if the boy's demons
burned him out and jumped to all of us."

Erek knelt and laid a hand on Rury's forehead as if
checking for a fever. Deanara snorted gently and drew
nearer, and Erek reached back and laid his free hand on
her velvety nose. He drew breath sharply after a moment,
removed his hands from Rury and Dee, and stood up.

"Find something?" said the Sergeant, frowning. Erek
sighed.

"Dee thinks he was something like a conduit for what
you and I and everyone else felt. I agree. When the King
was killed, when he and his bodyguard and their Companions and the other mounts were being cut down, the Companions knew it. Those directly involved *felt* their Chosen
pierced and dying, felt the pain and panic and death of
their fellows. They put out a combined mind-scream that
must have hit Rury like a thunderbolt. My guess is he threw
it back out over the army, probably translated somehow so
that even the least sensitive Valdemaran could understand
it." Erek stood stiffly.

"We can't find any trace now of his Empathic talents. I
think you're righter than you know when you say his
demons burned him out. What he did was an instinctive
reaction, but that's how we all felt the King's death at the

same instant. Whether or not he meant to do it, it helped turn the tide of the battle."

Krandal stroked Rury's head like a concerned mother. The boy's breathing evened out.

"Will he recover?"

"We need to get him to the Healers. You, too, for that matter. He'll certainly be affected, but no youngster goes through a war unchanged. With help and time, I think he'll be well enough." Erek paused and frowned. "We'd best keep this to ourselves, at least for now. The Companions will know, and some of the Heralds, but they won't gossip about it. I'll pass it on to those in the Guard with a need to know." Erek stopped abruptly as Rury opened his eyes and raised himself up on an elbow.

"How do you feel, Rury?" said Erek.

"My . . . head hurts." Rury replied. "But not like before."

Sergeant Krandal let out a long breath.

"At least you're alive, lad."

"I heard what you said," said Rury to Erek. "I didn't mean to send those feelings back out to everyone. It was like catching a red-hot iron. You just want to throw it back."

"I'm sorry you had to bear that, Rury," said Erek.

"I'm glad it happened, I guess." replied Rury. "I don't think I liked what I was feeling before that. Or maybe I liked it too much. When it hit me, it was like a basin of iced water in my face when I was having a nightmare." He paused and closed his eyes for a moment, then opened them. "And you're right, I can't sense other people's feelings now." Another thoughtful pause. "Is it true the King is dead?"

"It's true," said Erek soberly. He raised an arm and pointed to where a small group of riders picked their way down to where King Sendar lay fallen. At their head rode Princess, no, now Queen Selenay. "King Sendar's dead, but his kingdom still lives, and the Princess; thanks to you and all of us who fought today."

"I don't want to fight anymore," said Rury from where he lay. "And I don't want to kill. I just want to go home."

Erek smiled sadly. "That's all any of us wanted, Rury.

Perhaps when you sent out that cry we all truly realized what the Tedrel would take from us. Maybe that's why we won out in the end."

"Well," grunted Sergeant Krandal, "right now none of us look like we won." He reached up a hand and grimaced as Erek hauled him to his feet. "I'm getting too old for this." He tried his injured leg, winced, and balanced on his good one while Erek helped Rury up.

In the distance a body wrapped in the King's banner was borne and carried up the hill by Heralds and officers, followed by a young, new Queen. None noticed three ragged men and a Companion, upon whom the tide of battle may have turned, limping slowly away.

Years passed, and old veterans remembered their own golden valor, a heroic king and a brave, beautiful girl made queen. The memory of a searing cry piercing the thunder of war faded, until it was less than the distant calling of crows on a battlefield far from home.

STRENGTH AND HONOR

by Ben Ohlander

Ben Ohlander was born in South Dakota in 1965 and grew up in Colorado and North Carolina. After completing high school, he did a stretch in the Marines before attending college in Ohio. Upon graduation, he was commissioned as an officer in the Army Reserve, and is now serving on active duty in eastern Iraq. In his civilian interludes he works as a data analyst, part-time writer, and cat owner. He currently lives in southwest Ohio.

COGERN, Warmaster of the Nineteenth Foot, Hero of the Regiment, and Beloved of V'kandis, paced in the blazing desert sun. A distant smudge on the horizon drew his eye. He watched it a while as it spread laterally. The thought of an attacking force crossing the high desert at noon fell into folly, but he looked for it anyway. Folly, served judiciously, could be well employed. He'd employed it himself.

The smudge resolved itself. Not infantry. Dust storm. Typical weather for this time of year, but one of his least favorite things about his home country. He often wondered why they fought so hard to defend the place. The oft-heard comment was that the sun was the gift of V'kandis . . . too bad he'd been so generous. Dust storm looked like it would pass them by.

He wiped the sweat that rolled down his scarred head with his dog rag and checked the sentries. They were all alert and jittery. The village that lay hard by the oasis should have been brimming with life . . . children playing, women coming down for water. The presence of two thousand soldiers in the area should have meant a steady stream of fruit sellers, merchants, and the odd maiden intent on trading favors for silver.

Now, nothing. No bodies, no sign of the haste or force. Just no villagers. The place had been abandoned, as though everyone—man, woman, and brat—had simply walked away. The empty village wasn't central to their being there, but it felt bad.

Cogern wiped his brow again, tracing a clean streak in the dust that marked his forehead. He hated mysteries, especially when his regiment lay vulnerable . . . sprawled, with armor shed, in the thin shade of the date palms that clustered close to the oasis. He didn't need to look back to know that most men slept while others diced or talked quietly. All moved as little as possible.

He glanced to his right, seeing movement. A soldier made water, catching the fluid in a small bowl for the chirurgeon, who stood nearby. Cogern shook his head and stepped over. He would have dismissed the Valdemaran as a quack, just another foreigner with strange notions . . . had it not been for the man's skill with the arrow-spoon and scalpel. Cogern knew little about the chirurgeon, only that Tregaran had taken his service after some vague indiscretion back home. Cogern appreciated the man's skill and soft hands, but not his motives. That made him bear watching.

Cogern shook his head in polite disbelief as the man swirled the water in his bowl. The chirurgeon believed a good deal in piss.

"See, the dark water here?" the Valdemaran said, his accent mauling Karse's more sophisticated sibilants. His head and the trooper's leaned together, peering into the bowl. "These are your humors, growing cloudy. You need to keep them flushed out. Dark-yellow or brown mark a sure sign that your body's fluids are clogging up. Yellow is liver humor, light-colored, not so bad. Dark yellow, is bad. Brown worse."

Cogern, interested in spite of the obvious quackery, craned his head a little, to better see. "Then what?"

The quack with the soft hands looked at him and smiled.

"Ah, Warmaster. A little interest? If the humors get too thick, aren't kept flushed out, then they back up and clog the heart. You die."

The trooper looked worriedly into his bowl. "Ahm I gunna dic?" His homespun accent and credulity gave away his country roots.

The chirurgeon glanced sideways and smiled. "A laxative, a quick lancet to the wrist vein to bleed a little, and as much water as could be drunk oft fixes the imbalance."

The trooper paled. "Ah, lancet?"

The quack smiled. "Maybe not the lancet. Drink as much water as you can hold, and bring your bowl to me tonight. If it's clear, we'll hold the lancet for now."

The trooper nodded once and moved away. Cogern smiled as the lad headed for the Oasis.

The chirurgeon grinned. "The water seems the most needful. The laxative is only if the stools dry out and become too firm. The needle . . ."

Cogern understood. "Soldiers trade in blood, and hate to see their own shed. The trooper will drink to bursting to avoid being bled. Clever."

Cogern didn't have any use for chirurgeons, but he did admit this one knew his trade better than most. Most proved no better than butchers, and far too many enjoyed the blood shed. Though, to be honest, he did keep track of the color of his water now. No man but an enemy would bleed him, but drinking a little more water every now and again didn't seem to hurt. As for the rest. *"Feh. Pure quackery."*

The chirurgeon, understanding he'd been dismissed, eased away.

"Quit stalling, man," Cogern said to himself, as the quack stepped away to check on the next man. "Time to get it over with."

He crossed to the colonel's tent, passed between the sweating sentries with a nod, and entered. Inside, he drew himself up into full attention. "Sir, the warmaster requests permission to speak!"

Colonel Tregaran groaned once, then sat up on the low cot. He shook out the drowsiness and pulled the sleeping rug around his shoulders. He felt a twinge in the left shoulder, where the Hardornan's arrow had pierced the shield. He rubbed it ruefully. Sweat burst out of every pore, even from that small movement. He squinted at the warmaster.

Cogern's sudden affliction of formality did not bode well. He glanced at the shade outside, and shadows in the distance. Not much into the second watch of the day. Not even noon, and the heat already a blast furnace.

"Wine?" he asked, bending to pour some of the thin, sour stuff into a camp cup. "No?" He pointed toward the village with his chin. "Any sign?"

Cogern shook his head once. "No. Scouts have been out all morning. Solid trail, sir, going back up into the wadis, but no idea of why. Doesn't look like a threat. It's just . . . strange."

"Yes," Tregaran agreed, "but it's part of the reason we're here."

He felt Cogern relax. The commander's duty to set the orders, the warmaster's to keep them. Cogern was used to being aware of his colonel's thoughts, though, and Tregaran's refusal to include the warmaster this time had chafed the older man.

Cogern leaped like a stone-lion at Tregaran's opening, his bottled frustration spilling over. "Sir, what in the nineteen hells are we doing here?" Having started, his carefully rehearsed speech abandoned him, and the rest tumbled out in a heap. "We left our post, followed you across the high desert in summer, and laagered within a night's march from Sunhame. Why?"

Tregaran took a sip of wine, making a face at the sour bite. He looked down at the cup and the slightly oily surface of the liquid inside. He smiled, and made the decision to give it to the warmaster straight up. "The Black-robes have assembled a force . . . an army really . . . and are preparing to overthrow the hierarchs, and put one of their own on the Sun Seat."

Cogern prided himself on being unflappable, no matter the provocation. The slight widening of his eyes equaled most others' dropping jaw. He sat on the camp stool without being bid and reached out blindly. Tregaran smiled and handed him the cup. Cogern drained it, held it out for a refill, and emptied it as well. Tregaran watched Cogern work it out.

"But Laskaris must surely know. Won't he put a stop to it?" The warmaster shook his head, answering his own question. "No, he's too busy buggering boys, and the hierarchs are either too drunk to notice or well paid to look the other way." He chewed his lip, thinking. "The Black-robes will 'save' the faith, and our precious god hasn't put in an appearance so say what he thinks." He shook his head. "It's that simple. So, what's to stop them?"

Cogern played the role of the simple soldier, not too bright really, proof you didn't need brains to survive in the army. Tregaran knew the act for what it was. Not much got past the warmaster's washed-out blue eyes. He wouldn't have made thirty-five years in the line if it did. His blunt face, hare-lipped scar, and lisping gravelly voice all hid a quick and ready mind.

He let his silence answer for him. Tregaran reached for a second battered cup and poured more sour wine.

The warmaster's eyes tracked him, working it out. "Us?" A pause. "Us. Bugger me." He looked hard at Tregaran, sensing more to this.

"Why do we care? Laskaris the boy-lover, or some Black-robe. Thinning the herd among the Heirarchs has been a long time coming."

Tregaran nodded grimly. "It won't be just Laskaris, or even the Hierarchs who will die. When the Black-robes strike, they will have to take down all of the ministries, decapitate the entire government. They know that the Red-robes will have no choice but to fight. So, the Black shall strike down the Red. ALL of the Red-robes in Sunhame. I can't allow that."

Cogern exhaled deeply. *There it is. The real reason.* "So, then. This is for her."

Tregaran looked long and hard at him. "Yes. For Solaris."

Cogern's jaw firmed. He flashed back to the miracles performed, the regiment's adoration, Tregaran's increasing attentiveness during the months she had traveled with them. He had his own suspicions about the colonel's motives, but they owed her . . . dammit, HE owed her.

Cogern stretched his arms, corded muscle stretching. "Who else knows?"

Tregaran shugged. "Not sure. Delrimmon of the Thirteenth is close, I think a couple others. Hergram of the Thirty-first, probably.''

Cogern's face grew grim. "So, no orders, then." It was not a question.

Tregaran's pursed lips and single head shake made the word unnecessary. "No orders."

Cogern stood. "Sir, I want to make sure that I understand what we're for. We commit treason here, just by moving without orders. We strike against V'Kandis' own priests, and if the army splits, then we start a civil war. A civil war to protect one middle-ranking priest?"

Tregaran met his gaze, long and level. "Yes."

Cogern shugged and took a deep breath. "Okay, I'm in. Never liked any of those bastards anyway." He rubbed his hand over his face, touching the harelip. "How d'ya know all this?"

Tregaran smiled, measuring how far Cogern was out of depth by his lack of "Sir's". The warmaster, even in the worst battle, the line broken, and enemy in the camp, would never let the honorifics slip. Tregaran nodded over to the firecat, who lay curled up on the camp chest, quietly watching. He had finally gotten used to the 'cats ability to simply . . . be overlooked. He gestured to it, a sort of *"Well?"* Cogern's eyes followed his hand.

The cat chose to be noticed.

Cogern took a deep breath, air hissing between his gapped front teeth, as he registered its presence. "Is that a firecat? A real firecat? It told you?"

The 'cat, its tail kinked in annoyance, stretched and hopped down from the chest. *"Yes."* The creature's voice sounded clearly in their heads, irritation clear to them both. *"IT told him, and IT is hungry . . . and as you haven't even a saucer of milk for IT, IT is going to find ITS own damn dinner."* It stalked out of the tent, stiff-legged, tail still bent and flicking, a semaphore for a feline snit. *"IT. Peasants."*

Cogern jumped in his seat as the 'cat's mental voice sounded clearly in their heads, the offended tones fading as the avatar, insulted, stalked away. "What's got his tail in a kink?" He looked back at Tregaran.

Tregaran shook his head. Cogern was, if nothing else, flexible. In the space of a few moments the warmaster had

moved from an empty village, placed himself in opposition
to the strongest force in the land, and insulted the avatar
of the god himself, without seeming to show the slightest
concern.

He smiled, then reached into his pack for the carefully
rolled map.

"You're gonna love this."

Tregaran, followed by Cogern and the regiment's officers,
jogged hard up the hill. The late afternoon sun lay almost
directly behind them throwing long, red shadows. They
closed quickly on the ring of scouts who stared down at
what Tregaran first took for a pile of laundry. The circle
parted for them.

The townsman lay staked out in the sand, naked alongside the trail of the missing villagers. His belly had been
opened and the entrails carefully removed, so carefully that
none had torn, and there remained astonishingly little
blood. The man had most likely died from the exposure of
being staked out, rather than the vivisection. The corded
muscles and death rictus gave evidence of the man's agony.

The scout who'd marked the back-trail stood nearby. His
hands shook and his face was still pale, even after vomiting
into the sand. Tregaran didn't blame him. He was little
more than a boy, a stock thief saved by a stint in the army
from Karse's rough justice. Tregaran looked at his pale face
and shaking hands, and wondered if the boy thought keeping his hand now seemed a bargain.

Cogern toed the body with his boot, breaking into Tregaran's thoughts. "What does this mind you of?"

Tregaran was a few seconds late. Mindalis, a scout leader,
piped in first. "The man we found up by the border, Warmaster. The man with the horse."

"Yeah," Cogern said, in a troubled voice. "All we need
is a horse's head on a pike, and this'd be a perfect match."
He looked at Tregaran under his brows. "Absolutely perfect. This could be the same guy."

Tregaran studied the body, comparing it to a body found
in the borderland hills where Karse and Valdemar came
together in the regiment's Terilee River sector. The dead
Herald, staked and tied out . . . not naked, but with his

white leathers still about him to show what he had been.
He had similarly been tied, flayed, and left to suffer unto
death. Identically tied, once Tregaran saw what to look for.

"The Herald was little more than a boy," Tregaran said
slowly. "Whatever secrets he held would have been given
up early in the torment. What had taken place after that
had been for *fun*."

Yet, the Herald's surgical pain looked nothing to the out-
rages visited on the horse. The animal had been torn apart,
by a hatred strong enough to shatter equine bones. The
animal's head, blue eyes open, set on a spearstave.

He returned to himself and shivered. Cogern's marking
the spear as Karsite, and the presence high on the border
where Karse's brave defenders protected them from the
demon horses of Valdemar. The official version had paled
when faced with the reality. They did not protect Karse
from the demons . . . they protected the demons. A hard
moment, the worst of his life.

Tregaran bent to look at the man's hands. A laborer's
calluses, not a swordsman's. He lay near the trail of the
missing villagers, so was likely one of them. Whatever
caused this man to die, it was even less then the Herald.
That, at least, could be laid to spying. This? He could think
of no sane reason.

"Officers," Tregaran said, "file the regiment by. Let them
get a good long look at what they are fighting against. We
march at dusk. Blood for blood. Strength and honor."

The lead scout pounded in on a stolen . . . borrowed
horse.

"Sir, Thirteenth regiment reports having secured the
crossroads. They will drive on to the city's edge. They expect to ring the Sunlord's by dawn. No sign of the Thirty-
first yet."

The firecat beside him looked up. *Not to worry. Her-
grim's Thirty-first ran into more than they bargained for.
Hardornan mercenaries, of all things, serving the Black.
Most of the Black-robes' mercenaries are dead, the rest scattered. In the name of the Good God, they'll be at the city
by dawn.* It stretched and yawned, its job done.

"All right," Tregaran replied, to the scout. "Give the
Warmaster the same report and tell him to bring up the

rest of the regiment. Once we've secured the priory, we'll drive onto the city." He paused, looking over the scout's shoulder. "Never mind, the warmaster's here."

The older man, also on a "found" horse, halted in a spray of dust. The animal heaved and swayed. Cogern didn't so much ride horses as wrestle them.

"Sir," he said, while trying to control his snapping mount, "scouts report a village ahead. The trail goes straight in. Big fires. You'll see 'em on the horizon once you come up out of the wadi."

Tregaran shook his head. "No, our line of travel is north against the priory. That's were they've massed their strength."

Cogern shook his, a broad sweeping "no." "Sir, looks like the Black-robes are drawn out. Not at the priory. Troops, mebbe a couple hundred. Priests out doing the Fires. Scout says there are mebbe forty to fifty Robes down there, and villagers. Hundreds of them."

Tregaran puffed out his cheeks, thinking. "Okay, the village. Second Battle for the assault, hold the other two in reserve. It's going to be too tight in there for one than one Battle at a time."

Cogern nodded, rapping out orders to the under officers. The regiment shook itself out, moving from traveling order to assault column, then picked up Cogern's trot.

Tregaran, a little ahead with the scouts, crested the wadi, and saw the firelight glow from over the low hills. Pillars of smoke rose, then spread out forming a black layer like a roof over the burning. The lurid red flames flickered and danced against the smoke and clouds, giving the little valley a hellish cast.

Second Battle came clattering up behind him, shields at the ready.

One scout, momentarily highlighted against the flickering red background, swung a piece of cloth over his head. Any sentries placed were now dead.

Tregaran led his Battle forward, charging up out of the wadi, across the flat ground, and started up the slope to where the scout now lay hidden. He heard the rest of the Battle, some four hundred men, go to ground below them. They sounded like a herd of horses puffing and blowing after the exertion of climbing the hill.

He leaned his head up over the crest of the hill, and
peered over. The outer portion of the village glowed eerily
in the firelight. Flames from fires leaped high, at thrice the
height of a grown man. The firelight threw more red than
yellow, the bonfires set in a rough circle around the outer
court. The same pillars of smoke all but blocked the view
into the inner part of the village. Tregaran could see the
impression of more fires but little details. The rising smoke
formed a complete veil over the town square.

He shook his head. Karse, wood-poor as it was, lost a
treasure in the fires that night. An entire forest had to have
gone into creating this much burning.

A knot of troops, several hundred strong, came into view
from the village center. They formed a rough line, facing
the regiment behind the hill. They obviously meant to defend the village from the Nineteenth Foot.

"They're onto us, sir," said the scout.

"No kidding," replied Tregaran, then waved the horncallers to him. "Pass the word: 'Rise and Make Ready.' No
Horns."

The hornsmen scattered, running along the line and preparing the units for the charge. The Battle drawn into three
rough lines, stood ready.

Tregaran raised his sword over his head and cut it
down sharply.

"First sally. Go!"

The leading line of Second Battle gave the single shout
"V'KANDIS!" and charged. They crested the low hill and
sprang down the far side. The units' leading edges lost co-
herence in the steep slide down the hill, but training, discipline, and momentum carried them into the thin line the
Black-robes' warriors set to defend their chiefs.

The mercenary men fought like lions, but in the eternal
fight between soldier and warrior, soldier wins. The warriors, no matter how skilled, fought as singletons. The Men
of Karse, trained and blooded brethren, fought as part of
a larger unit. No shame in ganging two on one, three on
two, five on two. No honor in the line, just the imperative
of stab, guard, parry . . . shuffle step right to cover your
mate's exposed side. Thrust into the enemy's back. His bad
luck his mates didn't cover down.

The leading edge of Second Battle broke into the black-robes' line, fracturing it. Tregaran sent the second sally at that point, the men sliding down the steep slope. The reinforcements, piling into the first line, shattered the blackrobes' forces. They began to fall back. Warrior after warrior broke and ran as the fight turned south.

Tregaran still on the hilltop with the reserve, watched the enemy line fragment and fail.

He made a "come-here" gesture to the horncallers. "Blow 'Halt Pursuit. Form Double Line.'" He looked at the Battle's double squad of archers. They stood close by, weapons strung and ready. "Kill them," he said quietly.

The archers leaped into action. They used the new Rethwellen pattern bows, sinew and wood . . . all backed with horn. The weapons shot fearsome distances on a flat trajectory. The archers brought the weapons into play quickly, standing on the hilltop and taking a savage toll on the firelit men who fled. Tregaran noted that the archers killed as many as the line. The Black-robes' forces fell back into the village in disarray.

Tregaran's mind flashed to a place where a regiment used the bow to provide the bulk of the killing power, rather than just skirmishing. He had an image of a line of pikes with Reth' bows salted in, yard-long arrows in direct, flattrajectory fire, and two or three more rows of archers behind, shooting overhead. The pikes would hold cavalry at bay, likely enough, and the Reth' bows would punch through field armor for cert. If a half-company could work this slaughter, a regiment of bows would black the sun, and an arrow-storm that would shatter any unit closing. Valdemar's slow, heavy foot would never have a chance.

The "Cease Arms" call brought him back to the moment.

The last of the Black-robes' troops fled within the inner ring of houses surrounding the town square, depriving the archers of clear targets. Plunging fire remained an option, but there still remained at least one more fight tonight. Best to conserve arrows for the later fight.

He left a small detachment to guard the archers, and led the balance of the reserve down the hill. The horse they'd found for him plunged forward eagerly, not needing spur or goad. It nearly fell in the scree, and at one point sat down to avoid plunging tail over head.

The battle-line reformed quickly, the reserve moving to

its accustomed place. He passed their lines, his horse bucking a little at the soldiers' cheers. The troops' blood was
up. Winning did that, especially when the win laid low two
of three enemy with no loss on your side.

Tregaran led them into the Fire-lit streets, nearly staggering from the heat and smell. No wood fed these flames.
Instead, long bones marked the Fires' fuel. Each piled between knee and waist high, and all burning with an unholy
vitality. He was no stranger to battlefield carnage, enough
to estimate a death count, and his gut told him hundreds
lay slain just in the outer court. Most of the dead now
fueled these fires.

He heard the sounds behind him as the soldiers took in
the carnage and what burned in the fires all around. Their
morale would soften if he gave them too much time.

"To me," he bellowed. Then, "Charge!"

The Battle came behind him with a shout, and he led
them between the thick, greasy pillars and around the line
of buildings. The horse refused the flames, battling and
bucking to avoid being driven forward. He felt it slide in
the street, and fall heavily on one shoulder. Tregaran had
bare moments to kick free to avoid having his leg crushed.
He rolled away as the horse got its hooves under it and
staggered upright, slipping one more time, before bolting
in panic.

The troops, now ahead, rounded the corner. He grabbed
what remained of his dignity, picked up his blade and shield
from the street and ran to follow. His right leg still hurt,
for cert from the fall, and it was more of a limp than a
sprint when he cleared the corner.

His men already engaged hard, slamming into the fragments of the enemy battleline that still stood. A long line
of families stood behind, calmly lined up by a roaring bonfire. The furnace heat struck him like a hammer, and he
inhaled superheated air that brought him up short. Black-
robes stood scattered throughout the town's square.

Tregaran stood mute as more soldiers surged past him
and broke into the square, cutting into the remaining mercenaries. Behind the mercenaries' failing line, a priest
calmly tapped a man on his shoulder. Tregaran watched
helplessly as the man gathered up his daughter and, together with his wife and son, calmly walked into the center

bonfire. The man's flesh immediately burst into flames, but he stood without expression as the fires consumed him and all he loved.

Something about the smoke and rising sparks drew his eye. Tregaran slowly looked up, seeing the smoke from the fires bending together, blending into a single cloud, a maelstrom that slowly spun and turned, gathering the Fires into itself. He knew he should move, join the fight, but the overwhelming scene froze him. Decades of experience failed him as he took in something literally beyond his capacity. Failure and depression rolled over him. He had brought his men to this, failed them utterly. He tried to think of something to say, something to do, but his experience betrayed him as well. He simply couldn't move.

The Black-robes' last troops fell, and the soldiers broke past. They cut down priest after priest, and no few of the villagers as they turned to clumsily fight the veteran infantry. It became apparent to Tregaran than none of the victims moved of their own volition.

He shook himself out of his fugue. Now that he was aware of it, he could feel a heavy weight, like a blanket soaked in water, trying to descend on him. Its message was heavy, soporific. *"Listen to me. Do as I bid. Give over. You have failed. You are a failure. Just listen and all will be well."*

Tregaran tried to shrug the weight away, but now that he sensed it, he could feel it working its way into his mind. The depression built. He scanned around, frantically looking for the source of the oppressive weight in his mind. In the very center of the town square, next to the largest Fire, stood a priest working his stave.

A half-dozen soldiers cut their way through his final protection and pressed down on him. He raised his stave, and a *something* flowed out, moving like smoke. It coalesced in a few heartbeats, becoming a malevolent, envenomed whip, drawn from the end of the stave.

The first soldier swung his sword at the looping whip, his arm cutting smoke. Even in the distance Tregaran heard his high-keening scream. The man fell back, his arm boiling with blisters that ruptured. Maggots spilled from the wounds and chewed into his skin.

The second soldier charged full into the same sick smoke, then the priest whipped the thing on the end of his stave, carrying it through the other four. Each fell, screaming, flesh consumed by boils that burst into parasites that ate at their hosts. The men fell, screaming and writhing, still several feet short of the priest.

Tregaran looked around desperately, wishing he hadn't left the archers on the hill. His men continued their assault through the open center, slaughtering mercenary, priest, and townsfolk alike. Windrows of dead piled up near the Fires, as the defense failed against his men. The soldiers had cut down most every living thing.

It wasn't until he saw a tongue of flame bend, reach from the fire and engulf a fallen priest that he truly understood. Its movements were sentient, alive. The priests were *making* something.

He felt the touch of the firecat's voice in his head. *"Aye. And when they are done, they will bring it through. He thinks he can control it, but it is a master . . . not a slave. He seeks to use it to make miracles, to succeed where Laskaris has failed. Instead, he will be its tool."*

"Do something!" Tregaran cried aloud, as another of his soldiers fell to the smoking stave. Flames now licked around the arch-priest, swirling like a cyclone up above him.

"I cannot. You're halfway into its world now, where I cannot enter."

"Then how?" he screamed. He saw his soldiers slowing as the last of the minor priests fell, beginning to look around, and beginning to perceive the center of the holocaust they were now in. Most of the surrounding smoke now limned with flame, darting and dancing like things alive, as they licked and drew on the bodies of the fallen. A soldier dropped his sword in despair and fell to his knees. The weight of the voice, calling on them to despair, built now that blood cooled and panic built.

"Break the key, and break the binding that draws the thing here. Break the stave. That is the center."

Tregaran looked around wildly, seeing the first of his troops fall as the Fires, strengthened by the bodies of the fallen, lashed out at the living. A soldier frantically defended himself, using his blade to block the fist-shaped tounge of flame that grew out of the bonfire, punched through his armor, and immolated him. He had bare sec-

onds to scream before writhing on the scorched paving
stones, his body alight in sickly red flames. Tregaran heard
a second scream to his right a moment later, and saw a
third soldier fall across the square.

Tregaran knew then what he had to do.

He threw his shield away and gripped his sword tightly
in both hands. He shook off the last feelings of despair and
gathered his will into a single dart of purpose.

He lifted the blade over his head and charged the swirling pillar of flame.

Cogern with the First Battle just crested the hill and
started the running slide down into the fight when the detonation blew him backward onto the scree. The entire center
of the village, totally shrouded by flames and rising smoke,
blew outward, the pressure wave tossing the smoke aside
as it would a curtain. The lurid red glow that marked the
horizon faded then, to something more normal.

An under-officer, his armor scorched and one arm hanging free, staggered into him. "Warmaster! Thank V'kandis!
The colonel's down."

Cogern followed at a run, the bulk of First Battle behind.
They passed into the center square, where the bonfires had
been snuffed by the blast. A distant part of Cogern's mind
registered there was no wood in those fires, only bones.
Second Battle lay scattered around the square, some dead,
more hurt, most stunned from the detonation.

In the center lay Tregaran, held by an openly weeping
soldier. Nearby lay the blasted body of something with too
many arms, and a broken stave lay nearby.

Cogern fell to his knees next to what was left of Tregaran. Shiny skull showed at Tregaran's forehead and his
fingers and armor appeared burned away. Strips of flesh
hung from the colonel's ruined body, and sightless eyes
stared up. Cogern wept freely.

The chirurgeon appeared from behind the men, falling
to his knees besides them. He took a silvered mirror and
held it to where Tregaran's lips had been.

"By all that's Holy, he's alive!"

Cogern looked up, tears pouring down his sooty face.
"Will he live?"

The chirurgeon looked down, then up. "No. He's too

badly hurt. There's nothing we can do. He's probably not even aware of us."

The firecat, unnoticed, sat to one side. It had done what it could to take as much of the man's pain as he could. He opened the door to the man's mind and began to ease him away. Better to end this now.

Tregaran slipped into something like a dream. He walked on a wide plain, marked only by the dead Herald and the horse's head on the pike.

"It's not your fault, you know."

She sat on a rock nearby, her squarish jaw not a feature he liked. She stood, her acolyte's chiton flaring around her and settling back. Her long, lithe legs flashed as she jumped down from the rock and walked toward the Herald.

"You see this as what you fight for," she said. It was not a question. "You march your regiment from border to border, defending those who pervert the Way." She gently took his hand between hers. He could feel his scarred fingers rough against her smooth palm, feel the scribe's callus on the index finger against the back of his hand. "You lead your regiment to battle after battle. You execute traitors condemned by Laskaris' word, with not a peep in their defense. You start wars you know are wrong, execute orders you know are wrong, and sent many a brave soldier to their deaths for a Son of the Sun you don't believe in."

Each sentence, softly spoken, struck him like a physical blow. "Yes," he could but nod. "Yes."

Her cool hand brushed his face. "You saved those you could from the Fires, spared the wounded from pointless burning. You did as you were sworn to do, leading your regiment to battle to defend your country, and enforcing those laws placed in your hands to enforce. Your doubt of your orders came often afterward, in the full light of day, and in growing realization of error . . . when duty compelled and honor failed."

She smiled at him. He inhaled her scent, of honeysuckle and jasmine. "You have guarded your country, obeyed those you swore to obey, and held to duty when faith swayed." She leaned down to him and kissed his brow. "Your god is pleased with you, Tregaran."

"I love you, Solaris," he whispered.

And in Cogern's arms, he died.

The firecat lay still as the noon sun streamed down overhead. Tregaran's body had been removed in great honor. Cogern's men had worked their revenge, rooting out Blackrobe sanctuaries all over the outskirts of Sunhame. It would be a miracle if even a few survived who lived within a day's ride of the capital.

The 'cat felt the surge and heave of the god's presence, even this far from Sunhame, as He made His own appearance. By now, Laskaris would be dead, and Solaris, ascendant.

A small tendril of that power settled at the place where a man gave his life for a woman, for love.

A second firecat shimmered out of the void and stepped down. It didn't seem to know exactly what to do with its tail.

"Was that me?" it said, looking at the place where the colonel had died.

"Yes," said the firecat. "Your task now is to watch over her. She is handmaid to our Lord, and she must survive."

"I will," said the new 'cat.

"In the meantime," said the old, "let me show you the joys of field mice. They go best with toast."

The chirurgeon deserted the next morning. A month later, he knelt before his own bound liege.

"Arise, Healer, and report," said Queen Selenay of Valdemar. "What of Karse?"

THE BLUE COAT

by *Fiona Patton*

Fiona Patton lives in rural Ontario, Canada with her partner, a fierce farm Chihuahua, and inumerable cats. She has four novels out with DAW Books: *The Stone Prince, The Painter Knight, The Granite Shield,* and *The Golden Sword*. Her fifth novel, *The Silver Lake,* was published in hardcover by DAW in 2005. She has twenty-odd short stories published in various DAW/Tekno anthologies including *Sirius the Dog Star, Assassin Fantastic,* and *Apprentice Fantastic*.

SPRING had come late to the Ice Wall Mountains. Although the warm afternoon breezes had brought the first of the tiny purple-and-yellow flowers pushing up through the snow, the passes were still closed and the nights still frosty and cold well into the season. Two figures, each heavily bundled in hides and fleece and wearing thick caps made of the soft, luxurious brown fur that gave the Goshon clan its name, walked single file along a narrow, barely passable mountain path. Each carried a short hunting bow and several brown-fletched arrows in ornate quivers at their backs and long knives, waterskins, and a brace of rabbits at their belts. The older, just past twenty years in age, was tall and thin, with a short length of beard and long, dark hair, plaited in several thick braids and tied with bits of hide. The younger, closer to fourteen or fifteen, was clean-shaven, lighter in coloring and more compact in build, but still bore a striking resemblance to his companion. As the path widened to reveal a small, protected vale, they paused to study the tableau below them with an apprehensive air.

A stout hide tent stood in the lea of a copse of pine trees with four shaggy ponies cropping at the dry grass before a ringed fire pit. Two figures, one old, the other young, were the only people to be seen. For a moment, there was no sound except the piercing call of a hawk high above the trees, and then the sharp, painful birthing cries of their cousin Dierna that had driven the two men from the vale that morning began again. The younger backed up a step, but the older put his arm about his shoulders and drew him forward.

"There's nothing for it, Kellisin," he said, keeping his voice firm and even. "Take the hares and prepare them."

"But Trey . . ."

"I know." Treyill k'Goshon glanced over to where his brother Bayne stood guard before the tent's entrance. The other man met his gaze, then shook his head, and Trey nodded in resignation. "Shersi's doing all she can," he continued, handing Kellisin his kill. "Maybe a thick rabbit stew will help her and Dierna both, yes?"

Kellisin swallowed hard. "Yes."

"So go on, then, little cousin."

As the younger man made for the fire pit, his face clouded with distress, Trey walked the short distance to where Vulshin, the family's shaman, sat weaving his fingers through a thin trickle of water running down the rocks. As Trey touched him lightly on the shoulder, the old man raised his head, the expression in his rheumy gray eyes making words unnecessary.

Trey crouched beside him. "It's as you dreamed then," he said, studying the collection of stones and small bird bones lying on the ground before them.

Vulshin nodded, his seamed face gray and weary. "It's as we *both* dreamed," he corrected. "The baby's breached; Shersi can't make it turn, and Dierna's lost a lot of strength and a lot of blood just getting this far. Now the baby's in trouble. It can't breathe and there's nothing Shersi can do." He sighed deeply. "It's only a matter of time."

Trey picked up the largest of the stones, squeezing it in his fist with a helpless gesture before dropping it once more. "How long?"

"Dusk. No later."

Both men glanced up at the sun already well into its trek towards the horizon.

"Once there were so many of us," Vulshin noted sadly. "The voices of our people sang in my dreams like a chorus of sparkling water flowing down the mountains sides. Not like this pitiful little trickle," he sneered, waving a gnarled hand at the rivulet of water. "But like a torrent. Now sickness and clan-fighting have silenced their voices, one by one, until the Goshon are no more."

"The people are scattered," Trey allowed.

"The people are no more," Vulshin repeated sharply. "Their voices have left my dreams, I tell you. We are the last, and when Dierna and her child pass from this world so will the Goshon pass." Scooping the stones and bones into a small, hide bag, he fixed Trey with a stern expression. "When this is over, I want you to leave this place; you and Bayne and young Kellisin. There's nothing left for you here."

Trey gave the old man a worried glance. "There's yourself and Shersi, Shaman," he said.

Vulshin shook his head. "No. Shersi is old," he said wearily. "Old and sick. The winter was very hard on her. Too hard. And with our grandson Aivar's death coming before his child could even draw breath, the strength to carry on has left her."

His expression drew inward. "She used to love the meadow flowers in springtime, you know," he said, more to himself than to the younger man. "When we were children, so many years ago, we would go out seeking the earliest spring blossoms, even if we had to sweep the snow away to find them. Sometimes our fingers would be red and stiff from searching, but she would never return until she could bring a handful home to plait into our ponies' manes. Now she couldn't walk as far as the edge of the camp to find them, and my vision's so poor I couldn't see to fetch them for her even if I tried." He blinked a sudden welling of tears from his eyes. "She only waited this long to help Dierna bring her child into the world, but now . . ." He paused, and the two men glanced unwillingly toward the tent where Dierna's cries had become noticeably weaker. "Now, my Shersi won't last the week."

"Then we'll wait a week, and afterward you'll break camp with us."

"No."

"Shaman, you must. We need you." Trey scowled at the desperate sound in his voice but kept his eyes on the older man's face regardless.

Vulshin patted his arm with slightly more force than necessary. "No, you don't," he replied. "I've taught you all I can, Trey. Bayne will stand beside you as he always has, and Kellisin would follow you into a fire pit if you told him he could learn its nature. Rely on Bayne's strength, Kellisin's mind, and your own gifts, and you'll be fine."

"But my dreams aren't like yours," Trey insisted, trying to curb the sudden panic he felt at the thought of losing the old man's guidance. "They're hazy and unclear. And even when they're not, they don't make any sense."

"They will when you trust that they will. You're strong, so are your dreams; strong enough to lead the three of you to a new life." Vulshin passed a hand through the rivulet of water once again. "I have only one dream left now, and I don't want to see it through without my Shersi. I've never been without her, you see; I wouldn't know how." He raised his eyes to the sky. "In this dream I saw a storm of unusual fury bury the hills again as if it were the middle of winter. It will be our funeral storm. We'll wait for it and ride it into death like a mountain pony together, hand in hand." He returned his attention to the younger man. "By that time, you'll have reached the pass; it will be open, and you'll be safe."

"Pass?"

"The Feral Pass that leads south to the High Hills and the Terilee River."

Trey blinked. "The Goshon do not travel south, Shaman," he reminded him gently.

"Teach your grandmother to suck eggs," Vulshin snapped. "You'll travel south if I tell you to." His gaze drew inward again. "South to the river and farther still to a place of stone and timber where music and sunlight stream in equal magnificence, and where creatures of such magic and poetry as would take your breath away run freely over lush, green meadows; far away in the young kingdom of Valdemar."

Trey mouthed the unfamiliar word with a frown. "I've never heard of it."

"As I said, it's a young kingdom, and you're an even younger man."

"What clan holds its territory?"

"No clan. It lies far beyond their reach, but you will have to travel past clan lands to get there. Stay by the river, heed your dreams, and you'll pass through safely."

Trey shook his head stubbornly. "But what kind of life could we make in such a place even if we could get there safely?" he demanded. "What do we have to offer? Poetry and music have no need for trapping and hunting."

Vulshin's eyes narrowed. "The land and the people will be strange and foreign to you, that's true, but a sharp eye and a courageous arm are always welcome if they're offered honestly. It's their way. Besides, I dreamed you there." He closed his eyes. "Last night I saw you standing by bright water wearing a coat dyed the deepest blue of a summer evening sky." He opened his eyes again without noticing how pale Trey had suddenly become. "So you're going," he continued. "Don't argue with me, or I'll give you a good smack. When I . . ."

"Shaman?"

The two men turned to see Bayne gesturing to them, and Trey suddenly realized how quiet it had become. The old man nodded sadly. "It's time," he said. "Help me up."

Trey hesitated. "You don't think . . . ?"

"No, Treyill," Vulshin said firmly but not unkindly. "And neither do you. Their voices are no more. Come, make your first good-bye. It's what must be done and you know it."

With a reluctant frown, Trey helped him stand, then together, the two men made their way across the vale toward the now silent tent.

The next morning, after Dierna and her stillborn child had been wrapped in hides and buried under as many rocks as the three young men could pry from the still-frozen ground, Trey set Bayne to breaking camp. Vulshin and Shersi sat, huddled together before the fire pit without speaking and to Trey's eyes it looked as if they'd already begun their final trek, pausing only to wait until death could catch up with them.

Mouth set in a grim line, he began to wrap the season's goshon pelts in oilcloth. They would use them to barter their way south to Vulshin's dream kingdom of Valdemar. Whatever the old shaman believed, they were still trappers, that's what they did and that's all they had to offer a new life, regardless of their eyes or their arms. Beside him, Kellisin hovered about uncertainly until he sent him to help Bayne load Dierna's pony with their extra supplies. He could find no words to comfort him when he had none to comfort himself. Turning away from the injured look in the younger man's eyes, Trey picked up another pelt with deliberate care.

By the time the sun had reached its zenith, they were ready. Trey made one last attempt to convince Vulshin and Shersi to come with them, but the two older Goshon were adamant.

"It's our right as elders to choose whether we break camp or remain behind," Shersi said, her once strong voice weak and breathy. "It's the way of our people. You know that."

"Then choose to break camp with us."

"Treyill," Vulshin said sternly. "Come, it is time to make your second good-bye. Do it respectfully."

Trey would have continued the argument afterward, but finally, Bayne drew him away, setting his reins into his hand. His last sight of the vale was that of the hawk circling high overhead, sending its mournful cry into the wind. For good or ill, the last of the Goshon Clan were passing from its world.

The three kinsmen made their way in somber silence for the better part of a week, alternately walking and riding, following what paths were open, and heading roughly south. When they reached the Feral Pass, a thin, mushy path winding its way through a narrow canyon of high, jagged rocks, they rode cautiously, keeping a close eye on the walls of ice and snow that stretched high above their heads. When they finally emerged on the other side, they glanced back to find the sky above the mountain peaks had turned an ominous dark, slate gray.

"Vulshin's storm," Trey said heavily.

Bayne nodded. "We have to quicken our pace."

They made the shelter of a rocky tor just as the storm hit. Huddled behind their ponies, they waited it out and when they finally struggled free the next morning, the pass behind them glittered with impassible snow. Trey narrowed his eyes against the glare.

"Well, that's it, then," he said, his voice devoid of emotion. "There's no going back now."

Kellisin glanced over at him. "And Vulshin and Shersi?" he asked quietly.

"Gone. We should never have left them." Taking hold of his pony's halter, Trey made his way back to the barely discernable path without looking back.

Bayne shook his head. "We had to respect their wishes," he said to Kellisin, catching him by the shoulder and pulling him into a rough hug to take the sting away from his brother's words. "Life is seasonal, and everyone breaks camp for the ride into death eventually, little cousin."

"I know that," Kellisin said, his brows drawn down into a tight vee. "Dierna and the baby was hard for us all, but Vulshin and Shersi were old. Trey . . ." He shook his head helplessly. "It wasn't his choice to make."

"Trey's a shaman," Bayne explained. "They take responsibility for everything; so it's up to us to remind him not to. But in the meantime . . ." He caught hold of his own pony's halter, "we have to find a clear patch of fodder and some dry wood for a fire. Unless you want a cold breakfast?"

Kellisin smiled ruefully. "No."

"All right, then. Let's catch up to our ray of sunshine, shall we, before he falls off a cliff? Maybe some of your warm rabbit stew will lighten his mood."

Kellisin nodded and together, they followed Trey down the path.

That night Trey dreamed. He saw Vulshin standing in the midst of a winter storm so violent it blinded him. One hand shielding his eyes, the other stretched out before him, Trey reached out for the old man but, just as their fingertips touched, Vulshin vanished under a sudden avalanche of snow. Trey sprang forward and, falling to his knees, worked frantically to dig his old teacher free, but every time he thought he might have reached him, another deluge of snow buried him again. He cried out in frustration and awoke to find Bayne holding him tightly, rocking him back and forth as their parents had done when he'd been a boy. In the moonlight he looked so much like their father that Trey gaped at him, then the other man pulled back, and Trey was back on the cold ground south of the Feral Pass once again.

The next night he dreamed again, only this time it was Shersi who disappeared under a cascade of falling snow, then Dierna and her baby, then Aivar, then Vulshin again, night after night. He began to avoid sleeping altogether, sitting wrapped in his blanket, staring up at the moon for hours until exhaustion drove him to a few hours of broken rest. He became gray and gaunt, drawing farther and farther into himself and neither Bayne nor Kellisin could bring him out of it.

Finally, as the mountains gave over to rolling hills and valleys, Bayne joined him, sitting staring up and the star-cast sky before fixing his brother with a serious expression.

"You have to stop this, Trey," he said. "We'll be in foreign lands in a day or two and we'll need your insight."

Knees drawn up to his chest, Trey shook his head. "I can't."

"You have to. You're our shaman. We need you." Bayne frowned. "This isn't like you, brother. What is it?"

Scrubbing at the growth of beard along his cheeks, Trey took a deep breath. "Do you remember the nightmares I used to have as a boy?" he asked after a long moment.

When Bayne nodded, he continued.

"They were so real, so vivid; sometimes it was hard to tell if I was awake or asleep. I saw storms and floods and fighting and everything I saw came true. I saw our father's death as clear as if it were happening right before my eyes."

"I remember. That was when Vulshin began your training and the nightmares stopped."

"The nightmares stopped," Trey agreed. "But not because Vulshin began training me." He closed his eyes. "The dreams always started the same way. I was standing by bright, swiftly flowing water wearing a dark blue coat the like of which I've never seen among the Goshon. I looked

down into the water and I saw the future of our people."
His face darkened. "But our people had no future," he
grated, "and all I saw were bodies floating below the surface. And just as Vulshin heard them singing in his head;
so I saw them dying in mine, and it hurt worse than anything else has ever hurt before or since. One day it was
just too much, so I went into my dream and I took the
coat off, I buried it in a deep cleft in the rocks, and the
dreams stopped hurting. They became hazy and unclear,
sometimes happening before and sometimes afterwards. I
saw Aivar's death and Dierna's and their baby's, but they
didn't hurt. Not the dreams anyway," he amended.

"And Vulshin and Shersi?"

Trey nodded wordlessly.

"And the dreams are hurting again?"

"Yes. But there's more. The day before we left the vale,
Vulshin told me that he'd seen me in a dream standing by
bright water wearing a coat dyed the deepest blue of a
summer evening sky. His very words. Bayne." He fixed his
brother with an intense stare. "I never told Vulshin about
the coat. Does that mean it's back? That even though I
buried it, it followed me here?"

His brother gave him a skeptical glance. "It's not a predator like a mountain cat," he said.

"How do you know?"

"I suppose I don't." Bayne was silent for a moment, then
stared up at the stars again. "When I was young, I was
afraid of the dark," he said.

Trey smiled. "I remember."

"I still am sometimes."

"What?"

Bayne shrugged. "Why not? The things I thought might
attack me in the dark could still be there—now more than
ever since we're heading into foreign lands. But it doesn't
matter if they're there or not, and it doesn't matter if I'm
still afraid or not; I can't hide from the darkness anymore,
I have to stand against whatever might be hiding behind it
for your sake and for Kellisin's. It's what I do. I protect.
But I'm not that scared little boy anymore either, I'm a
man now with a man's strength, just like you are. And
predator or not, you may have to dig that coat up and put

it back on; make it a man's coat instead of a boy's coat and make it your own." He squeezed Trey's shoulder. "And whatever comes of it, brother, we'll face it together as kinsmen. As clansmen."

"And what if I see your death?" Trey shot back. "Or Kellisin's?"

"We'll face that together, too. That's what families do. They stand together so that no one has to stand alone, be they hunter, trapper, or shaman. Yes?"

Trey gave a long, resentful sigh. "Yes."

"Good." Bayne stood. "Then pull yourself together. You're scaring Kellisin."

That night, drawing on the warmth of Bayne's back pressed against his for courage, Trey reached out, past the avalanche of snow and the deaths of his people, and drew the blue coat from its hiding place. In his dream it was damp and cold and covered in dirt, much as it might have been in the waking world. Shaking it out, he studied the silver trim along its length, something he'd never noticed as a boy, before pulling it over his head. It settled across his shoulders with an all but forgotten familiarity, and once again he stood by the bright, swiftly flowing water of his childhood dreams. Taking a deep breath, he looked down, but instead of bodies floating beneath the surface, he saw a great walled city spiraling outward from a wide river valley. A broad belt of green land lay beside a beautiful structure of stone and timber and he could almost hear Vulshin's music and poetry in the distance. Fighting back tears of relief, he turned to the hazy figure standing in a meadow of spring flowers.

"Thank you, shaman," he breathed.

That night he had the first peaceful slumber since before Dierna's death, and two days later the three men left the hills and looked down upon a vast, open plain covered in tiny purple-and-yellow flowers. Beyond that lay a wide, swiftly flowing river.

Bayne glanced over at Trey. "The Terilee?" he asked.

"That's what Vulshin called it."

"Whatever he called it, I call it fresh water for drinking

and for bathing," Kellisin said excitedly. With a shout of joy, he urged his mount into a gallop, the pack pony close behind them.

The two older men followed more sedately, but neither of them could hide the pleasure the sight of the clean, blue water gave them as well.

That evening as they made camp, Trey collected a handful of the tiny blossoms and wove them into his pony's mane and that night he dreamed again. He saw a wide but shallow quarry where strangely garbed people labored to cut great blocks of stone from the ground which were then loaded onto rollers pulled by great horned beasts and then loaded once again onto three oddly-shaped flat-bottomed boats. The cloudless sky above promised a clear and storm-free day, but the dark forest beyond the southern bank whispered of hidden dangers behind the trees and the water below wavered with the hint of bodies beneath the surface.

He awoke with the familiar twisting fear in the pit of his belly. After a cold breakfast, they broke camp quickly and turned southeast, following the river with their bows near to hand. They saw no signs of settlements or encampments as they rode, but rather than have this allay their disquiet, after the initial excitement of reaching the river had passed, all three men began to feel both uneasy and exposed. The gently rolling countryside was too open and too empty for their passage to remain hidden, the strips of woodland that grew right up to the water's edge too dark and the underbrush too thick to maneuver in easily. Time and time again they had to leave the riverbank to bypass some soft and crumbling escarpment or boggy patch of ground and strike north.

After three days of this, Bayne's mood began to darken and Kellisin started to lag behind, his eyes constantly scanning the unfamiliar terrain. Trey was unable to break the tension. His dreams had become as impenetrable as the woodlands themselves, almost as if the blue coat were laughing at him for thinking he could overcome his childhood fears so easily.

However, nineteen days after they'd left the familiar peaks and paths of the Ice Wall Mountains, the river flowed through a series of lightly wooded hills, then opened up to reveal a group of huts built about a wide but shallow quarry. A dozen people labored to cut away great blocks of the exposed stone while a dozen more loaded them onto log rollers pulled by heavy-set horned creatures that looked like a cross between huge ponies and hairless mountain goats. Another dozen figures stood at key locations, obviously guardsmen protecting the settlement, while two women shouted orders from the first of three flat-bottomed boats tied up at a sturdily built wooden and stone pier. Two of the boats were already loaded with the stone blocks, the third half full.

Hidden just beyond the tree line, the three Goshon stopped dead and Kellisin's mouth fell open.

"Isn't that . . . ?"

"Yes," Trey answered.

"And look at the color the guards are wearing," Bayne added meaningfully.

Trey squinted down at the settlement.

"It's the wrong shade," he declared after a moment, trying to mask the sense of foreboding the sight of the bright blue uniforms caused him.

"Does it matter?" the other man asked.

"Yes, it matters," Trey snapped back with rather more force than necessary and his brother raised his hands in a sarcastic gesture of submission.

"All right, so it matters, but you have to admit, it's an interesting coincidence. Have you ever seen anyone wear any kind of blue cloth?"

"No I haven't, but until this moment I'd never seen anyone stand on floating rocks either."

Beside them, Kellisin stirred restlessly, impatient with the argument. "So, are we going down for a closer look or not?" he demanded. "If you dreamed this place, there must be a reason."

"True."

"Then, let's go down and find out what it is."

Trey and Bayne rolled their eyes at each other over his head.

"Life is always simpler for the young," Bayne noted sagely.

"Life is always slower for the old," Kellisin retorted.

"And life is always a pushy series of inevitable events for the shamans, old or young," Trey added.

"So we're going?"

"Yes, we're going, but cautiously," he added, grabbing the younger man's halter before he could go galloping down the hill. "Cautiously, little cousin."

All work ceased immediately as the three clansman broke from the trees and rode slowly into the open towards the riverbank. One of the guardsmen gave a whistling signal and, by the time they reached the pier, an older woman in a leather apron and a man in the guardsmen's bright blue uniform were waiting for them, ringed by people. Most held their tools or weapons loosely but resolutely, and Trey gave Bayne a casual, sideways glance.

"Keep your hands away from your own weapons, brother," he said quietly.

"Believe me, I'm trying to."

Reining up, Trey dismounted. "I am Treyill of the Goshon," he said. "This is my brother Bayne and my kinsman Kellisin. "We're traveling south. We have goods to trade. You understand, trade?"

The woman nodded warily. "I am Kith Arkarus of Waymeet, the Quarry Master here," she replied, her accent thick and exotic but understandable. "This is Captain Danel of the Valdemar Guard."

Trey couldn't help but show his surprise. "Valdemar?"

Captain Danel gave him a measured look. "You came through the Crook Back Pass?" he asked.

"The Feral."

"Ah, then you'll have passed through no villages to tell you. You crossed Valdemar's northwestern border some days ago. We're the farthest settlement in the area, and the newest."

"King Restil is expanding the palace," a new voice said excitedly. The three Goshon glanced up just as a young woman, perhaps a year or two older than Kellisin, appeared on the top of one of the blocks of stone on the half-loaded barge.

"This is Gabrielle Post," the Quarry Master said dryly. "My niece. Apprenticed to Haven's Master Builder . . ."

"My father," Gabrielle supplied.

"Sent north to gain experience in the building trades."

"Haven?" Trey asked.

"The capital of Valdemar."

"And you will float this stone there?"

"Tomorrow morning if the weather holds."

Trey and Bayne exchanged another glance.

"You'll be passing through a lot of wild country," Trey noted.

"Wild for the unwary, maybe," Captain Danel answered. "But we're not unwary," he added meaningfully, "and we're not unprepared."

Bayne smiled at the unsubtle warning.

"I'm sure of it," Trey replied smoothly. "I'm told that a sharp eye and a courageous arm are always welcome in Valdemar if they're offered honestly. For passage to Haven, I offer ours. If any of your people have heard stories of mine, you'll know that this offer is made honestly."

The captain and the Quarry Master exchanged a glance while both Bayne and Kellisin tried not to look surprised.

"We know of the Goshon in Waymeet," the Quarry Master acknowledged. "Though we've not seen any of your people in a generation or more." She tipped her head to one side, her expression speculative. "It's said that you have an uncanny ability to track and trap the creatures your clan is named for."

Trey smiled. "What's said is true, and yes, we have pelts to trade as well."

"I think we can come to an arrangement then, if the captain is willing."

"What a strange craft this is."

An hour later, with the negotiations between the Quarry Master and his kinsman complete, Kellisin lay stretched out on the pier, studying the underside of the barge intently as the setting sun cast long, orange fingers across the water.

Crouched beside him, Gabrielle bobbed her head happily. "It's a much better mode of transportation than sleds pulled by oxen," she explained. "The river does all the work, you see."

"Yes, I do see. But how does it stay on the surface with such a heavy load upon it?"

"Magic."

"What? Truly?"

Gabrielle's laughter rang out like the pealing of bells. "No, of course not. The barge is built to distribute the load evenly and since it's made of wood and wood floats, so does the barge and whatever is placed on it. Evenly. Do you see?"

He smiled up at her, obviously content to simply hear the sound of her voice. "Not really, Gabrielle."

She grinned down at him. "Call me Gaby."

"I shall." He glanced back at the barge. "What if winds or storms redistribute the weight?"

"Oh. Then the barge would sink."

"But if the barge sinks you'd never be able to get the stone up from the riverbed, would you?"

She shrugged easily. "We'd better hope it doesn't sink, then. My father said to bring him his stone or don't come home at all." She laughed again. "I'm mostly sure he was joking. Mostly." She cocked her head to one side. "Did you want to see how we load the stone upon rollers?" she asked, suddenly a little shy.

He smiled back at her, suddenly less so. "Yes, I should like that very much," he answered.

Seated by a small fire on the edge of the settlement, Trey and Bayne watched as Gabrielle tucked their kinsman's arm into hers and led him off toward the quarry.

"Well, it looks like he, at least, has ridden into our new life smoothly enough," Bayne chuckled.

Trey nodded wordlessly.

"That's good, yes?" his brother prodded.

"Yes."

"But?"

"But he isn't there yet," Trey said in a cautious tone. "And neither are we."

"Hmm." Staring up at the starlit sky, Bayne rubbed at a small scar on one knuckle. "This new idea of yours will likely see us there that much sooner though. I wasn't expecting to float our way south. When did you dream that?"

"I didn't, and it might be a terrible mistake, but . . ."

"But?"

"But as Kellisin said, I dreamed this place and its floating

stone boats for a reason. Vulshin told me to that my dreams
would make sense when I trusted them to do so."

"And do you?"

Trey sighed. "Not yet."

Standing, Bayne swiped at his trousers. "Well, let's hope
you do by the time we need you to. I'm going to check on
the ponies."

Left on his own, Trey scowled at the image of the blue
coat which seemed to form and reform in the flickering
campfire. "Yes," he said doubtfully. "Let's hope I do."

That night he dreamed of a hail of arrow fire coming
from the southern trees and the next morning, warned, the
settlement guards mounted an extra vigilant watch while
Gabrielle and the Quarry Master oversaw the loading of
the final barge.

After giving her a curt hug, the older woman held her
out at arm's length. "I'm sending you three masons and
three laborers to help unload at Haven, but I want them
back, understood?" she said. "And the captain has steady
company to see you safely there, so don't be afraid."

Gabrielle laughed at her. "Granite makes an excellent
shield, Auntie," she said in a condescending tone. "And
besides, I have my fine northern clansman to protect me."
She shot a dazzling smile in Kellisin's direction and the
Quarry Master scowled at her.

"Yes, well, be safe and come back to us if your father
allows it. You're a good worker. Tell my sister I said so."

"I will." Catching Kellisin by the hand, Gabrielle drew
him onto the lead boat, then waved jauntily as it cast off
while, beside them, Bayne and Trey shared another rolling
of their eyes.

"That's all we need," Bayne whispered. "Another colt
to look after."

"Shh." Catching hold of one of the ropes lashed to the
stones to steady himself, Trey elbowed his brother in the
side as the three barges began to move slowly out into
the water.

Once they'd made they way into the current, the barge
captain, an old man with a grizzled length of long, braided
gray hair, squinted across the river with an egregious expression. "We won't be able to hug the northern bank for

long," he warned. "Sooner or later we're going to have to move into deeper water."

Captain Danel nodded. "Let us know when it's to be," he said.

"Shafts!"

At Bayne's shout, Gabrielle and her workers dove for cover while the six guardsmen and three Goshon answered the hail of arrow fire with a volley of their own.

They'd been traveling for two days down the center of the river and in the last few hours had fought off three attacks from the southern bank. One of the masons had taken an arrow through the arm and another had caught a graze across the cheek before the barge captain had pulled him to safety. Everyone had gotten much faster at reacting but, as Trey made his cautious way to Bayne's side, he knew it wasn't going to last. Sooner or later they were going to suffer a real casualty.

His brother shot him a swift glance before rising slightly to send a shaft of his own streaking towards the trees. The answering volley showed plainly that the enemy had not yet broken off the attack. "It's a good thing they don't have any boats of their own or we'd be in real trouble," he declared.

"They likely do. They're just softening us up first, seeing if they can take out a few of our combatants before they make their primary attack."

"And thank you for that, my ray of sunshine. Do something, then. Dream us out of this."

"I have."

"What?" Bayne's head snapped around. "When?"

"Last night, but you won't like it, neither will Captain Danel. There's going to be a fog. We can either use it to slip past them or . . ."

An enemy arrow cracked the stone block just above Bayne's head and he turned an exasperated look in Trey's direction as he ducked instinctively. "Or what?" he demanded.

"Or they'll use it to mount an attack against us and, warned, we can set an ambush. Either way, we risk injuries and deaths."

"If it's either way, I'm all for an ambush myself."

"As am I, but there's a problem."

"What?"

"The fog won't be for two days."

"Will they wait that long, do you think?"

Trey gave the southern bank a narrow-eyed glare. "I don't know. But I'm going to find out."

That night, huddled beside the ponies tethered in the center of the barge, Trey struggled to sink down into sleep, but the unfamiliar movement of the deck beneath him and the faint sounds of guards maintaining a constant watch all around him kept jerking him back to wakefulness. With a growl of frustration, he pulled the blanket over his head. Everything he'd seen or dreamed and every decision he'd made since leaving the vale seemed to hinge on this one final night and it looked as if he were going to spend it fighting his own restless fears. In his mind's eyes the blue coat seemed to shimmer with life, hovering just out of reach, its silver trim sparkling in the pale moonlight almost menacingly.

"You may have to dig that coat up and put it back on; make it a man's coat instead of a boy's coat and make it your own."

"Yes, I know Bayne," he said wearily. "I'm trying." Using the soft, familiar scents of fleece and hide and ponies, he forced himself to relax. "We'll face it together like a family just as you said. But what if I see your death, or Kellisin's? There's been too many good-byes already. I can't face another one." He closed his eyes. "I can't."

Two days later in the early hours of the morning, three small boats carrying half a dozen bandits in each pulled up alongside the first barge in the covering fog. They swarmed over the low sides only to be met by total, empty silence. Padding cautiously between the great stone blocks, their leader made to signal that the barge had been deserted when a frightful apparition, dressed in hides and furs, rose up to catch his arm. A piercing whistle filled the air and suddenly the deck was alive with people. The apparition struck the leader down and violence erupted across the barge.

When the fog finally burned off in the wake of the morning sun, the fight was nearly over. Taken completely by surprise, the remaining bandits either surrendered or fled back to their own boats only to be shot down by a hail of arrow fire from the Valdemar guardsmen. Their bodies, floating just above the surface, bobbed against the barge side, and Trey stared down at them for a long time before turning away.

On the deck, the captain was kneeling before the body of one of his younger guardsmen. The boy had taken a knife slash to the neck and had died instantly. He glanced up as Trey approached.

"Your kin are all unharmed?" he asked, his voice thick.

Trey nodded. "Kellisin has a nasty cut in the left shoulder, but Gabrielle's bound it up. He should be fine."

"That's good." The Valdemar man stared out at the water. "The barge captain tells me that we should make the village of Deedun by late tomorrow," he said. "We can prepare Marik's body there and send it home to his family by road."

"He fought bravely," Trey offered.

"Yes, that will comfort his father." The other man sighed. "But not his wife."

"No."

"Your people fought bravely as well," the captain continued. "And your aid as . . . shaman," he said, hesitating over the unfamiliar word, "was invaluable. My thanks." He stared out at the water for a long time. "You said you were heading south to Haven?" he asked finally.

"Yes, I dreamed of it, so did the eldest of our people."

"Haven has a need for . . . what did you call it, sharp eyes and courageous arms?"

"Offered honestly."

"Yes. I would be honored if you would consider another offer made honestly. If the king agrees, there could be place for all three of you among the palace guard if you were willing."

"Palace guard? I thought your people were settlement guards."

"My people are *Valdemar* guards who go where they're needed," the captain replied stiffly. "Not just *settlement* guards. But I am palace guard, on loan to Gabrielle and her workers to ensure her safe return." He smiled faintly.

"The king values his Master Builder's peace of mind and the Master Builder values his incautious daughter's health and well-being."

Trey frowned uncertainly. "It's a fine offer," he began.

"But you need to think about it."

"And consult my kin."

"I understand. Take what time you need."

Later, after the barges had put in to the wharfs of Deedun and the Valdemar guardsmen had carried Marik's body ashore, Trey told Baync and Kellisin of Captain Danel's offer.

Tugging irritably at the edge of the bandage around his shoulder, the younger man fixed his cousins with a firm stare. "We should accept," he said. "This is good new life. Purpose, arms . . ."

"A girl," Bayne added.

"Yes, a girl. A home, family, eventually children. It's everything we came south to find."

"I agree. We should accept."

They both looked at Trey stood, staring down at the water with a pensive expression.

"Trey?" Bayne prodded.

"Yes," he answered. "You're right, we should accept."

"But?"

"But I don't know. There's something missing."

"You dreamed of Valdemar and of Haven, didn't you?"

"Yes."

"Then trust your dreams like Vulshin told you to. If there's anything missing you'll dream of that, too, and we'll find it together, yes?"

Trey took a deep breath. "Yes."

"Then go and tell Captain Danel that we accept, shaman."

Deedun was not a large village, but nevertheless it took Trey some time to find his way through the dizzying crowds of people on the docks. Finally he spotted one of the guardsmen he recognized standing at the entrance to a low, wooden building and the man escorted him into the hushed anteroom at once. Captain Danel stood before Marik's body laid out on a long table and the silver trim on his formal uniform tunic flashed in the afternoon sun as he turned.

Trey gaped at him in shock.

"I thought Valdemar guards wore bright blue," he said weakly.

"They do," the Captain answered. "Palace guards wear . . ."

"Coats the blue of a summer evening sky," Trey finished for him.

"If you like. We call it midnight blue." He came forward. "You have an answer for me?"

Still staring at his tunic, Trey nodded slowly. "Yes." He drew himself up. "We accept. If your king agrees, the last of Goshon Clan will join the palace guard and make a new life in the south."

The Captain smiled. "Welcome to Valdemar."

As he took his outstretched hand, Trey thought he saw a man and woman mounted on shaggy ponies with purple and yellow flowers in their manes. Vulshin and Shersi smiled down at him, then turned and melted into the distant mountains beyond.

SAFE AND SOUND

by Stephanie D. Shaver

Stephanie D. Shaver lives in Missouri with assorted cats
and wooden swords. She desings online games and web-
sites for a living, and has been very active in the develop-
ment cycle of the upcoming MMORPG *Hero's Journey*.
When she isn't talking to gamemasters and artists about
the lifecycle of dragons, she writes books, and hopes to
someday sell one. Or two. Or twenty. You can visit her
website at www.sdshaver.com.

"DO you think if I swallowed this whole book," Lelia
mused, eyeing the fist-sized volume of songs she had
taken off the shelf, "I'd get a bad enough stomach ache
that they'd let me postpone the performance?"

"I think the Healers would give you a bottle of preserved
plum juice and tell you to cheer up," Malesa replied, not
looking up from where she was scribbling away furiously
at her song. "And then the Chronicler would probably flog
you for eating one of her books."

"Mm." Lelia slumped in her chair, peering about the
Collegium Library with a disappointed scowl. "I guess
you're right." She opened the book to a random page and
grimaced when she saw the title.

"Bright Lady," she muttered.

"What now?"

"Sun and Shadow." Lelia closed the book with a thump.
"Everywhere I look."

Malesa shrugged. "It's a good story, made better by good songs."

"Exactly. Everything that can be sung about Sun and Shadow has been, and by better Bards, and yet *every* year some damn trainee thinks he or she can top the Masters."

"Ah, capricious youth," Malesa said dryly.

"So why compete?" Lelia railed on, ignoring her best friend and year-mate. "There are other story jewels to plunder." She picked up another volume, this one bound in brown leather. "Like this."

Malesa finally looked up. She frowned. "That's a journal."

"The journal of Herald Daryann, to be exact. It's fantastic."

"Sure." Malesa looked back at her sheaf of papers. "Except for the fact that she dies at the end. And while it's many things, it's *not* a story."

"It is *so*—"

"No, it's a *journal*. A *diary*. A collection of events without a discernable plot, antagonist, or resolution." She lifted her head and raised a brow. "Or did you miss that class?"

Lelia scowled and thumped Daryann's journal with her knuckles. "Story or not, it's the untold stuff between the lines that matters. Look." She flipped the book open to a point near the end. "Here. She mentions that her brother, Wil, got Chosen, too. And how proud she was of him. And then two pages later—last entry. Right before the raiders got her and her Companion."

Malesa leveled a look at her. "So?"

"Can you imagine being him? Wil, that is." Lelia's eyes glazed over. "I bet *he's* got a story, and I bet it's no Sun and Shadow."

"And I bet it's very sad. Why *is* it you have this morbid fascination with dead Heralds anyway?" Malesa asked suspiciously. "It's always Vanyel this, Lavan that . . ."

"Hey—if the Bards were right, Vanyel was quite a catch."

Malesa sighed and shook her head, glancing back at her parchments. "I'm done."

"What?" Lelia squeaked.

"I'm *done*. Eight verses, one bridge, and a melody already in mind." She looked up coyly. "You?"

Lelia groaned and buried her face in her arms.

"Oh, 'Lia," Malesa stood and patted her on the shoulder. "Just write the song and get it over with."

"But I don't know what to *write*," Lelia wailed into the table.

"You're a Bard—"

"—trainee—"

"—with a brother who's a Herald—"

"—*trainee*—"

"—I'd think you could cobble up *something* if you're so opposed to borrowing from the classics."

Lelia moaned inarticulately.

Malesa patted her shoulder again. "It'll come to you." She clutched her papers to her chest. "I'm off to practice my masterpiece."

Alone in the Library, Lelia lifted her head and stared at the scuffed leather cover of Herald Daryann's journal.

What did you do, Wil? she thought. *What did you feel, when you found out she was gone?*

She sat with her thoughts and her blank parchments until the Herald-Chronicler came around to put out the lights.

The next day didn't get any better.

It started with waking up.

Lelia emerged from a fitful slumber to the sound of someone knocking on her door. She sat up, papers sliding off her chest to the floor, and stared blearily forward as the knocking droned on. She knew with a grim, growing certainty that when she *did* manage to convince her legs to move, it would be to open the door and throttle whoever had chosen to wake her on a rest day.

"One moment," she moaned, coaxing her weary arms to pull on a lounging robe. She'd spent all night trying to pry a song out of her head, and bits of parchment with half-scribbled lyrics and notations were strewn here and there. They crunched underfoot as she crossed the room.

She knew before her hand dropped to the handle who was on the other side of the door. The warm touch of the bond she shared with her twin easily cut through her stupor.

The door swung open. Her brother stood in the hallway, dressed from head to toe in Whites.

"Is this some sort of joke?" she blurted.

"I did it!" he whooped, crushing her in a hug. "They voted this morning! Me and all my year-mates!"

"Gnhrr," she replied.

He set her down, grinning from ear to ear. She sat down slowly on her bed, her hands trembling. Whites. He'd finally earned his Whites. He'd be on Circuit soon enough. He'd . . .

Terror struck her, fast and hard. She managed to regain her composure as he shut the door, picked his way across the floor, and took a seat in the only chair in the room.

"You look great," she said at last. It hurt to smile, but she forced one onto her face. "Really . . . good."

His grin faded. "What's wrong?"

Their twin bond wasn't legendary, but it was strong enough. He knew she was worried about something. And *she* knew he wouldn't stop until he found what that something was.

"Enh." She scrambled for an excuse. It was ironic, really. Her whole training rested on communication, and yet she couldn't tell him that his becoming a full Herald was the one thing she feared most.

Her eyes lighted on the drifts of discarded paper. She couldn't talk about her worry. She couldn't lie to her twin. But she *could* be creative.

"I'm supposed to write a song," she said, looking more than passably worried. "And—"

"Can't write it?" A knowing look lit his face.

"Mm. And I know it's going to affect the Bardic Council's voting on whether I should be made a full Bard."

She shrugged, focusing all her fear and frustrations into this one thing. This song. This *damn* song.

She said, "You think if I threw myself in the river and caught pneumonia I wouldn't have to perform?"

His smile changed to a smirk. "I think some Herald would jump in after you, the Healers would stuff you to the gills with foul-tasting potions, and the Bardic Council would ask you to play from your bed."

"Drat." She flopped back onto her pillows and closed her eyes, then forced herself to ask the question she least wanted to know the answer to. "So when do you go on circuit?"

She heard him shrug. "Don't know. There are only a few Heralds ready to head back out into the field. If I had to guess—and if I'm lucky enough to be one of the first picks for my internship—I might get to go with Herald Wil when he heads out again."

Lelia's eyes snapped open.

"Go with who?" she asked.

"Herald Wil?"

She sat up and eyed her brother.

"Uh," he said. "What?"

She smiled. "Wishing you had that Mindtouch Gift, don't you?"

"Dear sister," he replied somberly, "I wish for that when I'm around *any* woman."

"That's him," Lyle said, pointing across the common room and speaking as quietly as he could manage amidst the din.

"Where?" Lelia asked. "The brunette?"

"No, the blond."

"Oh." She squinted, and then brightened. "Ooooh. Havens! He's not much older than us. Bwahaha."

"You honestly frighten me sometimes."

"Any idea where his quarters are?"

"You still haven't told me why you—"

Just then, a knot of Lyle's year-mates—all dressed in sparkling Whites—came flowing into the common room. One spied Lyle, and instantly he was surrounded and carried off. From the sound of things, they were all intending on heading into Haven to celebrate.

No matter. Lelia had her own work cut out for her. She eyed the exits, took the one closest to Herald Wil's table, chose a shadowy corner to stand in, and then stood vigil on the door until he strolled out, a book tucked under his arm.

She let him get a little ahead of her, and started to follow.

The sun was setting when she emerged from the Collegium, the humid air heavy with the promise of rain. Her quarry was advancing toward Companion Field, a white shape trotting out to meet him.

Lelia slowed to a stop, gnawing on her lower lip. Vexing. Very vexing. She couldn't shadow him, not with this much open land between them. He'd see her coming. And then—

What? She blinked, realizing she was being stupid. *He's a Herald. He has to like you.* She lifted her chin. *Go talk to him, ask him your questions, and write your song!*

Yes, that was *exactly* what she would do.

Herald Wil leaned with his back to the fence, his arms folded over his chest and his eyes half-shut.

"It's hot," he confessed.

:*Rain's coming,*: Vehs replied.

"Good. This weather is giving me a headache."

:*Bard's coming.*:

"What?" He opened his eyes fully to stare at his Companion.

Just then, he heard the crush and rustle of someone walking through grass. Turning his head, he saw a small form in rust-red walking toward him.

:*Worse than a Bard,*: he thought at his Companion. :*It's a Bard-trainee.*:

"Pardon me, m'lord Herald," the girl said. She was short and fine-boned, with straight black hair and dusky skin. Her voice was surprisingly low and mellifluous. "Can I ask you about Daryann?"

Wil stared at her for a moment, dumbstruck.

Then he gave her the best answer he could come up with on short notice.

Malesa looked up with a raised brow as Lelia stomped in and sat down.

"No song?" she asked.

Lelia growled inarticulately.

"I had to go back and rework a couple lines on mine," Malesa admitted, patting the parchments spread out on the Library table. "I found I used 'light' no less than five times in the first six verses."

Lelia mumbled and snarled.

"Silly error, really, but that's what happens when you write something fast—"

"I found Herald Wil," Lelia said.

Malesa blinked. "Herald Who?"

"The brother of Herald Daryann."

"Bright Havens! Where?"

"He's back from circuit," Lelia continued through gritted teeth. "I spotted him in Companion's Field." She was omitting some truth by phrasing it that way, but she didn't think Malesa would care that she had been stalking the Herald. "I went up to him and asked a question."

"And?" Malesa asked, chin in hand.

"He said no." Lelia looked down at the brown-and-gray quill Malesa had been using. "Do you think if I stabbed myself in the eye with that thing—"

"Plenty of stories about blind Bards playing harp."

"Maybe if I got ink poisoning."

Malesa smirked. "So he said no?"

"Emphatically." Actually, what he'd done was swung up onto his Companion and ridden off. And the look he'd given her!

Fit to freeze hellfires, she thought with a shiver.

"What did you say?" Malesa asked.

" 'Can I ask you about Daryann?' "

"Did you introduce yourself?"

"Not exactly," she said slowly.

"You just went up and asked him, 'Hey, about that dead sister of yours. . . .' "

"Well . . . when you put it that way. . . ."

Malesa put her head in her hands. "Oh, 'Lia."

"What?"

"It's a wonder sometimes that you're a Bard. You have the tact of a stud in heat."

Lelia bristled. "It was an honest question!"

"There's honesty, and then there's rude. Did you even stop to consider his feelings?"

Lelia scowled and stared at the table. She'd expected comfort and commiseration from Malesa. Not a tongue-lashing on the ethics of questioning a subject.

"I just wanted to know," Lelia muttered.

"So what are you going to do now?"

Lelia thought about it for a moment. "Seduce him," she said decisively.

"Please tell me you jest."

Lelia wiggled her eyebrows.

"Well, you have fun." Malesa stood up, collecting her scrolls. "I'm off to practice the bridge of my stunning piece of genius."

"Fine, leave me to my misery." Lelia waved her off, then leaned back in her chair and stared at the ceiling.

"This," she said to no one in particular, "is going to be a challenge."

Lelia was anxious and fidgety all through class and morning chores, most of which involved restringing harps and lutes. The humidity had broken with a brief rain, but the result had been many out-of-tune instruments and much trainee busywork.

At the lunch bell, Lelia skipped the Bardic common room and instead retrieved a bandolier of knives from her quarters and took herself out to the practice salle. Even the Weaponsmaster had to eat sometime, and there was no one outside to watch her as she threw over and over, the handleless blades landing dead center more often than not.

"Nice grouping," a voice behind her said as she was pulling her last knife out of the wooden target. "Didn't know they were teaching Bards these things."

Lelia spun, startled. Standing behind her, his face half in and out of the salle's shadow, was Herald Wil.

She regained her composure quickly. "My parents are gleemen." She pushed damp, sweaty hair out of her eyes. "I learned knife-tricks from my grandmother."

His brows lifted. "I see."

She tucked the knives away into their sheaths; anything to keep herself from fidgeting. "Um . . . about yesterday."

"Yes, about that." He pushed away from the salle. "I behaved coarsely. I . . . apologize."

She nearly squealed with glee, and had to resist the urge to fall on her knees and praise the Bright Lady. *You do exist!* she thought.

"Does that mean I *can* ask you some questions about Daryann?" she asked.

He smiled warmly, turned around, and started to walk away.

"Herald?" she called, her hopes crashing to the ground once more. "Is that a no?"

"I just wanted you to know that I'm not angry at you, and I'm sorry if I acted like a brute," he yelled back, waving his hand. "Good day, trainee."

"Wait—" she called desperately to his departing back.

He stopped, looking over his shoulder at her.

"I—" Her mouth opened and closed. "I *really* need a song."

"Do what every Bard-trainee does," he replied. "Write about Sun and Shadow."

And then he laughed.

He *laughed*.

She sat down in the grass, watching him disappear.

"Oh," she said, her eyes narrowing, "I think *not*."

Later, as Wil was taking an early evening stroll through the Field with Vehs, he caught a flash of red out of the corner of his eye.

It was the Bard-trainee girl. She was charging toward him as fast as the tall grass and her own short legs would let her.

"What . . . ?" he said.

"Herald!" she yelled. "I just want to ask you a few questions!"

"Good gods," Wil blurted.

:*That famous Bardic stubbornness.*: Vehs actually sounded *amused*.

"Get me out of here," Wil mumbled, swinging up onto his Companion's back.

:*At your service, m'lord.*:

As Wil was coming out of the library after a satisfactory read, he heard the slap of boots behind him.

"Herald!" a familiar voice called. "Herald, just a moment of your time!"

His legs were longer than hers, and in better shape. He outran her, but only just.

Alone in a hallway and coming back from lunch, Wil was startled when the girl popped out from behind a velvet curtain and flung herself on him.

"I just want to know!" she panted as he wrestled out of her grip. "I just have a few questions to ask!"

He managed to escape to his room again, and threw the latch in case she grew more ambitious.

After that, he was on the lookout for any trace of rust-red or boots peeking out from under curtains and tapestries, and quick to avoid the small, persistent girl the moment she came into view.

"I have to question the ethics of this—"

"Question all you want," Lelia said, tossing her hair and giving Malesa a glare. "He *laughed* at me."

"And *you're* inquiring about his dead sister. That's called tasteless."

"It's been ten years, Malesa!" She flailed her arms frantically. "Ten! Years! He has to have found peace with it by now."

"Would *you* if it was Lyle?"

Lelia flinched, but ignored the question, muttering, "She deserves a spot in the Bardic repertoire."

Malesa eyed her. "Are you saying that because you actually believe it, or because it justifies your behavior?"

Lelia snorted derisively.

"Besides, even if *you* think it," Malesa continued, "he obviously doesn't."

"He *laughed* at me. A Herald!" She pushed her head out of a window and yelled in the direction of Companion's Field: "Just what kind of people are you *Choosing* nowadays?"

A passing page gave her a strange look. She growled back, sending the boy scurrying away with a squeak.

"You worry me," Malesa said.

"Oh, go get Chosen already. You sound like my brother." Lelia stopped at a door. "Speaking of which . . ."

She opened it and stepped inside. Lyle never did lock his door; he was just so damn trusting, sometimes. Many of his belongings had already been moved to his new suite, but a few things remained. And yes, there at the foot of his bed was a chest, and inside—

Lelia laughed darkly as she pulled out a gray shirt and pants.

"Astera bless a fool," Malesa moaned.

Wil sat down at a table apart from the others. There was really no quiet place in the common room, but this was far enough away that he could hear Vehs think if he needed to.

He also had an excellent vantage of all entrances. The moment he saw a rust-red figure walk in, he would walk out.

:*Why not sit with the others?*: Vehs asked.

:*I like being alone.*:

Vehs gave a purely mental sigh.

Wil was wiping up a large lump of meat and parsnip with a chunk of crusty bread when someone sat down next to him. A voice purred in his ear, "Heyla, Herald."

He looked to his left, and into the face of the black-haired Bard-trainee. In Grays.

No. Not *uniform* Grays. Gray shirt and pants, but not Grays.

"Uh," he said.

"You can call me Lelia."

:*Did she get Chosen?*: he thought at Vehs.

:*Suuure. And I sprout gryphon wings in the moonlight.*:

"Uh," Wil repeated.

"Tell me your story, Herald," she said in a low voice. "That's all I ask."

"You're walking a fine line," he said, nodding to her gray (but not Gray) clothing.

Her hard eyes remained fixed on him. "One story. Won't take long. I just want to know what happened to Daryann."

Wil's blood boiled at the sound of his sister's name. He pushed away from the table. "Excuse me."

She made a grab for his sleeve. "Herald—"

He jerked his head to where Elcarth sat several tables down. "One more word," Wil growled, "and I tell *him* what you're up to. Bardic Immunity or not, I doubt very much the Dean would be pleased to see how you're behaving."

Lelia released his sleeve, and Wil slipped out.

Wil sat down on his bed and rubbed his eyes. The effort to calm down after his last encounter with the Bardic Pest had left him exhausted mentally and physically.

That damn *girl*.

:*We might be heading back to circuit sooner than antici-pated,*: he thought to Vehs.

:Poor Chosen. Poor, poor Chosen.:

:It's nothing to be amused about.:

:Oh, I disagree. I think it's hysterical.:

Wil sighed deeply. *:She's defiling Daryann's memory.:*

:By writing a song about her legacy? That's not really defiling.:

:It's not her place.:

:But don't you think it's time you told someone?:

A cold knot crept up from Wil's stomach to his throat. Memories welled up, unbidden. The acrid smell of herbs and wine—etched lines around dark eyes—the soft *shush* of hair sliding over crisp linens as her head turned toward him—the gaunt, pale face, whittled to a wax doll parody by pain—

He shoved the memory rudely aside.

:No,: he replied.

He stretched out on his bed, abstaining the covers. He preferred an old, loose shirt and breeches to smothering layers of bedding. Bit by bit, he drifted toward the borders of dreaming, relaxing gently into sleep's embrace.

It was strange, just *how* relaxed he was. And his feet—they were nice and warm and—

His eyes snapped open. Someone was rubbing his feet.

He yanked his legs back and sat up. Belatedly, he realized he'd forgotten to latch the door. There was just enough moon-and starlight coming through his windows that he could see an all-too-familiar fine-boned face at the end of his bed.

"That's it!" he roared at her, swinging out of bed and bearing down on her. "Get out! Leave me alone! Leave *her* alone!"

Lelia stared at him, her mouth wide open. "I—" she started to say.

"Out!"

She backed away from the murderous rage in his eyes, turned, and ran.

He heard a faint sob as she fled.

Wil slumped back onto his bed.

"Ah, Lord," he mumbled, rubbing his forehead. "Ah hellfires."

Lelia bolted back to her quarters, half-sobbing the whol

way. Wil's anger had been startling—overwhelming—terrifying. The only thing she could think to do was run from it.

She opened the door to her room, reaching for the laces of the gray shirt— Her twin sat in the chair by her bed, his hands folded in his lap. Lelia froze in place, the heat of embarrassment creeping across her cheeks.

"Heyla," Lyle said softly.

She shut the door, her hand falling to her side.

"That shirt doesn't fit, you know," he said, and then sighed. "What's wrong, 'Lia?"

She shook her head, sitting down on the bed and not looking at him. "Nothing."

"I'm worried about you," he said. "So is Malesa. She and I . . . talked tonight."

Lelia grimaced at the implications of that.

Lyle sat down next to her, putting his arm around her shoulder. "Thy heart is heavy, little songbird?"

The familiar, comforting sound of her childhood dialect crushed her pitiful attempts to shut him out.

"I think I did a bad thing," she whispered.

"What could be that bad?"

Her words emerged as halting, half-incoherent sentences. She told him her fear of never finishing the song that would make her a full Bard, her days stalking Wil, and the disastrous consequences of intruding on the Herald in his bedchambers; the frightening display of anger that had sent her scurrying for her room.

When she finished, Lyle sat quietly, mulling over her tale.

"In his *bedchambers*?" he said at last.

She ducked her head. "I didn't see anything—"

"You violated his privacy."

She slumped.

"You should apologize to him," he said.

"I should apologize to him," she echoed listlessly.

"And maybe I'll get him as a circuit mentor, and I can explain to him my crazy Bard-sib."

The word "circuit" crashed down on her shoulders like a lead church bell. In a fit of recklessness, Lelia blurted the words she'd never dared given breath before, *"You're going to die!"*

"What?" He knelt in front of her, taking her hands in

his. She Felt his concern and love down the line of their bond so fiercely it startled her. "No, Lelia."

"You'll be leaving me, at the very least," she said, half hysterical, tears streaming down her cheeks. "Gods, Lyle, do you know how many stories I know? Do you know how many times I hear about the Heralds who don't return from circuit? Do you know what happens to a twin when the other one . . ."

She couldn't finish it. The growing dread in her heart made her feel like she'd already said too much.

"I'm so selfish," she said, shaking her head.

"Y . . . eah," he agreed. When she gave him a startled look, he grinned. " 'Lia, it's not a bad thing. I see you as my balance. Given half a chance, I'd beat myself to death to help others. I need you to remind me that, sometimes it's okay to help myself." He touched her shoulder. "I worry about you, too, you know. In a few months you'll be wandering out there on your own . . . who knows what trouble you'll run into without me around to balance you out?"

"Why couldn't you have been a Healer?" she asked, not smiling. "Or a Bard? Why couldn't you be like me? We're supposed to be twins!"

He laughed, but there was a brittleness to it.

"Bright Lady. Bright Havens." She crushed his hand in hers. "How I wish you didn't have to go."

They sat together in the darkness, holding hands just as they had during thunderstorms as littles. She couldn't imagine a world without Lyle in it to give her comfort, to bear her through the storms. She just couldn't.

Lelia got up early the next morning, dressed once again in rust-red. She'd lain in bed all night, struggling to come up with a plan for dealing with Wil and the damage she'd caused.

Before breakfast, she hiked down to Companion's Field and went hunting.

It didn't take her long. The Companion she searched for was wide awake; he even seemed to be waiting for her.

"Heyla," she said, approaching him. "You're Wil's Companion, right?"

The stallion tossed his head.

"Well, I know very well you're probably smarter than me," she said. "I also know I owe some things to your Chosen." She reached up and scratched his neck. "So I need to ask you a favor." And she told him her plan.

Much to her surprise, he nodded in agreement.

Wil didn't see Lelia all the next day. Or the next.

As the candlemarks passed, his discomfort outgrew his ability to ignore it. By dinnertime he was wrestling with the twin serpents of guilt and anger. Why should *he* feel guilty? *She* was the one intruding on his life! *She* was the one who refused to leave him alone! *She* . . .

"Damnit," he muttered as he sat down to eat by himself in the common room.

It didn't matter what *she* had done. *He* had lost his temper. *He* had raised his voice. *He* was better than that.

Or supposed to be. *He* was the one with a cart-sized otherworldly horse on his side.

Dinner ended quickly, but the self-flagellation remained. He wandered back to his room, lost in the emotional push and pull of anger and shame.

He stopped in front of his door.

A note was pinned to it with one of Lelia's knives.

He gritted his teeth, took it down, and opened it up.

It read:

> *If you want to see your Companion again, come to the Grove Chapel in one candlemark.*
>
> *Signed,*
> *L.*

He stared for a moment, dumbstruck.

:Vehs,: he thought, *:where are you?:*

:Oh, Chosen!: Vehs thought back. *:Please save me! The evil Bard-trainee has me and—:*

:This is not *funny.:*

:She refuses to play anything but "My Lady's Eyes"! It's awful, Chosen!:

"This is ridiculous," Wil mumbled.

:Ah, gods! She's invented a chorus to it! Save me!:

"I'm going to kill you both," he sighed.

*   *   *

Lelia wasn't playing "My Lady's Eyes" when Wil strolled up. She *was* sitting on a stump and playing, but the song she'd chosen was one from his own sector of Valdemar; a piece by the Bard Faber called "Seven White Horses."

Vehs lingered nearby, a loose bit of rope around his neck. She'd tied him off to a dead sapling he could have snapped without breaking a sweat.

Her strings grew silent as Wil approached. She put the lute in its case, closed it with a snap, and walked over to Vehs, untying him and tucking the rope into her belt. She stood on tiptoe, whispered something in his ear, and then gave the Companion a kiss on one plump cheek.

Vehs looked away. To Wil, he seemed to be blushing.

Lelia approached Wil and looked up at him.

He steeled himself.

Be calm, he thought. *Whatever you do, be calm. Be gentle. You're a Herald, damnit. Act like one.*

"I'm sorry," she said. She patted him on the arm as she walked away.

Wil blinked stupidly, caught off guard. An ache started in his heart and throat, and grew the longer he stood there.

Damnit.

"Wait," he said.

Her footsteps continued to fade away.

"*Wait,*" he said again, turning toward her.

She started to run.

Lelia didn't want to know anymore.

She ran through the Grove like an arrow aimed at the Collegium. She'd write something—she had to—and it would be terrible—and unoriginal—and it would probably be about Sun and Shadow—and it would probably get her kicked out of the Bardic Collegium—and she would have to go back to juggling knives with her family—but she didn't care—she didn't care—she—

A white shape flashed to her right. Vehs leaped in front of her. She flailed to a stop, sliding in the grass and leaves, clutching her precious lutecase to her chest. She fell on her back and stared up at him.

Wil frowned down at her from Companion-back.

"Wait," he said stubbornly.

She blinked, flinging tiny bits of tears from her lashes.

He dismounted and sat down next to her. "Just—wait."

Crickets sang, nightingales warbled. Vehs' white coat shone like moonlight, a silent challenge to the growing darkness.

"She didn't die immediately," Wil said at last. "It took a month. Her Companion—he carried her all the way to Haven, and then collapsed. He—died. She should have, too.

"But she didn't. She held on. The Healers didn't know why for the longest time. And then one day she woke long enough to Mindspeak something vital—some bit of intelligence she'd been holding on to. I was there. I saw her eyes when she slipped away—to the Havens."

Somewhere, a frog gulped. Lelia said nothing and made no move except to breathe.

"The whole Heraldic Circle was in a fury," Wil continued. "Everyone wanted the raiders who did it to her. It was a mess."

He stared numbly into the darkness. To his surprise, he felt Lelia's calloused fingers close over his hand.

"She fought going," he said, "because of duty. She had to fulfill it."

"And to say good-bye."

He looked at Lelia, startled. "What?"

"To you. To say good-bye."

"To me? Why?"

She gave him a confused look. "Havens, Wil, she loved you. Why wouldn't she want to say good-bye?"

Wil blinked stupidly, thunderstruck by the obviousness of her statement. In ten years, the thought so simply expressed to him now by a Bard-trainee had never once occurred to him.

His shoulders tightened and the aura of a headache threatened. He'd avoided it for so long—the memory of that moment when Daryann's eyes had opened. The clamor of the Healers—the shouts for a Herald—Daryann's head had turned toward him, like a north-needle gravitating toward its inexorable position—

He pushed past the pain of the loss, and allowed himself to finally, really remember that moment.

She had *seen* him.

"She winked," he said slowly. "She winked at me."

Something inside him broke free. He felt as if an old weight—one he'd forgotten was there—had been lifted away.

Lelia's hand slid off of his. He heard the lutecase open and the hum of the disturbed strings as she pulled it out. Notes—bittersweet and haunting—rose from the belly of the instrument, hanging in the air.

Lelia sang.

"Bring them home," she began, directing the lyrics at Vehs. *"White guardian . . ."*

And it just kept going from there. She knew, as it bubbled out of her, that it wasn't a six-verse piece of genius. The lyrics weren't terribly clever. The melody had none of the flash of "My Lady's Eyes." But it came straight from her heart, the truest expression of what she felt. It was exactly the song she could write at that moment, it was complete, it was hers, and it was enough.

The Grove had fallen into silence by the time she finished.

"Not really about her," she said at last. "More *for* her than *about* her. I think the bridge needs work. And—"

"It'll do," Wil said.

She rubbed her lute's neck. "You think so?"

"I do."

She nodded. "Me, too."

The morning of her performance, Lelia got up at dawn and wandered down to watch as Lyle put the final touches on saddling Rivan.

"Where are you headed?" she asked.

"West," he replied. "Not quite Evendim, but close. Forst Reach. Don't know if you've heard of it—"

"Ashkevron holdings." Her eyes flashed. "I've always wanted to see the famous manor."

He smiled. "Ah yes. I forget that I speak with the Kingdom's greatest authority on dead Heraldic heroes."

"Only the pretty ones." She eyed her twin critically. "You'll say hello to Mother and Father?"

"Oh, hellfires. Are *they* out that way?"

"Lyle."

He grinned. "If I can."

"You'll stay away from trouble?"

"Of course."

"And at the first sign of danger, you'll ride straight back to Haven and let the Army handle it?"

He nodded solemnly. "I promise."

She smiled and stood up on tiptoe, throwing her arms around him. "Be safe," she whispered in his ear.

"If we meet not in this Haven," he whispered back, "we shall meet in another."

She let him go, and then turned toward Rivan.

"Bring him home," she sang to him.

The stallion tossed his head in a Companion's nod.

Wil strode in, decked out in riding leathers.

"Are you two ladies going to stand around clinging to each other all day, or are we going to leave?" he asked, glowering.

"I believe my instructor is not what one might call a 'morning person'," Lyle said in a mock whisper to Lelia.

"Surely," she "whispered" back, "he could take lessons in charm from Alberich."

"Bright Lady." Wil rolled his eyes. "I'll have to ask the Dean what I did to deserve this." He nailed Lelia with a look. "I need to have a word with your sister, Lyle. Alone."

"Yes, m'lord Herald," Lyle said, bowing his head and beckoning to Rivan. The two walked out, leaving Wil and Lelia in the Stable.

"Yes?" she asked.

He took a step forward, extending a fist. His fingers uncurled, revealing a silver necklace with the shield of Valdemar hanging off it.

"For you," he said. "For luck."

She blinked, reaching out and taking it gingerly.

His fingers closed over hers.

She looked up at him, startled.

"We'll come home," he promised her, then bent down and kissed her on the forehead.

"You'll come home," she agreed, her heart thumping in her chest.

He turned and started to walk away.

"You'll come home!" she yelled, running at him and

jumping on his back. He grunted as she threw her arms around his shoulders and hugged him fiercely.

Lelia slid down and stepped away, grinning like a fool. Wil looked back once, a faint smile on his face.

The hooves of the Companions chimed as the two Heralds rode out, heading for Haven proper and the rest of the Kingdom they served.

Malesa leaned over and whispered, "Nervous?"

"Nope." Lelia grinned, tapping her necklace.

"Did you finish your song?"

"Yes."

"And who gave you that lovely necklace?"

Lelia's grin widened.

"I see." Malesa raised a brow. "What makes you smile so, dear?"

"Because the Council's going to vote soon," she said. "And when I'm a journeyman Bard, I know exactly where *I'm* going."

"Really?"

"Oh, yes." Lelia smiled. "I've always wanted to visit the birthplace of the Last Herald-Mage."

SONG FOR TWO VOICES

by *Janni Lee Simner*

Janni Lee Simner has published nearly three dozen short stories, including appearances in *Gothic! Ten Original Dark Tales*, on the labels of Story House's coffee cans, and in the first Valdemar anthology, *Sword of Ice*. Her next novel, *Tiernay West, Professional Adventurer,* will be published in 2006. Visit her web site at www.simner.com.

GAREN'S Voice

This is not some Herald's ballad. We Holderkin are practical folk, and we know what matters: sun and land, wheat and hay, breaking horses to saddle, protecting those in our care. These are the things you should ask about, if you wish to know our ways.

The story you ask for instead ought to be none of your concern. Yet Holderkin pay their debts, and you say this is the only payment you'll accept.

Know this, then. I was content, even before Nara came. I care for my Steading, which was my father's before raiders sent him to the God, ten years past. I care for my first three wives, and my two brothers, and my oldest son, who works beside me in the fields. I care for my littles, even those too small to work.

I've seen you Heralds scowl. You think Holderkin men care only for themselves. Yet I know well enough the gifts the God has granted me, and I give thanks for them.

Just as I give thanks for the winter day last year, when I visited my cousin Jeth to trade a sure-footed plow horse

247

for some wool. As I followed Jeth into his hall, I heard a
high, sweet song, above the crackle of the fire and the whir
of the spinning wheel.

Birdsong, I thought—but the voice was human, a girl's
voice. I looked across the room and saw her, bent over the
spinning wheel, dark hair hiding her face. She sang of a
time when the Goddess freely wandered the fields, feet
bare and hair unbound, before she met the God. A woman's hymn; men do not sing it. Yet hearing her, something
inside me woke, and grew restless, and yearned to answer
the song. My fields and hall seemed suddenly small, simply
because her voice wasn't in them.

You say such things are known, in your ballads and your
lives. But they are not known here.

The girl looked up, and her hair fell back, revealing dark
eyes and pale skin. She looked at me without shame, and
I met her over-bold gaze. She fell silent then, her song
unfinished, and without warning she smiled.

I smiled back. Her face grew red, and she leaned back
over her spinning.

I knew, then, that I could not leave without her. I turned
to my cousin.

"Your daughter," I said, for this had to be one of his
daughters. "Do you intend to arrange a marriage for her
soon?"

Nara's Voice

You ask for our story. I do not know how to tell a story.
I only know that until I came to Garen's Steading, I was
not content.

I had my work, in my father's home: endless spinning,
and weaving, and cooking, and caring for littles. The work
needed doing; I understood that. I understand it still. Is it
different in the north? Here, we know that every person is
sacred in the eyes of the Goddess, put in the place we are
put, given the work we are given, because that work matters, and is meant for us.

Yet knowing this, I still longed to walk the barren ridges,
to look out over the narrow valleys, to feel the wind tan-
gling my hair. When I was younger, I'd spent my days outside on sheep watch, and been happy; but that was long
ago, before I was replaced by littles too young for other

tasks. By the time Garen came, my days were mostly spent indoors, with my mother and my sisters and the other wives of the Steading.

But the Goddess never gives us a task without also giving us what we need to complete it. And what She gave me was song.

I sang as I worked, hymns and teaching songs, songs no one could find improper. The work went better when I sang. The walls and roof felt less near, the wind and sun less far. I was fortunate; my father's firstwife welcomed my songs, perhaps because the littles also worked better when I sang.

Then a stranger entered my father's hall and met my improper gaze. And—I do not know how to say this. When I looked into his gray eyes, I saw open fields and the spaces between clouds. For the first time, I thought maybe marriage—the marriage I knew my father must arrange, soon or late—might be more than just another set of walls.

Garen's Voice

Of course I left without her, that day. There was the dowry to negotiate, and the priest to consult, and the ceremony to arrange. But at last we knelt together, beneath the open sky, the men and the women of our households around us. It was one of those rare spring days, when the sky is so blue you fear it will break in two, exposing the first level of Heaven above.

But I forget—you don't believe in Heaven, only in endless Havens and countless gods, with none to tell which is true.

The priest chanted the ritual prayers. We gave the ritual responses, and if my attention was more on the curve of Nara's neck and the sun on her bound hair than on my own words, still I meant those words.

At last the priest asked for our vows. "Do you, Garen Aranson, vow to serve the God and honor the Goddess? To defend your Steading and your fields, your brothers and sons, your daughters and wives?"

"I do so vow."

"And you, Nara Jethsdaughter. Do you vow to serve the God and honor the Goddess, and to obey your husband and your elder wives in all things?"

Nara smiled. "I do so vow."

The priest drew us to our feet. I looked into Nara's dark eyes; they seemed as large as all the sky. I could have gazed at her forever, but then she bowed, as the ceremony demanded, and stepped back to join the women of my household, showing she accepted her place as one underwife among many.

The priest sang a hymn then, recounting the first meeting of God and Goddess—when the Goddess grew restless, and wandered beyond her realm, and could not find her way back. Both households joined him in that song, all but me; the God gave me no gift for singing, and I knew my voice would be no tribute.

Nara stood with my other wives, her shoulders straight, her eyes cast properly down. She sang with my other wives, her voice no louder than theirs. Yet somehow her song rose above the others—and though I knew better, her voice still seemed not one among many to me, but its own, distinct.

Nara's Voice

I was happy, married. I did not expect that.

Garen's Firstwife, Latya, had work for me, of course, laundry and cooking, cleaning saddles, grooming horses, mending tack. But often that work took me outside, where I could linger over the blooming of orange paintbrush and purple lupines, where I could watch the shifting gray clouds. I sang beneath those clouds, and I sang in the hall, too. So long as the work was done, and done properly, Latya did not complain.

It is true that proper and improper matter a great deal more to Latya than to my mother, or even to my father's firstwife. Latya expects hair to always be bound, and collars to always be buttoned, and tunics and leggings to always be ironed beyond creasing. Yet I am dutiful, as much as I am able.

I did not see Garen often, those first months, save for mealtimes and the nights he came to my room; he had his work, just as I had mine. But sometimes, I would turn from grooming horses to see him in the stable doorway, silent, listening to me sing. He would smile, and I would smile back, and the stable walls would seem to fall away, as if we stood together beneath the sky, just as we had on our wedding day. My work somehow always seemed lighter, after one of those meetings.

But I am telling this out of order. Before the stables, there was the first time Garen came to my room, the night we were married. I was shy and afraid; my mother had told me to expect pain. Yet Garen was slow and gentle, as concerned for me as for himself. When we came together, I felt as if we were closer than skin and bone should allow; felt as if we shared a single body, a single space. Afterward, I pressed my body close to his, not wanting to let the feeling go, yet knowing that all things fade, in time.

Garen brushed my loose hair aside, and he whispered in my ear, "I am glad you have joined my Steading."

"I am glad, too," I said, and meant it with all my soul.

The times after have been like this, too, more often than not. Is it so for everyone, or only for us?

It seems immodest to ask.

Garen's Voice

Lying with Nara is not like lying with anyone else. My first three wives are dutiful. They give what is required. But they draw away from me when that duty is done, and I from them. I don't linger in their beds as I do in hers. I could lie with Nara every night, if not for my other wives. I could spend my days watching her, if not for the work of my Steading.

But that is not for you to record, and it is not for sharing with your fellow Heralds.

Say instead that spring turned to summer, summer to fall, the seasons in the order the God set them. Raiders attacked other Steadings and Holdings, but spared mine. Latya bore another son, and my second underwife, Isa, a daughter. Nara showed no signs of bearing children, but she was good with the littles. Like me, they seemed to listen for her song.

One stormy afternoon I entered the common room to hear Nara singing as she twisted dried grasses to rope, while wind pounded the walls and hail pounded the roof. The littles sorted grasses by length around her.

Nara sang of Jania's ride. You do not know this song; it is a Holderkin song, about a maiden whose brother was killed by raiders while they were on sheep watch. The raiders dishonored the girl, but she escaped, riding alone through darkness and storm to warn her Steading of the attackers. She knew her duty, you see. She delivered the warning first. Only afterward did she take her life, to keep her dishonor from her family.

Yet when Nara sang this song, I heard more than duty and honor. I heard the joy of hooves on stone, of rain on skin, of wind through hair. I longed to sing with my wife—but no, I'd not sully her verses with my rough voice. Instead I smiled as I listened, entranced as the littles.

Nara did not look up, but she smiled as well. Then Latya entered the room, her arms full of laundry. I looked away from my underwife, but not before Latya saw my lingering gaze. Latya's frown made that clear enough.

I see you don't understand. You know only that a holder is free to do as he will. And he is; the God made that clear long ago. But the God lives in His Heaven, with only His one Goddess. I have four wives, and Latya is first among them. She oversees the work of hearth and hall, waking before dawn to do much of that work herself. I value my firstwife, and I would not have her think otherwise.

So I decided I would be more careful. But my gaze drifted to Nara again before I left the room.

And again, it was Latya, not Nara, who saw.

Nara's Voice

One stormy afternoon, Latya changed all the tasks she set before me.

She did it abruptly, without warning or reason. At once my work was entirely indoors: scrubbing rooms, tending the fire (but not gathering the wood), mending clothing (but not mending tack). I saw Latya's displeasure clearly enough, though I did not know what I had done to earn it and she did not explain.

I did not complain of this. Instead, I turned to my new work and to a song, determined to regain the firstwife's favor. I sang of how the Goddess urged the sun to rise, in the God's realm, of how she coaxed golden wheat from the hard soil, to ease her loneliness far from home.

For the first time, Latya frowned at my song. "Dear

Nara," she said, "I know you've been lonely, away from your home, and so I've not spoken of your singing until now. But in truth, it is not proper, and it disrupts the work. I must ask you to stop."

I opened my mouth to protest; closed it again. I was a new wife, a young wife. I'd vowed before the Goddess to obey my elder wives, as surely as I'd vowed to obey my husband.

You look troubled by that. Is it true that in the north, a woman has only her one husband to obey, and no other wives?

In truth, I was troubled, too. I had not understood that obeying my other wives—obeying other women—might be harder than obeying my husband.

I told myself there was time enough for things to change. Latya's displeasure—whatever its cause—would wane, and I would be assigned other duties, performed in places where I could sing unheard, and trouble no one. I told myself I could wait. I reminded myself that the Goddess never gives us tasks we cannot handle.

Yet as the weeks went on, I felt as if my unsung words were choking me. My only comfort came the nights Garen visited my room, but that was a fleeting thing, gone once we parted, leaving me alone in a room that felt smaller every day.

Garen's Voice

Nara stopped working outside. She stopped singing inside. I didn't know why; I knew only that the days felt longer, without her voice. And the nights I went to her room, she seemed far away from me, even when I drew her close.

I asked if anything troubled her, more than once, but she just shook her head. Yet I knew something was wrong, knew it in a way that went deeper than reason.

Fall gave way to an early winter, though not before we got the harvest in. Silence and cold settled over my Steading. I had good offers on the geldings I brought to saddle, not only from Holderkin, but also from the villages to our north, who are learning that Holderkin horses bear work and bad weather with less complaint than their own.

I offered you one of those horses, but you wanted this story instead. A holder would have taken the horse and been long gone.

But what you need to know is, my Steading was prospering. Yet my fourth wife was not content, and I did not know why. I knew only that because of this, I was not content either.

It was with these thoughts that I set out with my oldest son, Ari, to fix fences on Midwinter Day. Understand that. I was worried about my wife.

Not about myself.

Nara's Voice

No one knows when the world will change—when an offer of marriage will come, or a woman grow heavy with child, or an early frost damage the crops and turn an easy year into a hard one.

I was uneasy all Midwinter Day. Once, I stopped at a jabbing pain in my leg, and nearly dropped the mugs I was carrying to the table. Latya asked if I was well, and I assured her I was, but my uneasiness grew even as the pain faded. I knew something was wrong.

So I was the only one not surprised, when the pounding came at the doors. I think I even shouted Garen's name— before those doors were opened. I don't remember clearly.

What I do remember is that Ari and a stranger in white carried Garen inside. Garen's clothes were splattered red; a raider's arrow jutted from his thigh.

Later I would realize that you were a Herald, and a woman, and that though you came upon the raiders by chance, you fought alongside my husband and his son. You broke three ribs doing it; you were injured, too, and would need time here to heal. Later, it would surprise me that a Herald would fight for Holderkin.

But just then, I knew only that I ran with the others to Garen's rooms. I kept thinking about the brothers I'd lost to raiders, and of how losing Garen would be so much worse. It would be like—like losing wind and sky.

I know that sounds foolish. I am sorry. I have no better words for such things.

Isa removed the arrow—her mother is a midwife, and

taught her some doctoring—whispering thanks to the Goddess that the point was not barbed. She cleaned the wound and bandaged it. Blood soaked through the white linen, far too fast.

I don't like to remember this. The coppery smell of the room, my husband's pained breathing, the unsteady beat of his pulse. I knew I could not lose him.

I knew I could not leave him. Latya argued with me; then she set me to watching over him instead. "But you are to call me the moment you see any change," she said, and I saw her own care and worry clearly enough.

You seem surprised. I don't see why. Do you think Holderkin women don't care for their husbands? If what you tell me is true, perhaps what Latya felt was not what I felt. But she would have mourned Garen's death, just the same.

For a time I sat by Garen's side. His eyes were closed, and I called his name, as if that would open them. Then I fell silent, chiding myself for thinking he might wake, just because I bid him to. What man had ever done anything because of a woman's voice? Instead, I took his hand in mine. I wondered how I would survive the long years ahead, alone.

I thought that: alone. In a thriving Steading, among many men and wives, I would be alone, without this one man. The walls of his bedchamber seemed very near. I thought perhaps I would go mad, indoors, alone all my days. I remembered Jania's ride, and for the first time, I understood its end. I understood the despair that led Jania to take her own life, and I knew that her fate could be my own. In that moment, there was only one thing I could do.

I sang.

Did you expect otherwise? I had not forgotten Latya's command. But disobedience could be punished and forgiven—later, when I stood safe beneath the light of day. Even if Garen were meant to die, I could not believe the Goddess wanted my life, too.

I sang Jania's song, softly at first. I lost myself in wind and rain, in the pounding of hooves. I forgot the ceiling and walls around me.

I did not forget Garen, though. When it came time for

Jania to take her life, my voice faltered. I heard again my husband's ragged breath. I felt his clammy hand in mine. I couldn't sing of death, not with death so near.

But then Garen squeezed my hand, though he shouldn't have had the strength for it. "Sing," he whispered, his voice hoarse and fierce.

So I sang. Not of Jania's death, but of a second escape: of how she knew she could not remain with her family, dishonored; so instead she retreated to the barren ridges and narrow valleys she loved well, and rode there all her days. A foolish ending, I know; it would not happen that way. But I have sung no other ending since.

My voice rose; I barely noticed. Garen's grip remained tight—remained strong. I sang the song through again, and again, my voice gaining strength with each repetition.

I did not hear the door open. I knew only that when at last my voice fell silent, you and Latya both stood in the doorway, watching me. I looked down, face hot, avoiding your stares, leaning over my husband instead.

His pulse was strong, his breathing even. He still held my hand.

"You—" Latya began.

"I am sorry," I said swiftly. "I was tired, and the watch was long—"

"You saved him," Latya said.

Again you are surprised. Yet Latya is not foolish. She understands what needs understanding. She knows, now, that my song was needful, and she will not forbid me song again. Holderkin women are practical. More practical, perhaps, than those who let white horses decide their fate.

That was disrespectful. I am sorry.

At any rate, you know as well as I what you said next. Your words were strange to me, are strange still.

"I did not realize," you said, "that there were lifebonds among Holderkin."

You said you wished to know our story.

I do not know how to tell a story.

Garen's Voice

Her song saved me. There is no other way to tell it.

I was ready to leave this world. No more, for me, the dizzying pain of broken flesh and lost blood. I wanted the

God's peace. I knew I could face His judgment without shame. The raiders were dead, after all, by my hand and Ari's and yours. I knew we owed you a debt, and that was an uncomfortable thought—but it was also a matter for others. I was done here.

Until I heard Nara's song, reminding me what it was to live, to ride beneath the sky. I knew, then, that whatever else was finished, there was something between Nara and me that was not yet done, something new and incomplete, something I was not free to leave. You call it a lifebond—call it what you will. What matters is that, though I am a man, I was not—am not—free.

I held to her song. I held to her. As if she were my only wife, the only woman in all the world.

So I lived. Through that night, and through the nights after, to this day when you say you have healed enough to be on your way. I asked how we could repay you, for I know Ari and I could not have killed those raiders alone. You told me what payment you would accept.

Now that payment is delivered, and I need not say more. I walk slowly with this cane, but I can walk, and since I can walk, I can work. I have three geldings ready to sell, and two mares in foal, and the fences still need fixing. There is much to do, and if Nara's song makes the work go better, that is for the good. It is as the God intended.

A man has many wives—many people—in his care. Nara and I are bound, but not only to each other. The God places many obligations upon us. We are not Heralds. We seek more than simply to be free.

You are not Holderkin. You do not understand.

Nothing has changed.

Everything has changed.

Nara's Voice

I am bound to Garen, yes. But I also serve the Goddess, and my elder wives. I have not been put in this place by chance; it is the Goddess' will. It is for a reason, even if I cannot always see that reason for myself.

You say this troubles you. Yet I think maybe Heralds know how to serve, too. I think you know about having your fate decided by powers beyond your understanding.

And I think perhaps the story you asked for ends here.

I can tell you this, though: last night, it was my turn to look after Garen. His wound still troubles him, and will for some time. I gave him medicine to numb that pain, and because it was late, and the day's work was done, he accepted it. As he grew sleepy he asked me, "Would you ride from this place, if you could?"

His words startled me. I thought he spoke of Heralds. "This is my home," I said, because it is true, and because it says all else I would have said.

"You wouldn't ride as Jania rode, then?" Garen's tone was light, but his gaze was not. If not for the medicine, he wouldn't have spoken thus.

"Jania rode these ridges," I said, "and these valleys. She did not ride in some stranger's land."

Abruptly, Garen grabbed my hand. "Nara," he said, "You must not be silent again. I must always hear your voice."

"Always?" I laughed, trying to make it a joke. "If the God and Goddess grant us years enough together, you might regret that."

"Always," he said, and he did not laugh.

Garen will not tell you this. Perhaps I should not tell you either.

But his serious voice made me feel strange, shy as the day we met. "I will not be silent," I promised. And then, shyer still, I said, "I wish something, too."

"What do you wish?" Garen asked, even though he need not do anything on account of my wishes.

"I wish to hear your voice. I wish—to hear you sing." He never had, you see, in all the months I'd been here.

"My voice is no gift from the God," Garen said.

"I wish to hear it, just the same."

So he sang the hymn from our wedding day. His voice was rough, and off-key, and perfect. I added my high voice to his low one, and as we sang together, I knew there was in truth a bond between us, and that it was not like other bonds.

You say the gods have put this thing between Garen and me. I do not know your gods. I know only one Goddess, who is lost and seeks a way home; and one God, who has offered her shelter and longs to keep her forever by his side. Yet nothing is forever; one day the Goddess will return home. One day Garen and I will be parted, for a time at least. If Garen leaves first, my only comforts will be my songs and my land, and even they will not be enough. Yet that parting will not be this day, and that matters more than any story can say.

But then, I do not know how to tell a story. I only know how to sing.

Garen does not know how to sing. But he is learning.

FINDING ELVIDA

by Mickey Zucker Reichert

Mickey Zucker Reichert is the author of such masterful DAW fantasy novels as *Beyond Ragnarok, Prince of Demons,* and *The Children of Wrath (The Renshai Chronicles* trilogy), *The Last of the Renshai, The Western Wizard,* and *Child of Thunder (The Last of the Renshai* trilogy), *The Bifrost Guardians* series, *The Legend of Nightfall, Flightless Falcon,* and *The Unknown Soldier,* her debut science fiction novel for DAW. She is also the coauthor (with *Jennifer Wingert*) of the spellbinding fantasy novel, *Spirit Fox.* Mickey lives in Iowa with her husband and three of their children, and divides her time between her family, her writing, teaching at the local university, and the assorted livestock.

A SWORD crashed against Elvida's with a force that nearly unseated her from Raynor's saddle. Trusting the Companion to tend to balance, she put her full concentration into harmlessly redirecting the strike. Her riposte followed naturally, training drummed into habit by Weaponsmaster Altorin. Her blade struck flesh with a sickening tear. Pain thrummed through her hands, her enemy a target more solid than mock combat had prepared her to expect. Blood splashed, throwing red spots and squiggles across Raynor's snowy neck and her own silvery gray uniform. The man collapsed, and a bitter thread of bile clawed its way up Elvida's throat.

Cursing the dark curls that obscured her vision, Elvida

wasted a motion tossing them from her eyes. She followed the sound of bridle bells to find the other two Companions, Tabnar and Leahleh, together. Surrounded by a mass of unmounted enemies, Herald Sharylle and her partner Anthea flailed wildly through the press. Scarlet splattered their Herald Whites and their faces, and the warriors bayed at them like blood-sick hounds.

Open for the moment, Elvida suffered a moment of terror. Her first mission was supposed to be routine, a leisurely ride through the Holdings, hauling a single cart. They would plant soaproot and blue bells, help organize the restocking of Waystations, and gather information to assure nothing troublesome was brewing just beyond the kingdom. Instead, danger had found them, in the form of a small and, as yet, unidentified army. One that clearly hated Heralds.

Sharylle screamed in clear agony. Her Companion plummeted, and both disappeared beneath the wild mass of warriors.

"No!" Elvida shouted, her cry lost beneath Anthea's louder one, raw with a pain so desperate and primeval it stopped the assault long enough for her to disengage as well.

"This way!" Anthea called out, and her Companion wheeled suddenly toward Elvida. "The cave."

Elvida remembered the dark hole they had passed earlier that day. Dank and jagged, it had seemed to radiate a chill that spiraled through her marrow, so unlike the myriad welcoming Waystations that had brought the three women and their Companions through so many warm, safe nights. Elvida had relished the camaraderie, opening up to the Heralds in ways she had never dared to in the past. For the first time in her life, she had felt as if she had real sisters, though she also found herself envying the bond the Heralds shared.

Raynor reared, spun, and galloped toward the cave. The suddenness of the movement added to Elvida's gastric distress. Mentally, she suffered her own terror, the rage of the enemies, and the deep, hellish agony of Anthea together. The mixture made her desperately ill. Leaning forward, she vomited, trying not to further soil Raynor or herself. It felt silly to concern herself with hygiene at a time when it seemed abundantly clear: They were all going to die.

Raynor's slender, muscular legs carried them at a speed the unmounted warriors could never hope to match. Apparently reading her terror, her Companion sent waves of encouragement that did not fool Elvida. Without the magical strength to Mindspeak, his Herald-in-training was limited to empathic communication, but she had learned that well. Raynor could try, but he would never wholly hide that his own courage was a thin veneer masking a fear nearly as strong as her own.

Leahleh loosed a frantic whinny, followed by a cry from Anthea. Raynor whirled in time to show Elvida that the Herald had fallen. Leahleh stomped and snorted, her empty stirrups flying, attempting to hold a band of men with waving swords at bay. Elvida saw no sign of Anthea. *Where is she? Where is she?*

Raynor nickered in question.

Elvida glanced around frantically, knowing every moment wasted meant one less in flight. She knew Sharylle and Tabnar were dead; Anthea would never have abandoned her partner if any hope remained. Now, Elvida searched for some radiating emotion that would assure her the remaining Herald still lived. Nothing came to Elvida's mental senses, but her wildly leaping gaze did eventually land on Anthea. The woman lay among the stones, blood trickling from one ear. Though clearly unconscious, her chest still rose and fell in obvious, living breaths.

Leahleh whinnied in agony.

"She's alive!" Elvida jerked Raynor's left rein. "We have to save her."

Raynor did not hesitate, speeding back toward the fray while Elvida wrestled her own decision. Magically Giftless, she had honed her weapons and Empathy skills, but she had little hope of standing against even two armed men, let alone several dozen. Nevertheless, while a Herald lived, she had no choice but to attempt a rescue.

"Move! Move! Move!" Elvida encouraged Raynor, leaning over his neck as if to add her speed to his own. Already the men had swarmed over Anthea's only other hope. Leahleh collapsed, her brilliant white fur indelibly stained, her mortal agony an unignorable screech in Elvida's mind. Even immersed in terrible pain, the Companion tossed her head toward Anthea's still form, as if to direct Elvida and Raynor to save her Herald.

Besieged by the physical and mental suffering of Herald and Companion, Elvida felt as if her head might explode. She wished she could comfort the animal, to rescue Leahleh or at least allow her to leave the world in peace. Her death, Elvida wanted to promise, would not be in vain. Instead, she waded through the morass of anguish to bolster the Companion, to entreat her not to give up no matter how awful the pain. If Leahleh died, they would lose Anthea also.

Elvida forced the thought from her already overtaxed brain, focusing solely on her own desperate duty. As Raynor skidded to a stop, Elvida leaped from the saddle and ran to the Herald. Aided by an anxiety beyond extreme, she managed to heft Anthea's larger still form and lug her toward the saddle. The impatient Companion barely waited until Anthea's body reached his side before shoving his nose under her and jerking his head upward. The Herald flew toward his saddle. Elvida scrambled to her seat, barely quickly enough to keep Anthea from flying over his opposite side. She steadied the older woman, still noting the shallow breathing, the stream of sticky scarlet trickling from one ear, the total lack of response to any of this frantic movement. *She, too, is nearly dead.*

Raynor lurched into a run. Still trying to position Anthea on his withers, Elvida slid halfway from the saddle. Panicked, she caught a death grip on Raynor's mane. A sword cut the left stirrup where her leg should have been, slicing a short gash in Raynor's side. Another blade slammed against his left hind leg, jolting Raynor with an abruptness that nearly sent both women tumbling to the ground again.

Strings of mane cut painfully into the Elvida's fingers, but she barely noticed beneath the all-encompassing waves of agony issuing from Raynor. Unable to run, he stumbled forward as Elvida clawed her way back into the saddle and steadied Anthea. She dared not look, trying her hardest to send encouragement to her mount. Raynor needed her to help him continue despite the extra weight on his back, the heavy burden of two lives relying on hooves that were no longer capable. Limping heavily, he rocked toward the cave, step after excruciating step, his pace barely faster than that of a running man. The enemy bayed at his heels, only one misstep from victory.

"You can do it," Elvida whispered fervently. "I have faith in you, my Beloved." She kept her attention on the warriors who, miraculously, looked to be losing ground. Raynor seemed all but motionless compared to her wildly racing thoughts and his usual speed, though he obviously moved quickly enough to stay ahead of the howling army, at least for the moment. With each step, the ache radiating from him became more intense, more excruciating, until it usurped all other thought. "You can do it, Heartsib. I know you can."

And Raynor responded, dragging his left hind leg in a blind haze of pain.

Elvida wished she could do something, anything, to ease his burden. Her instincts screamed at her to dismount, but she conquered them with logic. Doing so assured all three of their deaths. Raynor would not go on without her, and she would never find the strength to carry a full-grown Companion. It felt like an eternity before the cave came clearly into focus, drawing slowly and inexorably toward them. "There it is, Beloved! Only a few more steps."

Those last few seemed more like a thousand, then Raynor managed a last heave into the darkness before collapsing at the mouth. Anthea's still form rolled gracelessly from his withers and into the darkness.

We're safe! The thought was madness, Elvida realized with a sudden jolt of fresh terror. She alone could keep the warriors from simply running into the cave after them.

Seizing Raynor's bridle, Elvida closed her eyes to a grim focus and pulled. His weight strained every muscle in her arms and back, but she managed to drag him away from the opening and deeper into the cave. She stood poised directly in front of him, sword readied, stance balanced, hoping no more than two men could face her simultaneously through the crack. At least she might manage to hold them off for several hours. Gripping her sword in hands gone numb, she stood bravely at the mouth, waiting for the army to arrive.

*   *   *

The sun sank toward the horizon, leaving the sky awash in broad stripes of vivid, rainbow hues. Though still at the cave opening, Elvida gradually lost her demeanor of crouched expectation. Gripped in arms aching with fatigue, her sword wilted to dangle at her side. The army remained a respectful distance from the cave, their campfires springing up like gloating wraiths dancing in the gathering darkness.

For nearly an hour, Elvida watched the men butcher some large animal for their evening meal, hauling hunks of glistening meat toward the scattered fires. Her own empty stomach rumbled with a desire she could not contain. She imagined the sweet, fatty aroma that would soon drift toward her on the night breeze, and her mouth watered. Then, a group of men in the center triumphantly hefted the skin of the hapless creature: huge and long-legged, white as new-fallen snow. *Tabnar.* Revulsion struck Elvida in a wave so strong and vile her own saliva soured to poison. Once again, she found herself vomiting, this time with an agonizing savagery. Long after she lost everything inside, she continued to heave dryly until every muscle ached and tears fully stole her vision.

It's over. The sight of a Companion defiled in this manner destroyed Elvida's remaining will. Staggering mindlessly deeper into the cave, she dropped her sword and crumpled to the ground. Stone bruised her knees and scraped her palms, but these superficial pains went unacknowledged. She curled into a hopeless ball, weeping so violently she could scarcely breathe. All her shortcomings paraded through her mind: her magical weakness, her gross incompetence at mental communication, her total lack of any Gift. Sharylle and Anthea had clearly picked her as their travel companion from pity alone. And choosing her for his rider would soon prove Raynor's fatal mistake as well.

Two Heralds and three Companions. Elvida had always known her inability would get herself killed. She had never imagined she would cause the deaths of so many truly special, epically important others with her incompetence. *I deserve to die.* She did not seem worthy even of the same fate that would surely befall Raynor and Anthea. *I deserve to die* horribly.

:Stop it!: The words entered Elvida's head like a whip crack. Shocked senseless, she sat bolt upright, the tears dribbling from her sodden, hazel eyes.

"Who—who said that?"

:I did. Raynor. You quit wallowing in self-pity or, so help me, I'll struggle over there and stomp you to death.:

Dumbfounded, Elvida could only attempt the Mind-speech that had previously eluded her throughout her years of training. *:Can you hear me, too?:*

Raynor snorted loudly. *:What am I, mind-deaf? Of course I can hear you.:*

Elvida gathered her legs beneath her, the flow of tears ending and her vision returning in a blur. *:But this is the first time . . . I mean I never . . . how come I . . . ?:* She found herself incapable of completing a thought. Clearly, her newfound ability had something to do with the intensity of her current emotions. She had always believed she tried her hardest to communicate. Now, she knew, she had allowed self-doubt to hold her from truly giving it the effort it deserved. *:I can Mindspeak?:*

No answer followed, only her own bitter disappointment. Apparently, the ability had left as swiftly as it had appeared. Elvida wondered if she had to hit the depths of despair in order to awaken it again.

:Oh, I'm sorry. Was that an actual question?:

Relief flooded Elvida, and she managed a choking laugh. *:A damn silly one, obviously. I'm sorry, Raynor.:* The apology went far deeper than the ludicrousness of turning the self-evident into a serious inquiry. *:I'm sorry I'm worthless. I'm sorry I'm going to get the three of us killed. I'm sorry . . . I'm sorry . . . for being the world's most useless Herald-in-training.:*

:I told you to stop it!: Anger accompanied the sending, louder than the words themselves. *:Wallowing in self-pity isn't going to save anyone's life. And I resent the suggestion that I'm inept:*

The very idea sent Elvida reeling in horror. *:But I never said—:*

:You did! You said I couldn't pick a capable Chosen.:

:But I didn't mean . . .: Elvida paused, finally turning toward her Companion, who clearly had a point. Only then she realized she had been deliberately avoiding looking at

him. His pain had faded to dim background in her mind, but it haunted every thought, every action, and every decision. He lay on his side where she had dragged him, his fur clotted with dirt and speckled burgundy with the blood of foe and friend alike. His breaths came in pants, and his left hind leg lay at an awkward, swollen angle. Clearly, it was broken.

Elvida cried out, despising herself for not tending to him and Anthea immediately. Trapped in a web of her own grief and loathing, she had worried more for increasing her own burdens than for helping her friends. The realization only intensified her self-hatred; but, this time, she cast aside the morass of deprecation that held her inert at a time of necessary action.

Clearly riding with her on this journey of internal discovery, Raynor sent a quieter message. *:Little Sister, there's nothing you can do for me. A horse without a leg can accomplish nothing. Anthea is gravely injured.:*

:I wish I were a Healer. I wish my Gift—: Realizing she was still stalling, Elvida rose and walked to Anthea. The Herald sprawled in the dirt, her Whites smeared with grime. Dark blood matted her hair, but nothing bright red to indicate a current site of bleeding. Her breaths stirred slowly, oddly peaceful, as she lay in a state beyond sleep. A more thorough examination revealed no other injuries. All the damage remained inside Anthea's head, where no one other than a Healer could reach them. Injuries to the brain, Elvida knew, were always serious; and every moment that passed significantly decreased the Herald's chance for survival. *Leahleh must still live . . . barely.*

:Your Gift is not Healing, Elvida. Do not mourn what was never meant to be.:

Gingerly, Elvida stroked Anthea's hair. She doubted the Herald could survive the night. She asked hopefully, *:But I do have a Gift?:*

:You do,: Raynor confirmed, as so many of her teachers had before him. Yet, like them, he refused to elaborate.

Elvida repeated the familiar line, *:I have to find it myself.:*
:Yes.:

It seemed unfair in so many ways. Others were told as they trained and most had more than one. Now, it seemed, Elvida would die without ever knowing because her Companion was a stickler for rules at a time when such things no longer mattered.

Apparently reading her emotions, Raynor relented. *:I will tell you this much. It has something to do with communication.:*

Under less extreme circumstances, only that very morning, Elvida would have found the suggestion laughable. She who could not even Mindspeak had little education or talent for communication, magical or otherwise. Yet, now that the suggestion had come from the very one she had waited so long to talk to, it did not seem so absurd. *:This is no time for riddles, Beloved. Our lives may depend upon this nameless Gift.:*

:I gave you a hint. I won't say anymore.:

:Why not?:

Raynor turned his head with a snort and a toss of his filthy mane.

Elvida sat back from Anthea, heaving a deep sigh. She knew better than to fight a futile battle long. Repeatedly punching a stone wall accomplished nothing more than broken fists.

:Look.: Raynor spoke with clear caution. *:As I've mentioned, it's customary to put a horse without a leg out of its misery, and Anthea can't make another day without a Healer. Chosen, leave us. Do what you can to save yours—:*

Elvida refused to allow the stallion to finish. *:People kill horses because the animals don't understand the necessary treatment and usually wind up hurting themselves worse. You're not a horse. You're a sentient being, capable of deep thought and understanding.:* She dropped the senseless argument, dismissing Raynor's words as an attempt at heroism. Though only trying to save her, the Companion's words were nonsense. Elvida could never leave him to suffer alone; and, if he died, she surely would also. Besides, his value to the Queen far exceeded hers—and he knew it. *:I'm going to look for another way out of here. You let me know if anyone—:*

:Don't waste your time.:

Elvida rose, scarcely daring to believe she had heard correctly. *:What?:*

:It's the job of Heralds to detail every part of the world.

*I know of this cave—a Waystation once. It has a stream and
a back exit . . .:*

Elvida's hopes soared, only to be dashed by the rest of
Raynor's description.

*:Both cut off to anything larger than a mouse by a massive
cave-in. Ahead lies our only escape and, unfortunately, our
only water.:*

Elvida's lips went suddenly dry, and she licked them
thoughtfully. Her crazed bout of crying would only see to
it that dehydration overcame her sooner. She swallowed
hard, steeling herself against the same fog of hopelessness
that had earlier consumed her. Even if she never earned
her Whites, she would at least learn to die bravely. She
strode away from Anthea to look out over the camp of the
waiting army. *:So why haven't our enemies come after us?
What are they waiting for?:*

Elvida did not expect a reply to her mostly rhetorical
question, so Raynor's surprised her.

*:Morning. Daylight. They're a superstitious lot and worry
about monsters or spirits in the darkness.:*

Elvida shook her head. *:Too bad we're not monsters.:* She
shivered, not bothering to add ". . . or spirits." Soon
enough, they might become exactly that. She tried to understand their enemy, as the strategists had taught. If she could
get into their minds, perhaps she could find a way to outwit
them. *Enter the depraved world of men who attack Heralds
at peace, who slaughter and cannibalize Companions.* The
thought stirred an anger Elvida could not quell. She would
rather die than see the reason behind heinous and barba-
rous actions. *I don't ever want to know what stirs inside
those creatures in the guise of men.*

Elvida sank to her knees. She had never followed a religion, but now she bowed her head, fingers laced tightly
against her chest. *Gods, Lords and Ladies who sanction
goodness, I beg of you now to come to our aid. I will do
anything, suffer any trial if you will only rescue my friends,
these humble servants of the Queen.* She could feel her heart
thumping against her fists. *Please, anyone who's listening. I
will do whatever bidding you ask, you need only make it
clear. Save Raynor and Anthea. And, if it is your will, save
me as well.*

For several moments Elvida remained in this position, waiting for an answer, some sign to indicate any deity had heard her prayer. Insects hummed a steady chorus. The dull rumble of conversation, occasionally pierced by laughter and shouts, came from the enemies' camp. No other sounds reached her, not even the light breathing of herself and her injured friends. It seemed the gods took no interest in their plight.

Not that Elvida expected otherwise. She had known many people who extolled some god or goddess in every other sentence. These faithful believed that everything that went right in the lives of humanity was the work of whichever deity they personally worshipped. Any tragedy or mistake, they blamed on human infallibility. This, they felt, justified their beliefs in a mindless circle that defied Elvida's understanding. It had always seemed to her a certain path to self-deprecation and loathing; yet, she realized, she had felt equally low only moments earlier, without the help of any religious teaching or faith.

It's up to me and me alone to get us out of this situation. Elvida took a deep breath, unfolding her hands, her determination set. *:Raynor, I don't know much about Mindspeech, but I'm going to try to shout with all the power I can muster. With you being so close and all, I hope it doesn't hurt you?:* It was a question as much as information. Dismissed as incapable, she had never learned the conventions or details of the art.

:It won't hurt me,: Raynor assured with a mental smile. *:And I think it's a great idea.:*

Encouraged, Elvida clambered off her knees to sit firmly on her bottom. She lowered her head and breathed slowly and deeply, eyes closed, mind open and focused. She put every bit of mustered strength into her call, physical as well as thought, sending a message of need to anyone who might hear. It was, at once, a communication of desperation, filled with begging and demand, with need and hope. She called to anyone capable of listening: be they Heralds or Bards, Mages or Healers, apprentice or not-yet-discovered. With every fiber of her being, she prepared them for an army of brutal enemies and drew them toward the cave.

Elvida had no idea how long she sat in her chosen position, her eyes tightly closed and her mind outreaching. It seemed like hours before Raynor intruded with a thought that, in comparison, seemed a breathless whisper, *:Little Sister, look.:*

Elvida opened her eyes. Moonlight trickled through the cave mouth, and stars studded the sky. Then, from the depths of the gloom, she saw a vast sea of brilliant white horses, Companions, their eyes burning like angry sapphires, their hooves churning the brush into flying bits of torn stems. Astride sat Heralds of every description, their Whites as spectacular as their steeds, their weapons drawn and gleaming. Elvida gasped, staring in wonder as this massive force of Heralds descended upon the suddenly hushed camp of their enemy. She scrambled to her feet to watch in quiet awe.

:You did it, Elvida. You did it!:

:I did it?: Elvida had not known so many Heralds existed in the world, even throughout the entire history of Valdemar. Yet, they marched in formation before her very eyes, in a grim silence, prepared for a confrontation with an enemy no longer dealing only with three girls and their mounts, most already dead or badly hurt.

Screams rose from the enemy camp, filled with unholy terror. She watched them flee like frightened children, not bothering to grab their belongings, some half-naked in the growing chill. They left their fires blazing and their packs unclaimed, even the supply cart they had captured from the Heralds. They abandoned meals partially eaten in the dirt, their tents lopsided and incompletely pitched, racing without clear destination or reason in all-encompassing terror.

Something's wrong. This can't be happening.

Raynor's mind-voice cut through Elvida's doubt. *:Steady, Chosen One. Steady.:*

Elvida did not know what her Companion meant, but his interference knocked her thoughts askew. She continued to stare at the mass of Heralds as they streaked doggedly through the camp and chased their enemies far beyond her sight. *They did it. We're saved.* Only then, she addressed Raynor directly. *:What exactly am I steadying?:*

Elvida received no answer. Afraid unconsciousness had

claimed Raynor, she whirled toward the Companion to find him staring back at her, his pale eyes moist with a mixture of pain and joy. *:You did it!:*

:I did it,: Elvida agreed, finally allowing herself to feel a tinge of relief and happiness, despite the trials that still awaited her. *:I reached—:* Reality finally intruded. *:I reached what? How can this be? How could I draw in more Heralds than actually exist? How could they all have arrived so quickly, all at the precise same time. How . . . ?:* Elvida shook off the haze of doubts and questions. *:It's impossible.:*

:Impossible,: Raynor echoed. *:Is precisely what it is.:*

Elvida jerked her attention back outside the cave. The camp remained as she had last seen it: abandoned in clear haste and wild disarray. She saw no sign of the Herald army, not even a hoof print to prove they had ever existed. *:What . . . what happened? I don't understand.:*

:Your Gift.: Raynor raised his head, looking better than he had at any time since their arrival in the cave. Though battered and broken, he radiated hope.

:Communication. The ability to communicate pictures into the minds of others.:

"Illusion?" The word was startled from Elvida. She returned to Mindspeech. *:You mean that band of Heralds, that massive army was nothing but—:*

:A creation of your mind, yes. A glorious, amazing creation of your great mind, Beloved.:

Elvida continued to survey the ruined camp, knowing exactly what she must do next. She would have to reclaim the cart and drag her friends into it. She would then have to haul it to civilization. A lot of hard work remained, yet it all seemed so simple after the tragic events of that evening. *:But why wouldn't anyone tell me? Why did you risk our dying without my ever knowing?:*

:Because, Chosen One, doubt is the enemy of illusion. For it to work, it must be believed.:

Elvida still did not understand.

:Until today, you were ruled by your doubts. They would have foiled any attempt you made to use your Gift, just as they had your Mindspeech.:

Elvida considered, still grasping for comprehension. *:You mean, for any illusion to work, I have to believe it, too?:*

:Yes.:

Elvida sighed. It seemed her first great use of her Gift would also be her last.

Apparently reading her emotions, Raynor continued. *:Your teachers will train you to properly blank your mind. You will learn, but your first illusion had to come spontaneously.:*

Elvida shook her head. She still did not wholly get it. *:Why?:*

:Because, until you performed the first one, you would always doubt your ability. So long as you doubted, you would fail or, at best, succeed only weakly. You would never have learned the amazing power of your Gift.: He shook his mane impatiently. *:Little Sister, you are very strongly Gifted.:*

Elvida sank back to the stony ground. Her rubbery legs would no longer hold her. *:Please tell me last night was also illusion.:*

:I wish I could, Beloved. I wish I could.:

As so many times before, Elvida marveled at the wonder that was Raynor. Even through the emotional agony of the battle, even through his own physical pain, he had kept the secret of her power, knowing they all might take it to their graves. To do otherwise would have prevented the great miracle of the ghostly Herald army. *:Thank you,:* she sent, along with the awe of the universe.

:For what?:

Elvida did not bother to answer. She slid from the mouth of the cave and headed toward the camp. She still had friends to rescue. And no force in the world: no magic, no army, no doubt was going to stop her.

DARKWALL'S LADY

by Judith Tarr

Judith Tarr is the author of a number of historical and fantasy novels and stories. Her most recent novels include *Pride of Kings* and *Tides of Darkness,* as well as the "Epona Sequence": *Lady of Horses, White Mare's Daughter,* and *Daughter of Lir.* She was a World Fantasy Award nominee for *Lord of the Two Lands.* She lives near Tucson, Arizona, where she breeds and trains Lipizzan horses.

L ONG ago, after the magic went out of Valdemar but long before it came back again, the Lord of Forgotten Keep had a daughter. He was old and his Lady had thought herself past childbearing; his son was a man full grown and his elder daughter had children of her own. They were already eyeing their inheritance and reckoning the days until it came to them.

And yet in the twilight of their years, the Lady Beatrice found herself waking ill in the mornings. The Healer confirmed her wild surmise: she was, indeed, with child. In spite of her age and the Healer's concern, the pregnancy proceeded as it should, and all was well.

Word of the Lady's miracle spread through the region. One day, three months before the child was due to be born, a guest came to the Keep.

The Lady of Darkwall Keep had last visited Forgotten Keep when Lord Bertrand's daughter was married, five years before. She was not a great traveler and visitor of her neighbors; she lived alone in her isolated Keep, high over a dark river that ran through a deep and fertile valley, and ruled a domain of farmers and river traders.

Her hosts were somewhat surprised by the visit, but they were hospitable people and she was a not-too-distant neighbor. They received her with courtesy. She responded in kind, with manners that could not be faulted.

The Lord was charmed. The Lady was not, but her moods had been strange of late. Even she was reluctant to trust them.

Darkwall's Lady was an easy enough guest. She professed herself content to rest in her rooms until midmorning, take a turn around the Lady's garden until noon, then join the Lady and her women in their bower until the day's meal was served. Her conversation was light and pleasant, like the face she presented to her hosts.

On the third day, at last, she came to the point of her visit. She did so in the afternoon while the rest of the ladies plied their needlework and listened to their Lady's page, who had a sweet voice and a singer's gift. Her long white hands were folded and her expression was serene. She leaned toward Lady Beatrice and said, "I have a favor to ask—and favors to offer in return."

Lady Beatrice was tired and uncomfortable and her temper was not at its best. Still, she managed to raise her brows and say reasonably, "Perhaps you should speak to my Lord."

Her guest smiled with a touch of indulgence. "Oh, I shall, of course. But you and I know, Lady, that though a Lord claims to rule, his Lady holds the reins."

"In your Keep, that may be true," Lady Beatrice said coolly. Still, she was curious. "What favor can Forgotten Keep do for Darkwall?"

Darkwall's Lady bent her head. Her smile had warmed considerably. It was almost enough to allay Lady Beatrice's misgivings. "You know of course that I have no Lord, and therefore no heir. I have to come ask if you would consider an exchange: gifts and favors in return for your child."

Lady Beatrice's hand rose protectively over the swell of her belly. Her face hardened. "My child is not for sale."

"Oh, no," Darkwall's Lady said quickly. "We're no merchants, to buy and sell our own children. But we are highborn, and our best currency is the inheritance we leave our

heirs. Your son will inherit the Keep. Your daughter is
Lady of Mourne Fell. What is left for this gift of the gods?
A boy may make his fortune as he can. A girl may be
traded in marriage. Is either prospect more tempting than
the lordship of Darkwall when I am gone?"

It was indeed very tempting. But Lady Beatrice was not
a gullible woman, nor was she particularly softhearted.
"That's all very well for the child. What do you offer us
in return?"

"A percentage of the river trade," the Lady answered
without hesitation, "to begin as this agreement is concluded
and to continue unless or until your child chooses to end
it. A promise of military aid for the same term, when and
as needed. And, as earnest for the rest, a chest of gold in
the amount proper for a Lady's dowry—for it will be a
Lady, my heart tells me, though I would hardly look amiss
at a Lord."

Lady Beatrice knew as mothers might, cherishing the
knowledge that she carried a daughter. She eyed the Lady
warily. "It's a most tempting offer," she said, "but my Lord
must decide whether to accept or refuse."

"Of course," said the Lady with all apparent willing-
ness. Then she smiled and beckoned to the page and
asked for a new song—a joyful one, she said, in honor of
the hour.

The Lord's misgivings were no less than his wife's, but
he was neither as wealthy nor as well defended as he would
have liked to be. It was also in his mind that if this last
and unexpected child was a daughter, she would serve her
family exceedingly well as Lady of Darkwall. And if it was
a son, well then, all the better that he should have a Keep
of his own and blood ties to Forgotten Keep.

And so they made the bargain. Darkwall's Lady would
have claimed the child when she was born, but Lady Beatrice would not hear of it. "We will raise our own daughter," she said, "and teach her everything that you would
wish her to know. Send tutors if you wish, but she will be
fostered here. When she reaches the age of womanhood,
then she may go."

Lord Bertrand opened his mouth to upbraid her, but
Darkwall's Lady astonished him by inclining her head. "As

you wish," she said. "I shall send a nurse for her, and tutors when she reaches a suitable age."

Lady Beatrice could hardly find fault with that. She bent her head in return.

The alliance was made and the agreement concluded, and it was settled. The Lord's youngest child, with three months yet to go until she saw the world, was assured of a lordship and a future.

Lady Beatrice kept her misgivings to herself. She only spoke of them once, six years later, as she was dying. She summoned her daughter to her bedside and said, "Don't ask what this means. Only remember it, word for word. Walk warily. Trust no one. Always keep your counsel, and remember everything that you see. We sold you for gold and soldiers, and we will keep that bargain—but you can make a new one of your own. Remember." That last word came out as a sigh. "Never forget."

"I'll remember," the child said.

Not long after that, Lady Beatrice died. But the bargain still held. The child, whom Lady Beatrice had named Merris, continued to live in her father's Keep. Tutors from Darkwall came to teach her, and the Lady herself appeared once each year on Merris' birthday, to celebrate it with her and to see how she had been growing.

She always professed herself pleased, or least not too terribly disappointed. Then she always went away as she had come, leaving the child in her father's care.

But those days would not go on forever. When Merris reached her fourteenth birthday, the Lady would come as before, but this time she would take the child whom she had bought for so noble a price.

Merris ran up the stair at a pace that would have given her tutors palpitations. She meant to have her hair up and her skirts down and her breathing back to normal by the time she reached the schoolroom, but while she could, she gave way to the restless energy that had been tormenting her all day.

One month from today was her fourteenth birthday. Everyone knew what that meant. Her life in this Keep was nearly over. It was time, finally, for her to fulfill the bargain her parents had made.

She had been preparing for it since before she was born. She was not afraid, but her mother's words had never left her.

She was going into a house of strangers. No matter how many tutors she had had, or how much instruction she was given in manners, deportment, and the conduct befitting a Lady of Darkwall, she had never visited the Keep she was to rule. She knew every nook and cranny, but only in books.

Her tutors never said anything but good of Darkwall. Still, servants talked, and Merris had sharp ears. She only caught fragments, whispers of fear, rumors that had no real substance—but they were enough to keep her on her guard.

Halfway up the stair, she stopped short. It was time to make herself decorous for Master Thellen and Mistress Patrizia, but that was not what brought her to so abrupt a halt. While she stood frozen, the bell rang at the gate.

Preparations for her birthday celebration were already underway. People had been coming and going for days. This morning alone, the bell had rung half a dozen times to let in trains of provisions, companies of workmen, and a succession of messengers bearing replies to the Lord's invitation.

This felt different. It felt . . . bright.

She did not know what she meant by that, but she had to see. Even if her tutors set her a punishment, she reckoned it worth the cost. She turned and ran back down the stair.

There was always a commotion in the courtyard these days, but when Merris came out into it, there was a circle of unexpected quiet near the outer gate. Brightness filled it, shot through with the tinkle of bells.

She blinked hard. The blur of light resolved into a pair of white horses with bells on their bitless bridles, and a pair of men dressed in the same striking color. By that she knew that the horses were not horses, and the men were men, but not exactly ordinary.

Everyone knew about Heralds. Books and stories were full of them.

Merris had never seen one. Forgotten Keep was small and out of the way, and her father involved himself only rarely with affairs of the royal court far away in Haven. Except for the occasional Bard wandering through to sing his songs, Forgotten Keep was as forgotten as its name.

Now not one Herald had appeared in the Keep, but two. She found that her mouth was hanging open. She shut it with a snap.

Everyone else seemed as taken aback as she was. Just as it dawned on Merris that someone ought to at least offer the Heralds a greeting, one of them swayed and sagged against the other.

The dazzle of what they were vanished abruptly. The one who had fainted was old, she realized, and the one who held him up was young. Inside their shining Whites, they were human—and the old one did not look well at all.

She ran forward without even stopping to think, calling to people who stood around with their mouths open. "Rolf! Gerent! Take the Companions to the stable. Remember they're not horses, no matter what they look like. Danil— find the Healer. Move!"

People moved. Merris planted herself on the other side of the old Herald and took part of his weight, thinking distantly that one of the servants should do this. But she wanted to do something, however unsuitable, and that seemed like the most useful thing.

She met the young Herald's brown eyes over the bowed white head. They were deeply worried. There was nothing she could do to soothe that worry, but she could say, "Come with me."

The Herald nodded. He looked fairly done in himself, but he could walk. Between them, he and Merris carried the old Herald into the Keep and up to one of the guest rooms.

The bed was freshly made and the room was aired. The shutters were open to the late spring sunlight. Merris and the young Herald laid the old one carefully on the bed.

His breathing was rapid and shallow. His skin was clammy and his lips were blue. Merris opened her mouth to ask what had happened to him, but the young Herald staggered and sat down abruptly on the stool beside the bed.

The water jar was empty, but there was wine in the cupboard. Merris poured a few sips into one of the cups and made the Herald drink it. He choked and spluttered, but a little color came back into his cheeks.

"Good," said Merris, reclaiming the cup. "We don't need you passing out, too."

He drew himself up. Apart from the glamour of the Whites, he looked perfectly ordinary: not too tall, not too short, well built and sturdy, with a pleasant, blunt-featured face and curly brown hair. There was nothing noble or heroic about that face, and she doubted he was highborn. He looked like half the villagers around Forgotten Keep.

"I'm Herald-Intern Coryn," he said, "and this is Herald Isak." His accent bore out her suspicions. It had a hint of a drawl in it, a countryman's twang. "And you are . . . ?"

"Merris," she said.

"Thank you, Merris," he said. "We've lost our way, I think. Are we very far from the road to Nottaway?"

"It's a day or two west of here," she said.

He sighed, then sagged. She jumped toward him, but he had not fainted. It was relief, that was all.

He might have spoken or she might have asked questions, but the Healer arrived just then. She took in the scene with an all too sharp eye, shooed Merris out, and took both Heralds in hand.

Merris would have argued, but she had tutors waiting— and an extra hour's worth of exercises in correct etiquette at banquets for being so drastically late. The exercises were deadly dull, but there was no getting out of them. There was a bargain, as she never failed to remember. This was her part of it.

It was two wildly frustrating days before Merris could escape the stranglehold of duty and discipline. The Heralds were still in the Keep—she was able to determine that much.

The old one, Isak, was very ill. Something to do with his heart, she gathered. The Healer was doing her best. The young Herald never left his elder's side except for a daily visit to the Companions.

All this, Merris learned from obliging servants. Even with the flurry around her birthday, Heralds were a great excitement.

Merris' tutors seemed determined to keep her from ever going near them again. Mistress Patrizia insisted that she be fitted for a trunkful of entirely new and to her mind completely unnecessary gowns, which took untold hours. When she was not strangling in folds of silk and brocade, Master Thellen had her memorizing endless lists of names and dates and places from one of his beloved and deadly dull chronicles, none of which had anything perceptible to do with either Darkwall or Forgotten Keep.

She came terribly close to asking him questions she should never even think about asking. "Is it true the last Lady but three used to take a monthly bath in infants' blood? Are there really creatures of darkness in the caves below the Keep? Why has there always been a Lady but never a Lord, and how is it that she never marries but always adopts an heir?" Not to mention, "Why did she choose me? There are four Keeps between hers and ours, all of which have surplus daughters. What do I have that those ladies don't?"

But she kept her questions bottled up inside as she always had, because her mother had told her to trust her instincts, and instinct told her not to speak of such things. On the surface it was all ordinary, dull, dry facts and ancient history, and so many gowns she would need an entire train of pack mules to carry them all.

Late the second day, as Merris dressed for dinner, Mistress Patrizia entered without knocking as she always did, and dismissed the maid. Merris looked at her in what she hoped was innocent surprise. "Mistress! What a pleasure to see you at this hour. Will you be joining us for dinner?"

"That would not be proper," Mistress Patrizia said. She was a tall, thin, forbidding person at the best of times. Tonight she was ramrod-stiff. "I have a gift for you from our Lady."

Merris' brows went up. Such gifts were not uncommon, but usually it was a messenger from Darkwall who delivered them. As far as she knew, no such messenger had come.

As if in answer to her unspoken question, Mistress Patrizia said, "I have kept this at our Lady's behest. It is a small thing, but she values it. She would be most pleased if you would wear it."

She raised her hands. There was a small wooden box in them, such as jewels were kept in.

Merris took it slowly and opened it with fingers that for some reason wanted to tremble. She had had gifts like this before, but only on birthdays.

It was a pendant on a silver chain, a drop of dark amber in a spiral of silver. It felt warm in her hand and strangely alive, and the flecks in it seemed almost to move, swirling slowly around one another inside their prison of waxy stone.

It was a beautiful thing, but strange. The other gifts had been much more mundane: a book, a gown, a tutor. This made Merris' skin prickle.

She made herself smile and be as polite as she had been trained to be, speaking words of thanks that she was not at all sure she meant. Mistress Patrizia watched her with peculiar fixity. She was supposed to wear the thing, that was clear.

She let Mistress Patrizia fasten the chain around her neck, trying hard not to shudder when the stone touched her skin. She resolved to get rid of it as soon as she was out of sight.

She had a moment of breathless fear that Mistress Patrizia would decide to go to dinner after all, but she was much too proper a servant. Merris stopped in the passageway to the dining hall, fumbling with the clasp. Her hands were shaking and the clasp was stiff. It would not come off.

She almost gave up and let it be, but her peculiar revulsion was growing stronger rather than weaker. She gritted her teeth and pulled hard. The chain broke. She thrust the stone into the pocket of her sleeve, where a lady might keep small and discreetly useful items.

Amber was as light almost as air, but this weighed her down out of all proportion to its size. Merris stopped thinking and acted. She turned aside to the garderobe and let the thing fall out of her sleeve into the odorous darkness. If and when she was asked, she could answer honestly that she had lost the pendant.

She took a deep breath, barely even gagging on the effluvium of the privy, and went to dinner with a lighter heart.

*　　　*　　　*

After dinner, at last, Merris had an hour to herself. Her maids were still at their own dinner, and her tutors were wherever they disappeared to when their duty to their Lady was done. She shed her voluminous skirts in favor of much more practical ones. With no one to stop her, she ventured out of her rooms.

It was a bright night, warm and moonlit. The garden her mother had made, that her father had kept up in Beatrice's memory, was in full and fragrant bloom. Merris went on past it to the stables.

Companions had somewhat different needs than horses, according to the stories, but Forgotten Keep's stables seemed to suit them well enough. Their stall doors were open so that they could come and go, and they were well bedded in clean straw, with full mangers and fresh water drawn from the Keep's deep clear well.

The younger Herald was perched on a stool between the two stalls, cleaning bridles. They were ordinary bridles, belonging to the Keep's horses; not the lovely, bitless ones ornamented with silver bells that she had seen on the Companions. Merris squatted beside him and reached for one of the many scraps of leather that he had spread around him, and started working soap into it with her fingers.

He stared at her as if he did not know what to make of her. A long white head came between them, followed by a massive white body.

Companions were not nearly as ethereal in person as they were in legend. They were broad-boned, heavy-set creatures with substantial heads . . . and silver hooves and clear blue eyes and manes and tails like white silk. Merris looked up at that deceptively horselike face and sighed.

"Selena says," said the Herald, "that no, our life is not for you—but what you have ahead of you is just as remarkable."

"I know that," Merris said—a little sadly, because even in Forgotten Keep, a girl could dream of being Chosen. She reached up. The Companion lowered a soft nose into her palm and blew warm breath on it.

"She also says," the Herald said, "that you don't have much time. Whatever you do, don't wear the pendant."

Merris felt her eyes go round. There were all too many questions she could ask, but most of them were too foolish to bother with. She said, "Tell her I dropped it down the garderobe."

"Things of that nature have a way of not staying dropped."

Merris wondered if that was the Herald speaking, or the Companion speaking through him. Not that it mattered particularly. "What are you really here for?" she asked.

She peered around the Companion's head. The Herald lifted his shoulders in a shrug. "Isak took sick on the road. Your Keep was the closest place that was likely to have a Healer."

He was telling the truth, as far as it went. Merris could tell. Still, she said, "I don't believe in accidents."

"Neither do I," the Herald said. "Is it true what they say? You're heir to Darkwall?"

She nodded.

He frowned. "You're nothing like what I would expect."

"What, pretentious? Full of myself? Too far above it all to sit in a stable aisle, cleaning bridles?"

He laughed, then flushed. "Well, that. And . . . well. Darkwall."

"What do you mean by that?"

He shook his head. "I'm sorry. I shouldn't have said it."

"No," said Merris. "Tell me what you mean."

His head shook again. The Companion pawed, then butted him, knocking him off his stool. He lay in the aisle and glared. "I can't say *that*!"

The Companion shook its—her—mane and snorted wetly, not quite into his face.

He shoved her head aside and scrambled to his feet, still glaring. "Selena says," he said, biting off the words, "that I should say, 'You don't look like something that would rule Darkwall. You're too, well, *clean*.'"

"And that means?"

"I'm not even sure what it means," he said angrily, but his anger did not seem to be directed at Merris. "It's rumors, that's all. Stories and a few poorly rhymed ballads. Darkwall isn't just called that because it's built on a black cliff. It has a bad reputation."

"Why?" Merris demanded. "What do you know?"

"If the heir to Darkwall doesn't know it," he said, "maybe there's nothing *to* know."

She wanted to pick him up and shake him, but he was standing up and she was sitting on the floor, and he was a fair bit bigger than she was. She let her glare do it for her. "Suppose there's something I haven't been told, and a reason why. Tell me."

"I told you, it's just rumors. That the Lady is a socreress. That she keeps herself young with the blood of children, and rules a domain of magical creatures as well as humans."

"I've heard those rumors," Merris said. "I've also met the Lady. She's not particularly young, and she's been aging as she should."

"Do you like her?"

That was a most peculiar question. It was also peculiarly perceptive. Merris answered it honestly. "No. No, I don't. I don't like any of the tutors she's sent either. They're all so cold. All duty, no humanity."

"That's not like you at all," he said. Then he flushed again. "I'm sorry. I didn't mean—well, I did. But I shouldn't have. I have serious deficiencies in tact and diplomacy."

He sounded as if he was quoting someone—probably one of his teachers. Merris reflected that unlike her tutors, he was very likable indeed. She was thinking she could trust him.

Thoughts she had not been daring to think, and realizations she had not wanted to come to, were coming together in Merris' head. She pulled herself up, staggering on knees that were suddenly weak.

The Companion's shoulder was there, offering support. Over the broad back and arched neck, she met the Herald's eyes.

"I'm nothing like the place I'm supposed to take charge of," she said. "So tell me, why did she choose me? Why not someone who fits her better?"

Coryn shook his head. He did not know. Or—did not want to?

The Companion's neck bent around. The blue eye was very keen. It saw everything she wanted it to see, and everything else, too.

"There are no accidents," Merris said. "Please tell me you didn't half-kill a Herald just to provide an excuse."

The white head shook from side to side. Some things, the Companion seemed to be saying, were beyond even her powers—even if she had wanted any such thing.

"I have to go," Merris said. She was running away, of course, but it was all too much. She needed to be alone.

She did not pause to see if Coryn tried to stop her. The Companion did not, and that was what mattered.

Merris lay in her bed, staring at the ceiling. Her maids snored in ragged harmony. The moon was setting. Its light reminded her of the shimmer of a Companion's coat.

One reason why Darkwall's Lady might have gone so far afield in search of an heir was because the farther from her Keep she went, the less likely it would be that people would have heard the stories. The Keeps kept to themselves. When they made alliances, they did so circumspectly. People in this country were not given to idle gossip.

Maybe Darkwall fostered that. If sorcery existed, and if the Lady practiced it, what better way to protect herself than by creating a buffer all around her of domains that asked no questions and shared no tales? Even Heralds seldom came here, as if something kept them from noticing this country existed.

Merris drew into a knot. Her stomach felt sick. This was the wildest speculation, based on practically nothing at all. She was afraid, that was all, because in less than a month she would have to leave everything she had ever known. She was inventing stories and imagining horrors.

But the pit of her stomach did not believe that. Deep down, where her instincts were, she believed the stories.

Then why did the Lady want her? What did Merris have that Darkwall could use?

Youth, of course. Fertility, maybe. Maybe her innocence was meant to lighten a dark place and make a cold heart warm again.

Somehow Merris found it hard to believe that. What did sorcery want with innocence?

Blood of children.

Merris sat up so fast her head spun. The moon was almost down. Its last glimmer caught the box on her bedside

table: a small wooden box, very plain, such as jewels were
stored in.

She had not put it there.

One of the servants must have found it and, ever helpful,
put it where she could see it. It was only a box, simply
made and fit for use. It must be empty. She had dropped
its contents down the garderobe.

Something was in it. Something that made her skin creep.

She got up suddenly, picked up the box in a fold of her
nightgown and flung it out the window. It was a profoundly
childish and possibly dangerous thing to do, but she did not
care. Let the garden keep it. She did not want it anywhere
near her.

In the morning the heir of Darkwall announced that she
would retreat for a while to the shrine of Astera. She had
a great task ahead of her, and considerable responsibility.
She felt a need to invoke the Goddess' guidance.

"I'll be back before my birthday," she promised her
father.

Lord Bertrand was quite old now and growing frail, but
his mind was as clear as ever. He nodded. "Of course," he
said. "Of course you need a little time to reflect. These are
great changes which you face, and you are young."

He did not make her promise to honor the bargain. That
would have insulted them both. He met her eyes and nodded, understanding more than maybe she herself did.

With his blessing on her head, she left within the hour.
One of her maids rode with her, and a pair of guards. She
was gone before either of her tutors could have missed her.

It was not terribly far to the shrine—half a day's easy
ride in late-spring sunlight—and the road was well main-
tained if not much traveled. Merris found her fears receding
as she left the bulk of the Keep behind. In their place was
a growing conviction. This was the right thing to do.

Tonight the moon was almost full, riding high over the
guesthouse of the shrine. Astera's priestesses had finished
their night office some time before. The purity of their
voices still shivered in Merris' skin.

Merris' maid Gerda was a sound sleeper. Merris had chosen her for it. The guards had not been allowed within the walls of the shrine; they had had to camp outside in a place reserved for their kind. It overlooked the main road but not, she had taken care to observe, a track that wound away through the woods.

She had to go on foot—there was no discreet way to liberate her horse from the stable. She regretted that, but some things could not be helped. Dressed in the plainest clothes and the most sensible shoes she had been able to find, with a small pack and a full water bottle, she slipped out into the moonlight.

Her heart was beating faster than her brisk pace might have called for, and her hands were cold. She had put fear aside, but that did not mean she was calm. No one in the world knew what she was doing. This was a very dangerous thing to do—but she had to do it. There was no choice.

Past the first turn in the track, out of sight of the shrine, the moonlight grew suddenly, blindingly bright. Merris stopped, shading her eyes against the dazzle.

It faded as suddenly as it had swelled, distilling into a white horse-body and the dark shape of a rider. Merris looked at them in a kind of despair. "I'm not trying to run out on the bargain," she said.

"It looks as if you're running toward it," said Coryn.

He was not wearing Whites. His Companion's gear was dark and plain—an ordinary saddle and a leather halter with reins buckled to the side rings. The Herald must have raided the tack room in the Keep.

There was still no mistaking what his mount was, but Merris had to give him credit for trying. "I won't let you take me back," she said. "This is something I have to do."

"I know," Coryn said. "Selena knows, too. We won't stop you—but we won't let you go alone either."

Merris was ashamed to admit how deep her relief was. It made her voice sharper and her words more cutting. "What, you can't wait out your Internship before you get yourself killed in the line of duty?"

"Maybe you're right," Coryn said. "Maybe you're not. Either way, you should have someone at your back."

"Why? Have you Gifts that can help? Can you transport

me there instantly? Read the Lady's mind? Blast the Keep into rubble?"

His cheeks were bright red. "I'm nothing either special or spectacular as Heralds go, and the gods know I'm not highborn. But I am a Herald. The King's authority rides with me. If this bargain is unholy or unsanctioned, there are things I can do to put a stop to it."

"Yes," she said nastily. "You can die for being too stupidly brave to stay away."

He took a deep breath and squared his shoulders. "Maybe so. And maybe my death will count for something. We're going with you."

She hissed in frustration. If she pushed past, he only had to follow. He had a mount and she had none. He could gallop ahead and be there hours before her.

She stared him down until he stepped aside. When she went on down the road, so did he, with his Companion clopping behind like a common horse.

She wished they would go away—but she was glad they were there. If nothing else, and if they survived, they were witnesses. They could tell the world what Darkwall's Lady was.

It was strange to be walking roads that Merris had only known on maps, and to see the country come alive around her. For a while she walked, then she rode because the Companion insisted—saying through the Herald that she was flagging and the day was not getting any younger, and she had to have some strength left when she came to her destination. On that broad back she rode through a wilderness of trees, over stony streams and across sudden outcroppings of rock and scree.

She had chosen Astera's shrine because it was closer to Darkwall than Forbidden Keep, but it was still a long way. They were most of three days on the road, in rain and sun, camping by moonlight and starlight. Coryn had a useful Gift after all: he could start a fire out of anything, though when she challenged him to do it with a cup of rainwater, he responded with a flat stare. He had a sense of humor, but it had limits.

Late on the third day after Merris slipped out of the

shrine, they came around a curve in the road—which by
then was little more than a goat track—and looked down
on a valley she had never seen before in her life. And yet
she knew it as if she had grown up there.

Its walls were steep and wooded. A river ran through the
bottom, deep and wide enough for traders' boats. Villages
clustered along it. High above it on a black rock sat the
Keep, crouching like a raven over a rich store of carrion.

Merris had expected to find the valley sinister. She could
apply that word to the Keep, but the rest was beautiful.
The fields cut from the woods and the hillsides were rich
with ripening crops. Vineyards clung to the slopes higher
up, thickly clustered with grapes.

Darkwall wine was famous hereabouts. It was a dark vintage, strong and sweet. It was wonderful in winter, heated
with spices, or diluted and chilled with spring water in
the summer.

The memory was so vivid that Merris could taste it. She
swallowed and made her eyes lift past the vineyards to
the Keep.

It was black, built of the same stone as the rock it stood
on. A round tower stood at each corner. The flag that flew
from it was black, with the blood-red outline of a raven
flying on it.

The Companion moved without her riders' asking, picking her way down the steep track. On the road she had
found a mud-wallow, then a patch of brown dust to roll in
until she was covered from ears to tail. She was still white,
but she had managed to dull the brilliance of her coat.

It was a long way down to the river. The track brought
them into the village at the foot of the crag, in among a
cluster of houses. Fishing nets hung on walls, and boats
were drawn up in alleyways and along the riverbank.

There were people out and about. They looked much
like the villagers of Forgotten Keep, or like Coryn for
that matter. The strangers attracted glances, mildly curious but neither greatly interested nor hostile. There must
be enough trade on the river, and enough traders coming
through, that unfamiliar faces were not unheard of.

Merris had meant to find either an inn where questions
could be answered in travelers' tales, or a temple where
the priests might be welcoming to strangers. But there

was no inn. One or two places looked like taverns, but they had a peculiarly deserted look. And there was no temple.

Every village that Merris knew had a temple, if not two or more. There was none here. "So where do travelers rest?" she wondered aloud. "And where does anyone worship?"

"On their boats, I suppose," Coryn said, "or they go elsewhere." He frowned. "It is odd. Maybe there's a market town downstream?"

"I don't know of any," said Merris. "This is the chief town that answers to the Keep. Look, there's the marketplace." She pointed with her chin to an open space visible down the alley.

"Except there's no market," Coryn pointed out.

"It's not market day, then," Merris said, but her voice lacked conviction. "I could swear the books talk about the market. And there should be an inn—the Raven's Nest."

"I gather we're not encouraged to spend the night here," Coryn said.

He touched his heels to Selena's sides. She went forward obligingly, playing the role of ordinary horse with perceptible relish. Merris thought she overdid the floppy ears and plodding step, but these fishermen were unlikely to know the difference.

Their lack of curiosity was beginning to bother her. No inn, no market, no temple—did traders really stop here? Or did they unload their cargo and get out as fast as they could? There were no other horses in the streets, not even a donkey, and no dogs or cats. Selena was the only four-footed creature that Merris could see.

"No birds either," Coryn said under his breath. "Does the air feel dead to you?"

Merris started to ask him what he meant, but she changed her mind. She suspected she knew.

The sun was bright and the breeze was warm, with a smell of water and fish and baking bread, all very pleasant. And yet it felt hollow—false. As if it were a painted backdrop, concealing . . . what? A fane of monsters?

She almost laughed. Her imagination was running away with her. There were fish in the river: she saw one leap well out toward the middle, a silver flash. And yes, there were birds. Black wings circled overhead: a pair of ravens, flying high above the Keep.

She had to get up there. If there was nowhere to stay in town, travelers must be expected to stay in the Keep. She slipped down off the Companion's back, too quick for Coryn to stop her.

In a town with narrow alleys and people coming and going at inconvenient intervals, a man on a horse, or a creature like one, was at a distinct disadvantage. Merris gambled that the Herald would not leave his Companion. It seemed she was right.

Her back felt cold without Coryn and Selena to watch it. She clamped down the urge to run back to them. This was too dangerous to share with anyone else.

She was beginning to think she had miscalculated. There was nothing to put her finger on, but what she felt here was the wrong kind of wrongness. People were too quiet—too complaisant.

There were no children. No young adults, either. Everyone was older than she was—but not very much older. There were no old people, either. No white heads or wrinkled faces. Everyone seemed to be between the ages of twenty and fifty.

Young people could be in school, except there was no temple for them to be educated in. Old people should be sunning themselves in doorways or manning stalls in the market.

She hesitated at the bottom of the ascent to the Keep. It was supposed to be hers, but it felt completely alien.

Coryn was gaining on her. The Companion was faster than Merris had thought, and more agile at sidestepping people and obstacles. Merris bit her lip and started up the slope.

Part of the way was straight ascent, and part was a series of steps carved in the rock. There were no guards at the gate above, but Merris did not make the mistake of thinking it was not watched. What at first she took for carved ravens perched on the summit of the arch moved suddenly.

One spread its wings. The other let out a single sharp caw.

It seemed she had rung the bell. With clammy hands and thudding heart, she passed through the open gate.

The Keep was deserted. The passages were empty and the rooms untenanted. Cobwebs barred windows and flung sticky barriers across doorways.

Merris searched from dungeon to tower with growing desperation. The only inhabitants were ravens roosting on the battlements. From the thickness of dust in the rooms, no human being had lived there for years.

She dropped in a heap on the top of the tower. The wind blew cool on her sweating face, even while the sun shone strong enough to burn. "I don't understand," she said.

Coryn squatted on his haunches next to her. She squinted, but he seemed real. He was out of breath, as if he had been running to catch her.

"How can it be empty?" she asked him. "There is a Lady, or someone who claims to be. She visits me every year. She sends my father gold and soldiers. I've had nurses and tutors. They've taught me all about this place, the staff, the servants, and who or what belongs in every room. How can it be deserted?"

"The Lady must have another residence," Coryn said. "A manor, maybe."

"Then why don't I know about it?"

"I don't know," he said. Then he went still, as if straining to hear something faint and far away.

"After the sun goes down," he said, "Selena says, look below."

Merris frowned. "What? What does she mean?"

"Look below, she says. That's all."

"There are dungeons below," said Merris. "Caves, really. Part of the river flows through them."

"Then that's where we'll look," he said. "We can rest while the daylight lasts. There's no food here and I don't trust the water, but I brought provisions."

He held up the rucksack he had brought from Forgotten Keep. It was bulging. "Bread from the bakery in town," he said, "and the water we brought from the spring at last night's camp, and a few odds and ends. We'll be comfortable while we wait."

Merris was not hungry, but she was thirsty. She sipped from one of the water bottles while Coryn ate half a still-warm, crusty loaf with cheese melted inside.

It smelled so good that Merris was tempted after all. She managed a few bites. They helped more than she would have expected. She felt stronger.

When they had both had enough to eat and drink, Coryn said, "I saw beds below. Maybe we should get some proper rest."

Merris shook her head. "I need the sun," she said. "You go, if you're too tired."

"No," he said. "I'll stay with you."

"But your Companion—"

"She's down below," he said. "She'll be safe."

"As long as it's daylight," Merris said, and shivered. He looked as pale as she felt.

They propped themselves against the parapet, side by side but not touching. Merris tilted her head back and let the sun bathe her face. Her eyelids drooped shut.

"Merris."

She started awake. Coryn was bending over her. In the confusion of sudden waking, she wondered why he had been bathing in blood.

Before horror could consume her, she realized that it was not blood; it was sunset light. Coryn was his honest self, with rumpled hair and travel-stained clothes.

He was much more awake than she was. "I've been exploring. I found torches," he said.

She nodded. There were no words in her. She took one of the torches, leaving him with the other two.

The sun was sinking fast. She did not need Coryn's encouragement to follow him out of the open air into the dusty stillness of the Keep.

The shadows were thick there. Once or twice as they worked their way down from the tower, Merris thought she saw someone, or something, flitting around a corner. It must be a trick of the light.

No matter how often she told herself she had a right to be here, she felt more like an invader the farther down she went. She would have loved to run out the gate and away and never come back, but neither she nor Coryn paused there. They kept on going toward the entrance her maps had shown her, down below the gate in an empty and echoing hall.

Coryn lit the torches in that hall, laying a finger and a hard stare on each until it burst into flame. The light put the dark to flight but made the shadows somehow stronger. In its flicker, they seemed more like living shapes than ever.

Merris had to lead, since she knew the way. Coryn walked close behind her. He was a solid presence compared to the shadows that crowded thicker as they descended the narrow stair.

There was a cold smell in that place, like old stone and deep water. The air that breathed upward made the small hairs stand up on Merris' body.

She desperately wanted to stop, turn, run back into the last of the daylight. Every part of her that was wise or prudent was shouting at her to do exactly that. But she had come to find out the truth. She had to know. She could not seal the bargain without some knowledge of what she was agreeing to.

And if it killed her?

Then it did. She had been bound to this since before she was born.

It was a long way down. Her legs were aching and her breath was coming hard, well before she came to the end of the stair. Her torch lit nothing but a tunnel carved out of the black rock, and steps descending below her.

They must be at least as far down as the river by now, if not even farther. She was stopping more often, and it was taking longer for her legs to stop shaking before she could go on.

Coryn had not said a word in all that descent. She kept looking back, terrified that he had vanished, or perhaps worse, that his spirit had been taken away and there was nothing left to follow her but an empty shell. Each time, he met her stare with one just as tired and almost as wild.

Just when she was about to give up, the steps ended. She almost fell down, but Coryn caught her and pulled her back onto her feet. He was breathing hard himself. Even in the ruddy torchlight his face was pallid.

He rummaged in the pack he was still carrying and pulled out a water bottle. She drank gratefully, then handed it to him so that he could drink, too.

They were still in a tunnel. The cold, damp smell was stronger. The only way to go was forward, unless they wanted to climb all the way back the way they had come.

Merris strained to remember the maps she had studied. Her memory was good, but the darkness muffled it. She should be at the level of the underground river, or just above it, but she was not sure which. The tunnel branched—at least, she thought it did. One way wound through a succession of caves to a blind end. The other led to the river.

First she had to get to the branch. Then she had to remember which direction to take. She raised her torch, though her arm was as tired as the rest of her, and pressed on.

Right, she thought. *No, left.*

The tunnel branched as she had thought. But which way? The wrong one would lose them both in the bowels of the earth.

She closed her eyes. In the dark behind her eyelids, she tried to picture the map. It had been in a book that Master Thellen gave her to study, tucked away in the back with the dry notes and the endless rambling appendices. She could feel the book in her hands, the worn leather cover and the crumbling pages.

There it was. She almost lost it, she was so glad to have found it. She struggled to keep it steady, then to focus on the part that she needed.

Right. She should turn right. She almost turned left out of sheer doubt and panic, but she gritted her teeth and followed her first inclination. The cold smell was stronger in that direction, or so she told herself. It must be the smell of the underground river.

The passage widened some distance past the turn. Coryn moved up beside her. Her hand reached out and clasped his. His fingers were as clammy as hers, but they warmed with the contact. Hand in hand like children, they went on into the dark.

*   *   *

The tunnel did not divide again, which gave Merris hope that it was the right way. It twisted and turned like some vast worm's trail, sometimes doubling back on itself. Their torches began to burn low.

Merris was beyond exhaustion. One more turn, one more doubling—just one more. Then she would worry about the one after that.

She walked straight into a wall that should not have been there. Only slowly did she realize it was a door. She pushed. It gave, swinging outward.

There was the hall she remembered from the map, and there was the dark, oily slide of the river running through it. If the tunnel had been a worm's track, this had the look and feel of a dragon's lair.

All the stone in the Keep and the tunnels had been black, but this hall was golden red: the same color as the stone that Mistress Patrizia had given Merris. Curtains and streamers of waxy stone streamed down the sides and pooled in columns on the floor. It almost looked like flesh—even to the veins that ran through it.

It was calling to Merris. Even the little time that she had worn the stone had been enough. It had marked her—bound her. And, she realized in a kind of despair, it had brought her here.

Coryn's fingers tightened on Merris'. His breath hissed.

Merris willed him not to speak. There was something in the center of the hall. It looked like a depression in the floor, a long, shallow oval, with a statue standing over it.

The statue moved. Like the crows on the arch of Darkwall Keep's gate, it was alive. Slowly, in the fading torchlight, it took shape as a tall, narrow figure in a dark cloak.

The hood slipped back. Darkwall's Lady looked directly at Merris. She was the same as Merris remembered: gaunt, aging, not beautiful, though her features had a certain stark elegance. Her graying hair was loose, falling on her shoulders.

She smiled. "Welcome, my child," she said. Her voice echoed in the cavern, reverberating from wall to wall and back again, over and over.

Merris gasped and clapped her hands to her ears. Coryn had fallen flat.

"Your eagerness is charming," the Lady said. The echoes

were fainter now, fading away. Merris dared to lower her hands from her ears.

The Lady spoke again, this time without echoes at all. "Come here."

Merris found she could not resist. She left Coryn lying and walked slowly across the hall. It must be her imagination that the Lady's cloak was made of dark scales, and the bottom of it wound away in a long tail. It was her shadow, that was all.

The torch was guttering badly now. Both of Coryn's had gone out when he fell. That must be why the river looked as if it ran not with water but with blood, and the basin in front of the Lady brimmed over with glistening dark-red liquid.

"There's no one in the keep," Merris said. "All your gold and soldiers—where did they come from?"

"I do have a manor," said the Lady, "and loyal men in my villages."

It sounded like an answer, but it did not feel like one. When Merris tried to back away, she found she could not move.

The Lady came toward her. She could swear she heard the rustle of scales. The Lady's gait was eerily smooth— but ladies were trained to walk so, gliding in their long skirts. She could not be slithering over that too-smooth floor like a great snake.

Her hand brushed Merris' cheek. It was warm and dry. "So young," she said. "And growing quite lovely. We have not always been blessed with beauty. Your bravery is impressive, though some might call it foolishness. Is that your young man yonder? Or a loyal servant?"

"A friend," Merris said thickly. "It's just a friend."

The Lady's smile was as patronizing as any adult's in the face of a child's silliness. "Just a friend. Yes. We may keep him, if he pleases us. Every Lady needs a friend."

Merris bit her tongue. There was no way she was going to tell the Lady what Coryn really was. She had been very, very foolish—just how foolish, she was only beginning to understand. If she lived through this, she would never again sneer at a character in a story for doing something so demonstrably stupid that the veriest idiot would know better.

And no, she was not going to blame Coryn's Companion

for getting her into this. She had done it herself, with or without anyone else's advice.

The Lady's hands came to rest on her shoulders. They applied no pressure, but they held Merris rooted. Her eyes were black, glittering in the waning light. "So lovely," she said. "So young. Blood so sweet with innocence—and just a tang of arrogance. You highborn are so sure that the world is yours to own."

"And you're not highborn?"

The Lady blinked. Had it startled her that Merris could still speak? But then she laughed. It was not a pleasant sound. "I am much, much older than your Lords and princes."

Merris fought to get away. She could not move at all. The Lady's nostrils flared, as if Merris' anger and frustration and her swelling terror had an intoxicating scent.

"So sweet," the Lady said, almost a purr. "So strong. I did well when I chose you. Young blood is precious, but young blood that is strong—that serves me very well indeed."

"I'll never serve you," Merris said through gritted teeth.

"No," said the Lady, "but your blood and body will. It was most enterprising of you to come early. Convenient, too. Pomp and circumstance have their amusements, but the crowds can be distracting—and there are so many questions. I'll take you now, then, with many thanks."

Her grip tightened. Her smile had grown wide— unnaturally so. Her face was changing, stretching. It had a strange look.

A snake, Merris thought, getting ready to swallow its prey. Except, why swallow her own heir? What—

A snake also shed its skin. Suppose it put on another one. Younger, prettier, stronger—able to feign the appearance of humanity, and thereby to avoid suspicion while it fed on its people.

The Lady did not want Merris. She wanted Merris' body. And Merris had walked straight into her lair.

She must have been doing this for years—centuries. Life after life, body after body. But . . .

"Where are the children?" Merris asked. "The old people, I could see why they would go to feed you, but if there aren't any children, where is the next generation?"

The Lady stopped. Her face was almost but not quite stretched out of recognition. She could still talk, though the words sounded odd. "I was hungry. Had to feed—keep the body alive. The cattle will breed more. Soon. Now the new body is here."

Merris fought with every scrap of will she had, but she was bound fast. The Lady was not human any more; she was all mouth and supple, scaled body. She rose above Merris, maw gaping wide.

The world exploded in white fire. Someone was shouting—screaming words that made no sense at all.

The spell on Merris let go. She dropped like a puppet with its strings cut. A white wall reared above her. Silver hooves struck, battering the great worm.

It burst like a bladder. Black blood sprayed. The stink of it turned Merris' stomach inside out. Everything that had ever died or rotted was in that stench, and every festering sickness.

Selena trampled it into the cave's floor. Her teeth were bared and her ears flat to her skull. Coryn clung to her back, making no effort to stop her, though she went on long after there was nothing more than a wet smear on the waxy stone.

The Companion stood still. Her light had dwindled to a moonlit glow. Her ears were still slanted back and her nostrils were wrinkled in disgust, but her fury was gone.

She blew out her breath in a sudden and explosive snort. Coryn jumped so hard he almost fell off. Merris found herself on her feet, arms wrapped around Selena's neck, holding on for dear life.

A tiny part of her gibbered that she could be killed, too. She was the Lady's heir, after all.

But Selena was calming down even more, relaxing little by little. Her neck bent around, but only to nuzzle Merris' hair. She sighed into it; if she had been human, Merris thought she would have sagged in relief.

"We got here in time," Coryn said for his Companion. "Dear gods, that was close!"

"Did you know?" Merris asked. "What she was?"

"We suspected," Coryn said. He had the grace to look a little shamefaced. "Selena is sorry she let you be bait.

She's also sorry she took so long to get here. She had to wait for the change, to catch the thing at its weakest point, when it was completely focused on you. But still . . . that was close."

Merris thrust herself away from the Companion. The flash of temper warmed her, which was a good thing—she had been cold to the bone. "I did not *let* anyone do anything. Any stupidity I committed, I did entirely on my own."

:And bravery, too.:

That was not a voice, precisely. It was a woman's, or at least female. Blue eyes glowed in it.

The Companion's approval washed over Merris. It was a gift. Merris decided, after due consideration, to accept it.

By the day before Merris' birthday, Herald Isak was well enough to sit in the garden and enjoy his Companion's company. It was a beautiful day, not too warm for the time of year, and the roses were in full bloom.

There was still going to be a celebration, though Darkwall's Lady would not be attending it. People from Forgotten Keep were in Darkwall, helping its people to recover from their spell-born confusion and the grief and rage that came with it. Merris had come back from there the day before, because she needed to see her father and her childhood home again—and because Coryn's Companion had told her she should.

Selena was there, too, with Coryn. The Companion had allowed Merris to braid roses in her mane. Coryn seemed to think she looked silly, but she was pleased with herself. Selena was more than a little vain.

Herald Isak smiled at them. "It was good of you to come back," he said to Merris.

"I couldn't refuse a Companion's summons," she said, "and I wanted to be here."

He nodded. "You've done well. Darkwall will prosper now, I think."

"I hope so," she said. Something about his smile made her add, "It's true, isn't it? You didn't come here by accident. You were sent to deal with Darkwall."

"We were exploring the region," he admitted, "and we meant to investigate certain rumors that we had heard. We weren't quite expecting matters to turn out as they did. We were thinking more on the lines of saving an innocent from a terrible fate, then making what order we could."

"And so you did," she said. "I'm grateful."

"We're grateful to you for proving yourself so well fit for the office."

"Am I?" she asked. "I'm hardly more than a child. Now that . . . thing . . . is gone, someone else can take the Keep. Someone older. Wiser. Better fit to rule."

"But," said Isak, "you were raised and trained for it. It was meant to be a ruse, an elaborate lie, but it was well done. We've already sent our recommendation to the King, and we're sure he'll approve it. You *are* the Lady of Darkwall."

Merris supposed she should raise more of a fuss, but the truth was, she agreed with him. It scared her—and well it should. Darkwall had a long way to go before it felt like home. But with her father's help and maybe some assistance from the King as well, she could turn that poor broken valley into the prosperous domain it had pretended to be.

"And, of course," Isak continued through the babble of her thoughts, "now the spell is broken and these lands are open to us again, Heralds will come here more often. In fact, his majesty wonders if Darkwall would be amenable to the presence of one of his own for a while, to help as needed and guide when he can."

"I'm sure Darkwall would be pleased to accept such a gift," Merris said. Her words were cool, but her heart was beating hard. "You'll be coming to Darkwall, then? Are you well enough to travel?"

"I will be," Isak said, "but I'm not the one the King has in mind." His smile slanted toward Coryn. "There is one whose Internship is just about complete, who is ready for a posting. His Majesty wonders if, since he and his Companion have served Darkwall so well already, whether—"

It was the height of impoliteness to interrupt, and a gentleperson never let out a whoop, but Merris was guilty of the one and Coryn of the other. "Yes!" she said through his eruption. "Yes, we would be pleased."

She glared at him. He scowled back. Then they grinned. Selena pushed between them, snorting and shaking rose petals from her mane. Let them never forget, her every move said, to whom the credit really belonged.

"Never!" they said together—then broke out laughing.

It was going to be a very interesting association.

Not only that, thought Merris. Partnership, too. And above all, and perhaps most best of all, friendship.

NAUGHT BUT DUTY

by Michael Z. Williamson

Michael Z. Williamson is variously, an immigrant from the UK and Canada, a twenty-year veteran of the U.S. Army and U.S. Air Force, a bladesmith, and a science fiction, fantasy, military fiction, technical author and political satirist. He lives near Indianapolis with his wife Gail, whom he helped graduate Army Basic Training at age thirty-six, their children Morrigan and Eric, and various cats that will assist in taking over the world any day now. He can be found online at www.MichaelZWilliamson.com and www.SharpPointyThings.com

THE aftermath of a battle was always confusing and ugly. Arden rode through the fractured pockets of suffering, surveying everything with trained eyes. His concern was practical, casualties and effect; there was little pleasure in this aspect.

Pleasure came from a well-planned and executed attack, a lightning raid against a larger force that inflicted casualties while keeping his own troops whole, a good maneuver around the flank of a worthy foe, or a feint that misdirected an enemy so the Toughs cracked his shield wall or line of battle.

The burning huts, the moaning, writhing bodies and the indignities and rape weren't pleasurable to any but the crass, the coward, or the pervert. A common soldier could be forgiven a few hours' brutality in the aftermath, his partner's blood still splashed on his tunic. But pain inflicted against helpless civilians as a punitive measure was the mark of a scared weakling.

Crass, coward, pervert, scared weakling. Those words well described the Toughs' current employer, Lord Miklamar. Jobs had been few and far between, and it had been necessary to move farther south to find employ. But the quality of the ruler varied greatly, and Arden had little time to sound out prospects. His concern had been for good and reliable pay with enough action to keep his troops interested, not enough to wipe out them or his reputation. Here in Acabarrin, the petty lords paid well enough, and the action was steady. But with the King dead, the squabbling princes and heirs, vassal-lords and slavering, power-mad seekers were carving the corpse of the Kingdom to nothing. He'd known nothing of Miklamar's reputation when he accepted the contract. He despised the man now that he did.

Arden's reputation, and that of the Toughs, was still safe. Barring an occasional looted trinket and scavenged arms and armor, *his* soldiers had left the village alone, and were drawn back up in formation awaiting his orders. The colors of a household unit they had not, but discipline, pride, and the poise of professionals they did.

Arden grimaced a bare fraction of an inch; watching six of Miklamar's troops stretch a young woman, girl really, out on the ground. She screamed as they tore at her silken clothes. No mere peasant, she, but more likely the daughter of the chief or mayor, whatever he would be called around this land. Arden watched, acting as witness. Little he could do, other than remember the event. Nearby, others hacked a young man to pieces for the crime of having dared protect his house with a pruning hook.

Fire and blood tinged the air, turning the fresh breeze sickly sweet and metallic. Such a sunset was an ill omen for others. Arden turned his mount and headed out from the village, back past the lines of the allied force.

Ahead was the mounted figure he'd have to deal with, no matter how much it disgusted him. Shakis, the regional deputy to Miklamar, and the mind behind this battle. If "battle" could be applied to a bloody, one-sided slaughter and the present butchery.

He nodded in salute as he drew up. It was respect for

the rank of the man who had bought his services, and nothing more. The gesture was not returned, which was as he expected.

"Lord Shakis, I see no point in brutalizing such peasants as these. It hardly seems worth the effort." It was a hint, and far more diplomatic than he wanted to phrase it. "There are other enemies we could seek."

Shakis gazed at him. The sneering contempt he had for the "mercenary" was concealed, but cut through to the surface anyway, flickering firelight from a blazing roof making it an even uglier caricature.

"It serves many purposes. The peasants will spread the word, that resistance brings only woe. It improves the take and the pay for my men. And it allows them some release, to take vengeance on enemy scum. It ensures they will have the right mindset for next time."

My men, Arden thought. Only male soldiers here. Arden would say *my troops,* because one in twenty was a woman. That had been part of the contract negotiations, too, as had swearing fealty to their employer's god. Arden had conceded on a temporary allegiance to their god, whose name he'd already forgotten, but had demanded his women warriors be kept. He would have canceled the bargain otherwise. All his soldiers were worthy, and he wouldn't allow any suggestion otherwise.

The right mindset, he thought. That of the bully and the coward and the robber. His own sneering contempt was locked down deep. It was not something he would share. No successful mercenary did.

"After the evening's Triumph, will there be another movement?" he asked evenly.

Shakis missed the sarcasm, or ignored it, and said, "There will. Two more towns along this front require attention. Each will be a harder fight. Are your men up to it?"

"My troops are," he agreed. "If you are done with us for now, my troops and I will encamp for the night, about a mile south. We are in need of rest and to care for our gear and horses."

"As you wish, though the revelry will last all night." Shakis chuckled and licked his lips slightly. The man was handsome enough physically, but his demeanor would strike fear into any civilian wench unlucky enough to meet him.

Arden wished he'd known of that ahead of time.

"Rest, and care of our gear and horses," he repeated. "We have our own revels planned." With ale they'd brought and hired wenches who were part of the entourage. Women who didn't require a fight and wouldn't slice your throat if you passed out. Ale that wasn't poisoned at the last minute, or badly brewed and rotten. Though the vengeance and poison were part of Shakis' calculations, most certainly, so that he could exact a price in response. Unprofessional. A professional took pride in his work, but didn't needlessly create more.

Another day, another battle. The town of Kiri. Arden scarcely remembered which were which anymore. It was easy to remember the towns where tough, honorable battles were fought. Likewise the ones where they'd rescued an employer's forces. The little villages, however, were never memorable, which made him uncomfortable. They were people, too.

The price of honor, he thought. The stock in trade of a mercenary company was its competence and reliability. The ragged bands of sword fodder never amounted to much, nor earned much. Only the best units did.

Which made those best the equal of any state or nation's army in quality and outlook. Which offended said "official" armies and earned sneers. Sneers the Toughs and the few outfits like them knew were part jealousy and part ignorance. And once you knew you were morally above the people you worked for . . .

It was rough work, and a conscience was both necessary and a hindrance. The Toughs owed allegiance to each other only. They protected each other at work, and in the taverns and camps afterward. They thought not too hard about their opponents of the moment, who would shortly be defeated or dead as part of a cold deal and a week's pay and food.

So Arden, as Kenchen before him, Ryala before Kenchen, and Thoral who'd founded the Toughs tried for only the best contracts. Supporting a proud state at its border or chasing bandits were the choicest tasks. Caravan escort was boring but honorable, as was guard duty at a border town or trading center. But there were few such jobs, and between starvation and ethics was a gray line.

Once again the Toughs cracked the defenses of the town that stood in the way of Miklamar's plan for expansion or peace or world conquest or whatever his motivation was. Were Arden a strategic planner for a nation, he'd find that information and use it. As a mercenary commander, he stuck to the closer, more local concerns of food, support, and pay. Thinking too much made working for such people harder.

Once again, the rape, pillage, arson, and looting began, the cowardly local troops reflecting the manner of their leader, as was always the case.

Arden wheeled his mount away from the spectacle, assured his own wounded and dead was being cared for by their sergeants, rode through the healthy ranks, and nodded in salute. He always recognized his troops for doing well.

Shakis was waiting at the rear, as always. "Arden, you have done well again, for mercenaries," he said as Arden entered his tent.

Such a greeting. "Well for mercenaries." As if sword wounds felt different to the vanquished, depending on the colors worn by the soldier thrusting it home.

"I thank you," he said.

"The campaign proceeds. We will keep your men another month, as we asked."

"As long as they are paid, they will remain loyal to the contract," he hinted.

Shakis barely scowled and with a nod one of his lackeys dropped a sack of coin in front of Arden. Arden took the time to count it. Those two acts summed up the relationship perfectly. Arden didn't trust his employer, and the man was fervent enough in his religion to imagine that people should *want* to risk their lives for it.

Not for the first time, Arden pitied the towns falling to this excuse for a man.

Then it was out to ride patrol. Everyone took turns at the duties of camp and skirmish, even the squadron leaders and Arden himself. No good commander could understand the working soldiers without sharing in the menial tasks

Occasionally, he exercised his privilege not to, but it was good practice and good inspiration, so he dealt with the muck and tedium and did it most of the time.

He met up with Balyat and two newer riders. Balyat and he were the scouts for the ride, the others backup and messengers if needed, and would gain experience in the skill.

Patrol gave him the chance to explore the area consciously, and to get a feel for it inside. It allowed part of his mind to relax and tour the terrain—rolling hills and copses of trees with small, growing streams. It let him ponder the job they had contracted.

The work was "good" in a sense. It was honest fighting at their end, the pay decent, and they had the benefits of a real army nearby. All the mercenaries were in the pay of one lord, meaning they weren't killing other professionals. Of course, they were killing innocent people and leaving the survivors to suffer at the hands of that lord.

Fausan, Mirdu, Askauk, Shelin . . . tiny hamlets, nothing but farmers and hunters with a few basic crafters. Why it was necessary to fight them was beyond Arden. He would have simply bypassed them, taken control of a large city, say, Maujujir, and let the traders spread the word that there was a new ruler. The peasants never cared, as long as the taxes weren't extreme and they were left to their lives.

Of course, that required a leader with self-confidence and who was secure in his power. Miklamar was not, and therefore wasteful. He'd been pacifying a very small province for years, proving to be a petty lord in every meaning of the word.

Riders ahead! The message came from a small part of Arden's brain that never slept. He didn't react at once, but let his mind go over what he'd seen.

Caravan, small. Not uncommon around an engagement area. It was foolish and inadvisable to fight, though both groups would report the presence of the other. To clash four on two wagons and a carriage would mean certain death for at least one rider, possibly all. Nor was Arden, as a hired sword, expected to fight outside of his contract. The train was not a massive provisioning effort, so it was not a threat to the war.

Still, a challenge and meeting were necessary, to determine the intent of the others, and their origin. Arden reined back and slowed slightly, watching to see that the others did. They were ahead to the left, crossing obliquely. One of their numbers took the lead, presumably the troop commander.

Shortly, the groups were drawn up facing each other, a safe twenty feet apart; too far for an immediate strike, too close for a charge.

"Arden, High Rider of the Toughs," he introduced himself. "Patrolling my unit's line."

"Count Namhar, of the Anasauk Confederacy, escorting a Lord," the other leader agreed. He wore striking blue-and-black colors, and had a slim lance with a small pennant. His horse was armored with light hardened leather and a few small plates that were more a status symbol than protection. Of the four others with him, two shared his colors and two were in a similar blue, black, and gray, marking them as belonging to some side branch of the family.

"You are mercenaries. For whom do you ride?" Namhar asked.

"We are on contract to Miklamar, through his deputy Shakis." Arden wouldn't lie anyway, and the truth was best. Dissemblance could be seen as a sign of espionage.

One of the others, quite young, snapped, "You are the butchers of Kiri!" He reined his horse and clutched reactively at his sword. His partner extended a hand and caught him.

"Steady," the youth was told.

"Chal had friends in Kiri. He is still in mourning," Namhar said.

"I understand," Arden replied. "No threat offered, I take no offense."

"You're still a butchering scum!" the young man yelled.

"In Kiri," Arden said. "All we did was crack the defenses."

"You lie! I saw the desecrated corpses! The torn . . ." For a moment Chal was incoherent with rage.

"Shakis' men," Arden said. "We broke the line, as we were paid to, and he took what he calls 'retribution' on peasants too poor and weak to resist." Thereby showing the sum of his courage.

For a moment, there was silence. Emotion swirled in the air, all of them negative.

At once, Namhar dismounted. Arden nodded and did likewise. His two junior troops stepped down, leaving Balyat mounted, tall, bearlike, and imposing, but wise enough to be a good lookout. One of Namhar's men stayed astride his beast, too.

The soldiers faced each other on the ground, the tension lessened. A mounted man was much taller and more imposing, a greater threat. With the horses held and the men afoot, it would be harder to start trouble.

The shouts had brought the other travelers out. The teamsters dropped from their wagons and the passengers in the carriage hurried over. The young man's outrage was contagious, and in moments the shouts of, "Butcher!" and "Violator!" were ringing.

Arden and his troops stood calmly and firmly, though the younger of the two trembled. Balyat sat solidly on his horse and refused to move. Namhar waved his arms and got control. The others acquiesced to his voice and presence, and the trouble downgraded to hard breaths and angry looks.

"I had a cousin in Kiri," Chal said.

Balyat spoke, his voice deep and sonorous. "My thoughts are with you," he said. "We fight only armed men. Shakis slaughtered the peasants. He left none if he could help it. He thought to show the kind of man he was."

"And you let him?" Chal said, glancing between the two mercenaries.

Arden said, "The Toughs are hired to bear the brunt against the peasants. Against larger forces, we are skirmishers and outriders. If you know of our name, we fight as we are ordered, but the pillage and rapine are not the work of my soldiers. I would not hire on to such, nor is it worthy of my troops."

Namhar nodded, recognizing the words as being the strongest condemnation the mercenary would utter.

"How can you fight for such animals? Is money so precious?" The man asking was a well-dressed merchant turned statesman. An honorable man, but not one to grasp the mercenary viewpoint.

Arden said nothing. He looked around evenly, finding

only one pair of eyes showing understanding. Namhar nodded imperceptibly, but in empathy. He alone knew the conflict Arden faced, and why he could not unbind his contract. He wondered now, though, if Miklamar or Shakis were trying to ruin the Toughs' reputation, to tie them here for lesser wages. Probably not. That would be subtle, and subtlety wasn't something he'd seen much evidence of.

"It is the employment we have, until released, perhaps at month's end."

"Release now! There are worthier employers around." The merchant tugged at a purse to emphasize the point.

"That is not possible," Arden replied with a shake of his head. "We have troubled you enough. Good travel to you. I must resume my patrol. I will report this encounter with my other notes, after I return and care for my horse."

"Bastard!" Chal growled.

"Quiet, Chal," Namhar snapped. "High Rider, we thank you for the courtesy."

Arden nodded as he swung up into the saddle. It would be as easy to report the incident at once, but there was no threat here, and he had no orders to do so. He wasn't about to offer a grace before eating without pay or orders.

"If you do find your contract at an end soon, I can offer the pay of my lord for good skirmishers."

"I will remember that, Namhar," Arden replied. "Offers of support are always welcome."

Shakis appeared outraged when the message was relayed hours later.

"You spoke to what amounts to an enemy patrol, and not only didn't stop them; you report it to me after a leisurely dinner!"

"They were merely a lord's retinue. Surely you wouldn't wish me to attack possible allies?"

"Allies? There are no allies! Lord Miklamar will be the undisputed ruler, as is his right!"

"Then you need to deal with such things, not have me be your envoy, yes?" Arden asked with a cruel smile.

It took a moment for the petty underling to grasp the verbal spar. "Watch your tongue, mercenary," Shakis rasped.

Shaking his head, he continued, "There has been more

rebellion along the border. Lessons must be taught. I expect this entire village put to sword." He pointed at a map, and to the south. "Manjeuk. Only another day's march."

A lesson of slaughtered peasants. Yes, Arden thought. That would surely teach other peasants not to try to live their lives. If he were planning, he would kill the village militia, then wait with baleful eye for the rest to flee. It was harsh, but it was war. It wasn't as dangerous, tactically foolish or obscenely cruel as wanton butchery.

He reflected that Shakis was acting professionally by his own vulgar standards. He wasn't sparing the town for looting, burning, and rapine.

Though not every occupant would be dead after the attack. Those left would be subject to the most vile humiliations this twisted troll could devise, he was sure.

"Wouldn't it be more efficient to simply kill the armed men and drive off the rest? Why waste good steel on starving, rag-clothed peasants?"

It was a reasonable question. So he thought.

"Rider Arden," Shakis said, caressing a jeweled dagger before him, with a blade that would turn on canvas, never mind leather or iron, "the plans are made here. You and your mercenaries," that with a sniff, "are merely one small part of many in an engagement planned many hundreds of leauges away. All we ask, all we are paying for, is your men to swing their swords where we tell them to, and to not think too much."

That decided Arden. He knew what course to take.

"As you command," he said with a nod, and turned to his own camp. That order he would give. That exact order.

Before dusk, his troops were ready, aligned, and poised for inspection. The ranks were dead straight, the product of proud, expert riders. He felt a ripple of excitement. His troops, those of the unassailable repute. There was Ty'kara, the Shin'a'in woman, tall and quick and almost as strong as some men. Bukli, skilled at sending signals with flags, hands, or fires, and almost as handy with a sword. Balyat, tall and broad and powerful as an ox, with a cool, mature head. His troops, the best one could pay for.

His troops, under pay of a cretin.

Duty.

He turned through each rank, examining each raised arm, sword, or spear, to see that they fit his orders. All were clean, well cared for, and ready. All his troops quivered in eagerness and a little fear. The brave could admit fear. Fear was part of being human. Only the coward and the fool denied fear.

Every soldier, every weapon, fit and ready as he had demanded. And now to follow the orders of the cretin.

He passed behind the last rank, then turned between two troops. They flinched not a bit, nor did their horses shy, as he urged his mount, Fury, to a fair gallop.

Then he was through the front rank, and behind him came the snorts of horses and the "Yaaah!" of riders. Thunder rose from the ground, thunder that he commanded, thunder that shattered armies.

Far ahead, brave and fearful peasants in sorry, untrained formation prepared to die for their homes. They trembled in fear, armed with hooks and forks and an occasional spear. A handful with bows was arrayed in the rear. He respected them far more than the scum he worked for this night. But he did work for them.

Duty.

And he would see that duty done.

Perhaps five hundred yards, and the flickering lights of torches melded with a blood red sunset to set the mood for the work ahead. Manjeuk was the name of a quiet town in a forest meadow. Tonight, however, it was a dark-tinged collection of rude huts with little prettiness.

A hundred yards, and he could see faces, grubby and fearful and shifting in grimaces. That was just enough time to brace shield and lower sword. . . .

He hit the defensive line and burst through the front rank. These poor peasants were no match in any fashion for professional soldiers. He chopped down and connected with a skull, feeling the crack through his arm. He let the impact swing his arm back, then brought it into a thrust that knocked another man from his feet. He brought the tip up as he swung his shield out on the other side. Two men sprawled, one of them nudged by Fury's left forehoof.

Then he was through. That dismal line of men with inadequate stakes and pits had been the defense. They'd lasted not five seconds.

Urging Fury to a charge, he cleared the deadly, empty space ahead. Four good gallops did it, and no arrow came close. Few arrows came anywhere.

Then he was inside the town. A crone with a pitchfork thrust at him, and he dodged, slashing at her chest. She went down. Behind her was a cowering girl of perhaps twelve, who had dropped her stick and was whimpering. A slight poke was sufficient for her. A boy of fifteen or so wouldn't succumb to a single blow, and had to be hit three times. Stupid of him not to stay down once hit, but that wasn't Arden's concern. He reined back, turned, and galloped on.

An old man in a doorway didn't have time to raise his ancient, rust-caked sword. Two younger men drew out a rope. Arden cursed and ducked, snatching at it and twisting. The shock pulled them to the ground. Behind him, Ty'kara whacked one, dogged over and twisted, jabbed the other and recovered.

Then they were through the town and done. Few casualties, but no loot or anything positive to show for it. He sniffed in disgust as he waved his arm for the Toughs to form up.

Duty done.

Now to encamp again. They circled wide around the now flaming town. What was left was Shakis' concern. And Arden found that most amusing.

The camp was as it had been, patrols far out, pickets at the outskirts, the wounded and support armed and still a threat to intruders, even if not the heavy combatants the "regulars" were. Only half the Toughs were involved in any given battle. The rest, including recruits and their sergeants, supported them.

The regimental fire was huge, the heat palpable many feet away. Farther out, squadrons and smaller elements had their own blazes, then there were those for the watch. Toughs' Camp was a ring of fire, ever brighter toward the center, where Arden sat with his troop leaders.

Arden took a healthy slug of his ale. It was a good, rich brew that quenched and refreshed him. The bread had been baked that morning, with a chewy crust and nutty flavor. The cheese was dry, crumbly, and sharp. He dug in with gusto. Once Mirke had finished roasting that yearling stag, he would enjoy the flavor of it, the flavor that was already wafting through his nose and taking form.

Regardless of their orders, it had been a good night's work, and he was proud of it. Pride and prowess in duty. It was the only really valuable thing he had. He cherished it. A faint warmth and tingle from the ale made it sweet.

Then Shakis, that damned foppish envoy, arrived, his horse clattering with ridiculous flashy accouterments. Arden wasn't surprised, and knew exactly what his complaint was to be before the worm opened his mouth.

"High Rider Arden! Lord Miklamar is most displeased with your performance, if it can be called that, in Manjeuk!"

"We did as we were ordered," he replied, stonefaced. "As we swore to."

"You were ordered to put the village to the sword and spear!"

"And so we did," he replied. He refused to get upset with the likes of this. It would not be honorable. Emotion he reserved for those worthy, who might be allied or enemy, but whom he would count as men. This was not a man.

"I expected you would take your swords *out* of your scabbards before striking with them! And use the sharp ends of your spears!"

"Then perhaps you should have so specified in your orders," Arden said, smiling faintly. Behind him were snickers. No doubt everyone in Manjeuk had been confused to have the fiercest riders of the south gallop through, swatting and poking them with scabbarded swords. No doubt they were all bruised and broken from it. But none had been stabbed or cut. The orders had not specified that. And *had* specified the mercenaries were not to think too hard.

"Because of your cowardice," Shakis said, and Balyat and Ty'kara growled with flinty gazes. Arden laid out a palm to hold them. It was all he needed to command them, despite the mortal insult. "Because of your cowardice, our men took near twenty deaths."

"I lost a man, too," Arden replied. "Bukli, my best messenger."

"You have my pity, sell-sword," Shakis replied. He was reaching a frothing level within, Arden could see. "No matter. The town *was* taken, and now our men show them what it means to lose." The expression on his face was a combination of excitement and lust that was simply obscene.

It would have been better, Arden realized, to have killed the poor bastards quickly. He'd done them no favors as it was.

The grumbling around him rose to a barely audible level as Shakis rode out. Arden's troops were no happier than he.

For a week the Toughs were kept in camp as other units fought. It was an insult, and a further waste of resources. Arden concealed his contempt, but his troops were not so reticent. They'd fought for harsh men before, and torture and agony were not unfamiliar sights to any of them, but any professional soldier had his limits. The Toughs were barely tolerating Miklamar's strategy and the toady who relayed his wishes.

Something had to be done.

After nine days, Arden was called to a strategy meeting. He'd been shunned from the planning sessions even though he was merely an observer. That banishment couldn't help his survival or plans, and his inclusion now, being "ordered to present" himself was yet another slap. He had expected it, of course. He'd hoped his disgusted protest in the last battle would have led to the contract being let, but either Miklamar or Shakis was too stupid or petty for that. They wasted pay to keep the Toughs doing nothing.

Arden arrived and was ignored. Movements were planned, orders given, messengers and commanders sent. Silence reigned around Arden, with no word or acknowledgment given him by anyone. Commanders of units he'd fought alongside, and who mutually respected him, gave him only a glance and then studiously avoided further interaction. For two hours, Arden sat in cold drafts at the wall of the tent, watching the flickering lamp flames in meditation. He refused to get angry, for that was what Shakis wanted.

When orders came at last, while Shakis loudly chewed a

pork shank at his table, spitting and getting grease on his maps, they were insultingly direct.

"Arden, you have a chance before you to redeem yourself. This afternoon, we destroy the last vestiges of the old Kingdom in this district. You will strike in the van, and attack the village. That means, with your weapons in hand, with the sharp ends, fight as hard as you can. I will countenance no clever ploys this time, or I will have your men and yourself used for target practice by my archer regiment. You will fight any who oppose you, you will lay waste as your reputation demands, and once we are done, you will be sent on your way, since you are reluctant to help the rise of a strong empire. But I hold you to your contract yet."

"Yes, Shakis. I will do as you command."

There being no point in further discussion, Arden dismissed himself. Shakis was aware of his departure, but made no sign of noticing.

The orders created a conflict of moral outrage in Arden. He couldn't obey an order to slaughter innocents. It was unprofessional, cowardly, and unmilitary. Nor could he break his sworn oath and contract.

As he always did when troubled, he rode patrol. His thoughts drifted, and distance from Shakis made him feel cleaner. He'd had disputes with employers before, even if this scraped the hoof for lowness. He rode ahead of the three troops with him, just so he could feel more alone.

It was a cool night, slightly misty, and fires could be seen behind the town, of a small force preparing to support the town once attacked. Miklamar's only good strategy was to use his larger army to spread the threat of his neighbors. Though that might be accidental rather than strategic planning.

Count Namhar showed far better sense, with his force high in the defense, prepared to rush in on a force bogged down even briefly in the town below. He knew he couldn't save the village, so he'd use it as an anvil to hammer Shakis' force against. He'd do far more damage that way, including to the Toughs.

Arden wondered if he could arrange to be where the counterattack would happen, so as to have an honorable fight against a decent enemy.

Something crept up through his mind and coalesced into a thought.

Yes. He just might be able to do that. It would take courage, risk his life, and save his oath. That made it worth doing.

He wheeled Fury about and galloped back to camp, leaving the other three soldiers to catch up while they wondered what their commander was doing.

Count Namhar watched the unfolding battle from a hilltop. Part of him craved to be down below with his brave men, doing what could be done to restrain a horror. A horror that not only outnumbered them, but had hired crack mercenaries.

He was thankful that the leadership used both mercenaries and indigenous forces poorly.

His presence on the hill was for tactical advantage. He had a small device from the mages that could potentially change the course of a battle, if used well.

The tube was a magic Eye. Its rippling patterns, almost oily, resolved to crystal clarity when stared through. He could see events far across the field and send swift messengers to maneuver his forces.

The Eye only let him see things larger. It couldn't see things beyond obstacles, but did enhance anything within line of sight. And the mercenaries were just within that line.

It took only a moment's glance to cause him to grin. A surge ran through him, of respect for a mercenary who embodied every virtue a soldier should have. There was loyalty, and then there was honor. Above those was courage, and it took tremendous courage to do what Arden's troop was doing now.

Somewhere, they must have been ordered to attack the village. And that's what they were doing. Arden was a genius, and brave beyond words to offer such a tactic. Exploiting it would cost lives. But the tactic was suicidally foolish, and Namhar could exploit that at once. He could wipe out the Toughs to the last troop. Though to do so would be a shame.

Then the true nature of it hit him.

"Send Rorsy's force down to take them," he ordered the nearest of his aides.

"At once. At the charge, or dismounted?"

"No, take them alive," Namhar said. This had to be done just right. A man with a sword was still dangerous, and if he knew Arden as he felt he did, the man wouldn't simply surrender.

"My Lord? I am confused," his aide said.

"I will explain, but quickly. We have little time."

And indeed, there was a risk. If Arden was what he seemed, it could be handled rather quietly. But the flash of steel could turn it into the bloodbath it had looked to be from the beginning.

"Attack the town," Shakis had ordered. "Town" had two meanings; either the population and resources of the small settlement, or the physical structure of it. It was that way Arden had chosen to obey the order, and his troops had agreed, with hesitation and fear, but in support of their commander and in rebellion against the detestable creature who'd hired them and debased them. Their honor was their coin in trade. They would fight as hard to protect it as to earn it.

Arden kept his face impassive and hacked again, the daubed withes of the wall powdering under his onslaught. Yards away, Balyat crushed small beams with swings of his ax. The Toughs were arrayed along a front perhaps two hundred yards wide, surrounding the rude buildings and smashing them. To the south, Shakis' other forces were slaughtering the helpless. Arden had killed one dweller who'd faced him with a staff. The others had run. Some had seen the mercenaries senselessly beating buildings and taken the opportunity to run away, or to the battle farther south. One didn't question an enemy's error.

Behind Arden, there were men approaching, in colors that made them allies of Lord Namhar. Each swing of his head let him see their approach. They were moving to flank him and were unarmed.

So they were civilians, not a threat, he told himself, clarifying the strategy in his mind. He was playing games with his orders, and the risk was great. He probably wouldn't die at this point, though both revenge and charges of atrocity could lead that way. He might destroy a company that

had a decades-long reputation for honest fighting. If this
worked, he would indeed have employ, and stories told for
generations. But the chance for death or disgrace as an
oathbreaker hung on the other side of the balance.

But some lords were beneath any contempt. Duty bound
him to a contract. Only honor could make him respect a
man.

The two burly "civilians" closed on him, and he point-
edly ignored them. They were dressed in battle leather and
well scarred. Professionals themselves. They had orders,
and perhaps they understood those orders. If they didn't
raise weapons, he was under no compunction to fight them
under any oath he or the Toughs had ever sworn. "We
fight only armed men." But if they did, he would perforce
respond in kind. All his troops had their orders, all would
obey . . . but a panicky moment could lead to a close-
quarters bloodbath with horrific results for all.

All three of them knew how it must play out, and the
scene would replay across the front. Arden could not de-
cline to engage, could not offer to surrender to unarmed
men. If asked, he'd have to refuse.

As he drew back for another blow, one of the two lunged
at him. He spun, shifted, and made to take a swing. His
trained reflexes prepared to strike a blow that would cleave
a man.

Then the ground shifted and he tumbled, cracking his
head against his helmet as he crashed. His sword arms flew
above his head, and bashing fists broke his grip. He kicked,
snapping his right foot in a blow that elicited a pained
grunt. The fists rained down on his chest, driving the breath
from him.

"Mercenary, you are disarmed! Will you now surrender
to Lord Namhar's courtesy?"

"I will," he said.

There was no dishonor in surrender once unable to fight,
and he'd followed his orders exactly. His employer—former
employer—had been the lowest filth imaginable. To be captured thusly should make him feel proud. It didn't.

Surrender. The Toughs didn't surrender. A wrenching
pain that wasn't physical tore at him. Certainly, the fight
had been honorable, but it was a defeat in the employ of

a weakling. That cost dearly in reputation, in pride, in self-respect. Not to mention the hundreds of townsfolk who had been killed.

"I am to offer you employ with Lord Namhar, at Guild scale and with a bonus of one fifth. Or else you may have free passage to our northern border."

He heard the words, but there was no pleasure in him. He'd won this battle for his honor by losing the battle in the field. Even though he'd planned it that way, it was dizzying, shocking.

Slowly, he rose to his feet. One of the two had rushed to join a group of fellows beating Balyat to the ground. The bulky warrior needed six of them to restrain him before he finally acceded. Arden couldn't help but grin. It restored some small breath of life to the unit that even disarmed they fought so hard.

His remaining escort was panting for breath and bleeding from nose and lip. Arden had acquitted himself well enough, though he would have a hard time convincing himself.

"I am Captain Onri," his captor said. "If you will give your word of honor to be peaceable, I will escort you to Count Namhar."

"My word you have, Captain," Arden said, feeling a slight rise from the depths his soul had sunk to. He walked away from the village, smiling. He had lived through his oath to a coward. He had lost by his oath to a good man.

LANDSCAPE OF THE IMAGINATION

by Mercedes Lackey

Mercedes Lackey is a full-time writer and has published numerous novels, including the best-selling Heralds of Valdemar series. She is also a professional lyricist and a licensed wild bird rehabilitator.

TARMA'S stomach growled, and she tried to appease it with a long drink of water.

It wasn't fooled, and growled again.

The problem with being a low-level mercenary pair without an impressive reputation was that sometimes you wound up at the end of a job in a place where your talents weren't needed. And when that place was as law-plagued as this one . . .

They'd escorted a very nice old lady to the timid niece who was going to take care of her in her old age. An exceptionally low-paying job, but one that Kethry's sword Need had insisted that they take. Appropriately, as it had turned out, since the poor old woman evidently bore a striking resemblance to a very wealthy old woman in the same town, and kidnappers had decided erroneously that they were one and the same.

Still, it hadn't done much to fatten their purses; it had led them here, the Duchy of Silverthorn, possibly the *most* law-abiding part of the world that Tarma had ever seen, and no one wanted them. Worse, everything was horribly expensive because of the taxes on everything that paid the salaries of the lawkeepers and constables. Worse still, there were more than enough lawkeepers and constables keeping a jaundiced eye on strangers that when their money ran out and they had to leave their inn, it was obvious that it was going to be difficult, if not impossible, to acquire food for themselves by underhanded means without getting caught.

So the only way to handle the situation was to saddle up and move out, ignoring hunger pangs for the two or three days it was going to take them to get out of the Duchy. Normally it would only take a day at most, but—

But traffic was held by law to a snail's pace here. And constables enforced that as well.

The only members of the party that were happy were the warsteeds and Warrl. The 'steeds, because not only was grazing the road-verge permitted, it was encouraged. So they were getting enough to content them. And Warrl, because he was resorting to the usual food-source of wolves and things that looked like wolves in the summer.

Mice and rats.

And that, too, was encouraged. Once constables saw him pouncing and gulping in the ditches, they were perfectly happy to leave him alone.

:*You really ought to try these,*: Warrl said happily in Tarma's head. :*They're quite delicious. Fat, tender. I don't know why they have a rodent problem here, but I am certainly pleased that they do.*:

Tarma's stomach growled again, suggesting that at this point, fricassee of rat was sounding good.

But Tarma's brain went into revolt. No matter that she had eaten worse things. This was not something her mind wanted to contemplate, surrounded as they were by civilization. *There should be meat pies, stew, bread and cheese,* her mind insisted. *Pease porridge, bread, and onions at least.* It was not going to put up with the idea of eating mice.

You've eaten voles, she reminded it.

Those were clean wilderness creatures, her mind said primly. *Mice are not. You don't know where they've been.*

Well, her mind had a point. And if they couldn't afford to eat, they most certainly could not afford to get sick.

:They taste just fine to me,: Warrl said gleefully, as he pounced, tossed, and gulped. Their current pace—stalled, actually, while they waited for a big hay-laden cart to negotiate a difficult turn—was so slow that Warrl was having no trouble in hunting for such small prey.

Urg, said her mind, and she resolutely turned her thoughts away from the idea. Properly speaking, Warrl should have been Kethry's familiar, not hers. Kethry was the sorceress. Kethry was the one who had cast the spell to summon a familiar. But Warrl was his own *kyree* and he had decided that Kethry, who already was bound to the spell-sword Need that gave her fighting powers equal to just about any swordswoman Tarma had ever seen, did not need a familiar. But Tarma evidently did.

So the two of them were bound to exceedingly useful but occasionally vexing partners. Kethry to a sword that forced her to come to the aid of any female in jeopardy, and Tarma to a calf-sized wolfish-looking beast with a penchant for sarcasm, a weakness for Bards, and a distinct and unique sense of humor.

Usually at his mind-mate's expense.

The hay-wain was still stalled in front of them. Now the driver was arguing with a constable. Her stomach growled. She resisted the urge to ride along the verge; the last time she'd done that, the constable had threatened to fine them. The only reason he hadn't was because Kethry turned out their purses, proving they had nothing, and pointed out that if they were jailed, they would be housed and fed at the expense of the Duchy.

Mind, that was beginning to look attractive—

Except that the warsteeds and everything they owned would be confiscated and sold.

No. Not a good option.

Tarma was all in favor of laws, but this place was ridiculous.

Kethry couldn't even earn some money by performing minor sorceries, because she wasn't licensed as a magician in this Duchy. Which license, of course, cost money.

Kethry was looking around with impatience. The other side of the road—reserved for traffic going the other direction—was absolutely clear.

Well, of course it was. The hay wagon was blocking it.

"Is there any reason why we *have* to go in this direction?" she asked Tarma.

"Well, no, but—" Tarma didn't get to finish that statement. Kethry nudged Hellsbane with her heels, turned the warsteed's head, and set off down the clear and open side of the road.

:It's all the same to me,: Warrl said philosophically. *:There are just as many mice in that ditch.:*

Tarma had no idea where they were, and she didn't much want to stop long enough to find out. As long as they got out of the Duchy, that was all she cared about.

:We're heading for the Pelagirs,: Warrl remarked philosophically.

Oh, bloody hell— "Keth. Warrl says we're—"

"Headed for the Pelagirs, yes I know." The Pelagir Hills were as chaotic and magic-infested as the Duchy of Silverthorn was law-abiding. "That's probably the reason why these people are so law-obsessed. It's their way of dealing with the insanity on their doorstep." Kethry, who was usually far more cautious about venturing into the Pelagirs than Tarma was, seemed entirely cavalier about this idea.

"But why—"

Kethry turned in her saddle and looked back at her partner. "Because if I'd had to look for another candlemark at the back of that hay-wagon I was going to kill someone. Because they longer we stay in this place, the more likely we are to do something that gets us thrown in jail. Because my stomach is growling. And because I'm getting a faint twinge from Need that is sending my head in this direction."

Oh, bloody hell— "Oh, no. Oh, *hell,* no. Not this time," Tarma protested. "The last time is what got us stuck out here in the first place!"

"So we're due for a change of luck," Kethry replied, with no hint of irony. "She owes us one. Maybe she's responding to our hunger pangs by finding us a good client."

"Maybe you're living in a dream world," Tarma growled under her breath. "Not that it matters all that much. We still have to get out of here, and whoever this is, if they have food, we'll already be ahead of where we were."

In answer, Kethry nudged the gray flanks of the warsteed again, moving her into a slightly faster pace. Tarma knew that sign by now; the magical pull on Kethry was getting stronger.

They rode over the top of a hill and found themselves staring down a long flat slope that went on for leagues, until abruptly, as if at an invisible line that marked a place where sanity ended. The landscape changed abruptly, from the rolling, manicured fields to steep, rock-crowned hills, whose tops rose above a forest of trees so tortured and twisted it looked as if some sadistic giant had been wrenching their limbs about.

"In the Pelagirs, then," Tarma sighed, "Oh, hold back my surprise."

They were stopped at the border by guards who were immensely suspicious of anyone who wanted to go into the Pelagirs, and from the look of the fortified wall they were going to have to pass under, the Duchy put a lot of time and effort trying to keep things from the Pelagirs out.

After dealing with their questions for the better part of a candlemark, Tarma finally lost patience. She glared at the guards, and silently summoned Warrl, who rose up from where he had been hidden in the grass of the ditch

He moved in to stand by her side as the guards became very still. Tarma looked their officer in the eyes.

"We just want to go home," she said tonelessly.

Within moments they were looking back at the closed gate from the Pelagirs side of the wall.

"You know, they're never going to let us back in there," Kethry remarked in a conversational tone.

"I can live with that," Tarma replied. "At least there are enough normal animals in here that we can hunt."

Her stomach growled agreement.

At least Kethry didn't take off across country, following the sometimes-elusive trace that her sword would give her. She allowed Hellsbane to trot sensibly along what passed for a road here, which was a faint track among the trees. Tarma kept a sharp eye out for game, but just as importantly, so did Warrl. Warrl, with his keen nose and sharper eyesight, should be able to pick out what was safe for them to eat.

But the forest was deserted. She would have said,

"strangely deserted," but these were the Pelagirs, and nothing much was strange there.

Ever.

Her stomach growled.

"Mushrooms?" she suggested to Kethry. "Watercress?"

Kethry shook her head. "I wouldn't try it," she advised. "Very bad idea. You can have no idea what's been changed in the blasted things. Maybe they wouldn't be poisonous, but do you really want to find yourself in the middle of hallucinations or intoxicated to the point you can't stand up?"

Well, no.

Silent forest with the silence interrupted only by the far-off drip of water and the dull thudding of the warsteeds' hooves on the turf.

And, of course, by the growling of Tarma's stomach.

:I believe, mind-mate, I have found Kethry's goal,: came the familiar voice in Tarma's mind, at the same time that Kethry said, "By the feel of things, my target is—"

They rode up over a rise.

"—there," Kethry finished.

It certainly looked that way. In the valley below, in what looked like a temporary camp, was a woman. A particularly ageless-looking woman with a relatively unlined face despite a coiled mass of silver hair fastened in place with pins, a little plump, but otherwise in very good physical shape. There was no way of telling what she was from her costume, a well-made set of brown riding leathers with a split skirt rather than breeches or trews. There were three horses with her, all with saddles. There were two ominous mounds of earth off to the side of the camp.

She looked up and spotted them at the top of the ridge line, and regarded them thoughtfully.

Tarma knew what she would see: sitting on a matched pair of ugly gray horses, big-boned and big-headed, were two women. The one in the buff-colored traveling robes (also with a split skirt) or a sorceress of the White Winds school, had a pretty, soft face, a mass of amber-colored hair pulled back into a tail—and the end of a sword sticking up over her right shoulder. The other, in the all-black leather and armor of a Shin'a'in Swordsworn, had the hawklike features, black hair, prominent nose, and golden-tanned skin typical of her race. Her hair had not yet grown out, and only brushed the tops of her shoulders; it was held in place by a leather headband to keep it out of her eyes. A sword hilt also protruded over her right shoulder, there was a quiver hanging from her left hip, a bow in a bow sheath at the saddle, and probably far more knives than the woman even dreamed possible both hidden and openly sheathed on Tarma's person. Beside Tarma was Warrl, a *kyree,* a creature who came from this part of the world. About the size of a young calf, with a wolfish head, but a body more like that of one of the big, speedster hunting cats of the Dhorisha Plains, Warrl was a small army in and of himself.

Whatever was wrong, the woman did not appear to be in immediate danger. That was probably why Need hadn't been prodding Kethry with the goad of pain into speeding down the road at a breakneck speed.

She also wasn't intimidated by them. Which was interesting. Although there were not *many* female bandits, such things weren't unknown. Which implied that, whoever or whatever she was, the woman thought she could handle herself against two armed people and a large and dangerous beast.

They looked down; she looked up. Finally, she spoke.

"So," she said. "I don't suppose you're for hire?"

They rode down the slope slowly. Tarma was all for saying "Yes!" then and there, but Kethry, for once, was more cautious. "What happened here?" she asked.

The woman sighed. "I'm on my way to keep an appointment with a—colleague. I had two temporary fighters with me. While I was off taking the horses to water them, I left them here to set up camp, and something attacked them, I heard the commotion, but by the time I got back here, it was too late."

Tarma did not bother to ask "what," because clearly if the woman had known, she would have told them.

"Signs?" she asked instead.

"Something large with a lot of teeth and claws," she replied. "Magic; the aura was all over the place. And it didn't want to face me, so magic probably was its one vulnerability." She glanced away from them, up the road leading deeper into the Pelagirs. "I've been here before. That condition isn't going to hold for long."

Sensible, too. Once again, Tarma almost said. "we're available" when Keth forestalled her.

"Conditions of employment?" she asked coolly.

Well, that was a change. Need's prodding must be nothing but a little nag in the back of her head. The woman started to answer when Tarma's stomach announced to the universe just how hungry she was.

The woman looked startled, then laughed.

"First condition is that I feed you," she said, with a shrewd smile. "I'd much rather negotiate with the sleepy and satisfied than the lean and hungry,"

It was trail food: dried beef, bread you could drive a nail with.

Tarma didn't care. At this point she would readily have broken teeth into order to get something to her stomach. Her stomach wasn't objecting either. Negotiations and meal concluded about the same time; the woman drove a hard, hard bargain. Nothing up front; fee to be paid only at the conclusion of the journey.

On the other hand, what did they have to spend coin on out here? And finally they got their employer's name. Nanca Jente. Sorceress who claimed no particular affiliation.

"How do you feel about riding in the dark?" Nanca asked, as they shook hands on the bargain. "Full moon tonight, and I've lost most a lot of time here."

The two exchanged glances. "I've got no objections," Tarma said, "But I'm not the one that makes the decision on whether or not to move in the dark." And she cast a significant look at Hellsbane and Ironheart.

Nanca followed her look, and raised one silver eyebrow. "All right," she said. "If your horses refuse to move, we stop."

And as it happened, the moon rose large and bright, and though the warsteeds slowed their pace to an ambling walk, they were able to see well enough that they didn't actually object to moving through the night. At least until the moon began to descend. And at that point, both mares snorted and made their objections to going on in pitch dark known.

For her part Tarma was nodding off in the saddle, and though Nanca groused and grumbled, she didn't do so for long. The "camp" that they made was sketchy at best; they only unpacked their bedrolls, arranged the horses around them, and crawled into the blankcts in the dark

They were on their way again at dawn. Tarma got the impression of a certain amount of urgency, as if their employer had a deadline she had to meet. So she pushed the warsteeds a little more than she might otherwise have done, and with three mounts to switch off, Nanca was well able to keep up.

And so it was that they reached their goal on the second day, just as the sun began to set. Which was about at the point where Tarma gave serious thought to walking on their deal.

Because their goal was a Gate.

"You didn't say anything about a Gate," Kethry said, as the three of them stared down into the little valley. The thing was alive and active, too; the pillars on either side shimmered with energy, and the strange blackness that was the hallmark of any active Gate pulled and tugged on the eyes in a way calculated to make whoever was looking at it feel sick.

"You didn't either," their employer pointed out. "Is it an issue?"

"You don't know where those things come out," Tarma objected, with a glance at her partner.

"Ah, but I do," Nanca replied, with the faintest of smiles. "It comes out in the place where I am supposed to meet my colleague."

Of course it did. "And then what?" Tarma demanded.

"Then you continue to do what I contracted to you for. You guard me and fight off anything physical that comes to attack me and I deal with anything of a magical nature, until we reach my colleague, and once we are there, I pay you and he provides the exit point, which will drop you through another Gate relatively near the Dhorisha Plains." Nanca shrugged. "After that, where you go is your busincss."

That was another thing. Granted, Kethry was probably not the magician that Nanca was—but why forbid her to work magic at all?

Unless it was because the nature of what lay on the other side of that Gate was of such a strange nature that Nanca didn't want a sorceress unfamiliar with it meddling with it. . . .

Tarma and Kethry exchanged another glance. And finally Tarma fingered the mind-bond that held her to Warrl.

What do you think? she left lying on the surface of her thoughts.

:I think that I sense deception in her, but no harm. Whatever is going on here, she intends nothing unfortunate for us, nor does she foresee anything unfortunate.:

Hmm . . .

Nanca dug into her saddlebags and passed over journey bread to both of them. Tarma gnawed on it while she thought, looking and not-looking at the Gate. In the end, it was her full stomach that decided her. Nanca was certainly right about that part.

"Let's go."

Now it was Nanca who hesitated a moment, but before she could say anything, Tarma was already drawing her sword and parrying-dagger, and looping Ironheart's reins through the pommel hold on the saddle. She felt Ironheart shift under her into full alertness, ready to answer to leg and weight-shift signals rather than rein. She heard the sound of Need clearing her sheath and knew that Kethry was doing the same.

She turned her attention to their employer. "Shin'a'in proverb," she said. "It is better to prepare for an ambush and look foolish than not and look dead."

Nanca smiled broadly, and gestured. "In that case, after you."

Warrl went through first. Gates were probably Tarma's least favorite way to travel, and thus far she had only had to endure two. This was the third and, as usual, it was horrible. There was a sense of dislocation with the world, the bottom dropping out of everything, a freezing cold that wasn't really cold, blackness like the inside of the head, and a myriad of other sensations, all awful, that passed too quickly to be identified.

Then they were on the other side. There was an ambush. Warrl had already gone after them; the ambushers must not have counted on anything that wasn't human because he already had control of the group locked down. With a harsh Shin'a'in war-cry, Tarma waded in.

And it had to be the strangest bunch she had ever fought.

Somebody's retainers, because they were identically dressed. Buff trews, red surcoats, chainmail. Three archers, already down, and a dozen swordsmen.

But what was strange was the way they fought.

Exactly alike.

Every one of them had the same four-move fighting pattern. Overhand slash, shield block, underhand thrust, parry. Absolutely the same and in the same order. Once she realized that, Tarma had them down in no time.

And realized the second thing. No blood.

"Automata," said Kethry. "Constructs." And she looked directly at Nanca.

Nanca nodded. "These are the simplest. There will be more. I was about to warn you there might be an ambush, but you were already preparing for one, so I kept my mouth shut."

Now Tarma looked out at the land on the other side of the Gate, and found it no different than the part of the Pelagirs they had just passed through. Wooded hills. Plenty of places for more ambushes. The one difference was the nice, clear road that cut through the woods.

She looked at it and sighed. "I suppose we have to stick to the road?"

Nanca nodded. "It would be a very, very bad idea to get off the road," she said. "The landscape itself is not predictable once you get off the road. And at the same time, it's too predictable."

"What the hell is that supposed to mean?" Tarma asked, frowning.

"That features can appear and vanish at random, sometimes," Nanca told her. "But worse than that, landmarks . . . repeat. So that you can't tell where you are."

"Landmarks repeat." Tarma got a bewildering vision of identical trees, identical rock formations, repeating over and over again like decorative tiles and suddenly—

"Bloody hell." She blinked, and looked straight at Nanca as all of the pieces came together. "This is a game. And your colleague is really your opponent. And this—" she waved her hand at the landscape, "—is a giant playing board."

"Ha!" Rather than being offended, Nanca seemed delighted. "By the gods, you are smart ones!"

"And you can't tell us because that would violate the rules," Kethry said slowly.

Nanca nodded.

"But us figuring it out for ourselves is fine." Rather than feeling offended, Tarma was actually delighted. "Has anyone done this before?"

"I've never brought fellow players in here before," Nanca said, her eyes now very bright with interest. "Only the two constructs I'm allowed as helpers. But there was nothing in the rules that said I could *not* bring fellow players in, and when my constructs met an untimely end before I could enter the game-space—I thought maybe I would try putting out a gentle magical probe for help." She raised her eyebrow. "My friend and I invented this to keep each other sharp, but I must tell you that I would not have permitted either of you to come to serious harm. Practice is one thing, Being hurt—we both have ways to bring the game to an end. Still." She pursed her lips. "This game is timed, and we are already late. And it does get a great deal tougher, the closer we get to our goal."

Tarma felt a wide grin spreading over her face. "Let's see if we can win this thing, shall we?"

Now that they knew what to expect, Tarma concentrated on understanding the logic laws by which the constructed opponents they met operated. She sent Warrl out ahead, knowing that whatever he found was all they would have to worry about for the moment. And one of the first laws she determined was that there was a set distance at which the constructs "noticed" them.

They sat their horses just outside that predetermined distance and watched the constructed ambush party stand there like so many mannequins, while Tarma assessed them, and worked up a strategy. "The usual, I think," she said finally. "You sweep in from the left flank, Kethry. I'll come in from the right. Warrl circles around and comes in from behind—"

"Ah!" Nanca nodded before Tarma could add the last.

"And I keep their attention from the front, because I have better ability to strike from a distance. I'd never tried that before, but then, my constructs were never bright enough to operate with a lot of reliable independence."

"Heh. That's encouraging, then," Tarma said, with a grin. "Let's see if this works."

"Be prepared to retreat if you have to," Nanca urged. "There's no shame in that."

Kethry sighed and grimaced. "You just told a Shin'a'in Swordsworn that there is no shame in retreat. This is a trifle like telling the village drunk that there is no shame in putting the wine bottle down and walking away from the tavern."

Nanca laughed as Tarma made a face of her own. "I'm not *that* bad," she protested. Then added, "Am I?"

Kethry's silence and significant stare were answer enough. Tarma flushed. "Let's just do this, shall we?" was all she managed to say.

It would not be fair to say that they cut across the landscape like a team of experienced mowers across a hayfield. Nanca had been correct; the closer they got to their goal, the more difficult and numerous the foes became. And the closer to their goal, the more magician-constructs also appeared, designed specifically to neutralize or at least occupy Nanca herself.

This were the most clever and the closest to actual intelligence and Tarma was very glad that she and Kethry were not the ones directly facing the things. They were not coming out of this unscathed, that much was certain, too. At the end of each battle, they were at the very least completely exhausted. And the injuries they got were quite real. Yes, Nanca could and did heal them almost immediately, but they did hurt, and they did incapacitate.

But Tarma, at least, was finding something exhilarating about this. It was like having the perfect training scenario. You didn't learn anything in fighting by not getting hurt, after all.

And the closer they got to the "endgame" as Nanca called it, the more cheerful she became. "If we can pull this off as a draw," she said finally, "I will be happy. Quite, quite happy, actually. Coming into this handicapped—"

"I am not settling for a draw." Tarma had opened her

mouth to declare something of the sort, but Kethry, to her
astonishment, beat her to it.

"Eh?" the Swordsworn said, looking curiously at her
partner, who was at the moment looking rather the worst
for wear, with her robes more than a bit cut up, her hair
straggling out of its tail, and the beginnings of a black eye
that was just one of the many sets of bruises they had both
collected. Bruises, after all, were *not* incapacitating, and
Nanca's reserves of healing energies were limited.

"I am not settling for a draw. I think we can win this
one. But I'd like to suggest a strategy change myself."
Kethry settled an unsheathed Need across her lap. "Am I
right in thinking we are going to encounter your opponent
in this endgame?"

Nanca nodded. "Absolutely. And rather than relying on
the constructs going through their patterned moves, he'll
be directing some of them personally.

"That's what I thought." Kethry looked over at her partner. We've been taking out the weakest of the constructs
first, then concentrating the fighting of all three of us on
the strongest. This time I think we should ignore all that.
Instead, we all converge on this mage-friend of Nanca's and
take him out. Once he's down, the game is over. Right?"

"Right!" Nanca pounded a fist into her cupped hand with
delight. "And that is the last thing he is going to expect,
because we've been doing the opposite of that until now.
The essence of what is going to work is that we can't be
predicted!"

"Is there any way you can give us an overview of the
battle site?" Kethry asked.

"I don't—" Nanca began, and then—her eyes fell on
Warrl. And she began to grin.

Mind-mate, Warrl said, with alarm, backing up a pace, *I
am not at all certain I like where this is going—*

I knew I would not like where this was going, Warrl complained bitterly, as he hovered in place, four paws dangling
limply in midair. *If the gods had intended us to fly, they
would have made us gryphons.*

"Hush up and practice." Tarma admonished him. "Just
do what Nanca told you to do; run as if you were running
on the ground."

It's undignified. He protested, ears laid back flat, but obeyed.

Finally even Nanca was satisfied with what he was doing. "You're no Tayledras bondbird, but you'll do," she said with satisfaction. "Now just make sure Jendran doesn't see you, and you'll be fine."

I'm doomed, Warrl said bitterly. *I'm a calf-sized flying predator. How is he not going to see me?*

But he galloped clumsily up into the sky anyway.

Tarma closed her eyes and concentrated on what Warrl was showing her. The layout of the troops. The disposition of the "special" constructs that their opponent would be operating himself. And most importantly, the whereabouts of Jendran himself—

Ack! bleated Warrl, as suddenly crossbow bolts from three separate units came hurtling toward him.

And Warrl came hurtling back at top speed, now displaying a great deal more agility than he had going out.

Or at least, agility in the air. He landed like a sack of wet sand, three crossbow bolts sticking out of his improvised battle-armor.

And he glared at Tarma.

If you ever ask me to do that again, he said savagely, *I will bite you. I will remove a very large piece of your flesh. And forever after you will be known as "Tarma the Half-A—"*

"They know we're coming," Tarma said hastily. "The advantage of surprise is over. Let's move, people."

The victory feast was very real. It was held outside the game-world, in no small part because what was inside the game-world was not entirely real. Jendran had a small, but comfortable Keep literally on the threshold of the Gate terminus, complete with several servants and a really good cook, none of them constructs.

"Brilliant!" he kept saying with delight. "I don't know when I've had a better game! But, of course, now we're going to have to agree to ban all other players from the field except the two of us, or agree to incorporate an even number on both sides."

Jendran was a small, wiry fellow in person, not at all formidable. But Tarma had immense respect for his ability to think on his feet and strategically deal with the unexpected. They had won, but it had been a very near thing, and only the last-minute appearance of Warrl, who body-slammed the mage from the rear, knocking him off his feet, had given them the victory as quickly as they had it.

Warrl was inordinately proud of that fact. Tarma was more than inclined to let him bask.

"I just want you to keep us in mind at some point in the future," she said, polishing off a second slice of apple tart. "Being able to practice large-scale strategy like this—"

"It will be a while before we can manage something that is not so predictable," Nanca put in. "But—well, I, for one, would value your input. And that of any other fighter you feel you can trust."

The discussion went on long into the night hours, and in the morning, fully resupplied and with their fee jingling in the pouches, they rode off towards Kata'shin'a'in and hopefully, some work.

But their did remain one small question in Tarma's mind.

Did you really mean what you said about biting me if I ever made you fly again? she thought hard at Warrl.

The *kyree* did not look back over his shoulder, but she got the distinct impression of a glower.

:You are feeling, precisely, *how* lucky?: was his only response.

And on reflection she could only come to one conclusion.

Not *that* lucky.

Mercedes Lackey
& Larry Dixon

The Novels of Valdemar

"Lackey and Dixon always offer a well-told tale"
—*Booklist*

DARIAN'S TALE
OWLFLIGHT
0-88677-804-2
OWLSIGHT
0-88677-803-4
OWLKNIGHT
0-88677-916-2

THE MAGE WARS
THE BLACK GRYPHON
0-88677-804-2
THE WHITE GRYPHON
0-88677-682-1
THE SILVER GRYPHON
0-88677-685-6

To Order Call: 1-800-788-6262

DAW 26

MERCEDES LACKEY

The Novels of Valdemar

To Order Call: 1-800-788-6262

DARKOVER

Marion Zimmer Bradley's Classic Series

Now Collected in New Omnibus Editions!

Heritage and Exile
0-7564-0065-1
The Heritage of Hastur & Sharra's Exile

The Ages of Chaos
0-7564-0072-4
Stormqueen! & Hawkmistress!

The Saga of the Renunciates
0-7564-0092-9
The Shattered Chain, Thendara House
& City of Sorcery

The Forbidden Circle
0-7564-0094-5
The Spell Sword & The Forbidden Tower

A World Divided
0-7564-0167-4
The Bloody Sun, The Winds of Darkover
& Star of Danger

To Order Call: 1-800-788-6262

www.dawbooks.com

DAW 6

Kristen Britain

GREEN RIDER

As Karigan G'ladheon, on the run from school, makes her way through the deep forest, a galloping horse plunges out of the brush, its rider impaled by two black arrows. With his dying breath, he tells her he is a Green Rider, one of the king's special messengers. Giving her his green coat with its symbolic brooch of office, he makes Karigan swear to deliver the message he was carrying. Pursued by unknown assassins, following a path only the horse seems to know, Karigan finds herself thrust into in a world of danger and complex magic....   0-88677-858-1

FIRST RIDER'S CALL

With evil forces once again at large in the kingdom and with the messenger service depleted and weakened, can Karigan reach through the walls of time to get help from the First Rider, a woman dead for a millennium?   0-7564-0209-3

To Order Call: 1-800-788-6262

DAW 7

Tanya Huff

The Finest in Fantasy

SING THE FOUR QUARTERS   0-88677-628-7
FIFTH QUARTER   0-88677-651-1
NO QUARTER   0-88677-698-8
THE QUARTERED SEA   0-88677-839-5

The Keeper's Chronicles
SUMMON THE KEEPER   0-88677-784-4
THE SECOND SUMMONING   0-88677-975-8
LONG HOT SUMMONING   0-7564-0136-4

Omnibus Editions:
WIZARD OF THE GROVE   0-88677-819-0
(Child of the Grove & The Last Wizard)
OF DARKNESS, LIGHT & FIRE   0-7564-0038-4
*(Gate of Darkness, Circle of Light & The Fire's
Stone)*

To Order Call: 1-800-788-6262

DAW 21

Tanya Huff

Victory Nelson, Investigator:
Otherworldly Crimes a Specialty

"Smashing entertainment for a wide audience"
—*Romantic Times*

"One series that deserves to continue"
—*Science Fiction Chronicle*

BLOOD PRICE
0-88677-471-3
BLOOD TRAIL
0-88677-502-7
BLOOD LINES
0-88677-530-2
BLOOD PACT
0-88677-582-5

To Order Call: 1-800-788-6262

DAW 20